JookBoxFury

Kevern Stafford

JookBoxFury

Matador
9 De Montfort Mews
Leicester LE1 7FW, UK
Tel: (+44) 116 255 9311 / 9312
Email: books@troubador.co.uk
Web: www.troubador.co.uk/matador

Cover photography: Musical Memoirs and jukebox images by Sarahphotogirl.com
Cover design and badge designs by Andy Watkins at eko-create.com

ISBN 978-1848760-394

A Cataloguing-in-Publication (CIP) catalogue record for this book
is available from the British Library.

Typeset in 11pt Sabon MT and Magic Twanger by Troubador Publishing Ltd, Leicester, UK
Printed in the UK by TJ International Ltd, Padstow, Cornwall

Matador is an imprint of Troubador Publishing Ltd

For Ruth,
Corrina and Holly

You take some heartbeats, drumbeats
Finger poppin' and stompin' feet
Little dances that look so neat…
Rock 'n' roll will stand

It Will Stand, The Showmen

YER ~~SELLOUTS~~

JOOKIN'

INSIDE: SKOOL ROOLS!..EX-SPURTS!..SCORIN'..GO!

THE FILTH 'N' THE JookBoxFury!

Allo, Punks and all you other kids who know how to ROCK N ROLL. The scenes dead, it has got borin' and we gotta get somethin' new to spunk it up. Theres no point goin out to a club and hopin your gonna hear a new band that will blow your mind cos we've heard it all before - they're all crap.

SMASHED TO PIECES

And who wants to listen to a so-called superstar DJ playin' techno bollocks like he's some sort of f'ing prog rock guitar god. I don't and I know you don't neither.

JOOKBOX FURY?

We've got the NEXT BIG THING in this issue - JookBoxFury. It's not a band - it's a load of old rock ~~spunkers~~ experts going into a pub, having a few beers or maybe the odd JOOK (best new drink I promise ya) and playin the best sounds on the old pub jukebox there. It's a kind of competition. Like playin footy in the pub and the jukebox is the pitch, the records are the ball, and everyone whose listenin is the ref. So you're gonna hear Punk, soul, rock 'n' roll, cuntry, 60s, 70s, 80s, 90s 'and - get yer earplugs out - classic rock, jazz and eeezee. Whatever is on that jukebox, they're going to play it. And you've gotta vote for who's played the best tracks.

☆ WITH ☆

SIMON 'PONY BOY' ROGERS
☆
BABS GOLIGHTLY
☆
RIK 'GUITAR MAN' PEA-BODY
☆
NYE HILL (NYEHILLISM, MAAAN)
☆
ROCKIN' PROF
DR. ANNILESE ROCOCCO

It's a larf and we need you to listen and tell the ex-spurts (sic) if they really know anything at all about music - I doubt it.

So go out there and let's rip it up for the kids.

Loz
'Ead hitter

MERCHAN-DIES
BADGES
'N' STUFF

JookBoxFury

it's the
Theabodies

www.JookBoxFury.com

AND THE WINNERS ARE:

* THE JOOK DUKE OF THE JUKE

* THE MONARCH OF THE
ZEITGEIST

NEWS FLASH

HEAR SIMON 'PONY BOY ROGERS
LAUNCH JOOKBOXFURY
WITH A LIVE PHONE IN
ON LOCAL FM 275
6PM TONIGHT (WEDNESDAY)

USE THIS SPACE
TO DO YER →
OWN THING

COP OUT - HA! HA! HA!

DISC ONE, TRACK ONE

God Gave Rock and Roll to You

JookBoxFury – I loved the old punk fanzine thing they'd got going on. My boss's secretary, Jenny, picked up the flyer in a record shop at lunchtime and gave it to me because, 'It looks like your kind of thing.' She was right, Jenny was always on the case. I balanced *Jookin'* on top of the pile of folders stacked on my in-tray (marked, 'I'm in with the IN-TRAY'). Then, after a moment's reflection, I moved it into PENDING ('I go where the In-tray goes'). Decision making is crucial in my line of work.

I moved the flyer back to the in-tray. I wouldn't normally go out of my way to listen to Simon 'Pony Boy' Rogers, in fact, I'd normally go out of my way not to listen to Simon 'Pony Boy' Rogers, but a competition to pick the best songs on a jukebox – brilliant. Forget about the World Cup, the Olympic 100 metres, the Tour de France, the Heavyweight Championship of the World… The World Champion Jukebox Song Selector – The Jook Duke of the Juke – now that would be an achievement. I'd made more than a few scorching jukebox song selections in my time, so I thought I'd give old Pony Boy's phone-in a listen to find out what was going on. It wasn't every day that something like JookBoxFury launched in my home town, plus, really, what red-blooded male wouldn't go out of his way to see Babs Golightly? You know, 'those' pictures.

I popped the flyer back in the pending tray to make the push through the final hour and twenty-three minutes of the working day when my boss, Justin Quine, strutted into the middle of the office floor and clapped a couple of times. 'Ad hoc huddle, guys,' he shouted, 'my area in five. Full turnout, no excuses. It'll be a quickie, but it's a biggie.'

Great, an ad hoc huddle. As if the daily ten o'clock huddle wasn't enough. Something in Quine's tone suggested he was going to announce that he was starting a new life as a woman, but that was probably only wishful thinking. Usually an ad hoc huddle meant that Quine was launching a new initiative, or we were being resized as part of a departmental cost refocusing exercise.

Five minutes later I was wedged in the corner of Quine's area, an open-plan bunker that he had fashioned out of office equipment. I half leaned on a filing cupboard in the corner, next to a shining green shrub that looked plastic but had dead leaves scattered round the pot. They were probably plastic too, nothing there was real. Quine had a poster behind his desk showing birds swooping over a cliff with the words, 'They can because they believe they can.' Every time I got called in to see him I had to grit my teeth not to tell him, 'They can because they're birds, you tosser. Sit them behind a desk and ask them to produce a spreadsheet, then you'll see a bit of doubt creeping in.'

Quine was on his mobile, jerkily pacing the corridor, humphing and giving exasperated waves of his hand. After a few minutes he jabbed the phone off and strode into the middle of his domain, 'Guys, sorry, sorry, domestic crisis, out of my hands I'm afraid. The wife's only gone and run out of gas on the ring road. She does not get the concept of petrol consumption, absolutely does not get it. It goes through the roof. I don't know how she does it in her little runaround. She keeps asking for her own four by four but, Jesus Christ, I'd have to buy a petrol tanker to follow her around. Anyway, first things first, the huddle takes priority as you all know, I'll get someone out to rescue her as soon as. I'm certainly not putting this one on the back burner.'

Quine's speech drifted away and washed over me in the background hum, hummm, hummmmmmmmmmmmmmMMMMM MMMMMMMMMMMM… It was getting louder. Quine's drone and a hundred machines, a thousand machines, all humming now –

PCs humming, everyone has a PC, needs a PC. Ten thousand PCs hum. Without them, what would you do? You'd be like a carpenter without a saw, a baker without an oven, a farmer without land. The PCs hum and they never stop. The printers hum. The photocopiers hum. The fluorescent light strips hum. The lifts hum up and then they hum back down again. The coffee machines hum. The whole office hummmmmmmmms like a beehive. The workers hum to one another in ones and twos at their desks. In threes and fours at informal meeting areas like would-be passengers in an airport coffee lounge whose flights have been cancelled long ago. They hum in their little meeting rooms, in sevens, eights, nines, tens, elevens, twelves… someone else joined the huddle – 'I'll get another chair' – thirteens – 'It's OK, I'll stand' – fourteens – 'It's just a quickie'… they're all humming to one another. They're humming deadlines, spreadsheets, targets, matrices, objectives, strategies, deliverables, project initiation, opportunities, threats. I wish they'd make it stop, but it won't stop because as long as it keeps humming we're alright, but if it stops… who knows… but it never stops and it's driving me mad!

'Just switch that fan on, Jenny,' Quine told his secretary, 'get the air moving,' then he continued with his drone. 'We're going to build service excellence… focus on the customer… move forwards to delight… improve speed to market… vertical integration… horizontal integration… cost reduction… process efficiency… upscale quoefficiency… enhance plutocracy… decimate bureaucracy – through a matrix based approach… remove blockages… blockage removals… seek out improvals…' Onwards and upwards… to a higher and more beautiful place, where we shall at last find peace, and fulfilment. It's our grail, our holy toil and it must be done. 'By noon tomorrow, latest.'

As I got back to my desk the phone rang, which is quite an event in our department. I answered in what I thought was the spirited and helpful way that captured the essence of Justin Quine's motivational huddle: 'Good afternoon, Ray Mitchell speaking, how may I help you?'

The caller at the other end of the line said, 'Uncle Ray, why are you talking in that funny voice?'

It was my niece, Emily. I lowered my voice, 'I was trying to sound helpful.'

'Oh, that's good,' she said, 'because I need help with my project. I need to talk to you about what you're doing at work.'

She was only seven and it sounded like she was going to give me a performance appraisal. She said, 'I'm doing a project about what a grown-up like a parent or gardener does. Jade's daddy came into our class and told us about being a policeman and resting people, but mainly helping people. He put his handcuffs on Mrs Morgan and lost the key, which made us laugh. Sam is writing about how his mummy helps people at the hospital when they get an injury, like you did when you were playing football, even though daddy said you should know better at your age. I can't write about what mummy and daddy do because everybody knows what a teacher and a headmaster does, so I have to find someone else, and I've decided to write about you, Uncle Ray. So please can you tell me about your job.'

I didn't have the heart to tell her that I worked in The Department for Those Who Have Lost Hope. Collecting data from other departments, who are convinced they have better things to do, so I can update the reporting matrix and RAG rate everything. It all has to be red, amber or green. If I RAG rated my life it would be at red, nothing going right – a no-hope job, no girlfriend, a tiny flat, and years of dedication to the cause of rock 'n' roll with nothing to show for it but a huge collection of CDs, LPs, cassettes, singles and ticket stubs from the best bands to have toured in recent times. In my misguided youth I gave my life to rock 'n' roll, as a fan – I wasn't even in a band – that's true commitment. It's like the old Argent song: 'God gave rock and roll to you… put it in the soul of everyone.' Well, I gave my soul back to rock 'n' roll – kind of. It wasn't as if I sold my soul to the devil at the crossroads one stormy night in return for the secret of guitar pickin', riffin', and wailin' the blues. It was more a case of drifting into Woolworths one drizzly Saturday afternoon and buying a *Hot Hits* compilation with my pocket money, but something did change that day. I listened to the cover versions of cheesy Seventies pop smashes and dreamed of a life with the woman in the bright yellow bikini and Rubettes cap who leaned, shivering, over the bonnet of a sports car on the cover. I dreamed of a pop life. I think I dreamed too much, but it was too late to turn back. If I couldn't believe in rock 'n' roll, then I had nothing left. The situation was RAG rated red alright. I couldn't tell Emily that.

'I sit at a desk and work on a computer,' I told her.

'Do you mend the computer?'

'No. Someone else mends the computer if it needs mending.'

'Are you friends with the person who mends the computer?'

'I don't really know them. They usually mend it over the phone anyway.'

'Oh.'

'I type things on the computer, reports and things. It's a bit like when you write a story at school. I write stories about what people are doing at work, but I call them reports. Then I do some charts and graphs. I do some thinking as well, and ring people up, and go to meetings. My boss would say that I'm keeping a lot of plates spinning.'

'What do you do with all the plates?'

'There aren't really any plates.'

'Oh.' Emily was silent for a moment, then asked, 'Does anything fun happen that I can draw?'

'You could draw a coffee machine,' I told her.

'I might do,' she said. 'I'll check with Mrs Morgan. She might not want me to draw a job like yours. I've got to get ready for dancing now. Send me another CD of your funny music, like the *Teddy Bear* one, it makes me laugh. Bye.'

Bye. I moved the *Jookin'* flyer back to the in-tray. That's where the action was, out jookin', not stuck behind a desk. What they needed in the JookBoxFury contest was a real fan, not a bunch of has-beens and light entertainment wannabees. If anyone knew anything about how to pick the best music on a jukebox it had to be someone who had shown a lifetime of commitment to rockular music. It had to be. That's why I called Simon 'Pony Boy' Roger's phone-in and ended up going along to Xstatix that evening.

DISC ONE, TRACK TWO

Chanson d'Amour

As soon as I turned into the main street I spotted Pony Boy. You couldn't miss him. His haircut hadn't changed since 1972 and he was wearing a shiny lilac shirt with a cricket jumper draped around his shoulders, the cuffs turned back to hold the sleeves together. He was outside Xstatix, but the bar looked like it had closed down and he was about to leave and climb the steps of a gleaming tour bus. I ran down the street to catch him.

'Excuse me,' I shouted. 'Mr Rogers… Simon… Pony Boy…'

It was difficult to know how to address someone you'd invited into your bedroom so many times. On the radio, admittedly, but even so, I felt like he'd had his way with me and left me emotionally scarred because of his diabolical choice of music at a very vulnerable time in my life.

I tried again, 'It is Pony Boy isn't it?'

He turned round. 'That's my name, don't wear it out.'

I wouldn't even wear it around the house. 'I was on your phone-in earlier and you said to come here for the jukebox competition. I've come down to vote for the good stuff. I've got to make sure someone picking great music wins.'

'Ah, the caller with attitude. Ray was it? Great radio, I love a bit of banter. Sorry you got cut off, mate, it was the producer's decision. You know me, I love a bit of edge in a programme – as long as it's not over-the-top or offensive obviously. Super to meet you, mate. It's always good to meet the listeners, but I'm sorry to report that you've had a wasted journey.'

That was typical Pony Boy, never slow to disappoint.

A fire exit at the side of Xstatix crashed open and a stringy longhair stumbled into the street zipping up his flies. He loped over to us as Pony Boy said, 'That's right, JookBoxFury is off tonight I'm afraid, matey. There's been a small problemo with the venue here, some leakage in the outflow main. The stools are floating about in the bar and they've had to shut the place down.'

The guy who joined us said, 'Too bloody right, man, even the kitchen's knee deep in turds. The only thing going on in that place tonight is a sewage workers' convention. It's fucking horrible, nearly as bad as the bogs at the venues I was playing in the Seventies.'

Of course, it was Rik Peabody. THE Rik Peabody – the 'Guitar Man' himself. Standing right next to me in the street.

A young woman in a Velvets/Warhol banana t-shirt and a flower-print skirt with Doc Martens came to the top of the coach steps. She moved a strand of dark hair out of her eyes and smiled. 'Rik, Pony Boy, I've found somewhere else with a jukebox, isn't that great? Fran says we can go and have the competition there.'

A piercing woman's voice came from inside the coach, 'Can't I even trust you to explain the situation correctly, girl. What I said was that we would have a look at the alternative venue and assess the synergy it has with the Jook brand. This launch campaign isn't something I'm taking the lead on for fun, let's not forget that.'

'Too fucking right we're not doing it for fun,' Rik said. 'We're not the Girl Guides. We're doing it for fucking mayhem, man. Come on, let's rock 'n' roll.'

Rik and Pony Boy got onto the coach and the door started to close. I got my hand in and held it back. 'Can I come?' I said through the gap. 'If there's any chance… you know, if you've got any spare seats.'

'The more the merrier,' Rik said. 'There's fucking hundreds of seats. Ain't that right, Rhia girl?'

The woman in the banana t-shirt said, 'It's fine with me, Rik, but Fran might have something to say about it.'

Fran was the woman with the piercing voice. She screeched as if she was struggling to keep control of a Pony Club night out, 'Oh really, what is it now? I might have something to say about what?' As I climbed onto the bus she looked me up and down as if I had drifted in from the sewage leak.

'Don't you worry, Fran,' Rik said, 'he's with me. You've always got to look after the punters.' He dragged me further inside, 'Come on, man.' Fran shuddered and flicked her hand at some imaginary dust on her suede collar.

I'd made it. I was on a rock 'n' roll tour bus with Rik Peabody. I was finally living the life. Rik led me to the back of the coach, slumped into a seat and said, 'God, I need another piss.' He shouted, 'Hey, Rhia, where are those bottles of piss?'

Fran stood up and straightened her jacket. 'May I remind you once and for all, Mr Peabody, that what you insist on referring to in that disparaging manner, is actually a soon to be high profile greengage and absinthe-based alcopop which I have projected to make a major impact on the alcoholic beverage market following its launch. A launch which, I might add, we are paying you quite handsomely to support. So, moving forwards, I would appreciate a more appropriate response to the brand.'

'Yeah, yeah, whatever, man,' Rik said. 'Have you got any more of the fruity piss juice then?'

Rhia gave Rik a couple of bright green bottles. He popped the tops off with his teeth and handed one to me. The label said 'Jook' in a psychedelic swirl.

'Don't worry,' Rik said, 'It sounds like cum, but it only tastes like piss. You get used to it after you've had a few.'

If it was good enough for Rik Peabody, it was good enough for me. 'You've sold it to me, cheers.' I took a long swig of the Jook and then had to clench my teeth, suck my cheeks in and gulp hard to keep from spraying it back out. One way or another, with a taste like that it was almost certainly going to make an impact on the alcoholic beverage market.

Rik knocked his Jook straight back. I took another careful sip to see if it really did taste as bad as I thought. Then I took another. It actually tasted green. It wasn't pleasant, but it was compelling, like picking a scab. I took a couple more sips. It got easier with every mouthful.

Rik belched and wiped his arm across his mouth. 'You need to ignore that Fran,' he said. 'She's in charge of some bollocks, I've no fucking idea what, but I shouldn't bother about her. What she needs is some lovin'. Would you? You know, with her? It could be just what's required. I might have to take matters into my own hands if the situation doesn't improve – another public service from the Guitar Man. Rhia's alright though. She's Fran's Junior dogsbody or something, but if you ask me, she's the only one round here who knows what the fuck's going on. That guy sat next to Fran, in the black, that's Laurence. He's supposed to be an ad man guru,' – Rik made a 'wanker' gesture as he said it. 'Then you've got Pony Boy Rogers, nuff said. Guy down the front in the suit and the plimsoles, used to be at the *NME*, Nye Hill, the nihilism guy – writes all that crap that students like. Woman next to him, frizzy hair, big dress, that's Dr Roc. Dr Annilese Rococco, she's the rent-a-gob they have on Radio 4 to talk about the Spice Girls. A professor of rock? Bloody stupid, don't read about it, just fucking strap on an axe and rock, man.' Rik nudged me, 'And the blonde bird who's asleep, you know who she is.'

I sat up to look at the dishevelled blonde bombshell crashed out at the tables halfway down the coach. It had to be Babs Golightly, but without the magazine gloss she looked more like the girl next door.

Rik said, 'I know your game, boy. You don't recognize her with her clothes on. It's always the fuckin' quiet ones. That's Babs Golightly, as if you didn't know, you sly bugger. You're not looking at her face when you see those pictures are you, man?'

'Babs Golightly, I know. I recognise her – she looks really familiar.'

'She can get as familiar as she wants can Babs, man.'

The coach turned off the dual carriageway and then down a back street where a gang of kids were playing in the middle of the road. They stopped and pointed at the coach as if a flying saucer was coasting by, and then threw stones at us as we drove past. At the end of the street we turned alongside a run down garage that had 'Keep Out' daubed across the corrugated iron gate, and barbed wire running round the top of the breeze block walls. Across the road almost everything had been demolished. It was all scrub land covered in rubble and the only thing left standing was a big square pub. There was a huge car park at the front with one car in it, up on bricks, with the wheels missing and the windows and lights smashed in. The car park was covered in glass. Nothing was moving except chip wrappers and crisp packets that were blowing around by the remains of a wall.

The coach pulled into the car park, but nobody moved. Rhia stood up at the front and tried to be enthusiastic. 'OK, everybody, here we are – The Queen Victoria. It's a traditional local and the Assistant Manageress is dead keen on us having JookBoxFury here. Apparently they have something special on every night so we're lucky they can fit us in.' Still nobody moved. 'It's got a well-stocked jukebox… and we've been promised a free drink if the competition goes well and the customers like it.'

'Now you're talking, girl,' Rik said. He got up to get off the bus.

Fran said to the ad man, 'I've got some concerns about this, Laurence. I need to understand how this sits with your launch campaign plan? We mustn't lose sight of the big picture here. We need to focus on generating a context that is consistent with Jook's core values.'

Laurence stepped into the aisle like an ad guru superhero, dressed entirely in black apart from a weird pair of red and silver space age sports shoes. He smoothed back his wavy black hair to tighten his pony tail. He didn't have a hint of grey, which was suspicious, because he must have been about fifty. He told Fran, 'This is where things really take off, this could be the tipping point. It's real, urban, gritty. Sometimes you have to step back from the campaign plan and give it air to breathe. You know, follow the campaign where the campaign wants to take you.'

Fran said, 'Well, I suppose these are the matters we're paying the agency to guide us on, so if you're sure…'

She looked far from sure as she followed Laurence off the bus. When she got to the bottom step Rhia said, 'Mind that, Fran,' but it was too late. She stepped down onto a used condom.

'Euw, what is it?' Fran said.

'It's nothing,' Rhia told her, 'just some litter. I didn't want you to slip on it.'

'Someone's been slipping it in,' Rik said.

As Babs got off the coach she noticed me and peered at me for a while through her huge Sophia Loren sunglasses, then asked, 'Did I interview you once… about a video or something?'

'Not me,' I said. 'I'm not a celebrity or anything, so it wouldn't have been me.'

Babs ignored me after that.

Rik led the way into the pub. I started to follow, but Pony Boy called me back and asked me to carry a large cardboard box for him. 'It's the Bobbly Wobblers,' he said.

I could hardly refuse after they'd given me a lift, so I took the box.

The Queen Victoria's door had a steel panel over it and there were grilles over the windows on either side. A dusty St George's flag hung down inside one window. There was a broken pane of glass in the other, with a piece of cardboard torn from a pork scratchings box taped behind it

I pushed the door open with Pony Boy's box and went inside. It wasn't much different than it had been on the outside. A yellowing, handwritten poster, sellotaped to the wall by the dartboard, showed events for each night of the week. They'd all been scribbled out with biro apart from: 'Tuesday: Big Nev's Big Pop Quiz ' and 'Thursday: Topless Tina – Topless Barmaid.' We'd missed both.

The pub's one cavernous room was panelled with stately home effect plastic wood. A battered pool table stood on faded red lino at the far end, and decrepit chairs and tables lined the walls. It was more like a run down community centre in the Eastern bloc than a pub. A jukebox hung on the wall between the end of the bar and the door to the Gents. Four people were in the place, like the last survivors of the apocalypse. Two lads and a girl eyed us up from bar stools by the door and an older guy clung to the bar at the other end. I rested Pony Boy's box on a bar stool.

One of the lads demanded, 'What's in the box, mate?'

'It's nothing, it's not mine,' I told him.

He turned to the other lad, 'Did you hear that, Vin? The dozy twat's carrying a box with nothing in it, and it's not even his.'

Vin put his hand on the box and said, 'No, seriously, mate, what's in it? Just interested.'

What do you say? It's full of Bobbly Wobblers. It was bad enough having to carry the things without getting drawn into explaining what they were. I looked around for Pony Boy.

Vin said, 'You're alright, mate, there's no scum in here. If it's stuff you're shifting we might be able to sort you out.' He turned to the other lad, 'Eh, Psycho, we might be able to help him shift his gear?'

Psycho looked into his pint and said, 'Dozy twat.'

'Here, Tina,' Vin said to the girl who was sitting with them, 'customer wants a fucking drink here.' Tina stubbed her cigarette out, eased off the bar stool and dragged herself behind the bar. 'Sorry, mate,' Vin said to me, 'she's the worst fucking barmaid in the world. Come back tomorrow though and you'll see why she got the job. Topless night on Thursday, eh Tina? You want to come back tomorrow and order a pint of Guinness, then you'll see Tina's party trick.' He put his hand on the box and leaned towards me, 'She only draws the fucking shamrock on the top of the pint with her tits. Draws it with her nipple, bloody amazing control. In't it, Tina, bloody amazing? You should be on the fucking telly with a talent like that.'

Tina looked at me wearily and asked what I wanted.

I said, 'I'll have a Guinness.' It was an instinctive reaction, I wasn't really thinking. Oh no, she didn't think I was implying I wanted to see the party trick did she?

'You dirty bugger,' Vin said. 'She does it on a Thursday. I told you it was Thursday… although I suppose she might be persuaded.'

'Guinness is off,' Tina said.

That was a relief. 'What bitters have you got?'

'Lager.'

Pony Boy called, 'Over here with those, Ray mate, we need to set up.'

'Catch you later, mate,' Vin said, 'then we can sort something out about your gear.'

'Dozy twat,' Psycho growled to himself.

Pony Boy started to arrange a display of Bobbly Wobblers at the 'merchandising centre', which was a table he'd moved next to the jukebox. He spent ages faffing about getting them in the right position and asking me if I thought the mix of colours was right, as if anyone cared – although he did start off with too many of the orange ones. Before I knew what was happening, I found myself helping him with the Bobbly Wobbler display. They used to be a gimmick on his radio show in the Seventies, although, thankfully, I'd never seen one in the flesh before. Each Bobbly Wobbler had a strange fluffy head on a spring. They were all wearing small knitted bobble hats and stood on a base printed with the words, 'Don't Go Breaking My Hat'. I tried not to catch the eyes of Vin or Psycho at the bar. They were having a great time watching Pony Boy fussing around, standing back from the table to see how things looked, and telling me to move the purple ones a little to the left.

That hadn't been my intention at all. When I saw the *Jookin'* flyer that afternoon and decided to find out what JookBoxFury was all about, my intention hadn't been to become Pony Boy's Bobbly Wobbler assistant. After grinding through the rest of the day at the office, I got home and tuned in to the local radio show Pony Boy was doing about JookBoxFury. As soon as I heard Pony Boy on air I thought I'd gone back in time. He still sounded like he was jumping around the studio in his tank top and a pair of wacky specs. He started to get over-excited and said, 'We're at the beginning of an amazing journey tonight, girls and guys. In just a few days, I'll be back here on your radiogram with the grand JookBoxFury final. Some of my pop picking showbiz pals will be joining little old me to play you the poppermost jukebox classics you have ever heard. We're going to tell you once and for all what the greatest pop songs of all time are, and you can be part of it all tonight. I'm giving you all a personal Pony Boy invitation to join us for the first round of JookBoxFury at the Xstatix bar. Come on down and you can vote for your faves while our experts spin the tunes on the old jukebox record machine. That's not all that's happening. While you're there you'll be able to pick up one of the Bobbly Wobblers from the crazy days of the Radio Wonderful roadshow. Who knows, I might even be giving out the odd signed photo. So, come on listeners, let's get some callers on the air and hear what your jukebox pop picks would be. To get you in the mood, here's one of my own personal favourites from way back when. With their classic, *Chanson d'Amour*, here's the Manhattan Transfer. With a *rah dah dah da daaa* – take it away!'

I almost changed stations. I didn't need to hear Simon 'Pony Boy' Rogers wittering on about his Bobbly Wobblers, and still playing *Chanson d'Amour*. Hadn't the world progressed at all? There was no possible way that 'Pony Boy' Rogers could be involved in anything that was going to say once and for all what the greatest pop songs of all time were. He wouldn't know what they were even if they fell on him in the shape of big gold discs being sent down from pop heaven.

I had to speak out, so I rang the programme. I got put on hold, then, just as *Chanson d'Amour* was fading out, Pony Boy said, 'We've got our first caller on line one, it's Ray Mitchell. Hiya, Ray, you've rung in to tell us which buttons you'd be pressing on the old jukebox.'

'I wouldn't be pressing the ones that play *Chanson d'Amour*,' I said. 'You ruined my school holidays in 1977 by playing that garbage non-stop.'

'Well, come now, Raymondo,' Pony Boy said, 'the Transfer introduced a radical new direction in popular music with that release.'

'They didn't at all. That came out right when punk and new wave was happening, which was the most exciting music I'd ever heard. I was desperate to hear the new stuff on the radio, but you just kept plugging away with Leo Sayer and Chicago and Manhattan Transfer over and over again. It's not a radical new direction at all. Music can be thrilling and you've got a responsibility to keep it alive. You've got to play the good stuff. You can excite people, lift people, but instead you're talking about Bobbly Wobblers and playing the same old rubbish. You're killing rock and pop.'

'Strong views, Raymondo, strong views – which are great to hear because I can tell that you're as mad about pop as I am. Let me just correct you on one thing though and put the record straight, so to speak, because I really must defend myself against that accusation of not playing anything new. I've always been a big supporter of the latest sounds and if you were listening at the top of the show you would have heard me playing Cliff's newie, not to mention a real stunner off the latest Sting album…'

I'd just started to say, 'Cliff Richard? Sting? You might as well walk around wearing a big hat with "Wanker" written on it…' when he cut me off.

Pony Boy said, 'Well, there was a guy who really is as passionate about this fabulous business as I am. So, Ray mate, why don't you come down to the Xstatix bar for the JookBoxFury contest tonight and you'll be able to vote for your own faves from the tracks that our celebrity experts will be playing. You can even get your hands on a Bobbly Wobbler.'

I told the radio, 'Yeah – and if I get my hands anywhere near a Bobbly Wobbler they'll be round its throat.'

So I was as surprised as anyone when, a few hours later, I found myself setting out a display of Bobbly Wobblers on a pub table. It's difficult to explain. You've got to watch out for the aura of celebrity because it can do strange things to your sense of right and wrong.

Pony Boy was telling me to make sure the Bobbly Wobblers' hair was fluffed out properly, when Laurence called out, 'Come on Jook team, let's gather round for a quick briefing session.'

The Jook crowd pulled chairs over to sit by Laurence. I wasn't sure whether to join them. I looked over to Vin and Psycho at the bar. Psycho mouthed, 'Dozy twat.' I went and sat on the edge of the Jook circle.

Laurence said, 'Now, hopefully you all know what's going to happen. I'm sure you've all worked through the official JookBoxFury programme to familiarize yourselves with the competition format.' He handed round copies of a stapled fanzine, with the *Jookin'* flyer that I'd seen earlier as its front and back pages.

Pony Boy said, 'When I received this before I assumed it was a draft copy. Please tell me that the glossy version will be available from the merchandising area in time for the press launch tomorrow.'

Laurence said, 'Well, no, not as such. This is the look we wanted.

We had our top graphic designer and copywriter working on the project to develop a programme with a music related theme. Rather than do an all-singing all-dancing brochure – yawn, yawn – they came up with this leading edge fanzine concept. Pinch me if we're not winning awards with this one.'

'It doesn't look finished,' Pony Boy said. 'It looks like a kid has produced it in his bedroom.'

'Fantastic, absolutely,' said Laurence. 'That's it exactly. It's Punk Rock you see.'

Nye Hill, the ex-*NME* journalist, appeared interested for the first time. 'This takes me back,' he said, flicking through the programme. 'I think they were looking at *Sniffin' Glue* when they put this together.'

'Sniffing glue is no excuse for poor quality merchandising,' Pony Boy said.

'It's quite clever,' said Dr Rococco. 'I like the notion of subverting the corporate to attain a sense of the subcultural, and it's so much better than those glossy programmes costing five pounds.'

'Well, it will be retailing at around the five pounds per unit price point,' said Laurence, 'but we have put a lot of time and effort into getting it right. Authenticity was very important on this project. You see those pictures on the front page…'

We all peered at the blurry smudges on the cover.

'We spent hours in the studio bringing those images down so you can't quite make out what they are. It took hours. You see, what we wanted to do was make the programme look like it had been put together by a snotty-nosed punk rocker with ink stains on his fingers, sitting on his bed and stapling the pages together while he's thinking about his next scathing concert review, or being discovered by the *Melody Maker*, or he's thinking about his poster of Farrah Fawcett-Majors or whatever. It's all part of the creative process. I've no doubt that the JookBoxFury audience is going to appreciate the level of authenticity that we've delivered with this design. Why don't we all get a feel for that, have a browse through, have a good look at the rules section, and we'll take it from there.'

Babs Golightly flicked through the pages like a bored schoolgirl, then threw them on to the table. 'I'm not reading that crap, it's like the bloody school newspaper.'

Rik said, 'I'm with you. We need another drink if we're going to be reading. Let's get a Jook to lubricate the old green matter.' He handed round bottles from a display next to the Bobbly Wobblers. Fran declined, but everyone else took one. Rik raised his bottle and said, 'To JookBoxFury, because I'm burnin' with fury, baby, it's burning me up.' He put his lips around the neck, threw his head back, and drank a good half of it in one go. Everyone else took a cautious sip and sucked their cheeks in. Pony Boy coughed, spluttered, dribbled Jook down his front, wiped his eyes and tried to say something, but nothing came out apart from another dribble of Jook.

'Come on there, Rogers,' said Rik, slapping him on the back. 'I thought you were the fuckin' honey-toned voice of the airwaves, but the minute you taste the first kiddie-pop made out of absinthe and greengages you're lost for words.' He turned to Fran, 'Throw him off the tour, darlin'. You don't want anyone representing Jook who looks like an old alkie who throws up all over his shirt the minute he tastes the stuff. Here, let's get you cleaned up, boy.' He picked up a Bobbly Wobbler from the display and rubbed at Pony Boy's shirt with its fluffy head.

'Hang on there,' spluttered Pony Boy, grabbing the Bobbly Wobbler off Rik. 'Hasn't anyone got a cloth?' Rhia handed Pony Boy a bar towel which he took and used to carefully dab the Bobbly Wobbler clean.

I sipped my Jook, which I was beginning to get a taste for, and looked through the *Jookin'* fanzine at the pages I hadn't seen before.

ROOLS (FOR JOOK ROCKERS)

Some ponce made this up, we didnt. We hate rools and bein told to sit down at gig and stand in line and all that shit.

ONE
ALL the ex-spurts have a go to play 5 songs on the jukebox. Easy peesy.

TWO
The listeners - that's YOU kids - decide how good the songs are and give them marks out of 10 - it's just like bein at skool this ain't it. If your a swot you can use the score sheet, or write it on a piece of bogroll - I dont care, you can write it on your arse for all I care.

THREE
It's gettin' more like skool now - more rools, more notices to read out in assembly. This is good tho cos it stops the ex-spurts getting away with playing the same old crap we,ve heard a million times before. The marks are for two different things - ain't that cleva - every song gets marks out of ten for QUALITY - I for shit, IO for ace, & marks out of ten for ORIGINALITY - I for the kind of thing your mum hums, IO for something you've never heard but you want to play it again straight away, like the first time you heard the Pistols.

GO!
An accountant or some other drone goes and adds all the scores up an you've got your winners:-

THE JOOK DUKE OF THE JUKE
When it comes to playin' tracks on the old jukebox they rule!

THE MONARCH OF THE ZEITGEIST
The monarchy are f'ing morons, but there's one place where you want to be a king or a queen - on the friggin' jukebox. So whoever plays the song that gets the whole place rockin', they're the Monarch of the Zeitgeist.

THESE ARE MY OWN ROOLS

1 GET UP OFF YOUR ARSE

2 FIND A PUB OR A CAFF WITH A JUKEBOX

3 MAKE SOME NOIZE TO GET UP THE NOSES OF ALL THE STRAIGHTS

GO! AND GET YER OWN JUKEBOXFURY SESH GOIN'

JookBoxFury SCORIN'

Players and songs played	Scores		
	Quality	Originality	TOTAL
Rik Peabody			
Song 1:			
Song 2:			
Song 3:			
Song 4:			
Song 5:			
TOTALS			
Babs Golightly			
Song 1:			
Song 2:			
Song 3:			
Song 4:			
Song 5:			
TOTALS			
Nye Hill			
Song 1:			
Song 2:			
Song 3:			
Song 4:			
Song 5:			
TOTALS			
Dr Annilese Rococco			
Song 1:			
Song 2:			
Song 3:			
Song 4:			
Song 5:			
TOTALS			
Your Gran			
Song 1:			
Song 2:			
Song 3:			
Song 4:			
Song 5:			
TOTALS			

Jook Duke of the Juke: _____

Monarch of the Zeitgeist: _____

− THE PLAYERS −

We gave all the JookBoxFury ex-spurts a questionnaire to fill in to tell us how they discovered Elvis or saw the punk festival at the 100 club or whatever. These beer stained scrawls are what they gave us back.

LADEES AND GENNELMEN - YOUR JookBoxFury HOST

WHO ARE YOU? SIMON 'PONY BOY' ROGERS

WHAT ARE YOU KNOWN FOR?

ANYONE WHO'S YOUNG AT HEART WILL KNOW ME AS A RADIO WON-DER-FUL DJ FROM THE HEYDEY OF THE WONDERFUL BREAKFAST SHOW. MY TRADEMARK WAS THE PONY BOY BOBBLE HAT AND THE OLD BOBBLY WOBBLERS WHICH WERE ON SALE AT THE WONDERFUL BOBBLY-O-GILE AT THE WONDERFUL ROADSHOW - LOOK OUT, THEY MIGHT JUST MAKE A COMEBACK. AT THE MO I'M IN THE FRAME TO HOST THE EUROVISION UK ENTRANTS CONTEST.

WHAT'S YOUR ERA?

AS A FAN IT WOULD HAVE TO BE THE BEATLES - MOP TOPS, STILL LOVE 'EM. AS A DJ, DOING THE BREAKFAST SHOW WHEN WONDERFUL RULED THE AIRWAVES - ALTHOUGH BEING OUT ON THE WAVES ON THE PIRATE SHIP WAS A LAUGH, AND IT'S ALL ABOUT HAVING A LAUGH.

THE FIRST SINGLE YOU GOT

FRANK IFIELD'S YODELLING CLASSIC 'I REMEMBER YOU'

FAVE ALBUM SERGEANT PEPPERS

POP HIGHLIGHT

WITHOUT A DOUBT JOINING WINGS ON TOUR IN AMERICA FOR THE BREAKFAST SHOW AND JAMMING WITH MACCA ONE NIGHT ON HIS BALCONY IN MIAMI.

WHY ARE YOU TAKING PART IN JookBoxFury?

POP MUSIC'S THE GREATEST BUSINESS IN THE WORLD - I LOVE IT, LOVE IT, LOVE IT. DON'T MIND WHETHER IT'S PUNK, REGGAE, HEAVY METAL, WHATEVER, GREAT POP IS GREAT POP AND I LOVE IT ALL - APART FROM SOME OF THE MODERN DANCE STUFF BECAUSE THAT ISN'T REALLY MUSIC IN MY BOOK. (TALKING OF WHICH, LOOK OUT FOR 'JOOK SMASHES' - INTERESTING FACTS ABOUT CHART TOPPERS).

WHO ARE YOU? RIK 'the GUITAR MAN' Peabody

WHAT ARE YOU KNOWN FOR?

As a rock 'n' roll icon I'm ~~sinary eyon~~ Known for
The Peabodies 1964 smash VIOLENCE IS GOLDEN (BUT MY
Wounds still bleed) b/w WALK TALL, and of course
being the Guitar MAN and a bon vivante
and raconteur who does a bit of painting
and decorating on the side.

WHAT'S YOUR ERA?

Late 60's/early 70's - anything that knows
how to wear a pair of flared strides and ROCK!

THE FIRST SINGLE YOU GOT That wasn't yesterday
Man, I think it was Be Bop a lula, but it
might have been Diddley or Donegan, or Howlin Wolf.

FAVE ALBUM DISRAELIS GEAR - all you need
ROCK!

POP HIGHLIGHT

Recording sessions for Earth Mother, Moon Lover
were out of this world. So was Hawkwind at
Henge Free Festival. A space ship landed
right in front of the stage and these little
green women came out and joined in
on backing vocals - I wasn't the only one
who saw that happen. These green things
freaked me out man - sometimes I can
WHY ARE YOU TAKING PART IN JookBoxFury? still see them

Whatever it is you've got to
have someone on it who's
had a nearly chart topping
smash HiT and who knows
how to ROCK!

Nye Hill (ism)

WHAT ARE YOU KNOWN FOR?

I suppose it's my NME column's 'Nyehillisms' which are just out in paperback. I'm most excited by my new book on Rock and Pop Mythologies. It's based on Roland Barthes' 'Mythologies' – it reveals how imagery from pop music creates a reality that appears to be rebellious but is designed to maintain the status quo – or Status Quo come to that. The picture of Paul Simonon smashing his guitar on the cover of 'London Calling' is a perfect example.

WHAT'S YOUR ERA?

Anything from the moment Louis Armstrong first put his horn to his lips to the latest application of lip gloss by Girls Aloud is a crucial part of the world I inhabit and comment on. And of course, I'm always on the lookout for the next raw thrill – the one that pushes the envelope of musical exploration.

THE FIRST SINGLE YOU GOT

I was given 'Ernie (The Fastest Milkman in the West)' for Christmas, but my first informed purchase was Roxy Music's 'Virginia Plain'.

FAVE ALBUM

Can's 'Future Days' or Girls Aloud's 'What Will the Neighbours Say'.

POP HIGHLIGHT

Undoubtedly Kraftwerk's appearance on 'Tomorrow's World' showing how they'd invented machines to play pop music.

WHY ARE YOU TAKING PART IN JookBoxFury?

Maybe we'll get students to drink more alco-pops - result! Ultimately though, I feel sure that impeccable taste will see me through and I expect to come out a clear winner.

WHO ARE YOU? **Babs Golightly**

WHAT ARE YOU KNOWN FOR? Just being Babs! - I've always
been Babs. People ask me what it's like being famous.
but I used to be famous in my school so I've never
known anything else. I host Video Hits on channel 73
and - as if you need to be told - I've had a couple of
popular photo shoots which I still get complimented
on.

WHAT'S YOUR ERA?

Eciiiiiid!
Manchester Hacienda
♡? Mad 4 It !!

THE FIRST SINGLE YOU GOT

Rubber Bullets -10cc - I think it was actually my
older sisters. I ♡'d 10cc's I had a real crush on Lol
Creme - how weird is that?!

FAVE ALBUM
Massive Attack - 'Blue Lines'

POP HIGHLIGHT

Presenting the Brit Award for best video in
2001 to the Swizzlesticks for that one
where their heads are made of fruit!

WHY ARE YOU TAKING PART IN JookBoxFury?

Its a wicked idea - and it's going to
be put on your dancing shoes because we're
going to have some fUN!! ♡

Babs?
♡

Dear Mr Whyte,

JOOK BOX FURY QUESTIONNAIRE

Dr Rococco has asked me to send you these answers for her biography in the Jook Box Fury programme.

What are you known for?
I am probably Best known as the author of 'Between Rock and a Hard On: Groupies, Chicks, Songbirds and Women in Popular Music' the first serious study of the relationship between women and popular music. Another, less academic, claim to fame is that I did handclaps on 'Earth Mother, Moon Lover' on the first Brutus Trout album.

What's your era?
It would have to be the late Sixties. Change was in the air, music was its lifeblood. The 14 hour technicolour dream happening – it was about much more than music.

First single
The Shirelle's 'Will You Love Me Tomorrow?'

Favourite album
'Leige and Leif'. Sandy Denny's Fairport Convention.

Pop Highlight
Personally, spending time with Sandy Denny while I was researching 'Between Rock and a Hard On'. More broadly, although I questioned it at the time for its crassness I would suggest 13th July 1985, Live Aid. It was the day pop grew up and became responsible, and for that reason it is also the pop lowlight – from its inception a significant element in the appeal of pop has always been its irresponsibility.

Why are you taking part in JookBoxFury?
I think the jukebox has become regenerated as a symbol of the current moment in pop – what is the i-Pod other than a pocket jukebox? I'm hoping to understand that relationship further by taking part, and of course, it's always great fun to put a good song on a jukebox.

DISC ONE, TRACK THREE

Rock Island Line

I put the programme down when I'd scanned through it. Hearing what Rik and Nye and Dr Rococco chose was going to be interesting, Babs might even play some good stuff, but if they were struggling, well, I'd got a history of classic floor-filling party tape compilations to draw on that would be difficult to match anywhere. I could step in and give them a few tips.

Laurence looked around to check everyone had finished and asked Pony Boy if he would explain how the competition was going to work.

Pony Boy stood up to address us. There was a large green stain on his shirt where he had dribbled the Jook. He put his hand to it and the material fell away. He said, 'That's odd. Look at my shirt.'

'Too bloody right it's odd, man,' Rik said. 'A grown man wearing a blouse, you want to sort yourself out.'

'No, it's rotted my shirt.'

'That's what I'm saying, it's a fucking rotten shirt – get yourself some denim.'

'Shall we carry on,' Fran said.

Pony Boy wasn't happy, but he was a professional and he continued with his explanation. While he spoke, Fran palmed the Bobbly Wobbler that Rik had used to mop up the spilled Jook and surreptitiously dropped it into her bag. As she did, I saw that its bobble hat and the fluff on its head had withered away, leaving the Bobbly Wobbler peeping out of Fran's bag like a psychotic skinhead. Fran caught my eye and quickly zipped the bag.

Pony Boy explained the competition. 'While the songs are playing, and this is a super part, you sit back and actually watch the crowd's reaction as the discs spin. After all, they're the ones who will be giving you the marks.'

'Now, let me get this straight,' Dr Rococco said, 'there are separate marks for quality and originality, is that right? Can you expand on that a little?'

'I'll expand on that for you, darlin',' said Rik. 'If you play *Angels* by that fat tosser from Take That, you get nothing for originality, because my old gran can sing along to that and she's been dead for twenty years, and you get about one mark for quality, because it's mushy bollocks. On the other hand, play *Violence is Golden* by The Peabodies, and you're getting ten out of ten across the board because it's fucking top quality, but it's also a cult classic, so you're getting ten marks for originality as well.'

Pony Boy said, 'Unfair criticism of Mr Roberto Williams aside, I'm surprised to say that's actually quite a neat summing up. We add all the scores for your five selections together, and whoever's got the highest score is the winner – the Jook Duke of the Juke.'

'You're talking bollocks again now,' Rik said.

'No, it's the title we're giving to the competition winner,' Pony Boy said. 'It's the JOOK – DUKE – of the – JUKE, do you see?'

'You're just saying the same words over and over again. It's been coming for a long time, Rogers, but you've finally lost it.'

'No, it makes sense. It's the Jook, as in the alcopop…'

'Don't worry about that,' Laurence said, 'it makes sense when you read it.'

'He's not reading it, is he?' said Rik. 'He's just saying the same thing over and over again like a dribbling old fool who can't hold his Jook.'

'I take exception to that,' said Pony Boy.

'Oh, whatever, man – Jook, Jook, Jook, Jookin', Jook.'

'I will ignore that,' Pony Boy said, 'and tell you about the other big prize, and it's a bit special this one. Whoever picks the individual song that gets the highest score wins the Zeitgeist Award.'

'Whatever that means,' Babs said.

Dr Rococo said, 'Strictly speaking, I'm not sure it's being used in quite the right context here, but it means the mood of the times.'

'Who's in a mood all the time?' Babs snapped.

'No-one's in a mood,' Dr Rococo said. 'It's the zeitgeist. It's the mood of the times. I've always rejected the concept of the zeitgeist myself. The notion that you can represent an era through a simplistic media category is an anathema which ignores the real diversity of individuals and communities. The idea of the Sixties as swinging, for example: were the Sixties swinging for girls who were driven away from their homes by an inflexible patriarchal society for 'getting into trouble'? Were they swinging for kids leaving school at fourteen to work in unsafe textiles factories? Were the Sixties swinging for…?'

Rik had been reading the programme but he looked up and said, 'Oh, it was swingin', man. You know those were swingin' times, baby, you know it. Look at this...' He held out the programme opened at the page showing Dr Rococo's questionnaire answers. 'It says here that you were at the Brutus Trout recording sessions doing handclaps. Now those were swinging times, man.'

'I think you'll find that was the early Seventies,' Dr Rococo said.

'Seventies, Sixties, whatever – it was swingin', man, free love, oh yeah! When they recorded their first album, the Trouts – Brutus Trout – set up a studio at a farmhouse in Wales because it was on a fucking ley line or something. If there was a ley line there you couldn't see it for pig shit. Anyway, when they did the last track, *Earth Mother, Moon Lover*, they turned it into one big be-in, man. They got all the freaks down there. It was full of heads and chicks and it was a hell of a crazy scene. They got me to go down there to do some howling, howling at the moon, you know, like the howling at the end of *Violence is Golden*. They had the studio full of freaks, turned on, tuned in, you know. It was a scene, man, swingin', and it kept swingin' and swingin' and turned into a non-stop orgy for about a week – fucking nearly killed me. While I was recording my bit, there was one chick there who was really shaking what she'd got. I was at the mic, howling away, and she started doing this kind of

27

snake dance, really sensual snaking around. Then she got down on all fours and crawled across the floor towards me, flicking her tongue out and licking her lips. When she got to me she unzipped my strides with her teeth, took the old todger out, and started…'

Annoyingly, Dr Rococco interrupted. She suddenly stood up and said, 'I'm sorry everyone, but I'm just going to get a breath of air, it's so hot in here.'

I was about to encourage Rik to finish his tale of rock 'n' roll excess when Nye said, 'That's a bloody good idea. I don't know why we're even bothering to discuss this programme and the rules. Take a look around, this is a complete bloody farce.'

Nye had always been one of the *NME's* coolest journalists and he was too cool for the Queen Victoria. He wore his mod suit over a band t-shirt that was so cutting edge I'd never even heard of them. Obviously The Kirbygrips were the ones to look out for, but Nye didn't seem keen to look for them, or anything else, on the Queen Victoria's jukebox. I couldn't understand it. Even if you couldn't play The Kirbygrips, you could find something good to play, that was the whole point. He had the chance and he didn't want to take it.

'I don't understand you,' I said. Everyone turned to look at me.

Nye said, 'Hey, I don't know who you are, but what's it got to do with you?'

'That's right,' Fran said, 'this is a private discussion we're having about an important business matter and I'm not sure who invited you to take part.'

'Sorry, I… I was…'

Fran stopped me, 'Excuse me, but are you an expert on consumer targeting? Because I am, and I have serious concerns about the target audience we're hitting in situ at the present moment. Laurence, perhaps if you could get your creative team on the task, we could implement a local area-wide poster campaign and revive the event, but we don't have time. In these circumstances I really do wonder what we're going to achieve.'

'Thank you,' Nye said. 'Some sense at last. Let's pack it up, get back to the hotel and I can do some work on my rock mythologies without wasting time playing songs to nobody in here.'

Pony Boy said, 'I've got to be honest and say that I don't think I'm going to hit target on the Bobbly Wobblers this evening.'

'I'm with you,' Babs said. 'If we get back now we'll still catch the end of *Celebrity WAG Watch*. God, I hope Cheryl doesn't get voted off after what she said about Danii's extensions.'

'I don't give a toss,' Rik said. 'There's a bar here, there's a bar at the hotel. Just lead me to the fucking Jook. It doesn't bother me, man, but let's crack open another green one while we're thinking about it.'

Fran glanced around the pub. 'You know, I didn't need to be running the Jook campaign. The Executive Leadership Team made me the youngest ever Head of Brand at the brewery because I'm being fast-tracked for a board-level position. I have been told that the Directors were actually arguing about which campaign was the most important, so they could give it to me to cut my teeth on. James Hylton-James personally chose me to head up the Jook launch. On James' advice I brought Laurence in for the creative consultancy and put together a team that could deliver a new market via a minimal-cost campaign. I wouldn't have taken that on if I wasn't prepared to face challenges, but I've got to agree that my career defining moment isn't going to happen here. My Gerald would have a fit if he knew I'd set foot in a place like this.

'Rhiannon, once again you've surpassed your own stupidity by bringing us here – did you even look at those customer profiles I told you to prepare? Why don't I give you an ad hoc performance appraisal first thing tomorrow? I need to decide whether a high profile campaign like this really is a suitable environment for you to be smoothing off those rough edges we spoke about at your annual review. One thing is for sure, this godforsaken place isn't what Jook is about at all. Let's go.'

They started to move, but Rhia said, 'It's got a jukebox though.' She blushed. 'We didn't know Xstatix was going to have a sewage leak did we? I found somewhere else with a jukebox. Isn't that the point? We can still play the jukebox and start the launch campaign. At least we can make a start.'

I had to back Rhia up. 'That's right,' I shouted. 'I thought that's what JookBoxFury was all about – that's what it says in the programme. It's about playing the best music on the jukebox. It's about playing great rock 'n' roll and pop and showing why it's so special. You can't give up on that – that's why they killed *Top of the Pops*. I can't believe you want to give it up.' My heart was beating faster and everyone in the pub was looking at me, even Vin and Psycho were taking an interest.

'Fucking rock, man,' Rik said.

'You can play the jukebox to your heart's content if you want, mate,' Nye said.

'I don't understand you,' I told them. 'You live rock 'n' roll, but you can't even be bothered to play the music when you have a chance. If you stop caring about the music, then you might as well say rock is dead. Just playing the music is enough – it's more than enough, it's everything. You don't know how lucky you are. I sit in an office all day in a dead-end job that I can't even begin to describe without putting myself to sleep, and you're here on a rock 'n' roll tour. When we came here, that was the first time I've ever been on a tour bus. I've spent my life reading about what goes on on tour buses, but I'd never even been on one until today. I've never even been in a band. I love rock 'n' roll, but I've never been in a band. I've always been a fan, though, and I've been the best fan I could be. I love rock 'n' roll and if I had the chance to take part in JookBoxFury, I wouldn't care where I was, I'd jump at it. I wouldn't be saying the venue wasn't any good, or it was the wrong target market, or the Bobbly Wobblers weren't going to sell… come on, just play the records. That's what it's all about.' I calmed down. 'It's just about playing the music. The music is the important thing.'

None of the JookBoxFury team spoke. Over by the bar Vin gave a slow handclap. Suddenly Laurence punched the air and said, 'Dig it, dig it, dig it!' He grabbed my shoulder and turned me to Fran. 'Now we've got a campaign – this is exactly what I was talking about when we brainstormed the launch. Low budget guerilla marketing. Tapping into the fan's passion. You see? Equate that passion with Jook and the cash tills are ringing.'

'Now you're talking, man,' Rik said. 'Gorilla marketing – fucking brilliant. Would you use a real one or a geezer in a suit?'

Laurence ignored Rik and told Fran, 'This is exactly what the campaign needs to kick start it. I've seen this happen so many times. You have the creative spark, but then the campaign takes on a life of its own, and that's when you know you're really connecting with people – this is that moment for Jook.'

Fran said, 'If we don't connect with the people in a way that impresses James Hylton-James, then someone is getting hauled over the coals and hung out to dry, and I don't expect that someone to be me.'

'Oh, we'll connect alright,' Laurence said. 'I can feel it. We're connecting with the mass audience. This is going to have us cooking on gas. We've got a great angle here. I think we might be able to link Jook to urban regeneration somehow, just thinking outside the box, but this really does give us a chance to up the ante and take it on to another level. I had my doubts, I admit, but I can see it now. This is the defining moment of the campaign.'

'Defining moment, bollocks,' Nye said. 'There are only four people in the pub including the barmaid. There are more of us than there are of them. For all the good it's doing us we might as well let the locals choose the songs and we'll judge them. You can count me out.'

'Fair enough, Mr Hill, fair enough,' Laurence said. 'Let's put this gentleman in the competition in your place.' He pointed at me and asked, 'What's your name again, my good friend?'

'Ray. Ray Mitchell.'

'Ray Mitchell.' Laurence held his hands up and drew a line high across the room, like my name was up in lights. 'The voice of the music fan, the passion behind JookBoxFury.'

Fran tugged at Laurence's sleeve, 'Can we just have a word about this before we rush into anything we might regret? We had everything planned out to the letter and I'd be happier if we were to stick to that plan. Surely we can't risk just anyone coming and choosing songs on JookBoxFury. I thought the whole point of the launch contest was to associate the quality of our experts' choices with the quality of the Jook brand.'

'Why not give the lad a chance to prove himself,' Pony Boy said. 'Let him tell us which songs he'd pick.'

'What, off the jukebox?' I asked.

'No,' said Laurence, 'let's make it an ideal world scenario. Top of your head. Let's imagine the crowd is ready and waiting and you're there in the competition. Imagine you're in the JookBoxFury final, what are you going to pick? First choice, what's it going to be?'

Now, usually these things take time. Under normal circumstances you wouldn't be rushed into picking your five favourite jukebox songs without giving it some serious consideration, but these weren't normal circumstances, I had to stand up and be counted. First choice, go for a banker, grab their attention straight away.

'OK, first choice, *The Boys Are Back in Town*, Thin Lizzy.'

Rik said, 'That's a fucking rocker, man. Nice one.'

'Second choice, I'd go for *Midnight Train to Georgia*, Gladys Knight and the Pips.'

'I do like that one,' Fran said. 'Gerald's got that on a CD in his car.'

'Number three would be Stevie Wonder, *Superstition*.'

'*Superstition* is brilliant,' Rhia said. 'I want to dance every time I hear it. Is that the funkiest riff ever?'

'Number four, *Shine on You Crazy Diamond*, Pink Floyd. It's a long track, but it's worth every minute.' I think even Nye gave a respectful nod at that point. 'And I'd finish off with *Seasons in the Sun*, Terry Jacks.'

'That's just typical,' Babs said, 'it's a loser's song.'

'Super platter,' Pony Boy said. 'It used to go down a storm on the Radio Wonderful roadshow. Get everyone singing along to *Seasons in the Sun* and you were home and dry.'

'Bloody weird choice if you ask me,' Babs said.

'Well, you can't win them all,' Laurence told her. He turned to me, 'I think you've done enough to show you're up to the task in hand, Ray. Big responsibility representing the fans, but I'm sure you'll be a hit. Great example of a tactical realignment to the campaign while maintaining the strategic integrity. Let's get the show on the road.'

Nye said, 'Good luck to you. OK, you've found someone else who can press the buttons on a jukebox. Fantastic. I'm not sure that replaces years of journalistic experience, but it's your decision, it suits me fine, but it doesn't get over your basic problem – where's your audience? Four people does not constitute an audience as far as I am concerned. So, go on, voice of the fan, pick the best music you can and give the characters at the bar the time of their lives, but you might as well be playing the music in your bedroom for all the difference it's going to make to anyone.'

No way did being on the JookBoxFury panel with Rik Peabody and Babs Golightly compare to playing music in your bedroom. I was on the brink of being part of the competition and I wasn't going to let it slip away that easily. 'We can get an audience,' I said. 'I could ring a few people, or I could go into town with the coach and bring a load of people back. I could go to the student bars and get a crowd of people if I tell them there's a drinks promotion and a celebrity competition on. When I tell them you're all here people will want to come over to see what's going on. There'll be loads of people in town who would jump at the chance of being part of this. I'll go now – I can be back with a crowd in no time and you can get JookBoxFury underway.'

'Dig it, dig it, dig it. I love it,' Laurence said. 'Great work, Ray. Breath of fresh air for the campaign. We're taxiing along the runway now. Let's do it, I'll come with you. We're moving mountains here. Come on, let's go.'

Fran stopped him, 'I need you here Laurence, for a quick huddle on the direction we're taking. There's the big picture to think about. Rhiannon can go. Look lively, girl, get some posters, take some Jook, get into town on the coach and tempt people back here with the offer of a great night out and couple of free drinks, well, one free drink. And remember that I'm giving you a chance to redeem yourself, so I'd jump at it with both hands if I were you, young lady.'

Rhia was about to say something to Fran, but then she turned and grabbed a couple of posters off the table and almost ran outside.

I was about to go with her when the guy who had been standing on his own at the bar lurched past on his way to the toilets and bumped into the merchandising centre, knocking most of the Bobbly Wobblers over.

'Sorry about that, pal,' he said and picked up one of the Bobbly Wobblers. 'What's this all about then?'

'Those are £5 each, my friend,' Pony Boy said, 'special JookBoxFury promotion.'

'Jook what? What's that all about then?'

'It's a competition,' I said. 'It's all about playing songs on the jukebox – it's called JookBoxFury.'

'I'm shite at that,' he said. 'I'll tell you what though, you see these boots?' He was wearing a pair of fancy cowboy boots. 'Genu-ine snakeskin boots from the US of A. You see what I'm saying?' He took a step closer to me and swayed, 'You see what I'm saying, pal?'

'I'm not too sure.'

'Am I not talking sense? Are you suggesting that I'm not making sense?'

'Oh no, it makes sense.' I felt I was treading a fine line. He was tall, probably six feet four in his boots, grizzled, with a wild look in his eyes. The best course of action would be to say something uncontroversial. 'Nice boots,' I said.

'Do you want them?' He started to pull at one of the boots to take it off.

'No, no, I was just saying that's a good pair of boots.'

He stopped pulling the boot. 'Genu-ine snakeskin boots from the US of A. You see what I'm saying?'

I still didn't have a clue what he was saying. I waited, hoping he'd tell me, so I could avoid giving him an answer because I sensed I was going to get it wrong and upset him.

He put his hand on my shoulder. 'What I'm saying, pal, is Country Music. That's what you want to play on your jukebox. Listen, here's a tip – who's the greatest British country singer?'

I thought. Was it Hank Wangford, or the Rockingbirds? Elvis Costello even, he did a country album. I wasn't sure, there must be someone else. Perhaps it was a trick question and Hank Williams had been born in Wales.

The cowboy fumbled in his jacket pocket and pulled out a Woolworth's bag which he opened and took out a CD. He held it up to my face. 'There you go, Lonnie fuckin' Donegan. Greatest British country singer of all time, pal.'

34

'The King of Skiffle,' I said.

'That's right, the King of Skiffle. Look at that,' he pointed at the CD case. 'Track twenty-two, a bloody classic. I'm going to play that for you.'

I started to say it was OK, but then he questioned whether I really liked Lonnie or not, so I agreed that it would be good to hear the track. He went over to the bar and said, 'Here, Tina, let's have some real music on for once. Play track twenty-two on that will you, duck.'

Vin said, 'It's not more of your country shit is it, Cowboy?'

'Soft twat,' Psycho said.

'Best British country singer in the world this is, pal. Better than most of the Americans too come to that. Forget your bloody technical disco, and listen and learn.'

Tina put the CD on and it started playing. 'A touch more on the volume there, duck,' Cowboy said. He pointed at me, 'This feller wants to hear it.'

The room filled with Lonnie Donegan yelling, 'I got all livestock, I got all livestock…'

Cowboy came back over to me. 'You know this?' he asked.

'*Rock Island Line*, it's a Leadbelly song.'

'It's a Lonnie Donegan song. This is Lonnie now.'

'Leadbelly wrote it, Huddie Leadbetter, you know, discovered by John Lomax at the Louisiana State Penitentiary.'

'This is Lonnie fuckin' Donegan. Come on, let's hear you sing.' He started belting it out, '*Rock Island Line is a mighty good road, the Rock Island Line is the road to ride*.' He put his arm around my shoulder, 'Come on, let's hear what you can do.' He turned to me and put his face up to mine so our noses were almost touching. 'Chorus coming up, let's hear you.'

I thought I might have to attempt the chorus just to keep the peace when Rik came over, stood in front of Cowboy, whooped, and joined him on the chorus. They both sung the song at the top of their voices. When it finished Rik shook cowboy's hand.

'Lonnie fuckin' Donegan,' Rik said, 'best British country singer there's ever been. Not a lot of people know that. The King of Skiffle.

That takes me back. We used to do *Rock Island Line* in my first band – tea chest bass, thrashing away at a guitar I bought from the hardware shop for seventeen shillings and sixpence. *Rock Island Line*, bloody brilliant, man.'

He shook hands with Cowboy again and they got into conversation about the Quarrymen and where you'd get a tea chest from nowadays.

I got all the Bobbly Wobblers standing back up.

Sex and Drugs and Rock 'n' Roll

A few more locals had drifted into the pub, but there was no sign of Rhia turning up with a coachload of excited JookBoxFury fans and it didn't look like we'd be challenging the Last Night of the Proms for atmosphere. Fran muttered something about having to do everything herself and not trusting that girl to do anything, then she clapped a couple of times to gather us together. 'Guys! We're going to make a go of this. Let's get started. Are you ready, Simon?' Pony Boy nodded. She said to Laurence, 'Can you get them to turn this racket off and we'll get things underway.'

The Lonnie Donegan CD, which was still playing at maximum volume, stopped and *World Cup Willie* got cut off in its prime.

We took our places behind a couple of tables that we'd set up in front of the jukebox. Laurence placed a small trophy in front of Pony Boy. It looked more appropriate for a school swimming gala than the jukebox song selection world championships. He said, 'I must admit that the trophies were something of an afterthought.'

Pony Boy addressed the pub. 'Ladies and Gentlemen, welcome to the inaugural JookBoxFury competition here in the fabulous Queen Victoria. I think you'll all know who I am, but just to check let's try this.' He shouted out the first half of his old catchphrase, 'Saddle 'em up and...,' then he pointed towards the pub in general hoping they'd shout back the rest. No-one was even paying any attention, let alone wanting to be involved in any kind of audience participation. Pony Boy was undaunted and gave the pub the whole catchphrase himself, 'Saddle 'em up and ride 'em out!'

'Yee-haw!' Cowboy shouted back.

Pony Boy was encouraged by getting the hint of a positive response and he enthusiastically started to explain the rules, 'I'll be the referee…'

Psycho turned round from the bar with his hands above his head. He pointed towards Pony Boy and shouted, 'Who's the bastard in the black? Who's the baa-a-s-tard in the black?'

Laurence didn't pick up the referee reference and looked around, confused at what offence he might have caused. 'I gave those lads a couple of bottles of Jook, and that's the thanks I get.'

At least they were listening.

With a flourish, Pony Boy produced a multi-coloured bobble hat and we drew numbers out of that to determine the order of play.

Pony Boy introduced the contestants. 'First up we have our very own rocking academic, Dr Annilese Rococco, or as we call her on JookBoxFury – Dr Roc. I'm sure our next contestant needs no introduction to anyone who knows the Sixties classic *Violence is Golden* by The Peabodies. We're very lucky to be joined by the man himself, it's Rik 'the Guitar Man' Peabody.'

Rik stood up and punched the air. Cowboy shouted, 'Come on Pea Boy, do it for Lonnie.'

I was next. Pony Boy said, 'He's the people's champion, he's done a fantastic job sorting out the Bobbly Wobblers over here, and if you ever need any cardboard boxes shifting, he's your man – Ray Mitchell.'

I could see Vin over at the bar point towards me and say something to Psycho, who laughed and said something back, 'Soft twat,' probably. I wasn't too happy with the introduction, but I wasn't in a position to complain. I'd turned up to watch JookBoxFury and now I was in it. I could play the great music myself. I could win it. I could win it, and then surely they'd want to invite me to stay on the tour. I could live the rock 'n' roll lifestyle and go on to win the JookBoxFury final with some genius jukebox selections. Once that happened, who knows, I'd probably get offered a late night slot on Radio One. Even Radio Two would be OK, or Radio Six – I'd take any of them. If that didn't come off, I was bound to have made some contacts in the biz so I could get into A&R,

music journalism, something like that. Then in years to come I could say to my grandchildren, 'No, I never was in a band, but I did win the first JookBoxFury,' and the little scamps would rush over to my chair, looking up at me wide-eyed, 'You won the first JookBoxFury? That is soooo cool.'

It could happen. I'd got a good draw – get in there when the crowd had been warmed up, right as their enthusiasm was peaking. I just had to take it one step at a time. Win the first one and see where it went from there. Take my chance to end the days cowering behind my desk like a battery hen, having my feathers pecked off. Live the rock 'n' roll dream, be someone, be the Jook Duke of the Juke, even the Monarch of the Zeitgeist. That was my destiny and all I had to do was pick the right songs.

Pony Boy said, 'Finally, last, but she's certainly not got the least, I'm sure you've seen plenty of her before, and now you can see her in the flesh so to speak. It's the star of page and preen – Miss Babs Golightly.'

I could beat Babs Golightly. I could beat them all.

Vin stood up on his stool and cheered, 'You should come in here on Thursday and help Tina out behind the bar, Babs.' Babs waved towards him half-heartedly.

'Let's have a big round of applause for our contestants,' Pony Boy said, and clapped vigorously.

Cowboy gave a couple of claps and shouted, 'Yee-haw,' but no-one else seemed to think we'd done enough to deserve any kind of ovation.

Pony Boy asked Fran, 'Any word from Rhia yet? I'll make a show of it, Pony Boy never gives up on an audience, but we could do with a few more in the crowd because we're dying out there.'

Fran looked at her watch. 'Time's running out. You're going to have to run with it. If anyone can pull this around I'm sure you can, Simon. I certainly wouldn't hold your breath waiting for that foolish girl to come back.'

'Let's do it,' Laurence said to Pony Boy. 'Try and get them to buy a programme and see if that grabs their attention. Let's key into the audience's mindset and ramp it up from there.'

It was nice to see him demonstrating his confidence in the agency's creation. Pony Boy said, 'Right folks, the moment you've all been waiting for, our first JookBoxFury contestant will make her selections. If you could step up to the jukebox please, Dr Rococco.'

Dr Rococco faced the jukebox like a woman choosing olives at a deli-counter rather than the first contender to pick the greatest jukebox songs in the world. She went for a selection of neo-world music combined with a hint of zig-a-zig-ahh and chose *Exodus*, *Diamonds on the Soles of Her Shoes*, *Sisters are Doin' it for Themselves* and *Wannabe*. Obviously struggling by the end, her last track was the Chaka Demus and Pliers version of *Twist and Shout*. It wasn't a bad selection, but no-one sat up to listen, no-one stopped talking, no-one tapped their foot. There was nothing to compare with the impact of *Rock Island Line*. It was as if someone had just gone and put a few songs on the jukebox, without putting in the thought required to adapt the selections to the audience. It was going to take more than that to win JookBoxFury.

Rik was next to play and it was no-nonsense riffing from the start: *Duh, duh, duhrr. Duh, duh, dah, duhhrrr…* He went all out to rock the pub with *Smoke on the Water*. Rik played along with some virtuoso air guitar, but he stopped when a group of women wearing devil's horns, angel wings and t-shirts saying 'Monica's Minxes' tottered into the pub. There were about thirty of them, obviously a hen party, which promised to liven things up. The last devil/angel woman was followed by Rhia, who seemed to be trying to dissociate herself from the group who followed her, but they were proving hard to get away from. About fifteen morris dancers, dressed in white and ribbons, jingled in with bells on their legs, flowers on their hats, pewter tankards hanging from their belts, and big sticks in their hands.

Vin and Psycho were fairly interested as the hen party filed past them, but when the morris dancers came in, they really paid attention.

'Hey, backs to the wall everyone,' Vin said.

'What the fuck are you bunch of soft twats doing coming in here?' Psycho said.

'Bloody poofs,' Vin said. He grabbed one of the morris dancers by the shoulder and said, 'Here, let's try your hat on.'

Rhia came to the jukebox. 'That took some doing. No-one was in the least bit interested. I was in and out of every bar in the city trying to get people to come along, but no-one was bothered. I was about to give up when I found this hen party. I told them there was a celebrity competition going on, but they said they had other plans. Then I said there were free drinks and they started to get interested, so I told them there'd be a special limited edition free gift for everyone, and they nearly knocked me over in their rush to get on the coach.' She said to Pony Boy, 'I need to have a word with you about the free gifts.'

Pony Boy was concerned, 'What do you mean, free gifts?'

'Don't worry about that,' Laurence said. 'What about all these morris dancers? Did you bring them? I suspect that they're not consistent with our demographic.'

'Who? Oh, them,' said Rhia. 'I thought you might not notice them, they were a bit of a mistake.'

Over by the bar Psycho was trying to get one of the morris dancers to let him have a go with his stick.

Rhia said, 'They were in the same bar as Monica's Minxes. They were doing one of their rituals. Their leader, I think he's called Bilbo Baggins, heard me talking about the drinks promotion, and he told the others to get their sticks and follow me because there was free ale to be had. Their guy with the violin started playing a tune and it was like the Pied Piper. They all skipped out into the street and followed Monica's Minxes onto the coach.'

'I don't think we even had any morris dancers in the focus groups,' Laurence said, 'I'm not sure how this is going to play out.'

Morris dancers or not, it was standing room only in the pub by that point and things were looking more promising for JookBoxFury. One of the morris dancers put his tankard on the bar and said to Tina, 'What real ales do you have on this evening, my good lady?'

Tina said, 'Carlsberg or Stella.'

'No, what I mean is, what do you have in the way of cask ales?'

Tina raised her voice and spoke more clearly, 'We have CARLSBERG or STELLA.'

Laurence spotted an opportunity and went over to the bar. He talked to the morris dancer for a couple of minutes, then poured a bottle of Jook into the tankard. When Laurence came to sit back down he was very pleased with himself. 'Just in case any of these morris guys ask, Jook is made to an ancient medieval recipe by local craftsmen at a micro-brewery in Dorset. Thinking on your feet, adapting to the product life cycle, that's essential if you're going to have any kind of success in the advertising game.'

With the Queen Victoria full of people and noise, the atmosphere was starting to buzz and Rik's choices on the jukebox were lifting the mood higher. He followed *Smoke on the Water* with *Cigarettes and Alcohol* and then his own song *Violence is Golden (But My Wounds Still Bleed)*. He climbed onto his chair for the last chorus and got the hen party singing along. Then he went rock folk with Thin Lizzy's *Whisky in the Jar*. The morris dancer's fiddle player said, 'I can work with this,' and played along impressively, weaving in and out of the guitar solo. The Minxes clapped and jigged along.

Rik's final song started with a hip hop beat, but with a familiar tune over the top. Rik said. 'Fucking rap, I hate it. It's called *Earth Mutha Fucka*, it samples *Earth Mother, Moon Lover*. Listen out for my howling at the end – I'm getting royalties for this.'

Rik stood up and gyrated his hips to the music, then as the track ended, he howled along, still gyrating and thrusting to the beat until the record finished and he gave one last howl and raised his arms in celebration. Everyone in the pub roared back. Monica's Minxes were cheering, the morris dancers were clashing their sticks together and shouting, even Vin and Psycho were yelling for more. The live fiddle playing during *Whisky in the Jar* and Rik's howling at the end of *Earth Mutha Fucka* had grabbed everyone's attention. The Jook was flowing freely and JookBoxFury had become a real show. One of the Minxes shouted out, 'Come on, let's have some more music… and some more Jooky in the jar-oh.'

Pony Boy stood up. 'Ladies and Gentlemen, we certainly will have more music because next to make his selection is Ray Mitchell.'

'Who's Ray Mitchell?' one of the Minxes shouted.

'He's the soft twat with those fluffy spring fuckers,' Vin answered.

'We were all promised a free one of those for coming here,' the woman said.

'No, I don't think that's quite right,' Pony Boy said, 'there must be some mistake about that.' He looked towards Laurence.

Laurence waved his hand at Pony Boy to dismiss the idea and said, 'Come on, let's keep things going while we're trending on an upwards curve.'

Pony Boy announced me again, putting more into it, 'As I was saying, a special guest on JookBoxFury. For one night only, it's my very good friend, he's the voice of the fan, it's the fabulous – Raaaaayyyyy Mitchellllllllllllll!'

The silence was overwhelming. 'The soft twat with the fluffy spring fuckers,' how did I get to be that? I should have told Pony Boy about some of my other achievements. There was no point worrying about that when my JookBoxFury chance had arrived, I had to focus on the competition. I was going on at the perfect time. Rik had built the crowd up with some no-nonsense standards, plus two tracks he'd performed on himself, now I had to take it higher. Take that energy and use it, maybe give the crowd something a little quirky. I looked around the room as I walked up to the jukebox – in the world of JookBoxFury, that's the hardest walk you'll make. I wanted to look into the eyes of the audience, feed off their energy, but the only eyes I saw looking back at me were Cowboy's. His eyes were bright green. It was strange that I hadn't noticed before, but he had the greenest eyes I'd ever seen. Cowboy's stare gave me the inspiration I needed. I had to play some Country Music. That's what he'd said – Country Music. The music of the people.

I started flicking through the cards and it jumped right out at me, track thirteen, on the *Ladies of Country* CD – Bobbie Gentry's *Ode to Billie Joe*. It was an absolute classic, not out and out Country but a little off the wall, catchy but quirky, a great story – draw them in with that. I punched in the numbers to select it and flicked on through the cards, looking for my next track. I found it on Nirvana *Live Unplugged* – oh you beauty – it was inspired. I could play Curt Cobain singing *Where*

Did You Sleep Last Night?, another Leadbelly song. Absolute bloody genius. Cowboy was going to love the link to Lonnie Donegan there through the Leadbelly connection. I was on a roll. Keep it going, stay with that mood but give them something a bit more familiar. I got it, Lou Reed, *Perfect Day*. It was a Number One after that BBC charity thing, so everyone would be singing along to it and my credibility rating would go through the roof. No Velvet Underground, but get Lou Reed in there and you're away. Nye Hill was going to be feeling pretty foolish by the time I'd put my selection together. Yeah, but don't be over clever, perhaps go for a real crowd pleaser next, a kitsch Sixties pop classic, one for a real sing-a-long. It had to be Tom Jones' *It's Not Unusual*. Sweet, very very sweet. They'd be dancing on the tables when that came on. Plus, clever link with the previous track, 'It's not unusual' – 'It's such a perfect day'. The marks were going to be flooding in.

What to finish off with? I scanned the last few cards… how about… how about…? That's it, an anthem, perhaps the greatest protest song of all time – Pulp, *Common People*. When Jarvis Cocker sang the last section, 'Watch your life slide out of view', the locals in The Queen Victoria would know that I shared their spirit, they'd probably hoist me onto their shoulders. Genius selection, five great tracks, skilfully tailored to the specific audience and environment. Genius selection.

Ode to Billie Joe was playing as I sat back down, but the pub was full of chatter and no-one appeared to be listening to the song. You've got to listen to it to get the story and the whole business of the girl and Billie Joe McAllister throwing the baby, or the gun, or whatever it is, off the Tallahatchie Bridge. No-one was listening. Cowboy didn't even seem to have noticed that I'd played a country song. He had his foot up on a stool and he was putting all his effort into buffing his boot with a bar towel. At least *Where Did You Sleep Last Night* would grab his attention. When the Nirvana song started one of Monica's Minxes shouted, 'Come on, let's have some dancing music. Who put this miserable rubbish on?' Cowboy swapped feet and started buffing his other boot.

'Interesting choices,' Babs said. 'Who did put this miserable rubbish on?'

Perfect Day was my next track. I was sure that would win the audience over, but as soon as it came on a few of the Minxes started to boo. Vin sang along to a couple of lines, but in such an awful karaoke style, it sounded suspiciously as if he was taking the piss. 'I should get back to looking after your spring men, mate,' he shouted.

Pony Boy leaned over to me, 'It's up to you to choose what you play, Ray, 'but this is all a little on the sombre side. I hope you've got something a little more upbeat for the listeners coming on next, because I think we're losing them. Number one rule in broadcasting – never lose your audience.'

'It's OK,' I said, 'the next one's a winner. Everyone will be singing and dancing to the next one, it's a classic Sixties pop gem.' At least I hoped it was, my confidence in my own judgment was fading fast. Nye looked smug.

Laurence said, 'We're not doing much for the reputation of the Jook brand at the moment, that's for sure.'

Perfect Day finished. Even I was glad when it came to an end. There was a moment of quiet while the CD changed, and then the horns on *It's Not Unusual* started pumping out – 'Ba, ba dah. Ba, ba dah.' The mood in the room lifted instantly. It was an emotional roller coaster ride, I even began to feel good myself. When the track got to the part where Tom sings, 'It's not unusual to go out at any time,' a few of the Minxes looked at one another and squealed, 'Ba da ba da ba daaahh.' What did I say? It was a winner.

We were just coming into the second chorus and I felt that some serious dancing was about to break out when Vin shouted to Tina, 'I said turn it fucking down, I'm on the phone here.' Tina went behind the bar and the music faded to almost nothing. You could only just hear a very faint, 'Ba da ba da ba daaahh,' in the background if you really strained.

I stood up and said, 'You can't do that.'

Vin looked over to me and put his phone to his chest. 'I can do what I bloody like, mate, seeing as this is my local and you've never set foot in here in your life until you turned up tonight with your stupid fucking spring men.' Vin went on with his phone conversation and the chatter built back up in the pub.

I sat down. 'That's not right,' I said to Pony Boy. 'I should get to play that again because it was a real winner.'

'Smashing track by Jones the Voice, I agree,' Pony Boy said. 'I sympathize, but the rules are quite clear that each player may only play their tracks once. Perhaps you should ask your friend over there to hurry along with his phone call.'

I'd got one more track left to play and I needed the volume up. I looked over at Vin. He seemed to be winding up the conversation so I decided to leave it and not pressurize him. By the time he actually did finish and the music came back up, *Common People* was halfway through. As the track reached a crescendo I was waiting for the crowd in the pub to get into it. Vin got up from his stool and headed towards the toilets. As he passed me he stopped and said, 'This is bollocks. You know where it goes, "Smoke and drink and screw, cos there's nothing else to do"?' I nodded. 'Well it should be, "Fight and smoke and drink and screw." There should be bloody fighting in it.' He stared at me, 'Don't you agree? There should be fighting in it.' He kept staring, so I nodded again. Vin carried on to the gents.

Pony Boy said to me, 'Nice feller. You seem to have struck up a rapport there. Music is such a marvellous way of bringing people together.'

Great. I was sure Vin would be casting votes for me when we got to the marking, which wasn't long away, there was only Babs left to go.

Common People had barely finished when Pony Boy introduced Babs. Vin had just got back to his stool and he turned round and responded with, 'Way hay haaayyyyy. Way hay! Come on lovely.'

The Minxes cheered Babs. One of them shouted, 'Come on, girl, let's get this party started,' and the morris dancers clashed their sticks together. Babs smiled at the welcome and waved to the crowd.

Babs didn't take long making her choices and by the time she sat back down *You're the One That I Want* was playing. I smiled to myself. Olivia Newton John and John Travolta – fundamental error starting with a piece of pop nonsense like that, not even a hint of irony. She'd blown it.

It seemed that Monica's Minxes didn't agree, because almost

straight away they started bopping along and by the second verse a few of the morris dancers and locals were joining in. Everyone cheered when the song finished and as the next track started they kept dancing, in spite of it being Sting. Didn't these people have any standards? They were dancing away as if they didn't care. I couldn't believe it. The track Babs had chosen was *Message in a Bottle*, obviously better than Sting's solo stuff, but even so… Instead of booing and jeering, they were all loving it, dancing and singing along – 'Sending out an SOS, sending out an SOS.'

I'd be sending out an SOS if it carried on much longer.

When *Message in a Bottle* finished, Pulp's *Common People* started playing.

'Is this a mistake?' I asked.

'No, I chose this one,' Babs said. Then she stood up and dragged Rik out to join all the dancers who were still strutting their stuff in the middle of the pub.

'Is she allowed to do that?' I asked Pony Boy. 'I played it and the sound was turned down for half of the track, and then everyone ignored it. Then Babs gets to play it and everyone loves it.'

'Well, there's nothing specific in the rules to cover that particular scenario,' he said, 'and it does seem to be going down a storm.'

We looked over the room full of people dancing. *Common People* was getting to a peak and everyone started singing along: 'I wanna do whatever common people do.' Even Vin was off his chair, holding a bottle of Jook in the air and singing, 'Smoke and drink and screw, because there's nothing else to do.'

That was outrageous – what about the fighting? What about, 'Fight and smoke and drink and screw?' Where was the consistency? If you believe there should be fighting, you've got to stick to your guns. You can't have fighting in it one minute, and the next you're happy just to smoke and drink and screw. He'd gone down in my estimation.

Common People finished and we waited for the next track. No doubt it was going to be another very obvious crowd pleaser. Babs had probably forgotten that there were marks to be handed out for originality, I had to be way out in front on that score with *Where Did*

You Sleep Last Night? and *Ode to Billie Joe*. To my mind, originality was the category that really mattered. Of course, there was the Zeitgeist Award as well, although the way things were going Babs was probably in with a fair crack at that. The whole thing was becoming a complete farce.

The next track started with some mushy strings weeping around, then the vocals came in: 'I'm not in love, so don't forget it, it's just a silly phase I'm going through…' Babs had her eyes closed and her arms in the air, swaying along. Hearing *I'm Not In Love* was like smelling freshly cut grass. It took me back years, to a time when someone had played it to me in the bus station café in Sheffield. I snapped out of that when Monica's Minxes joined in on the chorus. They were all singing apart from Monica herself who'd gone to sit down. Maybe it wasn't appropriate to be singing along to *I'm Not in Love* just before your wedding, or maybe she wasn't in love at all, and the song had brought her face-to-face with her own situation.

I turned to Pony Boy to say, 'This is bollocks,' but he was swaying from side to side in his seat and humming along. When the track ended, he stood up and applauded saying, 'Superb choice, great memories, superb.'

Babs came and sat back down, slightly breathless, and said, 'There you go, that's how you make your jukebox song selection.'

Pony Boy looked at his notes and said to Babs, 'You've only had four songs. You've got another one to choose.'

'I'm sure that was five, the jukebox must be wrong. I can't pick another one now – I've peaked. How can I top that?'

'Well, you really need a fifth song,' Pony Boy said, 'or how are we going to do the marking? It isn't going to be fair.'

He'd suddenly become an expert on fairness. There hadn't been any evidence of that earlier on.

The chief morris dancer, Bilbo Baggins, came over and said to Pony Boy, 'Excuse me for butting in, but the young lady who brought us here said there was the possibility of us performing one of our dances for you. She said to come and have a word with you, and you might be able to sort something out. Would we be able to do that if you've finished playing the jukebox? By the way,' he said to Babs, 'your choices were absolutely splendid, just the kind of thing I like to listen to when I'm off duty.' He turned back to Pony Boy, 'If we could do a dance it would be a great honour, we're very keen to bring the tradition into new places to show people something of our heritage.'

Babs said, 'There you go then, that's my fifth choice – morris dancing.' She said to Bilbo, 'Come on then, let's see you shaking your bells and waving those sticks about.'

Pony Boy said, 'Strictly speaking, I'm not sure the rules really allow for one of the choices to be…' but he was too late, the fiddle player had started to play a fast and furious jig. The morris dancers lined up as if they were in a leafy green glade. It looked as though they were going to sing, the way morris dancers do when you accidentally see them dancing in a shopping centre. It wasn't a good sign. The fiddle player stopped and the dancers started their song, but instead of it being about a fair maiden a-romping o'er the hedgerows-o, or whatever it is they usually sing about, they belted out, 'Sex and drugs and rock 'n' roll, are all my brain and body needs.' They whacked their sticks together so hard it sounded like the pub was under sniper attack. The fiddle player started again and the morris dancers were off, smashing their sticks with such a crack that pieces of bark were flying off around them. The dancers weaved in-between each other at speed, leaping into the air and using every last ounce of effort to get as high as they could, even leapfrogging over one another, and generally looking like they were having a great time. In the middle of the dance they stopped to sing again and, continuing the Ian Dury theme, they sang, 'Hit me with your rhythm stick, two fat persons,' and clashed their sticks together three times for the 'click click click.' Then they spun off again into the dance.

Monica shouted, 'Come on, lads. Who needs male strippers when you've got dancing boys?' The morris dancers leaped into the air one last time and finished the dance with a powerful two handed smash of the sticks as more splinters fell to the floor. The pub burst into wild applause. When I had stepped onto the JookBoxFury tour bus I was hoping to hear about sex and drugs and rock 'n' roll from Rik Peabody, I never expected to hear it from a bunch of morris dancers.

Babs said, 'There you go, live music and dance, tradition, rock 'n' roll – it was all part of the plan. That's my number five. Let's get the marking underway because I have to say that I'm feeling good about this.'

Pony Boy said to Laurence, 'Let's collect the marks in.'

Laurence got up and spoke to Rhia. She started to make her way around the pub, stopping at tables and groups of Monica's Minxes and morris dancers, showing them the score sheet in the programme. After a few minutes, she came back to the contestants' table empty handed. 'Most of them haven't even got a programme, and the others can't be bothered to fill the score sheet in. A couple of people said they enjoyed the dancing, but that's about it. Oh, and they'd like some more Jook handing round and Monica wants to know what's happening about their free gifts.'

'Is the Jook proving popular?' Fran said.

'Well, there are plenty of people asking for more of the free green stuff,' Rhia said. 'Some of them were even singing, "Green grow the Jooksie-oh," for some reason.'

Laurence said, 'Now there's an encouraging sign.'

Fran didn't look too sure.

Pony Boy said, 'I've got it – the old clap-o-meter, like *It's a Knock Out*.'

'I think you mean *Opportunity Knocks*,' said Nye.

'You could be right,' Pony Boy said. '*It's a Knock Out* was where you could play your joker. The Radio Wonderful DJs did *It's a Knockout* for charity once, super fun. I had to go along a greasy pole dressed as a huge…'

'So is it a joker or a clap-o-meter?' Laurence asked.

Pony Boy said, 'The clap-o-meter's definitely the way forward.' He stood up and tapped his pen on the side of a glass. No-one took any notice until Bilbo Baggins spotted what he was trying to do and bashed a couple of sticks together until everyone quietened down. Pony Boy explained that each of the contestants would stand up in turn, and the people in the pub would have to applaud and cheer for their favourite to decide who had won Round One of JookBoxFury. That caused some confusion when it became apparent that Monica's Minxes and the morris dancers hadn't really understood what the competition was about because they'd arrived halfway through. That went a long way towards explaining their behaviour during my selections.

Pony Boy called out Dr Rococco's name. She smiled and waved but got no response, other than from Monica who said, 'My mother-in-law to be is wearing a kaftan dress a bit like that for the wedding.'

Rik was next. He took a bow and howled. Cowboy howled back and shouted, 'Lonnie fuckin' Donegan.' There was a sprinkle of applause, which registered at the bottom end of the clap-o-meter – Pony Boy was holding his arm at an angle and moving it in response to the applause volume. You had to give it to him that he was an adaptable host.

Pony Boy announced me, 'Ray Mitchell,' and I stood up to complete silence. People obviously hadn't understood what had gone on at all, so I decided it would be best to clarify things. 'There was a bit of a problem,' I said, 'because no-one was really listening properly to my first three tracks…'

'Because they were shite,' Vin shouted.

'… and then someone turned the music down when it got to my last tracks…'

One of the Minxes said, 'Typical man, always blaming someone else.' The other Minxes laughed, and a few of them starting booing and shouting at me to get off.

Pony Boy put his hand on my arm and said, 'I should leave it there, Ray mate.' He announced Babs, 'And last, but she's by no means got the least, she got us singing and dancing, and she even got morris dancers rocking the pub, which is something I've never seen before in my entertainment career – it's Babs Golightly.'

The pub went crazy for Babs, stomping and hollering until Pony Boy swung his clap-o-meter arm round to the max. When the applause had died down Pony Boy said, 'I'm very pleased to announce that the winner of JookBoxFury Round One is Miss Babs Golightly. Babs, will you come forward to collect the trophy?'

Babs stood up and there was more applause, which took on an edge when Vin and Psycho started clapping along and singing, 'Get yer tits out, get yer tits out, get yer tits out for the lads…'

Babs turned and gave them a stare, but they weren't fazed. Vin said, 'Come on darling – it's for the lads,' and they both started singing again.

Babs' confidence left her and she seemed unsure what to do. I waited for Rik to say something to Vin and Psycho, but he was looking the other way and sipping a Jook. Vin and Psycho kept singing, 'Get yer tits out, get yer tits out, get yer tits out for the lads.' Babs stopped staring at them and looked down at the floor.

I stood up and said, 'Hey, fellers, there's no need for that…'

Psycho shot off his stool, knocking it over, and came to stand right in front of me. His face was only a few inches from mine. He was slightly shorter than I was, so I thought that if things got nasty I was in with a chance, but he looked like the Hulk – not just because of his muscles, but because he had a strange green hue, as if he'd bathed in Jook. Then I saw his eyes – it was unnerving. He wasn't called Psycho for nothing. He wanted things to get nasty.

I waited for him to speak. If he said something like, 'Who the fuck asked for your opinion?' then maybe I could respond and try to calm things down. He didn't say a word. He just kept looking at me, pushing me backwards with his stare.

'Look,' I said, 'I don't want to fight about it…'

Perfect Day

I spent the night at the hospital. One of Monica's Minxes had a look at me and said I should get an x-ray.

At first, I didn't even know I'd been hit. I was lying on the ground not sure where I was and I heard Babs scream, 'You bastards!' The door of the pub crashed open and footsteps ran across the car park. Someone helped me to stand up, but I couldn't focus on anything. I didn't know it was possible to hit anyone that hard. He only hit me once, but I felt like my head was going to come off.

Babs said, 'Are you alright, Ray?'

I couldn't really see her but I said, 'I think so.'

'I get abuse like that all the time. You didn't need to do that for me.'

'I wish you'd told me that before.' I put my hand to my face to see if I was bleeding, but I couldn't feel anything. How could you hit anyone that hard without breaking all the bones in your hand? Maybe he had – that'd teach him.

'That's going to be a real shiner,' Pony Boy said. 'I'm going to get you over to the A and E, mate.'

'I think I'm alright,' I said. 'I'll just sit down for a minute.' I tried to clear my head. There was something I wanted to ask Pony Boy but I couldn't think what it was. I shook my head, trying to shake it clear – come on, focus. It came to me. 'Who got the Zeitgeist award? Who got that?'

Surely I'd got the Zeitgeist award for *Perfect Day*?

I never found out. I don't think they awarded it.

The last thing I heard as I left the Queen Victoria were the morris Dancers and Monica's Minxes joining together in a feverish chant of *'Green grow the Jooksie-oh!'* The sticks went, *clash, clash – clash clash clash*, and they chanted, *'Green grow the Jooksie-oh!'* The chant was still going strong as our taxi pulled away.

I felt better just sitting in the waiting area at the hospital. The smell of antiseptic was reassuring. My head pounded and the side of my face and my eye were swelling up, but I was finding it easier to focus.

The receptionist at the Accident and Emergency desk was talking to a policeman. Pony Boy said, 'We really should report the incident. We can't witness unprovoked violence and nothing gets done about it. I'll go and have a word with the officer there.'

I watched the TV that was up on the wall and my head throbbed in time to the music.

By the reception desk, Pony Boy talked to the policeman for a while. They shook hands and the policeman left, waving as he went.

Pony Boy came and sat back down. I asked, 'Didn't he want a statement or anything?'

'No, he just wanted an autograph. He'd have had a couple of Bobbly Wobblers too if I'd brought any with me. He was a big fan from the old days, never missed a show. He bought a Bobbly Wobbler at the roadshow in Colwyn Bay back in '76, but his wife threw it out when they moved house five years ago. I suppose I could send him one on.'

'What about reporting the incident?' I asked him.

'I don't think there's any point, mate – I doubt they'll be able to track that Bobbly Wobbler down now.'

After the doctor finally saw me he confirmed that I had a beauty of a black eye and the left side of my face was swollen to twice its usual size.

On films they could be in a massive scrap: thwack, thwack, karate kick, get punched again, crash through a window, roll down a bank, get hit with a piece of timber, thwack, thwack, thwack, get bashed against a tree and when it's all over, end up with nothing more than a slight cut above one eyebrow. I got one punch, went down like a sack of spuds, my eye was every colour of the rainbow and my face was the size of a melon. The doctor said it could have been worse.

It was morning when we left the hospital. Pony Boy took me back to the hotel where the JookBoxFury team were staying. I wanted to say my goodbyes and thank them for the experience – it's not every night you get the chance to be a victim of jukebox related violence.

They were all in the restaurant having breakfast. As we went in Pony Boy said, 'Here he is, the man of the moment, 'Sugar' Ray Mitchell,' and they all started to applaud.

Fran said, 'Ooh that looks sore, does it hurt ever so much? I once came off Prince during a point-to-point and I got a black eye. You poor thing.'

'That's a fuckin' beauty alright,' said Rik. 'I'd hate to see what the other bastard looked like after you'd finished with him.'

Babs slapped Rik on the shoulder, 'The other guy didn't have a scratch on him. They ran off, don't you remember?'

'Oh, I remember,' said Rik. 'The green mist came down and I was just about to wade in and get the bastards sorted out when they realized they'd bitten off more than they could chew. That's when they lit the green touch paper and retired.'

Laurence took a chair out at the head of the table for me to sit down and said, 'I've got a little proposition for you, Ray. Let me set the scene and then you can tell me how it grabs you. After last night's slight false start with the Jook launch, we've got three massively significant days ahead of us. Obviously, the final in London at the end of the week. That's live on the radio, national syndication, and we expect to build a high level of awareness from that. Tomorrow night, Glasgow, targeting the student-slash-indie audience. We're using that niche to initiate the viral marketing via the blogs and Facebook. And today, of course, we've got the press launch in Scarborough. You know, roll up your trouser legs, get a hankie on your head and work off Simon's roadshow vibe and create the buzz.

'What we've got lined up, and I think you're all going to like this one, is that we're holding the press call and the competition in a perfect 1950s themed café. Fantastic place, virtually unchanged since the Fifties: milky coffee in glass cups, award winning Knickerbocker Glories and, best of all, it's got a fantastic old jukebox full of 1950s and 60s discs which you guys are going to love – it's JookBoxFury heaven. We've got sixty or so movers and shakers from the leading press and magazine titles coming along and we should generate plenty of column inches because the journos are going to be very much a part of the competition themselves. They'll be voting for the winner, so they're experiencing JookBoxFury first hand and I've every confidence that they'll write some lovely pieces evoking the feel we want to create around the Jook space. Very much so.

'Now, this is where you come in, Ray. I've floated this one past Fran, and we think there's a huge opportunity to use you again in today's competition. Having a fan involved, it's a nice angle for the press. We'll keep it fairly low profile, it's no biggie, but it's a neat way of showing how we're linking the fan's enthusiasm to Jook. What do you say? All expenses paid of course.'

There was only one thing I could say. 'That's brilliant. And I can be in the competition again? That's great. Thanks, I really appreciate it. I really enjoyed it last night... apart from getting punched... and getting booed... and having my records called miserable rubbish... But that doesn't matter, you've got a great thing going here with JookBoxFury, and if I can stick with it for another day that would be brilliant. Thanks, thanks for asking me.'

'Just a note of caution though,' Fran told me. 'Laurence has persuaded me that this will benefit the campaign, but one thing we need to make crystal clear is that you can not be seen to get into any more fights. Negative publicity is one thing we really can't afford at this stage, so I must ask you to be a little more circumspect, Raymond.'

'I appreciate you giving me another chance in the competition,' I said, 'but I thought I did the right thing.'

'Can I just remind you, Raymond, that you will be a guest on the JookBoxFury tour. It isn't about giving you a chance, it is about giving Jook the best possible chance. As long as we think you can help us in our ambition to promote the brand, then we can work together. I do need to be sure that you will display behaviours that are compatible with the attributes of Jook.'

Rhia said, 'Ray was sticking up for Babs against those pigs, so I think we should be thanking him for that, not criticizing him for damaging the Jook brand.'

Fran said, 'And that, my dear, is one of the many reasons why you are the Junior Assistant on the campaign and I'm the Head of Jook Marketing. Let's put this issue behind us now and move on. Oh, and while we're on the subject of your participation, Raymond, although I'm sure it's wonderful to have you along as the 'voice of the fan,' as Laurence puts it, it wouldn't go amiss if you were to play some records that are a bit more fun...'

'Here, here,' said Babs.

Fran continued, 'Why don't you see if you can find something from one of the Disney soundtracks, they're always very popular and are hugely entertaining. Perhaps you could play one of those as we move forwards.'

Move forwards. It was like being at work, she sounded just like Justin Quine. He loved things to be moving forwards. Always move forwards. Never look back. Never stop to think. Move forwards. Quine wasn't going to be happy about me missing work. Surely I couldn't be expected to go to work in my condition, bruised and swollen, a night spent in hospital. I was still shaken. I needed to take it easy, maybe spend a day in a 1950s café by the sea to recuperate.

I rang Quine. When I finally got through I said, in quite a weak voice, 'Hi, Justin, I'm ringing in sick. I'm not well. I'm slightly involved in the JookBoxFury tour with Rik Peabody and Simon 'Pony Boy' Rogers as well, but the main thing is that I'm ill. I got punched in the face.'

Quine had been shouting to his secretary while I was talking. He wasn't interested in details. 'You're doing what? Having a day off? I'm sure I don't need to tell you what kind of havoc that is going to play with the Key Tasks Matrix. You do realize that we've got the Big One coming up in less than six weeks and we've got to keep all those plates spinning. Let's not forget that I'm taking the lead on a major new initiative that we mustn't lose sight of.'

Those new initiatives came along every few months to transform the business. If you missed one new initiative it didn't matter, there'd be another one along shortly, hyped up even more than the last one to cover its lack of substance and the fact that it was actually what we used to do before the previous new initiative changed everything around in the name of moving the business forwards. New initiatives were the emperor's new clothes – if you couldn't see their wonder, then you obviously weren't on-board.

'We've all got to be on-board going forwards,' Quine said. 'I need to know I can rely on you when the brown stuff hits the twirly thing. Christ, if I put in a sixty-hour week at the moment it feels like a holiday. There's no slack – I need you at your desk right now. Take a couple of paracetamol and I'll brief you on the new process change process at the ten o'clock huddle.'

I thought about Emily and her school project, drawing a picture of me being briefed by Justin Quine at the ten o'clock huddle. I told Quine I'd be back in a day or so and hung up.

JookBoxFury – I could because I believed I could. I would because I needed to.

candle in the Wind

After we'd been on the road to Scarborough for a while, Fran got us to sit together at the tables in the middle of the bus. She said, 'I'm determined that we should hit the ground running at the press conference this afternoon, so I've asked Laurence to run a short warm-up exercise to get us thinking about experiences we can relate to the Jook brand.'

Rik said, 'Well, there are a few occasions when I've had to drink my own piss…'

Fran stopped him. 'For the hundredth time, that is exactly the kind of comment that won't be helpful. This is precisely what I mean, Laurence. I hope your exercise will give Rik something to talk about other than… drinking his own… wee.'

'Don't get me started on that other stuff, man,' Rik said, 'they told me it was salty mayonnaise.'

'That wasn't you,' Nye said, 'that was Glen Matlock on tour with the Pistols.'

'Don't be so fucking sure, man. Where others follow, the Guitar Man has usually been there first. Talking of which, it must be time for the hair of the dog. I've got to admit that I woke up feeling pretty fucking green this morning. I just need a couple of the old Jookers to take the edge off.'

'Shall we move on?' Laurence said. 'When I came up with the idea of using JookBoxFury to promote Jook, I knew we'd found a way of tapping into something very fundamental about the pleasure we want our target market to associate with Jook consumption. It's very much the same process we've been using since we made those groundbreaking Levis ads back in the Eighties. By using a classic recording as the backing track you're instantly associating the product with a whole set of emotional responses that are already embedded within the consumer's psyche.'

'And ruining the song,' Nye said.

'Heaven forbid, if the song is ruined, the campaign is dead in the water. This is quite a different process. It's about the pleasure you get when you catch a great track on the radio, something you haven't heard for absolutely yonks, and then you hear it and it gives you a fantastic buzz. Let me give you an example, something that happened to me last weekend while I was driving out to the country to try and sort out the latest screw-up the builders had made on my barn conversion. I was motoring along with the top down, tense as anything, and all of a sudden that old Sade track, *Your Love is King*, came on the radio. It took me right back to when I was starting out in this game, and you know the stress just ebbed away and I remembered why I'd been able to afford the cabriolet and the barn in the first place. It put it all into perspective.'

Nye said, 'A beautiful memory of ersatz jazz as a representation of the Thatcher years. Very moving.'

'The Green Party,' said Rik, who was squinting through a Jook bottle at the skylight in the roof of the coach.

Laurence said, 'Well, yes, the Eighties, of course. That was only an example, although *Your Love is King* was quite a special track for me personally. What I want to achieve in this session is very much along those lines. I want us to get a feel for the power of music and how we can mobilize that for the benefit of the campaign. I want you each to share an example of a piece of music that has meant something special to you. It's as simple as that.'

He laid out a flip chart pad and some marker pens on the table. 'We've got plenty of flip chart so there's nothing to hold us back. Where shall we start?' He looked at me. 'Ray, your enthusiasm yesterday actually gave me the inspiration for this, so why don't you go first?'

I had still been thinking about how great it was to be on

JookBoxFury for another day and I was taken aback by having to do something. I started talking rubbish, 'Um, a song that means something, well, there's so many. Oh, God, which one do you pick? I'm not really prepared… could someone else go first?'

Oh, pathetic. Pathetic. My chances of making a mark in the competition were fading fast if I couldn't even think of one song.

'Nilche problemo,' said Laurence. 'Dr Rococco, would you like to start, and we'll come back to Ray at the end when he's had chance to think of a song. Sorry, Ray, it's not an easy thing to do, is it?'

Patronizing bastard. I started to put some serious consideration into coming up with a song that would restore my credibility, well, not even restore it, just give me some very small level of credibility. The first thing that came into my mind was *Wig-Wam Bam* by The Sweet, which was the first single I'd bought. It was too obvious, and I didn't have much to say about it. I thought I could tell them about a time I played *Seasons in the Sun* once, and a girlfriend walked out on me because of it. I couldn't though, not with Nye Hill there. What sort of credibility was I going to get in front of a super-cool ex-*NME* journo if I said my special song was *Seasons in the Sun*? I was already on shaky ground after suggesting it the night before as one of my ideal jukebox picks. I got away with it then, but it wasn't worth risking a second time. I couldn't use *Seasons in the Sun*. Not a chance. Come on – think.

Dr Rococco started talking about her piece of music without a second thought. 'I'm sure that what you say is right, Laurence, pop is most profound when it articulates… when it has that two-way articulative relationship with the listeners' own emotions. For that reason I am going to choose *Will You Love Me Tomorrow?*, which was the first single I bought. I was about fifteen or sixteen when I first heard it and for a young woman, and a young woman in love at that, *Will You Love Me Tomorrow?* encapsulated the way I felt… about decisions I had to make, and it really… well, it was my guidebook. I was a young woman growing up in South London and to hear other young women in America experiencing the same things, well, The Shirelles helped me. I won't tell you what decision I came to, that's between me and the young man concerned, but… The Shirelles, thank you.'

'Magnificent, wonderful,' said Laurence, 'great story. Nye, do you want to give us yours?'

'Sure,' Nye said. 'It's a funny thing, but when I think about musical memories, many of the special moments I recall come from seeing bands play. That's why I do what I do really. There's a thrill in seeing a great band, especially an undiscovered band, that takes me to another dimension. I can forget about being a critic and I'm a fan again. That's when it's most real, but when I think about those great moments, classic moments in pop even, that's all I'm left with – moments. So I could pick a track like *Pretty Vacant*, which I relate to the time I saw the Sex Pistols at that children's party they did one Christmas day in Huddersfield and John getting into a food fight with all the kids. They were all throwing Christmas cake at him. The kids didn't know he was public enemy number one, and they didn't care. Or I could choose something that reminds me of seeing Joy Division in the early days, while they were still called Warsaw, and being one of the first to recognize Ian Curtis's jerky intensity, in both senses of that phrase. Or seeing Jonathan Richman play *Ice Cream Man* at that legendary show at the Hammersmith Odeon, and the audience loving it so much, and Jonathan loving it so much, that every time the song ended the cheering swept him up into giving them more, doing another verse, until he'd reprised the song ten or more times, each time better than the last.

'Do you see what I'm saying? Those were great artists giving performances that were on another level, transcendental even. Those gigs would count amongst my best experiences, but all I really know about them now, when I look back, is what I've told you, just snippets. So I can think about those moments, but I can't really get back there. I could think about those moments all day long and I wouldn't get any closer to the feeling. But then, one morning a few days ago, I was in the kitchen getting my breakfast, perhaps making a pot of tea, and my eleven year-old daughter was there waiting for the toaster. When it popped up she sang, "Toast, just toast!" because she'd seen the Streetband singing that Number One of theirs on *Top of the Pops 2* a couple of days before. In that instant, that snatch of song gave me an intense feeling from the past, from when the song was in the charts. For some reason, for a moment, maybe even a fraction of a moment, I was taken to another time and another place.

'The thing was, I wasn't taken back to a specific event or thought – it was pure feeling. I felt like I'd felt back then, as if a tunnel to the past had briefly opened up and something slipped through from the other side. I wanted to grasp that fragment of the past, hold on to that feeling and be there, be me all those years ago with all that excitement of being young and starting out. But I couldn't get to it. As soon as I felt the past tug at me, it slipped away, and there was nothing there, nothing to remember.

'So why is that? It could have been the song itself, or perhaps it was because it was still dark outside, or the feeling you get from the time of year. Could it have been that? Or maybe it was the smell of the toast. I don't know, but why is it that my daughter singing a couple of words from some throwaway nonsense took me back so powerfully, when my memories of the best music I've experienced are nothing more than tiny… crumbs? So, that's mine – *Toast* by the Streetband. Thanks for the memories.'

'OK, OK,' said Laurence uncertainly, 'that's um, right. Um, interesting one. OK, well let's move on quickly shall we? Simon, would you like to give us your musical memory?'

'Love to, mate.' Pony Boy's cheery enthusiasm made him sound like he was presenting his radio show. 'I'm not sure whether it's going to be quite as profound as the examples from my intellectual pop pals here, but it is something that meant a great deal to me way back when. Some of you will guess it I'm sure – *Don't Go Breaking My Heart*, big smash for Elton and Kiki Dee way way back in the summer of '76 if I'm not mistaken. It was number one when we were doing the Radio Wonderful roadshows. My trademark was the old bobble hat, because it was brass monkeys out on the prom when we were doing the shows. One morning, while the fellers were setting up, I went into one of the fishing shops down by the sea front – it might even have been in Scarborough, we'll have to go and have a look. That guy won't believe it if he sees me turning up again, I bet he's still got the signed photo up on the wall. Anyway, I went in the shop and bought a woolly bobble hat and I started wearing it as a joke, you know, here's my British seaside summer wear – a bobble hat.'

'I thought there was a heatwave in '76, hosepipe bans, swarms of ladybirds,' said Nye.

'That must have been '77. This summer I'm talking about was bloomin' freezing.'

'Wasn't *Don't Go Breaking My Heart* number one in '75?' I said.

'I think you could be right,' said Nye. 'This whole bobble hat business sounds like a fabrication.'

Pony Boy was affronted. 'If you think it's a fabrication, then you come and have a look at the thirteen hundred Bobbly Wobblers I've got in these boxes.' He went to one of the boxes and pulled it open to show Nye. 'Come and have a look.'

'I don't need to look. I've seen them and they are a truly awesome promotional device. All I'm saying is the facts aren't stacking up.'

'Let's not get too hung up on the facts,' said Laurence. 'You were telling us about your bobble hat, Simon.'

'These Bobbly Wobblers have been a real money spinner,' said Pony Boy. 'And another thing, do you think there'd be any Red Nose Day if there hadn't been any Bobbly Wobblers? Just think about it for a moment.'

Everyone thought about it for a moment.

'The bobble hat?' said Laurence.

'Oh, yes, the hat,' said Pony Boy. 'I got this bobble hat, and it was a great laugh, and the kids loved it and they started coming along to the roadshows wearing them. Wonderful, great memory.' Pony Boy sat back down.

'I don't get it,' said Nye. '*Don't Go Breaking My Heart* was number one – possibly – and you may – or may not – have been moved by the heatwave to buy a bobble hat. Is that it? I can see why you said it wasn't profound.'

'Oh, well, that's the thing,' Pony Boy said. 'The kids picked up on it and they were coming along to the roadshows wearing bobble hats as well. So I started playing *Don't Go Breaking My Heart*, and I got the audience to yell out "Hat" instead of "Heart" – thousands of kids chanting, "Don't go breaking my HAT," and, you know, holding their hats up in the air on the word "hat". Great memory, bloomin' marvellous. I actually recorded it, all new lyrics,' and he sang, 'Maybe if I had a trilby – Baby, that's not your kind.'

'So you changed it quite a lot,' Nye said.

'Oh yes. I was hoping to get Annie Ashton from *The Golden Shot* to do the female part. I was going to do it on the *Pops* wearing lots of different hats, get Flick Colby to work out a whole routine for it with Pan's People. It was a sure fire number one after the coverage we'd got on the roadshow, but we couldn't get clearance to release it. If you ask me it was the label that blocked it, I'm sure it wasn't Elton because he was always up for a laugh. Anyway, that's my choice, *Don't Go Breaking My Hat*.'

'Another classic,' said Nye.

'Great, thanks for that, Simon,' said Laurence. 'Let me just capture these on the flip chart.' He wrote up *Will You* ❤ *Me Tomorrow*, *Toast* and *Don't Go Breaking My Heart/Hat* up on the flip chart. 'Right, good range of stuff so far. I'm liking this a lot, so let's keep it going. Babs, your turn next I think.'

Babs had her elbows on the table and her head in her hands. She looked up and said, 'What do you want me to do? A song? Cool.' She took a deep breath and started. 'I was going to say *Sorted for Es and Wizz* 'cos when I heard that at Glastonbury it was amazing, wicked, because I was kind of sorted at the time and I heard that and I was buzzing around like I was running around inside the song then it got to the line at the end "What if you never come down?" and God, what a bummer there I was high as a kite and Jarvis says, "What if you never come down?" and I was like "no way" and apparently started crying loads and got on a real downer and everything and it really freaked me out and we had to go back to the tent to chill out and missed loads of stuff – so I'm not choosing that. My tune is going to be *Can't Get You Out of My Head*, especially with that New Order backing track, I go mental on the dance floor whenever I hear that. If you want a song to get you up on the floor, that's the one, it's wicked.'

'Right,' said Laurence, who had already written *Sorted for Es and Wizz* on the flip chart, 'shall I cross this one off?'

'Yeah, cross it off. I hate that song. What if you never come down? What kind of crap is that?' Burned out, Babs put her head back in her hands.

Laurence wrote *Can't Get You Out of My Head* on the chart and said, 'OK, Rik Peabody, it's your turn.'

Rik was staring at the skylight again, rocking backwards and forwards slightly, with Jook empties wedged between the fingers of each hand. He looked like a man who might never come down.

'Rik, are you OK there?' Laurence asked him. 'Have you got a musical memory for us?'

Rik continued to gaze at the skylight. He suddenly flinched and screwed up his eyes. Babs nudged him, 'Are you alright, Rik?'

Rik snapped into life as if he'd just been transported from another planet. 'Oh, shit,' he said. 'What the fuck was that? Did anyone else see that?' He looked up at the skylight again. 'Oh shit!' He pushed himself back into his chair. 'Can't you see it now?'

We all looked at the skylight, but it was just a skylight.

'What can you see, mate?' Pony Boy asked him.

'All that green slime oozing out of the roof. It's going to trap us if we don't get out of here.' He stood up, but looked like he couldn't move. He looked down at his feet, 'The bastards are coming to get us. We're knee deep in it here.' He sat back down and pulled his knees up to his chest. 'I'm feeling a little strange,' he said. 'I'm feeling fucking strange actually.'

'What are you on, mate?' Nye asked him.

'I'm not on anything, man. I'm clean as a whistle now. I've only had a couple of these juices.' As well as the eight bottles Rik was holding between his fingers, there were as many again on the table in front of him, which we all looked at suspiciously.

Fran realized with horror what everyone was thinking. 'It's not that. It's not the Jook,' she said. 'We've gone through all the tests, EEC regulations, a full range of food standards tests, risk assessments – you can rest assured that all the ducks are in a row. We've actually got some results showing the health benefits. Jook wouldn't harm a fly.'

'The juice can make you fly?' Rik got to his feet and flapped his arms up and down like a nervous chick.

'Well, Rik doesn't look too good,' Nye said to Fran.

'No, I'm alright, man.' Rik kept flapping gently. 'I just need to get the hang of it. I think I just got a bit… you know… green. Yeah. Fine. You carry on. Don't mind me.' He gradually slowed his flapping and lowered himself back into his seat.

'Right,' said Laurence, 'well, it's your turn to choose a piece of music, Rik. Do you want to give it a go?'

'Sure, man, no fucking problem. Let me think for a minute.' He looked up at the skylight. 'OK, a song. Well, probably *Green Door*.' He thought again, still staring at the light. 'Or *Green Green Grass of Home*, or *Greensleves*. Any of those, those are my favourites, every one a fucking classic.' With that he stood up and lurched towards the back of the bus. He said, 'Look, I'm just going to lie on this nice green lawn for a couple of minutes,' then crashed down onto the aisle between the seats. Pony Boy, Nye and Babs rushed over to check on him.

'Let's get him in the recovery position,' said Pony Boy.

'No, he's OK,' said Nye, 'his eyes are still open.'

Babs knelt down next to Rik and took his pulse, 'He's alright,' she said, 'he's just having a little moment. I've had a few of those in my time.'

'I'm fine,' croaked Rik. 'I'm going to have a couple of minutes here and then up and at the fuckers. You lot get back to bed. Cheers, I'm alright.'

Fran didn't look happy with the way things were developing. Having a deranged greaser out cold probably hadn't been part of the launch campaign plan. She said, 'If we stopped what we were doing every time Mr Peabody demonstrated erratic behaviour we'd never get anything done. Come on, at least while he's sleeping it off we can continue without his foolish interjections.'

'Well, let's carry on, but someone keep an eye on him,' said Laurence. 'Rhia, are you going to give us a song or are we missing out the Jook team?'

'I'll give you a very quick one,' said Rhia. 'I've got one from yesterday morning, actually and I think it's a good one. The funny thing is, I'd never even heard the song before, but I'd read about it and then when I did hear it, it turned out to be brilliant. I mean, straight into my all time top twenty, maybe even top ten, and I just want to hear it again. You know Elvis's backing singers…?'

'The Jordanaires?' said Pony Boy.

'No, no, later than that – in the Vegas years. The girl backing singers. You see them on film with him, sharing a joke. They're on the concert film of *Suspicious Minds* I think. Well, they were a vocal group called The Sweet Inspirations. I'd read about them…'

'It's in the Peter Guralnick book isn't it?' I said.

'That's right, that's where I read about them. Before they joined Elvis, in fact the reason he wanted them to sing with him, was they had a single out called *Sweet Inspiration*. *Sweet Inspiration* by The Sweet Inspirations. So I'd heard of the song, but I hadn't actually heard it. Then I stopped for a coffee on the way to work.'

'No wonder you were in so late,' Fran said, almost under her breath.

'The music playing in the coffee shop was some old rock 'n' roll and soul and R&B kind of stuff, really good, not like the non-stop Elton John they sometimes play.'

'Yeah, sometimes all you hear in there is *Don't Go Breaking My Hat*, eh Pony Boy?' said Nye.

'You see how fast it's caught on,' said Pony Boy. 'I knew it was a smash.'

'Well, none of that stuff,' said Rhia. 'It was all great music, which I was enjoying a lot. Then a track started with a great little riff, kind of country soul guitar and crisp drums and the first words were, "I need your swee-ee-eeet inspiration." So I knew it had to be *Sweet Inspiration* by The Sweet Inspirations, and it was just brilliant. It was partly gospel and rock 'n' roll and soul and country, you know, it was all of them at the same time. In the middle of the song there was a section where the music dropped down and one of the singers took the lead, giving it this, well – heavenly to be honest – it was heavenly gospel singing. She cried something like, "When you call me darlin', sets my soul on fire," and one of the other singers comes back with the most soulful "Yeah" you've ever ever heard. I love hearing a soulful "Yeah" in a song. It was beautiful, and it kind of took my breath away. I sat there thinking, *life is great*, you know, life is so sweet. Sweet inspiration, it's a feeling I don't get from music all that often now. When you're a kid you just love so much music, and you really do love it.'

Nye said, 'It's like that line of Weller's, "…when you're young, you used to fall in love with everyone, any guitar and any bass drum".'

'That's it, that's it exactly,' said Rhia. 'I felt like that again, like a kid. Fantastic. And I sat there thinking, life – is – great. I've just heard one of the best songs in the world, and I'm starting off on this brilliant experience to be organizing the JookBoxFury competition…'

'Assisting organizing,' Fran said.

'Well, involved in organizing it and having the chance to meet all of you. It's quite daunting in some ways, being an ordinary girl who works in an office being with all of you, but I'm really excited about the whole thing, and that was all kind of encapsulated when I heard *Sweet Inspiration*. I just knew this was going to be a good experience.'

'Lovely, thanks for that, Rhia,' said Laurence.

'I thought it was only going to be a quick one,' said Fran.

Laurence asked Fran if she wanted to give a song.

'I don't listen to a lot of music myself,' said Fran, 'but my Gerald is a big rock fan. He's ever so proud of his Bang and Olufsen and he always plays lots of rock in the car when he's travelling around and he loves things like *Chicago*.'

'The band?' asked Nye.

'No, the soundtrack. Gerald likes a lot of music like that, *Chicago*, the *Wizard of Oz*, *Oklahoma!* He's very keen on the Disney soundtracks too, so I'm going to choose *Hakuna Matata* from the *Lion King*. Gerald always says that's our song because he took me to see the *Lion King* on our first date. That's a lovely song. It does inspire me as well. When things are difficult at work, and everything's getting on top of you, and your staff aren't pulling their weight,' she looked at Rhia, 'then listening to *Hakuna Matata* can make you realize that tomorrow's another day and things are going to be brighter going forwards. It is lovely. Oh, oh, and *Candle in the Wind* as well, for Diana.'

'OK, that's great, Fran. Thanks for sharing those special songs with us,' said Laurence.

There was only me left to go.

DISC TWO, TRACK TWO

Wig-Wam Bam

'Right,' said Laurence, 'back to you, Ray. Hopefully hearing everyone else's choices has given you a few ideas. Has it helped? Have you been able to think of a song? If you haven't that's OK. Perhaps it isn't fair to expect too much from you when you're not connected to the music business as the rest of us are, so by all means we can miss you out if you want.'

'I've got one,' I said.

What was he saying, not connected to the music business? He'd come up with *Your Love is King*, and then he had the gall to say that I might not be able to think of a song. 'Oh, I've got one alright,' I said, 'and it's a good one, a very good one.'

It had to be a good one, although I hadn't actually chosen a song. My mind had pretty well gone blank as far as choosing songs went. While everyone else had been talking about their choices, I'd been wracking my brain, but I found myself just thinking about thinking about songs, without being able to drag any actual songs into my mind. The only one that kept popping into my thoughts was *Seasons in the Sun* – I couldn't get rid of it. Shit, I was going to have to go with it. What the hell, Nye Hill had gone with a novelty hit, Rik Peabody had mumbled a couple of songs with green in the title... *Seasons in the Sun* wasn't that bad, just go for it. Oh no, I couldn't, there must be something else...

'Do you want to tell us what it is then?' said Laurence.

'OK... I'm going to go for *Seasons in the Sun*, Terry Jacks.' Everyone looked at me expectantly. It's possible that Nye's mouth was hanging open in amazement. I think Dr Rococco was smiling wryly.

'Not again,' Babs said from between her hands.

It was too late to turn back. I launched into the explanation. 'I suppose it's fairly maudlin in some ways, but my memory of it is of quite a funny thing that happened to me when I played that song once. It was on a jukebox actually, which is a co-incidence as we're here for JookBoxFury, so it's very appropriate really. I hope so anyway.

'It reminds me of a Sunday afternoon, years ago, at the bus station café in Sheffield. You know the kind of place: condensation running down the windows, one dried-up piece of chocolate cake and an egg custard in the display, a girl serving who's apparently never made a cup of tea in her life before, huge love bite on her neck if I remember rightly. There were only a couple of other people in there, and a little kid whining about something. Nothing going on really.

'I was in there with this girl I'd been going out with, Sandra – Sandra Daft. That was her real name, Sandra Daft. That's actually what started the whole conversation off because we started talking about getting the school bus, and…'

'Are you choosing a song or telling us your life story?' Fran asked me. 'Let's focus on the exercise, shall we?'

'Oh, OK. Well, Sandra was helping out in an old people's home for a summer job, and she'd gone in to check on one of the old dears and turn her radio off and everything for the night. While Sandra was tucking the bedclothes in, the lady grabbed hold of her hand with a really strong grip and looked right at her. The old lady didn't say anything. She just looked right into Sandra as if she was pleading for something, it was a kind of spiritual connection apparently. Then the old lady's grip went loose and the look went out of her eyes – like the light had been switched off – and she'd died. She died right there, holding Sandra's hand. And the song that had been playing on the radio, like a soundtrack to the whole experience, was *Seasons in the Sun*, you know – "Goodbye my friend it's hard to die, while birds are singing in the sky."

'Well, we were sitting there in the bus station café, and Sandra told me how this old woman died holding her hand, and how *Seasons in the Sun* was the saddest song she'd ever heard, and she started sniffling. I didn't really know what to do, so I went to get two more cups of tea. While I was waiting for the girl with the love bite to practise her tea-making skills, I saw the jukebox there on the wall by the counter. I thought, 'I'll put a couple of songs on to lift the mood.' As I was flicking through the records I spotted *Seasons in the Sun* and without really thinking I selected it. I didn't think really, I just spotted it and thought, 'Seasons in the Sun, we were just talking about that.' I got back to the table as the song started to play. Sandra had been crying and dabbing her eyes with a tissue and all that, but she looked up at me when the song came on and burst into tears again. Then she stood up, grabbed her bag, called me a…'

'Heartless bastard!' Babs shouted at me. She'd had her head in her hands all the time and looked as though she was asleep, but she suddenly stood up and shouted, 'Heartless bastard!'

That was a shock. Everyone else had got a fairly positive reaction to their songs. Even Pony Boy didn't get called a bastard for all that nonsense about bobble hats. It seemed a bit harsh.

'You're a heartless bastard,' Babs said again. 'What do you say to that with your oh-so-clever music choices?'

I was stunned. 'Um, well, I wasn't expecting… I mean… I don't think I was too heartless… that's what Sandra said to me at the time though…'

'I know,' Babs said. 'I know.'

'I'm sorry, I don't get you.' I was beginning to wish I'd gone with *Wig-Wam Bam*. What was it with *Seasons in the Sun*?

'No, you don't get me,' Babs said. 'You really don't get it, do you? You were a heartless bastard then, and you're a heartless bastard now. You think it's funny to come here and laugh about the way you mocked me for seeing that lovely old lady die, and you probably think it's funny that you walked out on me just because I played a song that wasn't cool enough for your oh-so-clever snobby music taste.' She spat 'taste' out with real venom.

What? 'Sandra?' I said.

'I suppose so, not that anyone calls me that now,' said Babs. 'I knew it was you as soon as I saw you, but you didn't recognize me did you? That's why I played *I'm Not in Love* last night, but not a flicker. You didn't even recognize me. Well, that's good, because I'm Babs Golightly now, not someone who would ever go out with a loser like you – even though I actually liked you for some bloody silly reason. I'm Babs Golightly, so you can forget that you ever knew me. I'm glad you didn't recognize me.'

I closed my eyes for a moment to try and understand what was going on. I was back in the bus station café, sitting on my own at the Formica table, not knowing what to do, while Sandra stood sniffling by the magazine rack. I didn't know what to do back then, and I didn't know what to do on the JookBoxFury tour bus. I opened my eyes to see Babs glaring at me. A lot of years had passed since I'd seen Sandra, and looking at Babs you'd have to say she'd undergone quite a transformation. I'd only really been out with her a couple of times – was I supposed to be some sort of memory man? There was no denying it though, underneath the peroxide and the cleavage and everything, she did look a bit like Sandra. I mean, it was Sandra. Shit, Sandra was Babs – those pictures – and I'd been out with her. I didn't have a clue.

Everyone was watching me, and Babs/Sandra still seemed to be waiting for me to explain why I hadn't recognized her. 'I kind of recognized you,' I said. 'It's just that you've, you know, you've scrubbed up so well. You're not…'

'I've what? I've scrubbed up well. What are you saying?' She held her hand out to me to close the conversation, then sat down and turned towards Laurence. 'I'm going to be talking to my agent about this. No-one said there were going to be losers on this show, heartless bastard losers as well.'

'No-one told me that either,' Rik croaked from the back of the bus. 'I'd have thought twice if I'd have known a load of heartless bastards were involved, because you can't trust those fuckers.' He stood up unsteadily and lurched towards us. 'Right, it's time to get to the bar.'

'Are you alright about the green stuff?' Nye asked him.

What a relief it was to be talking about the green stuff again.

'What green stuff?' Rik said.

'All that green slime you said was oozing out of the walls.'

'It sounds like you've been having one of your flashbacks, man. Right, who's ready for a little drinkie? I could murder one of those green thirst quenchers. Is anyone else coming?'

'I could use a drink,' said Babs. 'It's been quite a day so far.' She looked at me, 'And I certainly didn't expect to see you again, whatever your name is.'

'Well, perhaps I could join you for a quick drink and we can catch up,' I said. I needed to do something to try and retrieve the situation. Who'd have thought that making a bad choice picking a song on a jukebox would haunt you for the rest of your life?

'I don't think we've got any catching up to do,' Babs said. 'Come on, Rik, where's that drink.' Babs took Rik's hand and led him to the back of the coach.

Laurence said, 'Well, there you have it. Interesting exercise.' He started to roll up the flip chart.

'Are you going to do anything with that list?' asked Dr Rococco, 'because I could use it. Those songs are a marvellous illustration of meaning in use. I've been to a three day IASPM conference in Finland on interpreting meaning in popular music, and I didn't get as much out of it as I did from that session. What was interesting was the way almost everyone chose a piece of music not for the music itself, or the lyrics come to that, but for the part it played in memory. Do you see how we've overlaid our own experiences onto the music, and in doing so we've given the music a meaning that's quite unrelated to any desire or intention of the musicians themselves? Lovely. I can see a paper for the *Journal of Popular Music* coming out of this. Thanks, Laurence, lovely session.'

Fran said, 'It had its moments, although it wasn't quite what I anticipated.' She turned to confide in Laurence and in a stage whisper said, 'I'm still not convinced about your decision to put Raymond in front of the press. I wonder if he might prove to be more of a liability than an asset.'

'Not a problem, not a problem at all,' Laurence told her, which was a relief. 'A quick course of media training should do the trick, and then I think we can really boost that fan angle. The press guys are going to love it. Media training is the thing. I'll sort it.'

Laurence called to Nye, 'Mr Hill, just the man. I'm seeking a short burst of media training for our friend Ray here. As a gentleman of the press yourself I wonder if you might oblige with a few pointers to set him on the right track.'

Nye said, 'After the entertainment he's just provided, how could I refuse.'

'Splendid, we only need the basics to get him prepared. Obviously I expect the meat of the conference to be about the Jook product, but if Ray's on hand with a brand-boosting sound bite here and there it might just give us that little extra.'

'Yeah, I can do that. I hate press conferences myself, you really want to be one on one with the artist, but I've done a fair few, so I can talk him through what to expect.'

I joined Nye at his table. He said, 'Co-incidence, destiny, it could be both, or neither, but I've just been writing one of my rock 'n' roll mythologies on this very subject. They're loosely based on Roland Barthes' *Mythologies*, you know, the French theorist. I thought it would be cool to extend that kind of thinking to Mythologies of Rock and Pop. They're a follow on to the Nyehillisms, I'm thinking of calling them *Nyethologies*. They're about how the mythologies of rock and pop give us an ideology about the world in general that we take for granted, you know, the way the Man keeps control. I've done a few so far: *He Kissed Me and it Felt Like a Hit*, *Dead Stars Rock!*, *Sympathy for the Devil's Music*, *Far Out With Brutus Trout*, *Paul McCartney is Dead/Gorgeous*, *The Summer of Luv*, that kind of thing. Anyway, as luck would have it, this one is called *Drumbeat to Fleet Street: Rock Stars Talking Louder Than Song*, it's about this very topic. I'll run through that to give you the gist. The thing is, it all boils down to four classic approaches.'

At the back of the bus, Rik and Babs had started up on the Jook chant, clinking bottles together and chanting, *Clink, clink – clink, clink, clink* – '*Green grow the Jooksie-oh.*'

Nye nodded towards Rik and Babs, 'You see why the press get accused of making stories up – sometimes you have to. You never would with these four ways of handling the pop/rock press conference though. Let's start at the beginning. Number one, obviously, you've got the Elvis approach. Always polite, almost deferential: "Yes, sir." "Well, sir, I'm just making my records, I don't know why they like them really." "I'm just a country boy, sir." "I was driving a truck and on my lunch break I went into a little record store to make a recording for my momma, that's all it was, sir."

'You know, you watch films of Elvis talking to the press and to Ed Sullivan and those other TV hosts in the Fifties, and it's hard to understand why people found him so shocking. His music was being denounced as the work of the devil, and his records were being smashed in protest, but it didn't make sense because he was so polite: "Yes, sir," "Well, thank you very much for having me on your show, sir." He was a real nice boy, good to his folks, loved his mother. But then you look at what he's wearing compared to the TV host. The host looks like he just got home from the office, his hair's neat and tidy, like he's come straight out of a board meeting. In comparison, Elvis looks like he's landed from another planet – Planet Cool – in some crazy checked jacket, and even in black and white his shirt's pink. He's got a strand of hair falling over his eyes, which are very dark – "Is that boy wearin' make-up?" – and he looks out at the audience and the girls start to scream because… because, what else can they do? – "He looked at me." Because even though Elvis is saying, "Yes, sir, thank you for having me on your show, sir," his look and his smile, and – "Good lord in heaven's name above, do you see the way he's shakin' his legs?" – it says that he knows something that the TV host and all the other squares don't know. He's got a secret that only the kids understand, and they want to be part of it. That's why he was so thrilling and threatening. But he was polite – "Yes, sir." So you've got your first approach to press conferences right there: polite, deferential, but with a smouldering threat.'

I nodded, 'A smouldering threat, right.' I wasn't sure whether it was the kind of media training that Laurence had in mind, but Nye was on a roll, and I was getting to hear him virtually perform one of his articles straight at me. I wasn't going to stop him.

Nye got into the next one. 'It goes without saying that The

Beatles gave the second basic approach to the pop music press conference. "Listen, do you want to know a secret?" There was no bloody secret any more, the secret was out of the bag. They were four lads from Liverpool having a laugh. The deference had gone because they were in a gang, playing together, playing with the journalists, entertaining themselves and entertaining everyone around them because they were the Fab Four mop tops.

'The journalists are asking them things like, "When are you going to get a hair cut?" and they come straight back with something like, "I had it cut this morning."

"Is Ringo the best drummer in Liverpool?" – "Ringo isn't even the best drummer in The Beatles."

"Why do you get more letters than the rest of the band?" – "Because more people write to me."

'They even do it in their own film, "Are you a mod or a rocker?" – "I'm a mocker."

'They're having a laugh with it, being offhand, playing the game – but not playing *their* game. That's the thing, they're playing their own game... Is this helping?' Nye asked.

'This is great,' I said. 'I'm fine with those first two. Who's next?'

'Take a guess.'

'Dylan?'

'It has to be Dylan. He's the third. Sarcastic, edgy, talking back, asking questions back, smirking at the stupidity of it all. Affronted – "How could you even have the nerve to ask me a question like that?"

When the journalists ask him, "Are you a folk singer?" and, "What do your lyrics mean?" he pushes them back into a corner, breaking the time-honoured agreement and asks questions right back. "Do *you* think I'm a folk singer?" "Who said that?" He wouldn't give them the straight answers they wanted. "What's your message, Bob?" – "Always keep a clean head and carry a light bulb." He's saying, if I'm going to be part of this charade, then I'm doing it on my terms – this isn't a game any more, this isn't about entertainment. This is real.'

'That's the third. And the last one, I love this one, because I was there. I witnessed this first hand. The final approach? Fuck off with your approaches. There are no approaches any more. No respect, no trust, no fun. The Sex Pistols' press conference was a three-way exchange of bile: the journalists hated them, the Sex Pistols hated the journalists, and the Sex Pistols hated each other. They're not a gang having a laugh together. They're pissed, they're speeding, and they're telling everyone to fuck off because they're shit.

"What was that?" – "Nothing, a rude word. Next question."

"Go on say something outrageous." – "You dirty fucker. What a fucking rotter."

'There you have it, four approaches to the rock 'n' roll press conference: Yes, sir – I'm a mocker – what do you think it means? – you dirty fucker. You've got the history of rock 'n' roll in four styles of dealing with the press, and do you see why it's important? How many people would have heard the music if Elvis and The Beatles and Dylan and the Sex Pistols hadn't made such a stir when they were interviewed? The music was big, but when they talked they made it bigger. That's it... I hope it's been useful.'

I told Nye I really appreciated it. Maybe the press conference was going to be my chance to make an impact on JookBoxFury. If I could generate the kind of publicity Laurence wanted, then they might keep me on the tour for another day, even to the final. It was all falling into place. The filth and the JookBoxFury, as the programme said. Maybe that was the way to go at the press conference, live up to the billing, give it to them punk style – PukeBoxFury.

DISC TWO, TRACK THREE

Rhiannon

We drove into Scarborough along the sea front and the tour bus dropped us off by the beach. Rhia walked towards the sea and stopped just before the waves. Pony Boy shouted, 'Ray, can you give me a hand, mate,' but I pretended I hadn't heard him and went to stand by Rhia. She said, 'I love looking at the waves, they really make you feel good. However you feel, good, bad or indifferent, stand and look at the waves and you feel better.'

We watched more waves roll in, then turned away and crossed the road to a yellow ice cream café with a neon sign above the window saying 'Blue Moon of Ken's Tuck Inn.' A notice stuck to the inside of the window said, 'The Blue Moon of Ken's Tuck Inn will be closed today for a private Juke Box Furious event – we apologize for any inconvenience. Keep on rockin', Ken.'

Rhia shaded her eyes and peered through the window, then she tapped on the glass and waved. 'Here's Ken now,' she said.

A light went on inside the café and Ken came and unbolted and unlocked the door. He said, 'Rhia love, you're early. We're just sorting things out in the back. Lovely to see you though, come in, come in, you're very welcome. And your friend as well, come on in. Where's everyone else? I thought you said there'd be sixty of you? We're getting the food ready for sixty so there's going to be plenty to eat if there's just you two. You'll end up like me if you're not careful.' He patted his large stomach.

Ken must have been in his sixties. He had a full head of jet black hair swept back into a well-oiled quiff, but his huge sideburns were grey. He was dressed as a rock 'n' roll chef with an apron and chef's checked trousers, accessorized with a bootlace tie that had a circular blue disc as the clip, and he was wearing a pair of blue suede shoes. His crêpe soles were so thick they must have added three inches to his height, but he was still about six inches shorter than I was.

When Rhia introduced me Ken gripped my hand and looked at my black eye. 'That's a nasty one,' he said. 'I hope you've not been scrapping over the music you've been playing on your jukebox thingamajig, because I've got a strict rule about that. I had to introduce it after that business with the Mods and Rockers last bank holiday. A bit of banter's fine, but throwing punches over a Who record... I won't tolerate any silliness. You never said there might be any trouble, Rhia pet.'

'There won't be any trouble, Ken,' Rhia said. 'Ray was being a gentleman – that's why he got his black eye.'

'What, from one of them women's libbers?' Ken said. 'You held a door open for her and she lamped you? Women of today – I don't understand them, then again I never did. The female of the species remains a mystery to me, I'm afraid. Talking of which, I'd better go and give the missus a hand or I'll be getting walloped meself. You make yourselves comfortable, I'll be back in a jiffy to get you a cuppa, see how you want things setting up and the suchlike.'

I sat down at a table in a corner near the jukebox while everyone else came in. When Nye got inside he said, 'The Blue Moon of Ken's Tuck Inn? Are you kidding? That can't be the real name.' He let the door slam behind him and Pony Boy crashed into it with a box of Bobbly Wobblers, which he had to balance on his knee while he tried to open the door again. Just as I got up to help him he managed to flick the handle down with his elbow.

Rhia and Laurence were in discussion with Fran about where they were going to set up the competitors' table and seat the press. While they were talking, Fran's phone rang. She answered it, listened for a while, and then said, 'As the Head of Jook Marketing I'll be the one who makes the decisions about the Jook launch. Now, if you'll excuse me, I've got a press conference to organize, goodbye.' She ended the call and said to Laurence and Rhia, 'I can not abide the interference of jumped-up jobsworths who don't understand the boundaries of their role. Let's make sure this is a success, then I'll make that little upstart eat his words.'

Laurence asked if everything was alright and Fran was sharp, 'Why wouldn't everything be alright? Let's just get on with this.'

Watching them was too much like being back in the office so I looked around the café. It was the kind of place my mum and dad used to take me and my brother when we were on holiday and we were going to a café for a treat. There was Formica everywhere. The top of the counter was yellow Formica with chrome trim, and the sides sloped back to the floor with a crazy design of red, yellow and green circles and squares that were surrounded by lines and swirls. Bizarrely, it looked like the future, even though it must have been about fifty years old.

The Blue Moon of Ken's Tuck Inn was like being in the past, but at the same time there was an air of excitement about the future, perhaps the Sixties were the last time the future was exciting, rather than something to dread. It felt good to be back in the Sixties for a while.

The walls of Ken Tuck's Inn were mirrored, with gaps filled by ancient advertisements for ice cream and a comforting display of nostalgia. I could see myself reflecting into infinity between a framed Bill Haley LP cover and a sign advising 'Keep Fit by Eating Ice Cream Every Day'. I sat by a selection of saucy postcards. Busty blondes wearing revealing bright red tops and bright yellow mini skirts were at a holiday camp, with rosy nosed men in caps saying things like, 'Have you got a couple of nice hot crumpets?' On another: young woman goes into a grocer's. The ginger-haired, kilted owner is up a step-ladder putting biscuits on a high shelf, and the woman says, 'Ah, Mr McTavish, I see you have some ginger nuts.'

The centerpiece of the café was the jukebox, which was a world away from the box on the wall we'd used in The Queen Victoria. Instead of being a functional machine to play CDs, this jukebox looked like it had been part of Flash Gordon's space ship. A row of vinyl singles were housed inside a Perspex dome that had almost certainly been taken from the cockpit of a planet landing craft.

Below that there was a sheet of metallic effect, mottled pink Formica, with the name 'Chantal' above what appeared to be the grill of a Cadillac El Dorado. The model name was in chrome on the side: 'Meteor 200' – it really had landed from outer space, created as it burned through the atmosphere, before crashing through the roof, and then settling in the café to bring rock 'n' roll to Planet Earth.

I went over to the jukebox, planning to play a couple of looseners to get in the mood. I pushed the buttons to select the tracks, but nothing happened.

Ken saw me and said, 'If you want to experience her in all her glory, I'll switch her on.'

He leaned behind the Meteor 200 and flicked a switch. The jukebox hummed into life, and then took a moment to power up before all the lights flickered on. Beautiful. Ken randomly stabbed at some of the buttons, making a few selections. What was he doing? I looked around to see if the others were taking any notice. He could easily influence the competition by giving some ideas away with behaviour like that – I wished I'd never asked him about it. The record flipped on to the turntable and started to play. There were a couple of pops and clicks as the needle settled into the groove, but all that came out of the speakers was a muffled drone. It sounded terrible, like the mating groan of a hippo, you couldn't even make out what the song was. If this was what the competition was going to be like, we'd be better off going back to The Queen Victoria.

Ken must have spotted my horror because he said, 'Don't worry about that, son, she just needs to warm up. She's like all of us when we're getting on a bit, she takes a while to get going.' He patted the Perspex bubble that covered the records and said, 'Don't it girl, takes you a while to get warmed up?' He told me to put a few selections on and said she'd be right as rain, then he went back to the kitchen. I put on a couple of tracks that I was pretty sure I wouldn't be using in the competition, better safe than sorry, so I played *Walk in the Black Forest* by Horst Jankowski and *Hole in the Ground* b/w *Winkle Picker Shoes* by Bernard Cribbins.

'What's that bloody awful noise?' Babs shouted over to me. 'It sounds like you're getting ready for another sparkling performance with some more of your miserable indie drone music. Won't you learn?'

At least she was acknowledging me, and she had a point about the drone music, because with the jukebox not properly warmed up we were being treated to something reminiscent of John Cale's minimalist experimentation with the cello.

I looked through the cards on the jukebox to prepare for the competition. There was some great stuff on there. It wasn't a huge selection, but there was plenty of scope for some clever choices from a stack of rock 'n' roll, girl group and soul classics, plus a few rockers from the late sixties and some B sides that might add a bit of variety. I started to make a mental list of the tracks I might go for. After my experience the previous night it was probably best not to take any chances. I decided not to rush into anything, it was important to make sure I got the mood of the room right.

Ken brought out the teas and coffees. I declined. Rik had been handing bottles of Jook round so I had another of those. Ken came back with a couple of plates of multi-coloured fondant fancies. Dr Rococco said, 'Oh, wonderful, that's a lovely touch – I don't think I've eaten a fairy cake like that since the Sixties.'

Rik said, 'Fairy cakes are for the bloody fairies. The only cakes I was eating in the Sixties were hash cakes, man – a couple of those washed down with a mug of mushroom tea and you were away with the fairies. I don't suppose there's any chance of getting a plate of hash cakes in here, is there? What's the gaffer called? Ken? Oh, yeah, Ken's Tuck Shop. Here, Ken man, have you got any hash cakes behind the counter for old time's sake?'

Ken went over to Rik's table and said, 'We do a couple of hash browns with the Big Breakfast. We usually stop serving that at eleven, but I could get the missus to knock one up seeing as you're special customers, like.'

Babs said, 'It's alright, Ken, he's just messing about. These little fancies are lovely.'

Nye said, 'I've got a question for you while you're here, Ken. I love the vibe you've got going on in this place, but how the hell did you come up with a name like The Blue Moon of Ken's Tuck Inn?'

'It is a mouthful isn't it?' said Ken. 'It was the mother-in-law's idea, it came to her in a dream while she was listening to Bill Monroe and the Blue Grass Boys, so what can you say? I'm not saying my mother-in-law's bossy,' he turned round and looked towards the kitchen before he carried on, 'but if she tells you to call your café The Blue Moon of Ken's Tuck Inn, then if you want a quiet life, that's what you call it. Before we got this place I had a snack van on the A64, and that was called Ken's Tuck Inn, so it does make some sense.'

Rik said, 'You can't talk can you, Nye man? It makes more sense than calling yourself after a fucking concept. You're out of order criticizing someone else's made-up name.'

Nye was indignant. 'Nye Hill's my real name. The name came first, the Nyehillism came after. My old man called me Nye as a tribute to the Labour movement. Made-up name – I'm about the only person here with the name they were given at birth.'

Rik was indignant. 'My fucking name's my fucking name, man. I was christened Richard Peabody, so there's nothing made up about my name. Rogers is the man to talk to, he's the expert on made up names. Calling yourself Pony Boy – now I'd like to hear the inspiration behind that one, because that didn't come to you in a dream did it Rogers? That came to you in a fucking nightmare, probably with you riding bare back on a huge black stallion.'

Fran had been in discussion with Laurence, but she suddenly took an interest. 'I've only ridden bareback once,' she said, 'but it was absolutely wonderful.'

'I bet you rode it hard, baby,' Rik said. 'I can see you now with your head thrown back and the wind in your hair, screaming to go faster.'

'Well, not quite, you do need to be careful.'

'Yeah, yeah, the thing is,' Rik said, 'you didn't end up getting called Pony Girl, did you? You could have ridden bareback every day of your life, but you didn't get called Pony Girl.'

'Oh, I did love horses. I wouldn't have minded being called Pony Girl at all. I'd have much preferred it to Francesca. I'm sure things would have been so much better for me at school with a name like Pony Girl.'

'Tell me about it, love,' said Babs. 'I might not have been born Babs Golightly, but I've been known as Babs Golightly for all of my professional career, so I'm not about to start worrying about my old name or what those bitches at school used to call me. As soon as I got the chance, I became Babs Golightly.'

'Why that particular name?' Dr Rococco asked.

'Babs from Barbara Windsor, like in the *Carry On* films, and Golightly from Holly Golightly in *Breakfast at Tiffany's*. Babs and Holly – they're what I'm all about. I used to sit in class at school and the only thing that stopped me from being miserable was daydreaming about what I was going to be called when I grew up. I daydreamed being called Babs Golightly. I love my name now. Babs Golightly is my real name.'

Babs caught my eye and looked away quickly. She knew that I knew. That whole *Seasons in the Sun* business in the bus station café had started because of her name, because of being called Sandra Daft. It was in the bus station café when we were drinking our tea and looking out of the window at the buses that she had said, 'I'm sick of being called Daft. Being called Daft is bad enough, but now a gang of girls in my class have started calling me Shit Head because of it.'

I asked her, 'What's that got to do with being called Daft?'

'You know what some of those bitches are like. It started off with Dafty Duck, which wasn't too bad I suppose. Then it was Daft as a Brush, then it was Bog Brush, and all of a sudden that's turned into Shit Head. I hate going into lessons now because of them all shouting that at me.'

'Maybe you could change your name.'

Sandra was chewing some Bazooka Joe. She thoughtfully blew a big bubble until it popped, then said, 'I am going to change my name. I haven't decided what it's going to be yet. I might get married, and then I can change it. What's it like being called Mitchell? Sandra Mitchell sounds OK.'

That was all a bit too heavy. I'd only been out with her a couple of times. It wasn't really appropriate to be getting into a conversation about whether Mitchell was a good surname. I tried to change the subject and she said I didn't have any feelings, she kept asking me how I felt. I wasn't sure what she was getting at, whether I was supposed to say I loved her or something. I didn't say anything, so she told me I wouldn't know about feelings if I hadn't had any big emotional events in my life. I had to admit that I probably hadn't had any events like that, apart from losing my balloon from the fair when I was about four, but obviously that wasn't the kind of revelation she was after. I asked her what big emotional events she'd experienced, and that's when she told me about the time she'd seen the old woman die.

I needed to apologize to Babs because I'd probably over-reacted. Not because of playing *Seasons in the Sun*, that's a mistake anyone could have made, but after that. After she'd called me a 'heartless bastard' and stormed out of the café, she hung around outside in the rain for a bit. Then she came back in and started browsing the magazines they'd got on sale in the corner. She was still sobbing a bit and I didn't know what to do. I thought maybe I should go and comfort her, but then she went over to the jukebox, flipped through a few things, put her money in, and 10cc's *I'm Not in Love* came on. I thought, 'She's trying to tell me something,' and it was coming through loud and clear – she had no musical taste whatsoever. Appalling. I got up, walked out of the place, and I never saw her again, well, not until JookBoxFury. I probably got things a bit out of proportion.

I thought I'd put the whole affair behind me, but it was all coming back again. Being in a café with Babs/Sandra, and the jukebox over in the corner was like being forced to go through some sort of primal scream therapy.

The conversation had moved on from what Bab's real name was and Rik was telling Pony Boy, 'You see, Rogers, if you're going to make up a name, then make up a name, instead of pretending to be a fucking cartoon character. Here he is, kids, he's half boy, half pony – he's Pony Boy.'

'What would his super power be?' Babs asked.

'That would be his enormous schlong. If you were going to have a horse feature as a superpower you'd go for that every time. That's probably why you called yourself Pony Boy eh, Rogers? To try and hide your own inadequacy. That's what I've heard from some acquaintances who got to know you intimately, if you know what I mean.' He turned to me, tapped his nose, and said, 'Plastercasters is all I'm saying, man.' He turned back to Pony Boy, 'The word, as I've heard it, is that in the whole of broadcasting you're widely known as having the tiniest…'

'I didn't choose to be called Pony Boy, I didn't have any say in it. When I got out to the pirate ship for my first DJ job, I found they'd faked my signature as Simon 'Pony Boy' Rogers and sent out hundreds of promo shots with it on. That was it. I was being called Pony Boy before I even knew about it. Once you're in the public eye, then you've got to stick with the image or name that made you, otherwise you've got nothing.'

'Unless you've got talent,' Rik said.

Pony Boy ignored him. 'Later in my career, when I had a more adult audience, I tried to drop the Pony Boy but it was too late, I was saddled with it.'

Fran giggled, 'Saddled with it, that's very funny, Simon.'

Pony boy said, 'I wish I'd thought of this when I had a regular show, but we've got a super concept here for a phone-in, probably for the lunchtime show – you know, for the housewives. Get them to ring in and tell you how they decided to name their kids, and then find out where their own name came from. It could be called "The name game" or "Explain Your Name". We could even go to TV with it, Saturday evening slot, get a few celebs in every week. I think this one's got legs – let's give it a try.'

Pony Boy flipped into presenter mode, 'Dr Annilese Rococco, now there's an unusual name, there must be an interesting story behind a moniker like that.'

'I agree that considering how people get their names is intriguing,' Dr Rococco said. 'I sometimes wonder if there's a self-fulfilling prophesy about names. There's a kind of homology between the name parents choose, Liam or Colin or whatever it might be, and the person the child becomes. It is as if the child grows into their name and we say, 'He's a real little Liam, or he's a proper Colin?'

'That's a good point,' Nye said. 'If you call your children Fifi

Trixibelle, or Moon Unit, or Zowie, or one of those children of rock star names, you've got some expectation of what they're going to become. You're not working on the assumption that they're going to spend their life sitting behind the till at Kwik Save – although it would be good to be able to put 'Moon Unit' on your name badge.'

'Let's go back to Dr Rococco,' Pony Boy said. 'Tell me, how did you get that lovely name?'

'In my case, being called Annilese Rococco is a clear reflection of my heritage. Having a Portuguese father and a Trinidadian mother resulted in me being given a fairly exotic name, even compared to some of my contemporaries growing up in Ladbroke Grove.'

'Did people say, "She's a real little Annilese"?' Rhia said.

'They used to call me Annie. I have been called Dr Roc a few times, "The rocking author of *Between Rock and a Hard On* – Dr Roc." Some people like the sound of it.'

'I wouldn't be surprised if that's why they asked you to come on this Jukebox fiasco,' Nye said. 'That's about the level of organization we seem to be operating at. "Let's get an academic – OK, as long as they sound a bit rock 'n' roll."'

'Oh, that wasn't it at all,' Fran said quickly. 'That wasn't it at all was it, Laurence?'

'No, no, not at all. The selection process was all about credentials, academic credentials obviously, that was our watchword. Names didn't come into the discussion at all as far as I remember. Names, very interesting, yes. I'd like to be able to give you a story about my own name but I've never really thought about it, which is odd given that I spend so much time working on brand campaigns. You know, I've spent more time thinking about calling a new alcopop Jook than I did considering my own children's names... But I don't have a story, I'm afraid.'

Pony Boy said, 'You get that sometimes. There's nothing worse than trying to run a phone-in for the lunchtime show and you've got the news coming up, then you get a caller who's lost the plot. In that situation I always found that pretending to spill your coffee on the turntable was a good excuse to go straight to the news. Cut the caller off, fill in with a bit of banter with the newsreader about the weather, you know, "There's no news of earth tremors is there, because something made me spill my coffee," then you're back on track and you can move on to the next caller.'

Pony Boy slipped back into his DJ voice: 'Hi, we're back now with Rhia on line two. That's a beautiful name, Rhia, so how do you Explain Your Name?'

When he said 'Explain Your Name' he gave it the full game show host treatment, emphasizing every syllable of every word – 'Ex-plaaa-in Yo-uuuu-rrrr Naaaa-me!'

Rhia seemed slightly taken aback to be given such a build-up, but she humoured him. 'Well, Rhia's short for Rhiannon. My mum and dad got it from the Fleetwood Mac song, *Rhiannon* – obviously. They were a bit hippyish. You should see their wedding photos. If you want a laugh any time, come and have a look at my mum and dad's wedding photos. You've never seen so many cheesecloth dresses and crushed velvet loon pants in one place. Anyway, they were quite hippyish and one of their bands was Fleetwood Mac and they loved *Rhiannon*, so that's what they called me.

'I really like having my own song. If I ever hear it playing, it does make me feel good. There's a line in it that says, "She rules her life like a bird in flight," and I suppose that's what I've always wanted to be able to do. When I hear it, I feel like a little girl again, wanting to grow up to rule my life like a bird in flight. It reminds me of our family going on holiday somewhere in the car. My dad's playing a cassette tape he's made specially for the journey, and *Rhiannon* comes on, and my dad says, "This is where we got your name from, Rhia." He'd tell me some story about deciding what to call me, or seeing Fleetwood Mac play at the Marquee, or something about being a hippy. Then my little brother, who's called Peter, would start saying that it wasn't fair because he didn't have a song about him. My dad tried to fob him off once by saying he was called after the *Peter Gunn Theme* by Duane Eddy but it didn't really work – how can anyone get their name from an instrumental?'

Rhia thought for a moment. 'I ought to get in touch with my dad again. We sort of fell out and I haven't really seen him since…' She stopped.

Pony Boy said, 'You see, there you have it. There's your item. I really think we're on to something here. You tell your story. I play the song. Then maybe I get your father on the other line, you know, bring the two of you back together. That's great radio. I'm going to talk to a few people about that one.'

Rhia sniffed a little, stood up and said, 'Excuse me.' She went towards the toilet sign at the back of the café.

Babs followed Rhia, saying, 'I'll go and see if she's alright.'

Fran said, 'There she goes again, attention seeking. It's not my way – there's no place for waterworks in the office.'

'There fucking is if you work for the Water Board?' Rik said.

'It wasn't me was it?' Pony Boy asked. 'I was just trying the item out. That's going to be a great phone-in. Has anyone else got a story to tell because if you have then – Ex-plaaa-in Yo-uuuu-rrrr Naaaa-me. It's got a great ring to it. Who haven't we had, anyone who's got a bit of a happier ending perhaps? Ray, how about you?'

'There's not a lot to explain.'

'Oh, come on, mate, there must be something interesting about you. Were you named after a cricketing legend or a star of the silent screen, anything like that? There must be something.'

'Maybe your name was inspired by the Velvet Underground's *Sister Ray*,' Nye said. 'Instead of being into Fleetwood Mac, your folks were junkies, eking out an existence on the wrong side of town. Pale-faced waifs searching for their mainline, their only desire in life was their next fix, until their beautiful baby boy was born. And they called you Ray after *Sister Ray*, as a tribute to their former lives – the lives they escaped from so they could care for little Raymond. There's your item, Pony Boy, then you play *Sister Ray*, all seventeen minutes of it, with, "I'm searching for my mainline," bleeding out of your listeners' speakers while they're sitting at home eating their soup. And the band keep cranking the sound up until John Cale turns the organ right up, and it washes over everything in a distorted fuzz and the guitars are feeding back and squealing. You play it right to the end until your listeners are sitting open-mouthed, a spoonful of soup in mid air, and you say, "What a fabulous track. That was the very wonderful Velvet Underground with *Sister Ray*. We've got a treat for you now, Ray, because I've got someone here who you haven't spoken to for a long time. That's right, from the rehab clinic, we've got your father on the line..."'

As Nye was suggesting this version of events, Rhia came back into the room followed by Babs. When Rhia heard Nye say, 'We've got your father on the line,' she said to Babs, 'They're making fun of me,' and turned to go back out again.

Nye shouted, 'We're not making fun of you, Rhia, we were just taking the piss out of Ray and his interesting name.'

'We don't want to miss that, do we?' said Babs. She came and sat back down followed by Rhia.

'I'm not sure Nye's version is quite what we're after,' Pony Boy said, 'although we do need a bit more to flesh it out. You must have been called Ray for some reason.'

'I think my mum liked the sound of it. I don't think there's any more to it than that, sorry.'

'There you go, Pony Boy,' Nye said. 'Knock your coffee over and go straight to the news on that one, because the guy's struggling to make much of a connection. He's called Ray because his mother liked the sound of it – bloody brilliant radio.'

'You could maybe play Madonna's *Ray of Light*,' Laurence said. 'You've got a connection there.'

'*Ray of Light*?' Nye said. '*Ray Off Light*, more like. I'm sorry, but he was hardly a ray of light in the pub last night.'

'Now that's not fair,' Pony Boy said. 'Ray's been an absolute rock in helping out with the Bobbly Wobblers, which has been very much appreciated.' Then he turned to me, 'Although I could have done with a hand coming down here earlier.'

It was great being part of JookBoxFury, but I had to maintain some integrity, I didn't want to end up being introduced as his Bobbly Wobbler box shifter again.

'I don't mind helping out with the Bobbly Wobblers every now and then,' I said, 'but when you introduce me in the competition, would you be able to say something else, because I think I've achieved a bit more than that. You know, I don't want to be seen just as someone who organizes the Bobbly Wobblers.'

'Point taken, point taken,' Pony Boy said, 'although being associated with the Bobbly Wobblers has never caused me any problems. But no, point taken and I'll work up the introduction a bit. Give me your resumé and I'll see what we can bring in. Tell me, where have you come from, where have you been? What have you done?'

I tried to think of some of my major achievements that he could use. At work I'd been given the Employee of the Month award for coming up with a way of reducing the amount of times we had to re-order toner cartridges for the printer. It was actually a very clever idea, but I moved departments shortly afterwards and it never got implemented. Something music related would probably be better.

'Here's one,' I said, 'I've possibly got the third largest collection of vinyl on the Bam Caruso label of anyone in the North.'

'Right,' said Pony Boy. 'Which label is that again?'

'Bam Caruso – freakbeat, psych and garage.'

'OK, we could use that – and you've got the biggest collection?'

'Third largest collection… in the North… possibly – I recently heard that there's a guy in Rotherham who might have a couple of things I haven't got.'

'I'm not saying it's not impressive, mate, but we really need something where you've been the first, the best, the fastest, the highest. If we say you've got the third largest collection, people are going to be thinking, "Well, why haven't they got the guy with the largest collection here – he's the one we want to watch." We need something we can build up a bit.'

Rik had been studying the saucy postcards on the wall, but he looked up and said, 'I'll tell you who was the highest – our roadie, Smeggy. There was this one time…'

'OK, I've got you,' I said to Pony Boy. 'How about this – I was the youngest person in my school to attempt the Three Peaks Walk.'

'Now we're cooking,' Pony Boy said. 'That's one we can work with, it shows you've got grit and determination. You're well prepared for the endurance required by JookBoxFury because you were the youngest person to complete the challenging endurance test of the Three Peaks Walk…'

'I didn't actually complete it. I was the youngest person in my school to attempt it. One of the straps on my rucksack broke on the way down from the first peak, so I was carrying it with one strap. Then that strap went and the teacher, Mr Mason, said that if I kept messing about he'd get the back up team to take me home. There was a boulder that had been left in the middle of the path, and I tripped over it because I couldn't see where I was going, due to having to carry my rucksack in front of me. That was it. I was lying face down in the heather with a broken rucksack, and Mason said it was the last straw and I was off the trip for not showing enough awareness of safety measures.'

'Do you want me to use that for your introduction then?' Pony Boy said.

'I should,' said Babs. 'People like that kind of human interest – the youngest guy ever thrown off a school trip for showing a lack of awareness of safety measures. People love an underdog, so that might just win them over to Ray and his miserable music. Great plan.'

'I was only suggesting a few things,' I said, 'but it doesn't matter. Just introduce it how you want.'

'I'll work on it, mate,' Pony boy said. 'We'll come up with something, no problem.'

Lucy in the Sky with Diamonds

Rik had gained access to the Jook well and was handing bottles round at regular intervals, although I seemed to be the only one who was accepting them. I felt it was in the spirit of the day to support Jook. Nye was complaining because we could have had an extra hour in bed. Fran nearly bit his head off, 'Don't you realize how important it is to get this right? We're talking about people's futures here. I'll have you know that when it comes to the Jook press conference, "cock-up" isn't in my dictionary.'

Nye said, 'The way things have been going, you might want to consider writing it in on one of the spare pages at the back.'

Fran's mouth fell open. She pulled herself together and looked about to sink her teeth into Nye's neck when Laurence called over, 'Right, I've just heard that the journos are on their way, should be here in about fifteen, so let's get together for a final briefing session.'

Nye said, 'What's to brief? Let's just go for it. Jesus, if we were going to have a briefing session, couldn't we have done it an hour ago while we were twiddling our thumbs?'

'Fresh in the mind, Mr Hill, fresh in the mind. OK, let's take our positions.'

We sat facing five rows of chairs that Ken had set up. I was poked at the end of the line, almost stuck in an alcove by a display cabinet full of ice-cream making competition trophies.

'Righty-ho,' Laurence said, 'I'm sure you're all familiar with the press conference drill.'

'Been there, done that, got the full collection of t-shirts,' Pony Boy said. 'Both sides of the microphone, mate. When I was in the States interviewing Macca about writing a Bond theme he…'

Laurence cut him off, 'OK that's good. Is there anyone who is not fully experienced with the format? Ray, Nye's given you your media training, are you happy with that?'

I nodded.

'Good, good. We won't use you up front, but be ready in case I spot an opportunity to use that fan's enthusiasm angle that you've got going on. You know, Joe Ordinary, mixing with the stars, playing great music with the best of them, all because of Jook.'

Fran said, 'That's right, Ray, if you give a succinct answer to any direct questions, that will be more than adequate. Let's concentrate on using the big names we've got here to leverage the Jook brand.'

I'd got the entire history of popular music press conferences to draw on, but I could still be succinct.

Laurence said, 'That's pretty much it. The competition will be as before, but the journalists will be the judges.'

Nye said, 'So instead of morris dancers and a hen party, we've got a bunch of old hacks. Nice one – I don't think. From my experience on the street of shame, I'd say bang on a bit of Phil Collins and Celine Dion and you're into the home straight. There's no point being too clever with this lot.'

'I wouldn't be so sure,' Laurence said. 'We're going to have a real cross section here. I've got several specialists from the music mags and the style press on my list, so I think you're going to be pleasantly surprised. I've no doubt you'll all get a turn to say your piece, and we can get the message out right across the spectrum.'

A woman with big hair and a brightly patterned silk scarf came into the café, followed by four slightly bedgraggled men. The woman turned to the men and said, 'I told you this was the way.'

One of the men said, 'I knew it was here,' but the woman wasn't listening. She introduced herself, 'Estelle Campbell from *The Sun*, here to interview Babs.'

Laurence said, 'This is the press launch for Jook.'

'That rings a bell,' Estelle said. She looked around, 'Ah, there you are Babs, nice to see you again. Shall we talk over here?' She took Babs off to a table by the window.

Laurence asked the four men where everyone else was. The coach had collected the journalists from the station and he couldn't understand why there weren't more of them. 'There weren't any delays on the trains, were there?' he asked. 'Power lines down? Leaves on the track? Derailment? Anything like that?'

Laurence was disappointed to hear that there hadn't been a rail crisis, but he picked himself up and made introductions with the journalists who had turned up. They were a mixed bunch. The youngest was JJ from the *NME* who looked like he'd come straight from double English. He wore a pair of skinny jeans, belted at mid-thigh level, and kept flicking his head sideways to get his fringe out of his eyes. The oldest was Timothy Wintergreen from *Brewery News*, fiftyish, slightly fruity, wearing a checked waistcoat and a bow tie. He had a problem with his hair too, and had the public schoolboy habit of running his hand back through his hair to lay it in place.

The third journalist was Mike Statham from the *Observer Music Monthly*. His main concern seemed to be to find somewhere to hang his coat and scarf, but once that got sorted out – Fran asked Ken's missus to run upstairs for a coat hanger – he said he was planning to do a mood piece on the comeback of the jukebox.

The last journalist was Len Wiggins from the *Scarborough Advertiser*. His worn, brown leather bomber jacket had grease stains at the collar, and he looked like he probably spent most of his time hanging around at the courts waiting for local crime scoops. He told us to call him Wiggy and explained, 'It's because of Wiggins, not because I wear a wig, I hasten to add.' Until he said that, it hadn't crossed my mind that he might be wearing a wig, but once he'd denied it, I couldn't stop looking at his hair, which did seem abnormally well defined around the edges and surprisingly pristine. It was very difficult to say with any certainty whether it was a wig.

They were the journalists we were going to face at the press conference: one with big hair, one with a flicky fringe, one with the foppish brush back, and a possible wiggy in denial. Mike from the *Observer Music Monthly*'s hair wasn't really worthy of comment.

Rhia nudged me and whispered, 'Stop staring at that guy's hair.' I didn't even realize I was doing it. I'd developed a strange hair obsession, probably due to being on the road for so long – well, two days, but it felt like a lifetime. I'd have to check with Rik if that was the kind of thing that happened after being cooped up on the tour bus for days on end. Pumped up to a fever pitch by the thrill of the performance and then the comedown hitting you so hard that, before you knew it, you were in the depths of a hair obsession. The touring was physically demanding, too. After not having slept the night before I was dead tired and the side of my face was still throbbing. Plus, after knocking back a few Jooks during the afternoon, I felt like I needed to either go to a party or go to sleep. Seeing as the press conference preparations weren't generating a party atmosphere, I decided to settle down in my little corner, rest my head on the display cabinet and mentally prepare myself for the press conference. I closed my eyes, but instead of blackness I saw greenness. That wasn't normal. I opened my eyes and the room was bathed in a cool green light. I looked at Wiggy and saw a green light pulsing from under his hair. I closed my eyes again and it all went green, maybe not as bad as before, so I drifted off into the greenness to lie down on the green green grass of home. That was nice, so soft and green...

Ouch! I was jerked back from the comfort of the greenness by Fran clapping sharply. I jumped, cracked my head against the display cabinet, and a shower of green stars sprinkled around me. Fran clapped again, like a school teacher impatiently attracting the class's attention. When we were sitting quietly, we were allowed to listen to Fran describe how the Jook brand was an exciting new departure for just about everyone you could imagine. By the time she'd finished, I was ready for the Pope to come in, give Jook his blessing, and declare that they were going to start using it instead of Holy Water. Timothy Wintergreen from *Brewery News* had been taking copious notes, but the other journalists flicked through their press packs disinterestedly. JJ from the *NME* made a note on the back of his hand.

I was about to drift back into the greenness when the door to the café opened and a skinny guy with Buddy Holly glasses stepped halfway inside. He was wearing a green cagoule jacket over a crazy blue and orange Hawaiian shirt. He had a big camera case over his shoulder and was clutching a Matalan carrier bag. Everyone turned to look at him and he asked, 'Am I in the right place for the Chantal Meteor 200?'

Laurence said, 'I'm sorry, there's no Chantelle here, this is a private function – we're having a press conference.'

Hawaiian shirt said, 'That's right, the press conference about the Chantal – there she is,' he pointed at the jukebox. 'What a beauty, it's a while since I heard one of these in action. I'm Warren Watson from *Jukebox World* magazine, I've got my invitation here.' He came further into the café and took a crumpled letter out of his pocket and held it out to Laurence.

Laurence took a sheet of paper from a folder and scanned it. Rhia leaned over to point at something on the paper and said, 'It was a late addition.'

Laurence looked back to Warren, '*Jukebox World*, of course. Well, we're very glad to have you joining the party. I'm afraid you've missed the background on Jook but we can fill you in on all that good stuff later, so why don't you find yourself a seat and I'm sure Rhia will give you a Jook.'

By the time Rhia handed him a bottle, Warren was already aiming his camera at the Chantal, but he put it down and said, 'Don't mind if I do.'

Laurence handed over to Pony Boy for the introductions to the contestants. When he got to me I was dreading what he was going to say about my Bobbly Wobbler credentials. He started by giving me the full game show host build-up, 'And finally, the man of the hour, the man with the power, he's our representative of all the pop lovers out there. We call him 'Sugar' Ray, it's 'Sugar' Ray Mitchell. As you can see by the slight bruising around 'Sugar' Ray's eye, he's not afraid to stand up for what he believes in and he's always in the front line when classic pop and rock is under attack. There's one marvellous story about 'Sugar' Ray that sums up the character of the man, and if this doesn't epitomize the spirit of JookBoxFury, then I don't know what does…'

Fran looked towards Pony Boy, held her arm in the air, and tapped at her watch, but Pony Boy carried on. 'When 'Sugar' Ray was just a boy he had what was arguably the best collection of Bam Caruso records in the world at that time. They meant so much to him that he insisted on taking them everywhere he went. When he climbed the most difficult and dangerous of the challenging Three Peaks, he carried every one of those records on his back. The record collection was so heavy that, not surprisingly, 'Sugar' Ray's rucksack broke, but he battled on against the injustice and small-mindedness he was experiencing at that time and he continued to negotiate the boulder strewn paths until he achieved his aim. And let me tell you, not one of those records was damaged in any way, shape or form. Ladies and Gentlemen – 'Sugar' Ray Mitchell. Come on, I think that deserves some recognition.' Pony Boy started applauding with such enthusiasm that everyone else joined in, and I felt obliged to hold my hand up in acknowledgment. Pony Boy turned to me and winked. I nodded back.

I really should have thought things through before complaining about the Bobbly Wobbler introduction. Pony Boy had turned me into a weird obsessive. After he'd finally stopped applauding, we were into the press questions part of the conference. I wondered whether it would be best if I didn't get too many questions after all. I'd had quite a few Jooks by that point and I wasn't one hundred per cent sure that I would be totally lucid. What the hell, I could give them the Elvis approach without too much worry if required. Being polite wasn't going to be too difficult. I took another sip of Jook, which tasted ever greener with every mouthful. I was beginning to think that there was a connection between Rik's odd behaviour earlier and his Jook binge. The strange green light I'd been seeing had turned into an emerald fog that was curling into every corner of the café, and the green light coming from under Wiggy's hair had started to pulsate slowly.

Laurence asked if anyone had any questions for the panel. Mike from the *Observer Music Monthly* raised his hand slightly and put a question. 'Rik, what's it like being back in an old Fifties coffee bar like this? How does it compare with when you started out with The Peabodies?'

'Being back in the coffee bar is great, man,' Rik said. 'We weren't The Peabodies at that stage though, it was Ricky and the Rhythm Boys back then. We started out as Ricky and the Rhythm Method, but in 1958 that was a bit too shocking for some and no-one would let us play. We changed it to Ricky and the Rhythm Boys, and that's when we started to do the coffee bars. One place was Dino's in Kensington. We had Johnny on the tea chest bass, standing in the corner by the jukebox, Jimmy on the washboard and me on the gee-tar, banging away at the old favourites. We used to play skiffle stuff like *Rock Island Line*, Tommy Steele songs and a few of the early rock 'n' rollers.

'We wanted to get to the 2i's in Soho, that's where Tommy Steele got his break, but the main thing was you got paid in there. Over at Dino's we just got paid in coffee, milky coffee in glass cups. We drank so much of the stuff that by the end of the night we were pissing coffee – just like the way your piss turns bright green when you've had a few of these Jooks. I went for a wazz this morning after a night on the Jook, and you should have seen the colour…'

Fran was nudging Laurence furiously, but Laurence seemed enraptured by Rik's response.

Rik carried on, 'They tell you to eat your greens, there's no need to eat your greens when this stuff's around…'

Fran coughed loudly.

'… you get all the bloody green you need from the Jook. It's like that old joke – what's the difference between roast beef and pea soup?'

Fran whispered urgently to Laurence and pointed at Rik.

'…You can roast beef but you can't pee soup. I tell you, a few of the Jooks and you're peeing like the bloody soup dragon…'

Laurence finally got the message from Fran and intervened. 'OK, Rik, thanks for that great anecdote about the coffee bars. Shall we have another question?'

Fran stood up. 'Can I just say that you'll find full information about the health benefits of Jook in your press packs. Rik is such a joker, he's been making jokes like that ever since he came on the tour, he really is keeping us entertained. But seriously, Jook is full of antioxidants and vitamins from the fruits and herbs – it's all in the press pack so it's well worth having a look at that.' She looked at Rik, smiling sweetly for the journalists, and said, 'You're such fun, Rik,' then sat back down looking like thunder.

The next question was from Timothy Wintergreen, *Brewery News*. 'That's an interesting point about the health benefits of Jook. Does this suggest a new trend in the brewing and alcohol-based drinks industry, and if so, what makes you think consumers of alcopops are going to respond positively?'

Laurence said, 'Very good question. Fran, do you want to pick up on that?'

Fran picked up on it enthusiastically and responded with waves of facts and figures about all sorts of different trends, qualitative and quantitative research, focus groups, tasting panels, nutritionists and recommended daily allowances. When she mentioned the recommended daily allowances, Wiggy's hair seemed to bounce a little higher on the green light and he butted in, 'What the people of Scarborough want to know, is whether there is a recommended daily allowance for these alcopops before the youth of the area turn into lairy hooligans, vomiting and urinating into every shop doorway in the town.'

Fran said, 'Our own research clearly shows that the demand amongst consumers is for a sophisticated drink brand with a fun image, that can be consumed in a responsible way by adults.'

'That's all well and good,' said Wiggy, 'but the reality is that it's no longer possible for law-abiding citizens to go out for a quiet drink without gangs of louts and ladettes shouting out unwarranted comments such as, "Like the rug, Slappy." So I'd like to know how you can promote an alcopop with a game about fury, and a contestant sporting a black eye and a boxer's name, without contributing to the violent binge drinking culture?'

Fran was about to answer, possibly with more facts about demographics, when I realized that the comment about my black eye gave me a way in. It was time to use Nye's media training, and I felt strangely confident about doing it. What would Elvis have said?

I went for it. 'Well, sir, I was just driving a truck when I was invited to appear on the JookBoxFury. I didn't mean no harm to anyone or nothing.'

Laurence laughed nervously and said, 'Have we got any more questions?' but Wiggy still wanted an answer. 'What I would like to know is how this gentleman got his black eye, and whether your alcopop-fuelled fury is going to lead to a wave of violence in the streets of Scarborough?'

'You see, sir,' I said, starting to introduce the hint of an American accent, 'this here black eye was nothin' more than a little accident. I was jus' mindin' my own business…'

'That's what you say,' Babs chipped in.

'…Yes, sir, I was mindin' my own business and jus' playin' my records, and if people like 'em, well that's sure fine with me.'

'The trouble is they don't like them if you play that drone music, do they?' Babs said.

I ignored Babs' comment. I was quite pleased with the way the Elvis answers had gone so I added, 'I guess I just want to say a big thank y'all to my fans here in Scarbor-o, and we look forward to seeing you all again real soon.'

Laurence looked at me for a moment then said, 'OK, thanks for that, Ray. Hopefully you've got that out of your system and we can press on. Do we have another question about the Jook launch?'

Mike had another question. 'What I'd like to do for the *OMM* is a piece about how the jukebox is a kind of shrine for the real aficionados, the dedicated music collectors. I'm quite interested in this angle of…' he looked at his notes, 'Ray it was, trekking across the windswept moors, struggling over these huge boulders with an enormous collection of obscure vinyl – it would probably make quite a nice photo piece if we could recreate it. Whatever made you want to do that, Ray?'

The initial thrill of being asked a question was slightly undermined by it being about Pony Boy's flight of fancy in the introductions. I glanced at Pony Boy who appeared to be quite unconcerned that he'd dropped me in it. Who'd do the Three Peaks Walk with their Bam Caruso collection? Ludicrous – where would you plug in your turntable? I had to answer quickly or I'd lose my chance: either deny it and sound like a politician wheedling out of their own two-faced incompetence, or go with it and risk a future exposé. What was there to lose really? Just go with it, answer in the spirit of the question, be irreverent but fun – like The Beatles. Be a lad from Liverpool having a laugh. Press conference approach number two.

I must have been thinking about how to respond for too long because Laurence said, 'I think Ray's a bit thrown by that one, so why don't we move on and perhaps come back to it later if there's time.'

'No, that's OK, wacker,' I said (I was struggling a bit to get into character). 'John had a rucksack full of records, and Paul had a rucksack full of records, so I got one too.'

'John and Paul were part of your gang were they?' Mike asked.

'Oh, yeah, we were like a gang, which was gear at the time.'

'Gear, as in outdoor equipment for the walk?'

'No, GEAR – it was fab. We was all fab.'

'So you did well on the trip?'

Tripping? He was going all *Lucy in the Sky with Diamonds* on me and moving on to The Beatles' later period. Well, why not? I said, 'The trip was beautiful, man. We did well in the sense that it opened our eyes to a different way of seeing things – that's when we decided to go to Rishikesh.'

'And I assume Rishikesh is one of the stops on the Three Peaks Walk?'

Nye said, 'Rishikesh is where the Beatles went to see the Maharishi. I don't know what the point is that Ray's trying to make, but he's talking bollocks.'

'That's when George took up the sitar,' I said. 'I had a rucksack full of Bam Caruso recordings, and he had an enormous bloody sitar strapped to his back.' I didn't think I'd quite captured the spirit of the Beatles press conferences but my Liverpool accent was getting better all the time, so it was swings and roundabouts. 'Ringo couldn't come because he was ill, like, and John was in a mood. After a while he refused to carry anything and he just stayed in bed…'

'Shall we leave it there, Ray?' Laurence said fairly sternly. He glanced towards Nye, who gave an innocent shrug.

I said, 'I was only answering the gentleman's question in the best way I knew how.'

Fran said, 'I'm sorry about this everybody. Raymond is a music fan who we invited along for the day and he's a little nervous being in this situation. Why don't you have a break, Ray and take a walk around the block while we finish. I'm sure we can manage without you?'

'I'm fine here,' I said. 'Don't mind me and my feelings, you carry on.'

'OK, back to business,' said Laurence. 'Any more for any more? Can we expand further on the Jook experience?'

It was a bit harsh getting cut short like that because it seemed to be going rather well, but they were starting to get tetchy so I decided to let it go.

Warren said, 'There is a question I'd like to ask on behalf of the readers of *Jukebox World*. There's some controversy on the scene about this, and I don't want to offend anyone, but I feel I have to ask it because it's been pointed out to me by a couple of owners. I'm not saying it's my own opinion, I'm just the messenger here, if you like. I'm not sure how to put it, so I'll jump right in, so here it is – and you'll have to forgive me if this does cause any offence – but the question the readers of *Jukebox World* would like to hear an answer to is, do you find that the Meteor 200 is taking a while to get going these days? That's something I've heard from a couple of owners, that it takes a while to warm up.'

Laurence said, 'I'm sorry, but I'm not sure that I understand what you're asking.'

Didn't these people know anything? I said, 'Laurence, he's asking about the jukebox, Meteor 200 is the make of jukebox. Ken knows all about it, he told me earlier.'

Laurence looked round for Ken, and seemed relieved that he wasn't in the room. 'I'm sure the owner can fill you in on the background to the jukebox later,' he told Warren.

'I know about it,' I said. 'I can answer that one, Ken explained it to me.'

Fran put her hand to her head and muttered something to herself.

Laurence said to me, 'Well, go on then if you do know the answer, but keep it brief.'

I took a swig of Jook and weighed the question up. It was obviously one for the Dylan approach. I took another swig and a tingle of green-tinged confidence flowed through me. I leaned towards Warren, 'How do you even have the nerve to ask a question like that?'

Warren was taken aback and became defensive, 'I'm just asking on behalf of the readers of *Jukebox World*, it's not my own opinion.'

I challenged him again, 'Well, where did you pick up an opinion like that when it's not even your own? Who are these people who are giving these opinions – do you trust them to tell you what the truth is? Do they know the truth? What are you looking for when you meet these people?'

'I met them at the last Jukebox World show,' Warren said nervously. 'They seemed to know what they were talking about.'

'I think you and I both know what the truth is, don't we?' I sat back in my seat.

Warren nodded and started to adjust his camera. I felt that I'd cleared things up rather nicely.

Laurence said, 'I suppose it was brief, but I'm not sure that really gave Warren the information he was looking for. We'll get Ken to talk to you about the jukebox later, Warren.'

Warren said, 'I don't want to be any trouble. I was only saying what a couple of other box users had said to me, it's nothing more than a rumour on the circuit.'

I couldn't help but give a dismissive, 'Pah!'

Laurence quickly said, 'I think we've got time for a couple more questions about the Jook launch and then we'll get into the real business of the day and play JookBoxFury. A question anyone?'

Mike had another. 'It's quite an esteemed panel of contestants you've assembled, and I was particularly intrigued by Dr Rococco's involvement. Obviously I've read *Between Rock and a Hard On* and found it to be very perceptive, and I wanted to ask you to comment on one point you make in the book, Dr Rococco.' He pulled a hard backed book from his bag and turned to a page marked by a train ticket. 'You say, and I quote, "Within music and music-related practices, as within the broader cultural landscape, the male hegemony is sustained by facts and figures: knowledge of chart placings, catalogue numbers and years of release, take precedence over the experiential tactics more commonly employed by girls and women when using music. In this context, dancing, loving and sharing to popular music, are subsumed by a knowledge of who recorded the original or some other expression of an empty authority." Obviously it's a while now since you wrote those words, but I wondered how you would apply those sentiments to the contest you're currently taking part in?'

Dr Rococco pursed her lips and nodded thoughtfully. 'I've no doubt that the statement is as true today as it was when I wrote the book, but how does it apply to JookBoxFury? That's an interesting theme, because, of course, over the past couple of days I've been exploring it heuristically. We only have to consider the composition of the panel here – myself and Babs outnumbered by the guys – so there's already an imbalance which reflects the inherent hegemony, and as a result of that it seems intuitive that the songs played will favour the more masculine approach. However, I should point out that when we played JookBoxFury last night, Babs did win the contest and, to turn the machismo on its head, she well and truly whupped the guys' asses, so to speak. The way Babs won was to play music that the audience could enjoy singing and dancing to. So that very much supports the notion of women wanting to experience music, rather than treating it as a style-conscious version of train-spotting. It will be interesting to note who wins the competition today. We seem to have a fairly male-oriented audience, so I'm intrigued to see what response Babs gets from the male members.'

'Always a positive response to Babs from the male member,' Rik said, 'always very uplifting.'

Warren took this as a cue to take an active part in the press conference again. 'I did want to ask Babs about that. I'm a big fan of those pictures you did a while back, Babs, and I wondered if you might be able to do something similar for the readers of *Jukebox World*, you know, perhaps posing with the Meteor 200. Our readers would love it if we had a centre spread of you, perhaps in some frilly lingerie, sort of leaning over the jukebox picking a record with a kind of "oooh" expression.' He rolled his eyes, put his finger to the side of his mouth and pursed his lips to demonstrate. It was quite grotesque.

Babs was clearly annoyed, 'I really wasn't expecting this…'

Warren said, 'That's OK, I've come prepared. I went shopping on the way here, that's why I was late, but I picked out something which I think would be perfect for the readers of *Jukebox World*.' He reached into his Matalan carrier bag and brought out a hanger with a shiny red and black bra and thong set. There was a card round the top of the hanger saying, 'Reduced'.

Babs said, 'If that's perfect for the readers of *Jukebox World*, you'd better get *them* to wear it.' She stood up and said to Laurence, 'I don't have to put up with this – it's either him or me.'

'Understood,' Laurence said, and asked Rhia if she would escort Mr Watson from the premises.

Warren grabbed his camera bag and lingerie and went without any trouble at all, as if it wasn't the first time he'd been in that kind of situation. As he went out of the door of the café he shouted back, 'The Meteor 200 does take a long time to warm up you know,' and he was gone.

Babs said, 'I was feeling sorry for him while Ray was being ridiculous about the jukebox warming up, but I'm glad he got a hard time now. Snivelling little weasel.'

Laurence said, 'Right, that's probably as good a time as any to wrap things up. Has everyone got what they wanted?' He looked at JJ and said, 'JJ, you haven't asked a question, is there anything you want to put to the guys, and ladies of course, that would be of interest to the readers of the *NME*?'

JJ looked at Laurence like a bored teenager would look at his Head of Year when asked where his form for the sponsored walk was. He flicked his head a couple of times to get his hair out of his eyes and then, with his head tilted slightly to one side, he said, 'The readers of the *NME* want to know what's new, what's bubbling up, what's skimming, who are the jim jams? Not this old bollocks. Look at this place – I wish I'd brought my Grandad with me, he'd have loved it. Forget the nostalgia shit, let's move on. Come on people, what about Freeze Dried Man Juice, AF Notions, The Carcinogens? Every one of them has been a download of the week but I don't see them getting played by any of you, because you're all living in the past, in your own rock 'n' roll wet dream. Let's Hear Something Fresh Lords Above Hoylake Ice Cream Baby Sounds Enticing Wake Up Smell The Coffee Get With The Programme?'

I'd heard of a couple of the bands he mentioned, but I'd have struggled to hum any of their tunes, and by the end of his diatribe, I was struggling to follow whether he was listing the bands, describing them, or giving us instructions. Either way, I wasn't happy about his attitude. He'd come into The Blue Moon of Ken's Tuck Inn as if he owned the place, drunk our Jook without saying a civil word to anyone, and then slagged off the competition that I was putting my heart and soul into. I wasn't having that. You couldn't call classic rock 'n' roll records 'nostalgia shit', and honestly say you'd rather hear Freeze Dried Man Juice – what kind of crazy mixed up world were we living in? We'd been through the punk rock wars so people like JJ would never again have to listen to rubbish, and they were just pissing it all away. It was time to turn the tables.

I sneered at JJ, 'All those bands, they're heroes of ours, ain't they?' JJ looked at me without any expression. He didn't appear to have picked up my clever Sex Pistols/Bill Grundy interview reference – that's what I was having to deal with all the time.

'Yeah, we luuurve those bands,' I snarled. 'We think they're fucking hilarious.'

JJ flicked his hair. This was proving difficult, I was trying to feign punk indifference and he was genuinely indifferent. Still, stick with the programme. I took an insolent swig of Jook and then sprayed it out towards JJ.

Laurence said, 'Now hold on a minute, Ray, we're not in the playground.'

'I think we'd better have a word right away, Raymond,' Fran said.

JJ flicked his hair a couple of times.

'Fucking hilarious,' I said. 'What was that, a rude word? Carry on, next question.'

Laurence got to his feet, 'I think Ray's still a bit shaken up after what happened last night, so why don't we take a short break there and then we'll get straight on with JookBoxFury.'

Fran said to Laurence, 'Never work with children, animals or the general public. That guy is an absolute liability. I don't know what I was thinking of when I let you persuade me to bring him along. Rhiannon, get him to calm down and then I want to talk to him.'

I stood up and my chair fell over. I stabbed my finger towards JJ, 'You fucking rotter, you dirty fucker.'

Rhia was next to me and put her hand on my arm, 'What's going on Ray? What are you saying that for?'

'I was just making a point.'

'You're not making it very well then. You should probably apologize to JJ before you talk to Fran.'

'How do you mean?'

'Fran's not very happy with you. She wasn't in a good mood to start with so having you fooling around and insulting the people we're trying to impress isn't going to help. It's only down to Laurence that she let you come along, so I think you've had it. You could try to smooth things over, but I don't think it's going to do you much good.'

That wasn't part of the plan at all – sometimes I felt my best efforts were completely wasted. I decided to try and resolve the situation quickly. I went over to JJ, who looked up at me through his fringe. I held my hand out to him and said, 'Sorry about all that, no offence. I didn't mean to call you a "fucking rotter", I just got carried away.'

JJ flicked his hair. 'No problem, mate, nice attitude, I can use some of that. All that shite about brand synergy, what do I want to put that in the *NME* for? But an arsey bastard – that's what it's all about.' He shook my hand and said, 'Look, I've got to get a train over to Liverpool to cover The Kirbygrips backlash, but good luck with the competition.' He waved at the room in general, said, 'Later,' and left.

'There you go,' I told Rhia, 'all part of the plan. All smoothed over. Will you tell Fran or shall I?'

'You tell her. You're the one who's been acting up. What are you actually on?'

I held up a bottle. 'Just the green nectar – from the well of nature's goodness, if everything I've heard about it is true.'

Fran walked past, tapped me on the shoulder and said, 'Step outside with me for a minute.'

I followed Fran out of the café. She turned on me as soon as we got outside. Talk about punk attitude.

'I don't know what you think you were up to, Raymond, with those awful accents and the obnoxious behaviour, but it had very little to do with promoting Jook. What you don't seem to understand, is that we've got a major new drink brand to launch, and I'm not having either the good name of Jook or my own career put at risk by someone like you. We invited you to participate in the press conference – I honestly don't know why, perhaps Laurence will explain it to me again, after you've gone – but that has been a big mistake. Just get out, before things get any worse. Get out of my sight, I don't want to see or hear you again.'

'I'm sorry. I felt a bit strange. I wouldn't normally behave like that, but…'

'No buts, read my lips – you are no longer a part of JookBoxFury. You can count yourself lucky that you're not an employee, because if I could charge you with gross misconduct, you'd better believe that I would. And don't think this is over, if this launch fails, I'm holding you personally responsible.'

'But…'

Rhia came outside holding a phone. Fran said, 'Can't you see I'm busy, Rhiannon.'

Rhia said, 'It's Mr Hylton-James. He's just come out of a meeting of the Executive Committee and he says he needs to talk to you on a matter of importance.'

'Well, why didn't you say so, girl?' Fran snatched the phone off Rhia and then waved her away. Fran's tone changed completely when she started talking on the phone and in a sickly voice she said, 'James, this is Francesca, how lovely to hear from you. I've been meaning to put a call in to let you know what a success we're having with the Jook launch.'

It was making me queasy just listening to her, but her tone

suddenly changed. She almost sounded desperate, 'But, James, no, no, no... but, if I could just... No, I can't understand what you're suggesting... No, it would be wholly inappropriate to consider withdrawing Jook at this stage... the timing is... no, the timing... we're right in the middle of the press conference. We're really ramping up the publicity drive at this very moment. The press are very enthusiastic about everything they've heard, absolutely everything. Particularly the trade press. I've no doubt we're going to exceed the targets by some considerable margin.'

Fran listened for a while and then said, 'Well, those morris dancers and the hen party weren't even supposed to be part of the launch. They turned up in the middle of our promotional contest and if you ask me they were drunk when they arrived. In fact, if you had seen the way they were dressed you would have said they were on drugs, so I would take any comments from them about the effects of Jook with a very large pinch of salt.

'Absolutely everyone involved in the tour is having a great time. I'm no stranger to product launches, and this is undoubtedly the smoothest campaign I have been involved in... Violence? I must say they really have been letting their imaginations run riot. No, it was a very pleasant atmosphere... No, no, no-one got hurt... that's right... I can assure you quite categorically that all the product testing was thorough. I admit that I did expedite the process to achieve an early launch, but that was purely to attain the right market position for Jook. In no way did I cut any corners in terms of product testing. This launch is far too important for me to take any risks like that... Of course. I can assure you that if I had witnessed any problems whatsoever with the drink then I would be the first to raise my hand and say, "Guys, I think we've got an issue here. Let's delay the launch while we carry out further tests." But there is nothing whatsoever to give me even the slightest sense of doubt in the quality of the product we're putting to market. I know that personal taste shouldn't come into this, but I've been drinking Jook regularly and I've never felt better.

'My recommendation is that we press on and dismiss these ludicrous claims, which wouldn't surprise me to have come from our competitors because they know we've got a sales category champion on our hands. I'll be back to base next week with a pile of press cuttings and indicative sales figures to show that I've delivered you a winner... Thank you, James, I appreciate your support. I certainly will give you a daily update... Thank you, although I don't expect we'll be needing any luck – this is all running perfectly to a very careful plan.'

Fran closed the phone, held it to her chest, and took a deep breath. She muttered, 'Bugger, bugger, bugger. Oh, what would daddy say?' She blew her cheeks out and shook her head a couple of times as if to regain her composure, then turned to go back into the café.

She jumped when she realized that I was still outside with her. 'Ah, Raymond. Did you...? When I... did you? Oh, those builders. I do wish they wouldn't keep ringing me about my patio at times like this. They've no idea have they?'

She took another deep breath. 'Listen, Raymond, what we were talking about previously, about your involvement in JookBoxFury. I've been thinking about it. I thought your, um, witty remarks in the press conference were good fun... Just what the campaign needs. So why don't you stay on the tour for another day? You should do that. I'd be so pleased if you would. Come to Glasgow with us for the next date. If you did that then I could make sure you stay on the JookBoxFury panel. I'm the one who's running the Jook launch, so as long as the launch goes ahead, then I want you to be in JookBoxFury. Not that the launch isn't going ahead... but we are a team aren't we? And we need to support each other... because that's what teamwork is all about, isn't it? That would be best for both of us if we could do that. You do want to stay on the tour don't you?'

Moral dilemma. I asked her, 'Will I have to play any Disney soundtracks?'

'No, no,' she said. 'I was just being silly when I said that. Gerald's always saying that my sense of humour will get me into trouble. The music you played was super. I loved it. I've been meaning to ask you who those songs were by so I can get them on

CD for Gerald's birthday. You can play what you like as long as the tour goes on… which it is doing… because I'm in charge. Is that OK?'

I didn't say anything.

'Good. That's good then. Why don't you pop back inside and get ready for the competition. I'm sure you'll find some more of your interesting songs to play because you're so good at that. You go on, I'm just having a breather out here for a minute and I'll be right along to listen.'

I started to go back inside. Fran called, 'Oh, Ray, if there's anything else you need, just let me know. The team has to stick together.'

The Jean Genie

When I stepped back into The Blue Moon of Ken's Tuck Inn, Pony Boy shouted, 'Ray, where have you been? We're just about to get going – ding ding, Round Two.'

Everyone was sipping Jook, apart from Rik, who was gulping it down like it was the last Jook he'd ever taste. Maybe it was. He opened a couple more bottles and handed me one. I said, 'Perhaps you should go a bit easy on this stuff, Rik.'

Rik held his hands up in horror. 'Rock 'n' roll, boy, rock 'n' fuckin' roll. I don't believe what I'm hearing. The Guitar Man doesn't *go a bit easy* on anything, man. Take it to the edge and then just fucking keep on going.'

He clasped the Jook bottle in his teeth, tipped his head back and swallowed the contents down in one. 'Come on, boy. Are you jookin' or are you sitting there looking like a pussy?'

It was either Jook's potential side effects, or not being rock 'n' roll. I tilted my bottle towards Rik, then took a drink. As soon as I tasted it, green flashes sparked around me. As I took another sip Pony Boy said, 'You're on first, Ray.' He announced me and I stepped up to the Chantal Meteor 200 and scanned the cards. I hoped the Chantal was on my side because if it wasn't warmed up, I was in trouble. I couldn't afford another experience like the night before. I needed all the help I could get.

I closed my eyes and took a deep breath. Everything went green – I kind of greened out for a moment. It was obvious that there was something weird about the Jook. Fran knew it and I knew it. What

115

if everything stayed green for ever? I should stop everyone drinking it, but there wouldn't be any JookBoxFury without Jook. If there was something wrong with the drink, how bad could it be? What was a little green flash of light here and there compared to being on the JookBoxFury tour.

I opened my eyes and looked at the circular song list inside the Perspex bubble. List G was at the front and number fifteen was emitting a luminous green glow that grew brighter as I watched it. It was a sign. It was the Jook talking – but it was talking to me. I pressed the buttons to select the track and the G15 disc flipped down onto the turntable and started to play. It was a shame Warren hadn't stuck around because the speed was spot on. The song was *The Weight*, The Band, entered the charts in 1968, unless I was very much mistaken.

The Chantal had a wooden disc protruding out of the front and you turned that to move the track list around inside the dome. I gave the disk a spin and stopped it with my finger. A new track glowed green in the selection frame: H19. I pressed the buttons to pick it, and did the same again for B3, F5 and E9. Each one shone with a green glow as it came into the window.

I sat back down while *The Weight* was still playing. The Band sang, 'Aaahh, aahh, aaand – you put the load right on me.' On me. It was my responsibility. Fran knew and I knew, but Fran wasn't going to do anything. 'You put the load right on me.' The Band sang about judgement day. A Sunday school piano played. They were down home preachers, telling it like it is. Shoulder the weight – I had to take responsibility for what was happening. That's what the song was telling me.

The next track started. Tom Jones singing, 'It's good to touch, the green, green grass of home.' The green *is* good, the green's great. Everything's comfortable in the green, green grass, and walking down the lane with my sweet Mary. Then it changes. Why does it change? Tom, what are you saying? 'Then I awake and look around me, at four grey walls that surround me.' I'm only dreaming? I'm going to prison. Tom sings on, the sad old padre is coming for me. I took a sip of Jook. They're going to lay me *beneath* the green, green grass of home. I can't believe… I can't believe they'd execute me. They couldn't do that because I'd kept quiet about an alcopop problem, could they? What if hundreds died though? Thousands could be poisoned, and they'll change the law. The first public execution in fifty years. I need to talk to the padre before it's too late, but the track fades and the padre has gone. I needed to talk to the padre. What if there is no absolution?

Voices of angels surround me. Either I'm in heaven or the next track has started. The voices of the angels are the voices of the Beach Boys, telling me, 'Don't worry, baby, everything will turn out alright.' The angels sing, 'I don't know why but I keep thinking something's bound to go wrong…' That's it, something could go wrong. I've got to take control, but… angels tell me, 'Don't worry, baby, everything will turn out alright.'

There wasn't anything to worry about. Worry? Why would I worry? The next track began with the sound of a sax drifting from an upstairs window on a hot summer night. Barbara Lynne's smooth soul, yearning to do the right thing. Knowing the answer – 'If you should lose me, oh, yeah, you'll lose a good thing.' I couldn't lose Jook. If I walked away from Jook, I lost JookBoxFury. I lost being with Rik and Babs and Nye and Dr Roc… Rhia. I even lost being with Pony Boy. Why throw that away? Don't lose a good thing.

'STAY!' The next record hit me. It didn't leave any room for debate – 'Stay! Ahhh, just a little bit longer.' I punched the air and whooped, 'I'll stay as long as you want.'

'What's that?' Pony Boy asked me.

'Oh, nothing. Stay – great decision, I mean, great track… even if I do say so myself.'

Rhia said, 'It is a great track, Maurice Williams and the Zodiacs, *Stay*. I love the bit in *Dirty Dancing* where this plays.'

There's no need to spoil it, I thought. *Stay* was only one minute thirty-six seconds long, but it was pure spiritual joy. The spirit of Jook got Maurice Williams and the Zodiacs to tell me to stay with Jook. I had to do what it took to stay with JookBoxFury. I could make it happen. I relaxed into the green haze again and the confusion drifted away. *Stay* was the greatest song in the world.

As the song played, the café door flew open and Fran strode back inside. She went straight to Laurence and said, 'I've been thinking, it's all going so well that I suggest we keep Ray on the tour. He's been such a breath of fresh air, just what the Jook launch needs. A nice angle, as you mentioned earlier.'

Laurence lowered his voice, but not enough, and I heard him say, 'I'm surprised to hear you say that because I'm not sure that experiment really came off one hundred per cent. I hold my hands up to that one, I really do. Some of those comments from our friend were perhaps just a little too quirky for…'

'Quirky,' Fran said, 'that's the word. Isn't quirkiness one of the Jook brand characteristics we want to promote? I do believe that Ray is making an important contribution. This is all going so well. I've just spoken to the Chief Exec and he is so pleased.' Her voice started to get louder, 'It's all going so well. The Jook launch is such a huge success. I'm so excited, I really am.'

Fran went to the back of the café and paced backwards and forwards across the room a few times. After a few laps, she suddenly sat down and started to massage her temples.

The rest of the competition went by in a green blur and, even though they weren't up to the standard of my selections, every single track had something going for it. Rik tapped into his coffee bar roots with Tommy Steele's *Nairobi*, followed by Guy Mitchell's *Singing the Blues*. The mood in the room was good. Rik got us to join in on the whistling section of *Singing the Blues* while he sang, 'I've never felt more like singing the greens,' a couple of times. Then he rocked it up, playing prime British rock 'n' roll with Johnny Kidd and the Pirates' *Shakin' All Over* and the Kinks' *You Really Got Me*. He rounded off his selection with *Purple Haze*. 'Fucking green haze more like,' Rik said, ''Scuse me while I kiss the sky.' He leaned backwards to blow a kiss up to the ceiling and fell off his chair. He spent the rest of the song lying on the floor, staring upwards and weaving his hands in the air to Jimi's guitar.

Rik's choices were good for the coffee bar, but my tracks were going to take some beating. Their otherworldly selection meant it was almost unfair to compete. The journalists were making notes on their score sheets so it even looked like we were going to get some proper results.

Dr Roc went third and played *Casablanca* by Kenny Ball, something about her mother really liking it, and *Hey Joe* by Jimi Hendrix. It seemed risky to have two Hendrix tracks so close together, but she said she chose it because she had so much respect for Patti Smith and she'd have chosen her version if she could. I was going to point out that the original version was by The Leaves, but after what she'd said in the press conference I decided it was best just to experience it, and not appear to be trying to establish any kind of empty authority. Then she played, *I Just Don't Know What to Do with Myself*, Dusty Springfield, 'Because of Dusty's inner strength.' She followed that with *This Wheel's on Fire* by Julie Driscoll and the Brian Auger Trinity, because it reminded her of the time she saw them at a happening with Brutus Trout. She finished with *You Send Me* by Sam Cooke, because he was a very beautiful man.'

I got the impression that the Jook spirit hadn't been guiding Dr Roc in her selections. Was I the only one? I asked her how she'd chosen her tracks and she said, 'I simply chose the music I wanted to hear, the same as last night.'

I decided not to tell her about the green light, it was best to keep that to myself.

I was sure I was still in the lead.

Nye's choices were impressively eclectic. He started with *Theme from Z Cars*, I've no idea who it was by, but it had to be a contender for most unusual choice. He followed that with *Tom Hark* by Elias and his Jive Flutes – two instrumentals in a row was taking a gamble. Next he went for Tess and the d'Urbervilles' doo wop psychedelia with *Angel Clare*, and drove strongly for the finish with The Standell's *Dirty Water* and the Stones' *Have You Seen Your Mother, Baby, Standing in the Shadow?*

I was sure Babs would be choosing a Beatles track, the whole of card 'A' was Beatles. True enough, her first track was The Beatles but, credit where it's due, she'd gone for a B side and played *This Boy*, the instrumental version plays in *A Hard Day's Night* when Ringo goes walkabout. It was brilliant. She followed it up with the Marmalade version of *Ob-La-Di, Ob-La-Da*. Was playing a Beatles cover after The Beatles deliberate? That wasn't the kind of thing that Sandra would have done, but Babs was very different to Sandra. I wasn't going to ask her because she was still pretty cool towards me. *My Boy Lollipop* by Millie was her next track. Was that deliberate – a song about a Jamaican, followed with a song by a Jamaican? If it was all deliberate, then surely she'd have a Faces track next to connect to the fact that Rod Stewart played harmonica on *My Boy Lollipop*. She didn't. There you go, it was all chance. Bab's next two tracks were *Big Girls Don't Cry*, The Four Seasons, and Elvis's version of *Shake, Rattle and Roll*. I couldn't work out any obvious connections there. She'd gone for the crowd-pleasers again, but she'd made some great choices all the same. I loved JookBoxFury, and with the green spirit guiding my way, JookBoxFury loved me back.

We had a break and mingled for a while. Pony Boy collected the score sheets in and Ken brought out a huge pile of food. As we prepared for the results a flash of green hit me and I felt an overwhelming responsibility to try to alleviate the Jook problem. I went round the room collecting in all the bottles of Jook that were left. I took a half-finished bottle from the table in front of Rik who said, 'Hey, slow down there with all the bloody tidying, man, I haven't finished that.'

I said, 'I'll get you something else. I was just helping out clear away.'

Rik put his hand on the bottle. 'Never come between a man and his Jook.'

Another bottle probably wasn't going to make too much difference in Rik's case so I left him with it. I collected up the rest of the Jook and asked Ken if there was any chance of getting some tea and coffee and soft drinks. Ken brought me tea in a cup with a pattern of musical notes on the saucer and round the top of the cup. If I was able to read music, I could have said what the tune was. I held it up to Rik and asked, 'What's this?'

He said, 'That, my friend, is a cup – I'm a teapot, and I'd like to give you a big fucking welcome to our world.'

Pony Boy announced, 'JookBoxFury Round Two, we have the scores. First of all, many thanks to the esteemed members of the press who have been so kind as to judge for us this evening.'

'Most pleasurable,' Timothy said.

'If you think that was good, wait until you hear this, because I am now ready to give you the results of the second JookBoxFury contest as played on the Chantal Meteorite 2000 at the Blue Moon of Ken's Tuck Your Shirt Inn Lad or I'll be Having Words With Your Mother, and away we go. Bringing up the rear in fifth place, obviously the *Z Cars Theme* didn't get the old nostalgia bells ringing for everyone as they did for me, we have Nye Hill. Just ahead of Nye in fourth position, playing some fabulous sounds but taking a big big JookBoxFury gamble with Kenny Ball and His Jazzmen, it's Dr Annilese Rococco.'

There's a lesson. Don't play theme tunes and songs your mother likes. It had done me a favour, though, because I'd made the top three at least.

Pony Boy tried to whip up more of a frenzy about the big big top spots. 'Now this is a real first. We've never had this situation before on JookBoxFury and it really goes to show just how tight the contest has become.' Pony Boy was beside himself with excitement. 'It's absolutely amazing because, quite remarkably, we've got a tie for the next spot. In second-equal place, playing some of the old coffee bar classics, it's Rik Peabody. And would you believe it, on exactly the same number of points, he may have been acting strangely during the press conference, but he certainly knew what he was doing at the jukebox – it's 'Sugar' Ray Mitchell.'

Obviously Babs had won again, but second-equal was pretty good.

Pony Boy announced that the song with the highest points total was *Stay*. I'd got the Zeitgeist award. Great result, second equal overall and best song of the night – the force of Jook had taken me there, it had to be part of a bigger plan. I'd made it through the second round against all the odds, but that's what you'd expect from someone who'd taken their entire Bam Caruso collection across the Three Peaks Walk.

When Pony Boy announced Babs as the Jook Duke of the Juke she gave an elaborate curtsey, 'There you go, boys, listen and learn. Like you said, Dr Roc, another ass-whupping for the guys, and another night out on the town for the girls.' She gave Dr Rococco a hug and then said to the journalists, 'I will be available for interview about the secret of my success following the victory celebrations.'

'That's the spirit, girl,' Rik said. 'Let's crack open a Jook and I'll drink to the winner, whether they're male or female, and whatever the colour of their skin, whether they're green, green or green. Jooks all round.'

'I've got an idea,' I said. 'Forget the Jook. Why don't we ask Ken if we could celebrate with some ice cream floats or something instead.'

Rik was enthusiastic. 'Ice cream floats, nice one. Eat ice cream every fucking day for health. I'll have a long tall glass of Jook with a scoop of mint choc chip – I'm calling it the Greenie Jean Genie.'

I said, 'Well, Ken might not have any mint choc chip ice cream…'

Ken was walking through and said, 'Mint choc chip? The mother-in-law makes that one herself to a secret recipe. I'll get some out of the freezer.'

At least I'd cleared the Jook out of the way.

When Ken came back he was holding a large ice cream tub. 'Mint choc chip anyone?'

He put a glass down on the table along with the tub of ice cream. Rik pulled a bottle of Jook from inside his shirt and prised the top off with his teeth.

I said, 'I shouldn't have that now, Rik. It could be a bit much, you know, the effect it might be having.'

Rik said, 'No-one tells the Guitar Man what his body can handle – the more effect it's having the better as far as I'm concerned. Who the fuck wants a drink without any effect? It's not worth the effort of swallowing it, as the actress said to the Bishop.' He tipped the bottle of Jook into the glass and said to Ken, 'I'll take two scoops in there, man.'

Ken dropped a scoop of mint choc chip into the Jook, which fizzed with the intensity of a chemistry experiment a teacher was showing off with on open evening. Rik peered into the glass, then pulled his head back as a jet of steam shot from the top. He wiped his hand across his face to get rid of most of the green foam.

'Bollocks to your side effects – special effects is what it's all about.' He downed the Jook, slammed the glass onto the table, and followed it with his head. He was out.

Ken took a long look at Rik, then at the tub of ice cream in his hand, then back at Rik. 'That's a drink and a half. Is the feller going to be alright?'

Fran covered her face with her hands, but it was still possible to hear a faint, 'OhmyGodohmyGodohmyGod…'

Mike Statham sniffed a story and asked Fran, 'Is there something else you want to tell us about Jook? Secret ingredients? Unexpected side effects? I've got to say, that with Rik Peabody's legendary capacity, that has to be a powerful concoction to put him out. If the stories are true, Rik's got the constitution of an Ox and…'

Rik sat bolt upright and snorted a couple of times. He frowned and squinted to look round the room, not seeming sure where he was until he saw Laurence. He said, 'When's that fucking gorilla turning up?'

Rik looked at the gently steaming glass in front of him. 'The green genie lives in a glass. I'll take another of those pops, Ken man. Nice one.'

Mike Statham said, 'That stuff put you out cold, Rik. Surely you're not thinking of drinking any more of it, not after what just happened.'

Rik said, 'I can't remember what happened in nineteen hundred and… um… I can't remember what happened in… when something *was* happening, man. So there's no fucking chance of remembering what happened today, yesterday, tomorrow, whatever… All I remember is, it's going to be fucking green, and that suits me. Hey, Lozza, is the monkey bringing its own bananas or should I go and get it some? Not all bananas are yellow, man. Some of the best ones are those fucking green ones. I'll get it some of those. They're like the ones in the jungle anyway.'

Rik half stood up, but he couldn't make it all the way. He dropped back into the chair and said, 'One for the road hey, Ken.'

Fran stopped saying, 'OhmyGod,' and blew her cheeks out. She straightened her jacket. 'Rik's such fun. Such fun. Perhaps he's too much fun… he makes me laugh so much.' Fran looked as though she'd never laughed in her life. 'He's the Wild Man of Rock. That's what he is, isn't he, Laurence? That's what you said. He's the Wild Man of Rock. This is just the way he is. I know what you're trying to suggest, but there's nothing wrong with Jook and there's no reason why it should be recalled. It's just Rik. He's the Wild Man of Rock isn't he?'

Mike Statham said, 'Do you mean to imply that Jook could be recalled, because that isn't what I said? I came here for the launch of a new alcopop and you're already telling me that it could be recalled.'

'Oh no, it couldn't,' Fran said. 'It's not… no, there's nothing… Laurence, it's not being recalled is it?'

'Well, that's certainly not part of the plans that I have been privy to. I'm very sure that this is a brand that is going places. I'm very confident of that fact.'

Fran said, 'You've all sampled Jook haven't you? I mean, you're all fine aren't you? You'd know if there was any kind of problem… which of course there isn't.'

Wiggy said, 'Well, now that you mention it…' The green light was still pulsing from under his hair.

Fran said, 'There's Raymond – Ray – he's our special guest. He's a member of the public, so he's quite impartial. Ray could probably give you a quote because he was with us on the tour last night. He joined us then, didn't you, Ray? And because you were so drawn to the whole Jook experience, you decided to stay with us. You've sampled Jook haven't you? You could comment on the drink's quality. Jook's a perfectly ordinary drink – well, not ordinary, in the sense of being a weak brand, but normal. It's like any other market-leading absinthe and greengage-based alcopop isn't it?'

The journalists looked at me, waiting. Would the Elvis approach help? Or The Beatles, or Dylan, or the Sex Pistols? I looked at Wiggy's green light.

Fran said, 'Why don't you tell everyone what you think about Jook, Ray.'

'It's a perfectly normal drink,' I said. I blinked and green stars showered around me. 'I really like it. You've tasted it – it's not like anything else. It's special as a drink, but it's just a drink. You know, all things in moderation and all that. Jook's a great drink. I've had quite a few over the past couple of days and… well, it's become my favourite drink. I'd recommend it to anyone.'

The green light wrapped around me.

Mike Statham closed his notepad and said, 'We'll see.'

Jook, Baby, Jook

By morning the green haze had almost disappeared. I went to breakfast early to make sure I didn't miss anything. As long as Fran and the Jook spirit were with me, I could make it to the JookBoxFury final. If anyone deserved to be in the final of JookBoxFury it was me – I was the voice of the fan. I only had to keep on top of things and I could make it all the way.

The restaurant was empty, apart from Rik, who was fast asleep, slumped in a corner of the red velvet seating that ran along the wall. The table in front of him was set for breakfast.

As I sat down, a waitress who had been squeezed into a uniform two sizes too small bustled up to the table. She asked if I wanted tea or coffee, then pointed to Rik and said, 'Is he a friend of yours?'

'That's Rik Peabody from The Peabodies,' I told her.

She said, 'I don't care if he's Sammy Slipper from the Shoe People, I don't want to be doing nights again and hear him singing, "Jook, Baby, Jook," over and over again.'

'It shouldn't be a problem because we'll be on our way after breakfast.'

'Thank goodness for that,' she said, and told me to help myself from the buffet.

The others came into the restaurant one by one without having too much to say until Pony Boy arrived with a cheery, 'Morning, morning, morning. How are we all on this fine JookBoxFury morn?'

Rik woke up with a jump and straight away started to sing in a rockabilly style.

'*Jook. Jook, Baby, Jook*
Come on, Jook. Jook, Baby, Jook
You know I love that green stuff
It's the-uh secret of eternal youth.'

Then he took it down a little, singing more quietly and started clapping to accompany himself. '*Jook, oh Baby Jook, come on a-Jook, Jook, Baby, Jook, uh huh Jook, yeah-eah Jook, Jook-ah, Jook-ah, Jook-ah, Jook, Jook Jook Jook Jook, ohhhh Jook, that's right, Baby, Jook, oh-oh Jook…*'

It didn't look like he was going to stop, until Nye said, 'What's this one about then, Rik?'

Rik stopped singing, surprised that we were all there. 'Oh man, where the fuck have you all been? I've been waiting for you. Listen to this, I've got a new song inspired by some of the shit that's been going down.'

He started to sing again, '*Jook. Jook, Baby, Jook…*'

Nye said, 'I feel like I've heard this one before.'

Rik said, 'You've got to listen to it, man, you've got to hear the line about standing by the record machine. Here, get this, *Jook. Jook, Baby, Jook…*'

The waitress came over with a toast rack and said, 'Please, no more of the "Jook, Baby, Jook." We had that for six hours non-stop last night. He kept coming to the bar and asking for Jook. I told him there's no such drink, but he just kept on asking for it, with ice cream in it and all sorts of serving suggestions that I'm not going to repeat now. Then he started singing about it and he would not stop. No offence if he's in your party and he's one of the Shoe People, but it's a bit much at breakfast to be honest. So if there's any chance of asking him to lay off it for a while that would be a blessed relief.'

Rik started to sing again, '*Jook. Jook, Baby, Jook…*'

The waitress leaned down to Rik and shouted, 'For heaven's sake, will you please SHUT UP!' Rik stopped. The waitress straightened and said, 'Thank you. Now can I get anyone more toast or drinks?'

Rik said, 'I'll have a…' but before he could get the next word out the waitress stuffed a piece of toast into his open mouth and walked off.

Rik took the toast out of his mouth and looked at it disdainfully. 'That's not been buttered. There's not even any fucking preserve on that.' He picked up a knife and opened a packet of butter.

Pony Boy said, 'That's a catchy number, that "Jook, Baby, Jook".'

'Please don't start him off again,' Dr Rococco said.

Pony Boy said, 'I thought Rik's song,' and he mouthed the words, 'Jook, Baby, Jook,' as if he was in the presence of a small child, 'might work as one of the filler tracks for the spin-off album I've been thinking we could put together. I thought we could record a few tracks for an EP, maybe even an album. Call ourselves The Bobbly Wobblers and lead it off with *Don't Go Breaking My Hat* and cover a few other classics, maybe have Rik's *Jook Baby* song on there, too. What do you think?'

No-one spoke for what seemed like quite a long time until Nye said, 'What else are you thinking of putting on it? *Wherever I Lay My Hat (That's My Home)*? *It's a Hatache*? Maybe get Johnny Thunders and the Hatbreakers to guest. Why not get the Village People and Jay K from Jamiroquai involved, because they're famous for their hats? People are crying out for an album on the hat theme.'

'They are, aren't they?' Pony Boy said. 'Do you think we can do it?'

'It's pretty much in line with your other suggestions,' Nye said, 'because it's a concept from cloud cuckoo land. Who's going to buy something like that? Oh, and one other thing – how exactly do you break a hat? You might squash a hat I suppose. Wouldn't *Don't Go Squashing My Hat* be more appropriate?'

Pony Boy said, 'There's no need for that. I'm just trying to inject a little of the old Radio Wonderful magic into what is, to be perfectly frank, a slightly flagging campaign if you hadn't noticed.'

'A slightly flagging campaign?' Fran was horrified. 'This is all going so perfectly to plan that we couldn't have scoped it out any better, could we, Laurence?'

Laurence hesitated, 'Um… no… it's as if our storyboard for the campaign came to life.'

'Some storyboard,' Nye said. 'You get a punter to join in on day one and he gets knocked out by a member of the audience. The press conference is a farce, and then Rik has some sort of Jook-induced collapse.'

'No, it wasn't the Jook,' Fran said. 'I thought we'd made that clear.'

Rik sang, '*Jook. Jook, Baby, Jook. Come on, Jook. Jook, Baby, Jook, a-huh Jook…*'

Dr Rococco said, 'I must admit to becoming somewhat concerned about the effect Jook appears to be having on our Mr Peabody. I appreciate that Rik perhaps isn't an ideal control sample, but even so, his behaviour has been somewhat bizarre.'

Rik was still singing, '*… now we're Jookin', baby.*
The Jook it gets to you, man.
Stay green just as long as you can.
Jook's true, like a record machine
Back…'

Dr Rococco said, 'Really, listen to the man. Is that normal behaviour?'

Fran said, 'That's just Rik being Rik. Jook's fine.'

Rik stopped singing, 'Too right Jook's fine. That stuff's fucking inspirational. I've written a new song about it, man. It's the first song I've written in ten years, so you just keep the green juice flowing, baby.'

'That's not an issue is it?' Fran said to Dr Roc. 'Admittedly, Rik's song might not be comparable to the Disney classics, but there's nothing wrong with writing a new song is there? That hardly suggests there's a problem with Jook, and I'm sure no-one else has experienced anything untoward.'

No-one spoke. I wasn't about to admit that my life was possibly being guided by a green spirit force.

Fran nodded at me slightly. She said, 'We really need the team to get right behind Jook and make this launch a big success, for all our sakes.' She nodded at me again, 'For the sake of JookBoxFury.'

I took her cue. 'Jook's brilliant. I think I was saying that last night, how it's just a great drink. And obviously I've no reason for saying that because I'm just here as a guest – it's not as if I work for the brewery or anything. I just like it on a very rational level, and I suppose if I went into a bar today, it would be the drink I'd order out of choice... and it would be choice... it wouldn't be as if I felt I needed it... I just like it, and it's an honour to be associated with the launch campaign, so thanks to Fran and everyone for letting me come along for the past couple of days.'

Rhia looked at me and pursed her lips, but Fran seemed pleased enough. She said, 'You've been such a special part of the launch, Raymond. I'm so glad that Laurence persuaded me to let you join us, and it's a real boost for everyone that you're coming to Glasgow for tonight's event. You've become such an inspirational part of the Jook campaign that I'm beginning to think that I might be able to find a permanent position for you in the Jook brand team. We must discuss that later.'

Rhia shook her head slowly.

DISC THREE, TRACK TWO

Do You Believe in Magic?

At the motorway services, halfway to Glasgow, I found myself queueing at the coffee shop with Babs. She picked up a muffin and asked me, 'Aren't you getting anything to eat?'

It was the first time she'd spoken to me since I had recounted the *Seasons in the Sun* experience and discovered who she really was. I told her, 'I think I'll just get a cup of tea. I haven't got all that much cash on me.'

'What a sad case,' she said. 'Get yourself a cake. It's my shout anyway, after that horrible custard tart you treated me to in the bus station café that time.'

'Oh, that. I've been meaning to… I wanted to say sorry about all that. Sorry about the *Seasons in the Sun* stuff… for both times. I didn't mean to be insensitive, it's just…'

'It's just that you haven't got a bloody clue. You can't go through life thinking pop music's the real world or you'll never have much of a clue about anything, will you?'

'I don't think pop music's the real world.' I thought for a moment. 'I think pop music's a sort of magic – it's kind of outside of the world.'

'For Christ's sake,' Babs said, 'it's worse than I thought.'

'I liked what you played in the competition last night though. I really enjoyed it.'

'Did you?' Babs said suspiciously.

'Oh yeah, it was all good stuff. Playing *This Boy* by the Beatles was inspired, it's a great track.'

'Well, there you go,' Babs said. 'That's the sign of a real winner – when even your mistakes come off. I meant to play the other side, whatever that was, but I must have pressed the wrong numbers. Still, who cares if you win, hey?'

I cared. What's the point in picking great songs by chance? Where was the skill in that? The connections she made between the songs when she went from The Beatles to *Ob-La-Di, Ob-La-Da* to *My Boy Lollipop* were probably all down to luck, too. I said, 'I thought it was good the way you picked the songs so they'd have a little connection in them that people would get.'

'Oh, you liked that did you?' Babs said. 'I thought it was pretty smart.'

'It would have been good if you'd have gone from *My Boy Lollipop* to *Itchycoo Park*, indirectly pick up on the Rod Stewart connection. That would have kept it going.'

Babs said, 'Hey? If I'd done that, I wouldn't have played *Big Girls Don't Cry* and that was the whole point.'

'I don't get you,' I said.

'You haven't changed at all have you, Ray Mitchell? *Big Girls Don't Cry* was supposed to be for you, like I was saying, "I'm different now." I'm not the same person you knew before and who got upset when you played *Seasons in the Sun* that time in the bus station. I wouldn't get upset about something like that now.'

'Yeah, of course, *Big Girls Don't Cry*.' It was probably best to pretend I'd picked up on the *Big Girls Don't Cry* message rather than the whole Beatles / *Ob-La-Di, Ob-La-Da* / Jamaica link. As suspected, that had all been a fluke. 'Um, yeah, you are different, very different… but still the same in some ways – you're still the same person.'

'I'm not really the same person at all. Once I became Babs Golightly that was it for my old life. I never go back there, I never see anyone from that life. I see my sister once in a blue moon, but apart from that, no-one who knew Sandra Daft knows me, and that's the way I like it. That's why it was such a nasty surprise to see you again. This is my real world now, and at least its not some magic fantasy world made of pop music. How sad can you get?'

'It's not sad. It is magic, but it's as real as anything else. The thing is, if I see someone holding a guitar, slinging it over their shoulder and strumming it, making music and singing – it is magic to me. It's not of this world. I don't really know… I can't understand exactly what they're doing, but I think that when they play – not just when they play like they've learned to play and they put their fingers in the right place and everything, but when they really play – then they're connecting directly to the human spirit. It's not just the soundtrack to our lives, it *is* our lives. Music is a pure representation of life. I don't just mean some ethereal, spiritual music, and I don't just mean *Astral Weeks* or *Pet Sounds* or one of those albums that are exalted as being things of beauty. I do mean those, but I mean *Wig Wam Bam* and *Jeepster* just as much. It's like when I first heard those songs, I didn't really know what pop music was. I was on a school camp and one of the other lads, someone with an older brother or sister probably, had a cassette tape with those songs on it, and to me they sounded like they'd been beamed down from another world. It was magic. Not a magic trick, but a force that I didn't understand. At the same time, I understood it completely because it sounded like my life. Not because of the words: "Hiawatha didn't bother too much, 'bout Mini Ha Ha 'n' ha tenda touch," even though I loved those words. It was because somehow that music sounded like being me, or being what I wanted to be.

'Maybe it's because I've never been in a band and that's why I think anyone who can make music is a magician, and anyone who makes bad music is betraying what is good in life itself. That's why it pisses me off so much when I hear someone going on about how much they like Sting or Westlife or whatever. Do you know the Lovin' Spoonful's *Do You Believe in Magic*? That's what the song's about. There's a line in it that goes, "It's like trying to tell a stranger about rock 'n' roll." You know, if you believe in it, you get it, and if you don't believe in it, then there's no point in trying to explain it because you're never going to get it because… well, because you're one of those people… the people who don't get it. That's why pop music's so important. It's the force for good in the world becoming tangible for a moment and capturing the spirit of life. Pop music is magical.'

133

'If you feel like that why do you keep playing such a load of old rubbish?' Babs said. 'The music's from this world, isn't it? I should stop worrying about it being from another world and concentrate on this one, because it's all you've got. You're still talking the same old nonsense. You always used to say stuff like that before.'

'Well, like you say, that was another life, wasn't it?'

'It was for me, I'm not sure whether you've changed much, although you could start by promising not to play *Seasons in the Sun* again. It's too sad. I don't want to hear it, and you're sad if you play it.'

'Why would I play it again? I've learned my lesson. I'm sorry, and I promise that you won't hear me play it again.'

We sat down at a table with Rik and Nye. Rik said, 'That was a bloody good day that was, yesterday. The Blue Moon of Ken's Tuck Inn really took me back. Bloody good day.'

'It might have been OK for you,' Babs said. 'You had your lovely reminisce about the good old days and your milky coffee in the glass cups and all that. I had some pervert wanting me to strip off in front of the jukebox. As if that wasn't bad enough, we had to sit through Ray's weird answers to every question that came up. What was all that about with the weird accents and everything, Ray? You sounded like you were living in your magic fantasy land.'

I said, 'Oh, it was nothing really. I was just trying to give some interesting answers.'

'Interesting to who? When you started having a go at that Jukebox weasel guy – you didn't even know he was a perv? It was embarrassing. What did you say? "How do you even have the nerve to ask me a question like that?" You'd offered to explain what Ken had told you about the jukebox, and then you go and say, "How do you even have the nerve to ask me a question like that?" What's that all about?'

'It's fucking Bob, isn't it?' Rik said. 'It's in the film of Dylan's tour of Britain. He's in a press conference and he fuckin' goes right off on one and says to the journalist, "How do you even have the nerve to ask me a question like that?" Bob was always saying stuff like that. Half the time you couldn't have a sensible conversation with him. You'd say something like, "Do you fancy a cuppa, Bob?" and he'd give you all that, "How do you even have the nerve to ask me if I fancy a cuppa?" He could be a bit of a miserable bastard in that way, you never knew where you were with him. That's why I decided not to go on the Rolling Thunder Review.'

Incredible. 'You were going to be on the Rolling Thunder Review?' I said.

'It was mooted. I knew him from years before. I first met him when the follow-up to *Violence is Golden* got into the American Charts. I helped him out a bit one evening and after that we kind of kept in touch.'

It was the rock 'n' roll inside story I'd been waiting to hear. 'You helped Dylan out? How did you do that?'

'I'm not sure if I should say too much about it really because of the Fab Four being involved and all that.'

'You helped out Dylan and The Beatles? Amazing. There's got to be something you can tell us about it.'

Babs said, 'He can't tell you because it didn't happen, did it, Rik?'

'It bloody did happen, man. There are only two people who could ever really tell you the truth, but your luck's in – one of them is sitting in front of you right now.'

'Well, why don't you tell us all about it,' Babs said, 'and then the next time we bump into Bob Dylan, we'll ask him for his version of events.'

'That's exactly how it fucking happened, man.' Rik seemed to forget any kind of responsibility he had towards the Fab Four in terms of maintaining confidentiality. 'I bumped right into this geezer, sent him flying, and when I picked him up it turned out to be Bobby.'

'It was when The Peabodies had gone to New York for the first time. The furthest we'd been before that was Dundee. We were doing radio interviews all over the place, with Murray the K and all those guys. We had to do this TV show where they wanted us to dress up as fucking peas – you know Pea-bodies – and all the band were going to be like peas in a pod. Bloody ridiculous, but we didn't know any better at the time because we'd never been to America before.

135

Someone gives you a pea suit and your Manager, useless tosser, tells you it'll be good for sales so you go and put it on.

'We were back at the hotel – somewhere on Park Avenue where all the English groups used to stay when they went over there, bloody nice place – and I thought I'd give the pea suit a try. It was a huge round green body kind of thing, fucking stupid, but I got myself into it. Our drummer, Jimmy, took one look at me and said, "You need to make sure you can get through the door with that on." Jimmy was always good at thinking things through like that. He said I should test it, otherwise we could all be dressed as peas, and when they called us on stage at the TV theatre we'd be stuck in the dressing-room because we couldn't get out of the door. So I'd got the suit on, and I tried to go through the door of the hotel room and, true enough, it was a tight squeeze. I had to hold the sides of the costume to squeeze it in a bit, and I was squeezing and squeezing, and pulling on the door frame, and all of a sudden I popped out of the door like a fucking champagne cork. I shot straight across the hallway and right into this wiry little guy who was walking past. That was Dylan. I helped him up as much as I could, which wasn't easy being dressed as a pea. He started getting all sarcastic about it, and I wasn't having that. I said he was lucky I had the pea suit on or he could have got hurt, but then I realized who he was so I told him I was a fan of his work. I explained about the suit and everything and it turned out that he liked *Violence is Golden*, he used a bit of the riff on one of his songs – can't remember which one it was now. Anyway, we struck up a conversation and he told me that peas were his favourite vegetable but he hated butternut squash, which I'd never even heard of at the time. I don't even know what the fuck it is now.

'We got on to discussing vegetables in general, and while we were talking he started rolling a spliff, but he was making a bloody pig's arse of it – the paper was all crumpled and bits of grass were dropping out all over the place. When he'd finished, he held it up like it was a fucking amazing achievement. I said to him, "Bob man, that's a bag of fucking chips." I took the stuff off him and I rolled an absolute beaut. He was really chuffed with it and he said, "Look, man, this is for The Beatles, I'm just about to meet them. Why don't you come along, you must know those guys?" That's how I met Dylan – barged into him dressed as a fucking pea.'

I said, 'That must have been the time when Dylan gave The Beatles their first taste of cannabis. That's a historic moment – and you were actually there?'

'In spirit, man, in spirit. There was a bit of tension between me and Lennon after he accused me of hitting on Cynthia at the *NME* Poll Winners' party, so I kept a low profile.'

Nye said, 'That story about Dylan giving The Beatles a joint – it's just a myth.'

'Isn't this where we fucking came in? I was there, so I should know. You hear all sorts of people saying they were involved in that incident, but do you ever hear about the man in the pea suit? Never. You don't, do you? There's your fucking proof, you see. Dylan's management kept it quiet because it would have ruined his reputation if it got out that he was out-rolled by the Guitar Man. You know, "Take me on a trip upon your magic swirling ship – but hang on a minute while I get someone else to roll a doobie for me." Still, Bob never forgot it, and once again I made a major fucking contribution to the future of rock.

'We went and did the TV show that night wearing the pea suits and we got panned. Even the host of the show was laughing at us when we waddled off – which took bloody ages because Jimmy got wedged in the pea pod. People weren't ready for it. A couple of years later and it would have been psychedelic, but we just looked like overweight rejects from Robin Hood's band of merry fucking men. The single peaked at seventy-nine and by the end of the week we were on the plane back home.'

Nye said, 'That's a good one, actually. I might be able to use that.'

'Use what?' Rik asked him, but Nye had got up and was on his way back to the coach.

As we walked back, Babs saw the kids' playground and ran off to it. The playground had an elephant and a motorbike attached to big springs so the kids could sit on them and bounce about. Pony Boy wasn't around, otherwise I'd have pointed them out as a possible

Bobbly Wobbler development opportunity. Babs ran past the wobblers and sat on a swing and shouted over, 'Here, give me a push.'

I went over and pushed Babs on the swing.

I kept pushing and Babs was squealing with pleasure – how many guys who'd seen those pictures would like to be able to say that? You've got to know what pushes the button. Babs shouted, 'Swings are so cool,' then suddenly said, 'Stop, stop.' She jumped off the swing and ran to the edge of the playground where an old pushchair had been left half on and half off the wood chips.

'Here,' Babs shouted, 'get in this and I'll give you a push.'

I sat in the pushchair, which wasn't easy – it seemed to have been designed for a child. I pulled my knees up so I could get my feet on the plastic footplate. Babs started to push, trying to run, and said, 'God, you're heavy.'

I said, 'He ain't heavy, he's my brother.'

'It's a shame I'm not pushing him then.'

We started to get a bit of speed up, Babs was surprisingly strong. We took the corner round the end of the playground at pace and nearly ran into a woman in a big brown skirt who was walking past holding a pink plastic potty in front of her. I put my feet down, the wheel of the pushchair caught my foot, and I tipped out onto the path.   The woman looked at me sternly, 'You're old enough to know better. And you,' she said to Babs, 'should think about what it's like being a mother before you steal someone's pushchair and try to destroy it with your antics.'

Babs said, 'It isn't anyone's pushchair. It was abandoned by the playground.'

The woman said, 'I suggest you learn the difference between "abandoned" and "placed carefully while its owner is emptying a potty".' She grabbed the pushchair, 'I'll take that, thank you very much. I hope for your sake that it hasn't been damaged, otherwise my husband will be over to speak to you. He is a barrister, you know.'

After a few routine checks it seemed that, apart from a divot stuck in the braking mechanism, the pushchair was OK. Babs ran off towards the coach and shouted back, 'It's not even a nice pushchair.' It was very childish.

I was left with the woman. I said, 'I'm really sorry we took the pushchair. We thought it had been abandoned.'

'It is a Silver Cross, you know,' the woman said. I told her I realized that now, apologized again, and left before her husband turned up and initiated any kind of legal proceedings.

Back on the coach, Babs sat down and laughed. 'That was funny. And the swings, it's years since I've been on a swing and I don't know why I ever stopped. When you grow up why do you stop doing things that are fun? Swinging's wicked, isn't it? I love it. I used to be on the swings all the time when I was a kid, just swinging up to the sky as high as I could. You can forget everything that's on your mind when you're swinging because your head's moving too fast. I once spent hours and hours on the swings when I ran away from home. My mum was supposed to be taking me to my dad's but I didn't like going there. I didn't like his new girlfriend. So I ran away from home and spent hours at the park swinging. I went back home ages later, when I thought it would be too late to go to my Dad's and we'd have to call it off. I got back and my mum was just putting my bag in the car and she said, "That's perfect timing, Sandra. Go and wash your hands and we'll be off." She hadn't even realized that I'd run away.'

'I ran away from home once,' I said. 'Well, kind of, a bit like you really. I got up one morning and I felt like I needed a bit of space. I think I was about nine or ten at the time so I wanted to break out, become my own man. Plus, I was getting a load of grief because I'd spilt some Ribena on the front room carpet. So I got up early one morning, while everyone else was still in bed, and packed a bag with some comics and a block of cheese. Then I put a note on the kitchen table saying, "I have run away from home. I think it will be best for all of us. Please feed Goldie. Best wishes, your son, Raymond." Once I'd done that, I was a bit worn out by all the planning so I went back to bed for a while. I wanted to make sure I was fully rested because I thought running away from home would be quite tiring – because of all the running. When I went back downstairs later on, there was a policeman in the kitchen, my mum was in tears, and my dad had gone out to check the bottoms of ditches. I got even more grief for that than I did for spilling the Ribena.'

'Why didn't they check your bedroom to see if you were there?' Babs said.

'You know what parents are like, panic first, think later. I only ran away that once, and I didn't even get out of the house.'

'You're such a rebel.'

'I'm good bad, but I'm not evil.'

'What's that supposed to mean?'

'It's the Shangri-Las,' I said. 'From *Give Him a Great Big Kiss*: "He's good bad, but he's not evil."'

'Whatever,' Babs said.

I looked out of the window. It was good to talk to Babs. At least I'd put the *Seasons in the Sun* episode behind me. It was a shame there were still the potential fatal side effects of a new alcopop crisis to worry about, but, life goes on, I'd decided to stay. The way things were going I could have two more days of rock 'n' roll and I'd be in the JookBoxFury final. From zero to hero.

There was a big hold-up on the opposite carriageway, hopefully not an accident. We couldn't risk any accidents. JookBoxFury could be wiped out in an instant and no-one would be any the wiser. Unless it made our names – the JookBoxFury heroes taken just as their talent was blossoming. All those people sitting in the traffic jam didn't know what was going on with JookBoxFury, but on the bus it was the centre of the universe. It was for me, anyway. I felt like I'd been on the JookBoxFury tour for six weeks at least, but we were only into the third day. Six weeks packed into three days. Time was speeding up. It was difficult to remember what life was like outside of JookBoxFury. I didn't want to think about going back to the routine. All those people on the other carriageway were stuck, but as long as I was on the JookBoxFury tour I was going somewhere.

I Want to Hold Your Hand

As soon as we got to Glasgow, Fran insisted that Laurence and Rhia took her to the venue to walk through the plan. As they were leaving, Fran said, 'Ray, why don't you join us so I can keep an eye… so you can cast your expert eye over things?'

Nye tagged along. He was seeking the perfect vibe.

We stopped outside a place with 'No More Heroes' written across the middle of the window in crimson paint, the bottom of the letters dripping like the spilled blood of fallen heroes. The sides of the window were covered in flyers for bands and DJs.

We were about to go inside when Fran's phone rang. She put on the sickly, 'Ah, James, so good to hear from you,' but dropped it quickly when she said, 'That is a complete fabrication. Will those journalists stop at nothing? If your assistant could fax the details to the hotel I'll sort this one in no time. We really do have more important things to worry about than some jumped-up little man trying to make a name for himself.'

She finished the call and told Laurence they'd have to get back to the hotel sharpish to develop a damage limitation strategy in response to ludicrous assumptions being made by the press. She told Rhia, 'I never thought I'd be saying this, but you're in charge, Rhiannon. Ray will keep an eye on what you're up to. Raymond, don't let me down on this one.'

I carried the weight of responsibility with me as I followed Rhia and Nye into the bar. Inside it took a minute to adjust to the subdued lighting which filtered out from orange beehive lamp shades. The jukebox stood by the entrance, playing slow, intense sounds that I didn't recognize.

The furniture in No More Heroes had probably been retrieved from a 1970s disco club called Tiffany's or Roxy's. There were high stool chairs with chrome legs along the bar and smaller stools were set around tables that stood on a single chrome leg. Along the wall opposite the bar was a long high-backed bench upholstered in grey vinyl. In the area by the window were diner-style booths. At the other side of the room, in the corner by the jukebox, was a small raised area with more benches and stools and a huge St Andrew's flag covering the ceiling above it.

The decoration must have been done by a group of art students with conflicting notions and a limited budget. The back wall was red with kaleidoscopic harlequin figures made from multi-coloured triangles. The side wall was aquamarine with a series of framed paintings of island beauties. Individually, the paintings were car boot material, but together they were strangely alluring.

There were only a handful of people in the place. A couple of girls at a table by the window were looking out into the street, commenting on passersby. A couple of guys with bleached stringy haircuts and interesting jackets were sitting at the bar talking about situations, gig bookings and planning quotations. They were obviously in a band. The barman was reading, but when we approached he put down his book and came over to us. He had the look of a young Clark Kent, probably without the powers and definitely without the acne control. He had a greasy wave of hair falling over his eyes and wore black-rimmed NHS specs and a charity shop v-necked pullover on top of an old school shirt. If he wasn't working behind the bar he would probably have been in an underground bunker somewhere, writing a computer programme that would save the world.

Rhia said to the barman, 'Hi, I'm Rhia, this is Ray and Nye. We're here for JookBoxFury.'

The barman said, 'The jukebox is over there, best jukebox in the world. £1 for five plays, help yourself.'

Rhia said, 'No, it's for JookBoxFury – the competition. We will be using the jukebox, but it's a competition. It's for the Jook launch campaign. I talked to the manageress about it before.'

The barman reflected on the situation. 'The competition? The jukebox drinks promotion thing? Aye, right enough, I remember that. I thought that was next week.'

'No, it's tonight.' Rhia sounded slightly worried. 'It's definitely tonight.'

'Is it tonight then? I don't know, I've been away. It's best to talk to Minnie, she's the boss. She's away for a while right now, but she'll be back.'

'That's it, I spoke to Minnie before,' Rhia said.

'Aye, she organizes everything, so you're best talking to her. Will you be having anything to drink?'

Nye got a coffee and went to set his laptop up by the window.

Rhia and I took our drinks and went to sit on the dais in the corner by the jukebox. It was separated from the rest of the bar by a wooden rail and probably doubled as a stage for DJs or acoustic sets.

'This is where you'll be for the competition,' Rhia said. 'It's perfect isn't it? I picked No More Heroes as a venue. Fran wanted to go to Edinburgh because her aunt lives there, but luckily Laurence backed me up to come here. The music's brilliant. Have a look and tell me if you've ever seen a jukebox with a more obscure selection.'

I went to take a look. The jukebox was an NSM Ultimate and was obviously from a different era to the Chantal, it played CD albums instead of vinyl singles for a start. It didn't have the space age glory of the Chantal but at least there was more to it than the box on the wall in The Queen Victoria. It still looked like a proper jukebox. The NSM Ultimate must have been from the 1980s, the decade of the CD, and on the front it had an Eighties design of cold blue and black dots, broken by a cracked mirror effect.

I pressed the arrow button to move through the CD covers and handwritten track listings. The new cards slid over the top of the previous ones like a deck being shuffled. All the music on the jukebox was from the world that creatcd or came from new wave, and it was specifically new wave rather than punk – they'd got PiL on there but not the Sex Pistols. It was an anti-Rock collection that was proudly indie.

I got a feel for the music we could choose from. Rhia was right, it was fairly obscure. It was going to be a challenging JookBoxFury. There were a few classics like The Smiths and Joy Division, and a good proportion of Scottish bands, plus the MC5 and The Stooges. There were also artists whose names I knew, but that was about all, and, I hate to admit this, there were a few artists I hadn't even heard of: The Come Ons, Errors, Terra Diablo, Equally Humdrum. They must have been local bands. It was a tricky situation. Reputations could be made and lost in an environment like that. Babs' approach of playing music that was fun was going to be easier said than done. I certainly wasn't going to be the only one who would be struggling with the selection available on No More Heroes' jukebox.

I sat back down with Rhia. 'Couldn't you find *Seasons in the Sun* then?' she asked me.

'Very funny,' I said. 'There's plenty to choose from on there. Not a problem at all, it's good to have a different challenge.'

I wondered whether I should go and find an internet café to catch up on the happening sounds of Errors and Equally Humdrum. You had to put the work in to get the results. I was considering that when a woman who looked about fifteen came from behind the bar and over to our table. I don't know if you're supposed to say this, but she was really short, tiny, very, very small. She had wispy blonde hair in bunches and wore a pristine nylon overall with white collar and cuffs that made her look as though she had turned up to work at the wrong place. She said something very quietly. Her voice was as small as she was and I couldn't make out any words, only faint sounds in a strong Glaswegian accent.

Rhia said, 'I'm sorry, I didn't quite hear you.'

The woman spoke again. We leaned towards her, but it was impossible to understand what she was saying.

Rhia said, 'I beg your pardon, it's the music, what was that again?'

The woman repeated what she'd said, slightly louder and it was just possible to pick out the word 'Minnie.'

Rhia said, 'That's right, we're waiting for Minnie. I'm organizing the jukebox competition so we just wanted to check that everything was alright.'

The woman smiled and put her hand out to Rhia. She shook our hands, then said something else.

Rhia nodded, then said, 'I'm sorry, I didn't quite catch that.'

The woman spoke again, but it wasn't any clearer.

Rhia said, 'I'm really sorry, I couldn't hear, I've had a bit of a cold. Could you speak up a bit.'

The woman said something, and pointed to the jukebox and then at the bar.'

Rhia said, 'The jukebox, great. We're here for JookBoxFury… um, yes, so we'll use the jukebox. There's a few more of us coming in later and we'll get started about eight-thirtyish.'

The woman said something, nodded, smiled and went back behind the bar and through a door at the back.

'Do you think that was Minnie?' Rhia asked me.

'I don't know,' I said. 'She didn't come across as being the manageress type.'

'Do you think she was giving us the OK? She seemed fairly positive, I don't think she was asking us to leave was she?'

'No, she seemed quite positive.'

'I was going to put a few posters up. I don't want to do that if we haven't got the OK.'

'I should do it. They'll let you know soon enough if they're not happy about it.'

'I'll go and check with the barman.' Rhia went to the bar and showed the Clark Kent guy a poster and talked to him for a minute. When she came back she said, 'I think it's OK.'

'What did he say?'

'He said I need to check with Minnie. He's been away for a while. I asked him if that was Minnie we'd just been talking to and he said, "Aye, that's Little Minnie right enough." So I think it's all OK.'

I said, 'If that was Little Minnie, maybe there's a Big Minnie, and she's really the one we need to talk to. Perhaps you ought to check whether there's a Big Minnie.'

'I just asked him if that was Minnie and he looked at me like I was daft. I'm not going back to ask him if there's a Big Minnie. I think it'll be OK… I don't know though, what do you think?'

'What would Fran do in this situation?'

'What is it with you and that woman? All of a sudden you're Fran's big pal and she's asking for your opinion on Jook and telling you to keep an eye on me. No offence, but it's a bit strange because Fran's never that nice to anybody, at least not anybody who can't help her career.'

It was a bit strange. 'You don't think there's anything odd about the Jook do you, Rhia?'

'Why? Do you think there's something odd about it?'

'I was just checking,' I said. 'I wanted to make sure it wasn't bad in some way. It couldn't be harmful could it? It wouldn't be possible for a drink like that to make everything go green would it? What if it did that, and everything stayed green for ever? That couldn't happen could it? I was wondering if that's the kind of thing that was happening to Rik.'

'I've been seeing some weird flashes of green light,' Rhia said.

'Flashes of light, green stars, wisps of green fog and a green glow everywhere? That couldn't be dangerous could it?'

'I know this sounds ridiculous,' Rhia said, 'but did you ever get the feeling that Jook was somehow telling you what to do, as if there was a green spirit guiding you?'

I almost hugged Rhia. I said, 'Thank God, I thought it was just me – and probably Rik.'

'Why didn't you say anything before?' Rhia asked me.

'Why didn't you say anything?'

'It seemed too silly. I wasn't even sure if there was anything there at first. It was only a faint green haze. It was nothing really, well, not at first, but now I don't know. Something isn't right. The Jook has affected Rik hasn't it? It's strange that no-one else has said anything. I mean, what about Bilbo Baggins and all those morris dancers, and Monica's Minxes. They were all knocking it back. Why didn't it affect them?'

I told Rhia about Fran's phone call with James Hylton-James.

She started shaking her head as I told her. When I got to the bit about Fran telling me I was part of her team and we had to stick together Rhia said, 'I don't believe it. I thought you were OK. You seemed like a nice guy, but you've gone and stuck up for Fran so that she can make the launch a success and be made a Director of, or whatever her big ambition is. What if Jook really is harmful, and you knew about it and you didn't do anything? I should have said something myself. Why didn't I say something as soon as I saw the green haze the first time? I mean, what if it actually makes people ill and we're responsible?'

'You're right. You're totally right,' I said. 'I wasn't thinking straight. When Fran told me I could stay on JookBoxFury I just… I've never had a chance to do anything like this before. It's been brilliant. Just being on the tour, meeting Rik and Nye and finding out that I used to know Babs, and then when I thought I could maybe be in the final… I got too caught up in that. I thought it would make up for having a rubbish job if I could tell people I'd won the JookBoxFury final, or even been in it. I didn't want the tour to end so I…'

'I don't want JookBoxFury to end,' Rhia said. 'I organized most of it. There was hardly any budget, but I found the venues. I even suggested having some sort of jukebox competition to Laurence in the first place. I don't want JookBoxFury to end. Especially not now, because all the No More Heroes music is going to make the competition even better. It's going to be the best – you might even be in with a chance. Then there's the final, the classic old jukeboxes at the Jukebox World show are going to be unbelievable. I don't want to pack up and go home…'

'Neither do I.'

'… but I don't want to find out that everyone who's been drinking Jook is going to spend the rest of their life crouching in a corner trying to hide from the green fog.'

'I found the fog quite comforting,' I said, 'but you're right, you wouldn't want to be stuck in it for ever. We should do something about the Jook, like let the brewery know, or warn everyone about it.'

Rhia said, 'If we do that, and Jook gets withdrawn, then there's no JookBoxFury. What have you got? BoxFury – what's that?'

'It sounds like a man kicking a box around. It's not going to be the same. But what if we could organize it so no-one overdoes it on the Jook? Then there shouldn't be a problem with any kind of side effects, and we've still got JookBoxFury. Would that be OK? We can sort it out. Fran said you were in charge anyway. We could restrict it to one bottle per person. That's got to be OK. I'm pretty sure Dr Roc and Pony Boy haven't been affected by the green spirit force and they can't have had more than one or two bottles a night.'

'We need to check. We could ask them, and then I suppose…'

I offered to go and have a word with Nye. Rhia said she'd get in touch with the others. We had a plan. Rhia took her phone out and I strolled over to the far side of the bar. Nye was leaning back from his laptop, smiling. I sat opposite him and asked, 'How's it going?'

'Oh, pretty good,' he said. 'I've nearly finished another of the *Nyethologies*, so it's going well. I like to do them in places like this because it's more inspiring, it's somehow closer to the heart of rock 'n' roll than sitting in a hotel room.'

I said, 'You could smash your hotel room up and chuck the TV out of the window. That would be rock 'n' roll.'

'That's another rock mythology, actually. I might use that. Anyway, I've just got to make a call, keep an eye on the laptop, will you?'

Nye went outside. His media training based on *Nyethologies* had led me into a bit of bother at the press conference and I really needed to get a proper grip on the concept. I tried to look at Nye's new article in the hope that it would give me an insight, but the laptop was turned away from me and I couldn't quite see what was on the screen. I nudged the laptop slightly to try and get a better look, he had said keep an eye on it after all. The title at the top of the screen was, 'The Beatles First Spliff and The Birth of Rock.' I looked outside and Nye was on his phone, deep in conversation, walking backwards and forwards, waving his arm every now and then. I gave the laptop another nudge and leaned round so I could read the screen more easily.

The Beatles' First Spliff and the Birth of Rock

The incessant drip drip drip places me in a state of perturbed dislocation. If I could reveal the essence of the phantasmagoria that started the moment Dylan passed a marijuana cigarette to The Beatles, then we would be in inhaling distance of understanding why Rock became and why it remains. On record, the moment is the toke in every chorus of *Girl*. Lennon sings, 'Girl,' and inhales sharply. He's stoned by the girl and he's whispering a secret to everyone in the know: 'We're in on it too. We're the beautiful people'.

When Dylan first met The Beatles he already thought they'd been singing, 'I get high,' in *I Want to Hold Your Hand*, but until they met, taking drugs for the Fab Four meant popping pills to play all night at the Star Club. That moment at the Delmonico Hotel, New York, August 1964, when Dylan gave the Beatles their first taste of psychedelics, was about more than looking at the ceiling and giggling – it was the mythical moment when Rock music was born.

Far out! On the way home from the trips festival why not stop off for a nice cup of tea and a biscuit rather than recall having experienced anything so profound as a Dadaist happening with its discordant subversion creating a sense of unease that questions normality. Is it that, or is it simply a release valve, playing into the hands of those who make the rules and rewarding them with joyous, simplistic optimism? You had pop from the mop top shakin' Fabs – 'She loves you, and you know that can't be bad.' Paul and George come together at the microphone to 'whooooooooo'. And the audience screams 'RingooooooooooPaullllllllllllllGeorgeeeeeeeeeeeeeeeeeeJohnnnnn n.' Sobbing uncontrollably, or helplessly covering their mouths in awe, staring, pinching themselves and looking at their friends to check that this REALLY – IS – HAPPENING and then screaming again. 'Whoooooooooo.' Music for the people?

Dylan loved rock 'n' roll, might even have been a rock 'n'

149

roller if things had worked out differently, but then he got folk. Tunes handed down from generation to generation, songs that were stories about people and their connection to the land and the sea and the sky, and maybe she does love you, but there's no way you should be glad because it's going to turn out bad and she's going to the gallows. Music of the people?

Stop... stop for a moment... will you turn that down? Just TURN IT DOWN and decipher this empty billboard, the façade over the dream, the map over the landscape that hides the true nature of... of what? Of me? Of you? Of Dylan or The Beatles or whichever entertainer stands before us with a 'message'? Whether it's their own message, or some more sinister force, the effect is one of pure sensation. For the message itself has no deeper meaning than to represent itself as a 'message' for the diversion of bohemians as they dance beneath the sky with one hand waving free, or whatever the latest fad is, before it turns into a nightmare.

The Beatles started playing sdrawkcab sepat and yesterday, today and tomorrow never knows. Instead of the 'Whoooooo' and the screams they say something profound about the truth. Ha ha ha. They started to sing about something other than she loves you / she doesn't love you / I love you / I don't love you / do you love me? / don't you love me? / love me do – they sang about fields and roads and sky.

Awaking soaked in sweat, facing relentless temptation or the recurring guilt of a temptation not resisted until the cry 'No future' is the greatest hope we have. Hegemony, hegemony, I think you got the better of me. Give in and take the easy way: 'far fucking out!' instead of 'no fucking way!' Lay another platter on the turntable, maaaan. Click the i-pod on to shuffle and just lay back, soak it up and try to regain a defiled innocence. Fake surprise at the inevitable barrage of good news / bad news and welcome the new candidates, same as the old candidates, kick back and discuss, at considerable length, their haircuts, of considerable length. It's a bummer. That's all, so file it away with the other bric-a-brac or start to decode, if it's not too late already, and then stop because it all ends up here, no STOP – because it all ends up here – in the name of love, I said STOP!"

Hairway to Steven

I had to page down a few times to get to the end, and I have to admit I didn't quite get it all. That was always the way with Nye's stuff. Sometimes you weren't a hundred per cent sure whether you were getting it all, or even whether it was there to get. I was going to have another read through when the door to the bar swung open and Nye came back inside. I quickly tried to scroll to the top of the document and turn the laptop round before Nye saw me. The laptop beeped and I leaned away nonchalantly.

Nye sat down and looked at the screen, 'What's happened to it?' he asked me.

'What's happened to what?' I replied innocently.

Nye pointed at the screen. The document was completely blank.

'Have you been touching this?' Nye said. 'I asked you to keep an eye on the laptop, not delete my article.'

'Haven't you got it saved?' I asked him.

'I was going to save it when it was finished.'

'You should always save your work as you go along,' I said. 'You never know what might happen. It looked finished anyway.'

'How would you know? Were you reading it? That's just fucking… you dozy… That's all inspirational stuff. That's not going to come back to me again in the same way, if at all. You've read a private document and then deleted it. Jesus Christ.' He seemed quite annoyed and was about to stab at the keyboard with his finger.

'Stop!' I said. 'Don't move.' I took hold of the sides of the laptop and very very slowly turned it towards me.

'What the hell are you doing now? Wasn't deleting my work enough for you? Are you going to destroy the bloody…?'

I put my finger to my lips. 'No noise, no sudden movements,' I whispered. I'd started to sweat and my breathing was shallow. I wiped my palms on the side of my trousers and then carefully, very carefully, moved the pointer on the screen over the back arrow. I held my breath, and clicked.

Phew. The text came back onto the screen. I slumped back into the seat and let out a deep breath. That had been close. 'There you go,' I said, 'I should save that now.'

'You lucky bastard,' Nye said. 'If that had all been lost… I'd have… you'd have been a sorry man, that's for sure…' His tone eased and he asked me, 'What did you think of it, anyway?'

'I thought it was good,' I said. 'I'd probably need to read it again. I don't think I got it all the first time. You don't mention the man in the pea suit, either.'

'Yeah, I thought about the pea suit thing – I wondered if that might make it a bit confusing.'

'Oh, I don't know. Anyway, I'll leave you to it.' I slid out from the table to get away before Nye's laptop had another glitch. As I was going I remembered my mission. 'Oh, Nye, you haven't noticed anything strange about Jook have you?'

'It tastes bloody strange,' he said.

'Apart from that. Have you had any side effects? Like the way Rik's been behaving.'

'No offence to Rik,' Nye said, 'he's done some good stuff in his time, but you don't need me to point out that he's a couple of Portaloos short of a festival. Rik might be having a strange reaction to Jook, but that's Rik. I've been no saint myself when it comes to the mind altering substances, but I always knew when to say enough was enough. Rik never stopped, that's his problem. I'm not in that league. Jook's a run of the mill alcopop. It's not even worth drinking as far as I'm concerned. Why do you ask?'

'No reason really. Just checking Rik's OK I suppose.' I pointed to the laptop. 'I'd get that saved if I were you.'

I joined Rhia. She was looking at a list of the JookBoxFury

contestants. She had ticked Dr Roc and Pony Boy and there was a big asterisk next to Rik and a question mark next to Babs.

'Nye's clear,' I said.

Rhia gave him a tick. She added our names and gave us small asterisks. She said, 'That's three with some possible Jook effect, three with no effect, and one don't know. That's Babs. She'd gone for a walk in the park and when I rang her, she said that being asked whether everything looked green was a bloody silly question in the circumstances.'

'I think we can risk it,' I said. 'The three who haven't drunk much Jook are fine. We'll get the bar staff to limit it to one bottle per person. We can ask them to use vouchers or something.'

'Good luck with that,' Rhia said. 'We don't even know whether we've been talking to the right Minnie.'

'Don't worry,' I told her, 'I'll go and sort it out.'

I went over to the bar. The barman put his book down and I said, 'That was Little Minnie we saw before wasn't it? We were just wondering whether there was another Minnie?'

The barman said, 'Oh aye, there's Big Minnie.'

'Will she be back soon?'

'You never know with Big Minnie, hold on.' He went through the door at the back of the bar and came back with Little Minnie. 'This guy wants to know if Big Minnie will be back soon.'

Little Minnie answered. It must have been about Big Minnie but I couldn't understand it. When she finished I said, 'I'm sorry, I didn't really catch that.'

She said it again and I listened intently. There was possibly something about the Florida Keys or she'd lost her keys or something. I couldn't ask her to repeat it again. 'It's annoying when that happens,' I said. I thought was a reasonable response if someone had lost their keys, less so if they'd gone on holiday to Florida. 'Anyway, we wondered if it would be possible to sort out some sort of voucher system for the drinks promotion tonight so that everyone just gets one bottle… because it's in such big demand. So I wondered if you could arrange that?'

Little Minnie spoke to the barman and he laughed. Then she

said something and half waved her hand towards me, smiled and went back through the door. The barman picked his book up.

I went back to Rhia and she asked me, 'Is that the right Minnie then?'

'I'm not sure. There is a Big Minnie, but I think she's lost her keys. I did ask if they could organize a voucher system for the Jook though.'

'And?'

'And she kind of did that,' I demonstrated Little Minnie's hand waving gesture.

'What's that supposed to mean?'

'I took it to mean she was going to sort it out. I'm pretty sure she went off to do it. I'll check again later.'

Rhia started to question my belief in No More Heroes, when the rest of the JookBoxFury team turned up and decided to order food. I went for the Hero Burger with curly fries, Rik ordered the all day breakfast, and Dr Rococco had a Greek platter with aubergine dip, marinated olives and hummus. Rhia asked me if she could share my fries, I said she could, so she had the spicy sweet potato and coconut soup. Nye had chilli, and Pony Boy had bangers and mash with onion gravy. Laurence was still trying to decide whether No More Heroes would have a decent Chardonnay to accompany the fish pie when Fran grabbed the menu off him and said, 'I don't have time for this nonsense. This isn't a Sunday school picnic. The Jook launch is absolutely in the balance at this moment in time and I really don't think I can afford to sit here listening to any more of this inanity while there are journalists out there making unfounded accusations. Laurence, we need to go somewhere where we can get a bit of peace and quiet and walk this through again. When the going gets tough, the tough get going. Come on.'

Laurence said, 'I don't suppose there'd be time for a glass of chilled…' Fran's stare stopped him. He said, 'The tough get going.'

Fran said, 'It looks like you've got everything under control here, Raymond. Rhiannon, don't let me down… again.'

After they'd gone Rik said, 'What was all that about? Is she getting more fucking miserable every time we see her?'

155

Little Minnie came out from the bar and said something. We looked at each other and shook our heads. Babs said, 'I'm sorry, love, you'll have to say that again.'

Little Minnie repeated it. It was possibly about the bangers and mash, but Rik said, 'You're going to have to speak up, Darlin', you're just mumbling. No-one can understand a fucking word you're saying.'

Little Minnie stepped up to Rik and made a comment that was quiet but forceful, then she gave him a stinging slap on the cheek and went back behind the bar.

'Who the fuck was that?' Rik asked.

'That was Little Minnie,' I told him. 'She's probably the manageress.'

Rhia said, 'You're lucky Big Minnie's not here, she's lost her keys, otherwise you could have been in real trouble.'

'I bloody could have if she's anything like the little one. She's got a temper on her she has. That's the last time she gets the benefit of the Guitar Man's feedback.'

While we were waiting for the food I said, 'Have you seen the jukebox? It's a bit different to what we've had so far. It's obscure stuff.'

'Worried about another defeat are we, Ray?' Babs said. 'Getting the excuses in early this time, very wise. As the reigning Queen of the jukebox…'

'The Jook Duke of the Juke actually,' Pony Boy said.

'Whatever. I'd better take my responsibility seriously and go and see what pearls of musical wisdom I'll be offering my subjects on JookBoxFury tonight.'

Babs stood in front of the jukebox for a minute flicking through the albums and then said, 'You have got to be kidding. It's not April the first is it? What is all this crap? Is this music? I don't know who any of these bands are, but look at the names. Look at this,' she pointed to one of the album covers, 'The Butthole Surfers with *Hairway to Steven* – sorry, but am I missing something? And You Will Know Us By The Trail of Dead – is that a band or a history essay? The Butthole Surfers?' She said to me, '*Hairway to Steven*, would you listen to that? I bet *you* would, wouldn't you? You probably think they're great don't you?'

'I don't really know them,' I said, 'you can't listen to everything, can you? In the past you could know pretty much all the important music, but now there's just too much, there are whole genres you have to miss out. You might have forty-seven days' worth of music on your i-Pod – you can't seriously listen to all of that. I've even got songs on my mp3 player that I don't know, I don't know what they are. I've got the technology to carry music with me all the time that I've never even heard. It's not so special any more.

'It just isn't the same as when you were fourteen and you bought an LP and you'd read the sleeve notes on the bus before you got home – you loved it before you even got it home and played it. Then you play it, and you're a bit disappointed at first. It doesn't live up to expectations because you've built it up so much, but you keep playing it and it grows on you. At first, your favourite track is probably the single, side one track three, so you keep putting that on, but after a while you realize your favourite track is the one after the single. Then you decide that side two is even better than side one – and side one is brilliant – and you're telling everyone it's the greatest album you've ever heard, and you listen to it over and over again until you know every note and every word. Years later, you've bought a remastered version on CD with a load of bonus tracks that actually drag the whole thing out a bit too long and spoil it, and it doesn't sound as good as it used to. It ends up on your mp3 player next to something that you don't even know what it is, just because that's next alphabetically. Is it me, or is pop music not as good as it used to be?'

Babs said, 'So does that mean you like the Hairy Buttholes or not?'

Dr Rococco said, 'That's a very interesting point, Ray, this whole issue of popular music being defined in such a way that arbiters of taste, whoever they may be, can judge it as being good or bad in some absolute sense. They might even say that popular music is finished, come to that – and the notion that music that is popular is 'dead' is equally intriguing. Coincidentally, I've been working on an article for the *Journal of Popular Music* which is sub-titled, "mp3 and the Death of Pop," very much the topic you were alluding to, Ray. I'll pass you a copy if you're interested, I'm keen to know whether there are any points of commonality between the fan's perspective and that of the academic. Not that all academics share the same perspective, heaven forbid,' she laughed.

'Not that all fans share the same perspective,' I thought, and chuckled to myself.

While we'd been talking, Rik and Nye had been looking at the jukebox. They came back to the table and Nye said, 'I like it. It celebrates an alternative history. Instead of coming from the blues and Elvis, you've got music inspired by art and experimentation. The shock of the new, very sweet. I don't even mind if I play tracks that I don't know, because that's the thrill of it all. Discovering a vibrant new sound excites me more than regurgitating all the hackneyed Beatles and Stones and the same old dadrock.'

'I thought you were a dad,' Babs said.

'I may be someone's father, but when it comes to unearthing new sounds, I've got the wide eyed innocence of a child digging in a sand pit.'

'Let's hope you don't dig up a turd, 'Rik said.

'I've decided what I'm going to play,' Babs announced. 'As we've only got the choice of drone music by bands I've never heard of – And You Will Know Us By The Trail of Dead? The Butthole Surfers? You can't be serious? Anyway, seeing as I've only heard of about one band on this jukebox, I'll be playing anything with a happy sounding title. *Hairway to Steven* won't be on my list, I'll tell you that for nothing. I might as well try and get a bit of fun in before we all die of boredom.'

Little Minnie came back to the table to bring the food. It all looked good, although there weren't any bangers and mash which Pony Boy got a bit agitated about. He went and spoke to the barman. When he came back he said, 'Apparently I need to talk to Little Minnie, she's coming to see me in a minute.'

When Little Minnie came over, she brought one of the guys with the dyed stringy hair who'd been sitting at the bar earlier. She said a few words very faintly which seemed to be an introduction, because the guy shook hands with all of us and said he was Parker from Equally Humdrum. Little Minnie said something else, which may possibly have been to do with a delivery of anthracite, but who could tell? If it was about anthracite then, as far as I was concerned, it wasn't our problem, but Rik agreed with her and said, 'Too right, darlin', I'm with you all the way on this one.'

Little Minnie looked pleased and didn't slap Rik again. She went back to the bar, but Parker stayed and sat down at our table.

Pony Boy asked him, 'Have you got any news about my bangers and mash?'

Parker said, 'Sorry, I don't have any news of that kind. I'm the singer in Equally Humdrum. We've got a residency here and Minnie wants me to be in your jukebox competition because all the punters know me from the band. So, what's it all about? What do I have to do?'

Pony Boy said, 'I'm not sure how easy it will be to bring someone else in at this stage. We have got a panel of experts here and, no disrespect, but you may be a little out of your depth in this company.'

Well said. You couldn't have any upstart coming along and playing JookBoxFury – there was more to it than being in a local band. If you're in a band, then stay in your band, and leave the jukebox selections to the people who know what they're doing. At last Pony Boy was sticking up for some principles in the competition.

'I'll take a chance,' Parker said. 'It's our PA you're going to be using for your announcements anyway, so… you know.'

Rhia said, 'I think it's fine for Parker to be in the competition. It's nice to have someone from the local scene involved, it keeps things interesting. Unless anyone's got any major objections, let's welcome Parker to JookBoxFury.' She told Parker, 'We're just about ready to start. Pony Boy will explain the rules, there's nothing to it.'

Nothing to it? What had she done? What little indie rock advantage I had could easily be destroyed by someone with local knowledge. I leaned back in despair. The blue on the St Andrew's flag hanging from the ceiling had taken on a luminous green hue. The spirit of Jook was back, not as powerful as before, but it was there. Maybe there was a way... Parker might have bitten off more than he could chew.

Love is Strange

By a quarter past eight there was a buzz of expectation in No More Heroes. I went to the bar to check whether, by some crazy serendipity, Little Minnie had organized a voucher system for the Jook allocation. I asked the barman and he said, 'The vouchers, oh aye, that's all sorted, pal.' He gave me a catering size margarine tub full of vouchers printed with the words, 'One drink,' and a couple of rubber hand stamps. He told me, 'Little Minnie says you've got to help out with the vouchers. What you need to do is you give everyone a voucher and stamp their hand so you know they've had theirs. They bring the voucher to the bar, we give them a bottle of your stuff in return. Simple. Will that do you?'

It was so simple it was ridiculous. It was as if it had been planned.

Rhia and I split the vouchers, took a batch of programmes each to give away, and started working round the bar in opposite directions. As I moved through No More Heroes, I got the sense of being in a student union bar. Nearly everyone was around nineteen or twenty years old and wearing a range of student gear, from a girl in a University of Strathclyde hoodie, to the guy who'd been sitting at the bar with Parker, with his carefully tousled hair and army surplus store red ceremonial jacket. I gave him a voucher and a programme and stamped his hand. He looked at the programme and said, 'This is awesome. Our singer Parker's in this so he'll be getting my vote.'

I said, 'You should wait and see what all the other contestants play. If you don't vote for the tracks you hear, then it defeats the object.'

'Oh, aye, no problem. I'll vote for what I hear, sure I will, but Parker likes the same kind of stuff as me so I'll be surprised if I'm not giving him top marks. I've got an open mind though, no problem, pal.'

I carried on giving out vouchers and stamping the hands of girls with basin haircuts and red pumps, and imitation 1940s starlets with feather boas and diamante broaches. Guys wearing brown belted tweed jackets and tennis shoes, ski jumpers, even jeans and leather jackets. All student life was there. A couple more people asked me if Parker was in the competition. I told them he was, but so was Rik Peabody of The Peabodies. That drew a blank.

When we'd finished, Rhia said to Parker, 'You seem to have got plenty of fans here. There's quite a few people said they wanted you to win.'

Parker shrugged. 'It's because of the band, and I do DJ sets here now and then, so it's all local support.'

I laughed and attempted to say a cheery, 'I wonder if it's worth the rest of us taking part when you're such a local hero?' but it came out harsher than I intended and sounded quite bitter.

Parker patted me on the knee and said, 'Of course it's worth taking part, pal, don't worry about it. You can't go wrong with this jukebox if you're into the post-rock feel. Every album's a gem so you've got plenty of quality to choose from. I should know, I help Little Minnie pick what goes on there.'

It was an outrage. If Pony Boy had heard that I felt sure he'd be cracking down on what were clearly extremely unfair practices. Instead, he said, 'Right, let's get ready to rumble, team. Who wants to start this time?'

Parker said, 'I don't mind going last, pal. I don't want to steal anyone's thunder.'

Steal anyone's thunder? Cocky upstart. 'I'll go next to last then,' I said.

Babs, Rik and Dr Rococco didn't mind when they went, and Nye slotted in before me. Parker switched the PA on and gave a microphone to Pony Boy. Pony Boy tapped the mic a couple of times, then switched it on and tapped it again. He explained the rules, told people to see Rhia at the edge of the stage if they hadn't got their Jook voucher, and made the introductions. The response Parker got from the crowd was totally over the top, almost embarrassing. One girl shouted, 'We love you, Parker,' and Pony Boy quipped back, 'I think we've got Lady Penelope in the house tonight.' Hilarious.

Rik was on first. After he'd made his selections, he sat down and said, 'In spite of No More Heroes looking rock 'n' roll, trying to pick five tracks that rock is easier said than fuckin' done in this place, but once again the Guitar Man has worked miracles.'

His first track was *Kick Out the Jams* by the MC5. His next track was *Ramblin' Rose* by the MC5. That was two torn-out pieces of rebel-rousing bad-time fuzzed-up rock about being part of the solution. When the third track came on and it was also from the MC5's *Kick Out the Jams* album, Pony Boy said, 'Tell me, does anyone else think all the groups sound a little samey nowadays?'

Rik said, 'These are all by the MC5, man. Kick out the fuckin' jams. Those guys knew how to put it on the line and kick it over the edge.'

Rik's last two tracks were also from *Kick Out the Jams* and the crowd in the bar was getting a little restless with the MC5's relentless proto-grunge. The guy in the red ceremonial jacket came over to Parker and said, 'When are you playing your stuff, Parker guy? I can't take much more of these songs your grandmother taught you – I thought you chose the albums that go on the jukebox.'

Parker said, 'Big Minnie insists that this stays on, so what can you say?'

The final MC5 track finished with a messy, free-form jam that sounded like the collapse of an early form of civilization. When it stopped there was an almost audible sigh throughout the bar.

Babs took the next turn and spent a surprisingly long time at the jukebox. The first track came on while she was still choosing, it was *Fun House* off *Funhouse* by The Stooges. More loud and messy, primal rock. Rik heard it and said, 'This is the fucking business, man. I'd have played a bit of this if I'd seen it.'

When Babs came back to us she asked, 'What's this bloody

racket? It can't be one of mine because I chose five songs with nice, happy titles.'

I was just about to say what the track was when Parker told her, 'This is The Stooges, it's called *Fun House*.'

'*Fun House*,' Babs said, 'that's right. I chose it because it's about fun. It doesn't sound like much fun living in their house though, that's all I can say. Choosing five fun and happy songs from a long list about sick, death, blood, vomit, dark, violent and dying wasn't very easy. Don't even ask me what they are because I can't remember.'

The next track started. I recognized it, but while I was trying to place it Parker got in first, 'This one's *Golden Porsche* off Mogwai's *Happy Songs for Happy People*.'

Babs said, 'You see, you'd be happy if you had a golden Porsche, wouldn't you? *Happy Songs for Happy People* they say, but just listen to it – depressing songs for people who are just about to get a migraine is what it sounds like. I'll tell you what I could have picked as well off the same album.' She went to look at the cards on the jukebox. When she came back she said, 'Right, you could have had *Killing All the Flies* and *Boring Machines Disturb Sleep*. How are those supposed to be happy songs for happy people? Get a life, that's all I'm saying.'

Babs' next two selections were throwbacks to early-Seventies singer songwriters, possibly early-Seventies singer songwriters who were waiting for a bus in the rain. They were, according to Parker, *Greatest* by Cat Power and *It's a Sight to Behold* from Devandra Banhart's *Rejoicing in the Hands (of the Golden Empress)*.

'I quite like these actually,' Babs said. 'I could listen to this. Cat Power? Is that like girl power for cats, because if it is I'm all for it?'

Parker said, 'She recorded this album in Memphis with some old soul musicians. We've just written a new track that's got this sort of feel.'

Babs said, 'I'd like to hear that. If you play your cards right, I might be able to give it a play on *Video Hits* – if you've got a video obviously, there's not much point if you haven't.'

Devandra Banhart's wistful strumming finished and was replaced by an attack of distorted grunge power. Babs was horrified. 'What the hell is this?'

Parker said, 'This is *Halloween* by Mudhoney off *Superfuzz Bigmuff*.'

'Halloween's good fun isn't it?' Babs said. 'Trick or treating, parties, fancy dress, bobbing for apples. I'm not sure about Superfuzz Bigmuff though, I prefer to wax myself.'

'Superfuzz Bigmuff is the distortion pedal the band uses,' Parker said.

He was starting to show off a bit. Anyone can know it all when they've put the albums on the jukebox. He was in real danger of overstepping the line with that whole male power-trip.

Babs said, 'You're not telling me they're using special equipment to make them sound like this on purpose? I never meant to play such miserable songs, so sorry, everybody. I like Cat Power though. Cats rule.'

Dr Rococco went to make her selections. She played a fantastic run of post-punk with choppy guitars and earnest declarations: The Gang of Four's *At Home He's a Tourist*, The Au Pairs' *Come Again*, The Raincoats' *In Love* and Public Image Ltd's *Public Image*, followed by PJ Harvey's *We Float*.

After the first couple of tracks had played, I said to Dr Rococco, 'I wouldn't have thought this was your kind of thing.'

She said, 'I have a lot of respect for this challenging agit-rock. There was a lot of music played in the faculty during the late-Seventies and early-Eighties. It was a very vibrant time when the music really did seem to be questioning the status quo both on a macro and a sexual-political level. I see this music as the soundtrack of our opposition to Thatcher. Of course, it wasn't long before romanticism returned and vacuous songs about girls on film, drinking cocktails and dancing on the sand were in vogue and it was apparent that, although pop songs were a factor in social change, they could never be relied upon to promote an alternative agenda.'

Nye wrote in a notebook as he made his selections. When he came back to the table, he flipped it open and said, 'In the true spirit of the musical adventurer I've chosen five tracks I've never heard before. I'll tell you what they are because I suspect that if I don't know them, you're not going to know them either.'

Nye read his list:

'The Amphetameanies with *Bedroom Holiday* from *Right Line in Nylons*.

Pink Dust by Magoo from the Chemikal Underground compilation, *Out of Our Heads on Skelp*.

G Plan, *There's People Lying Dead in the Stairwell* from *All Roads Lead to This*.

We Will Become Sillhouettes by The Postal Service from *Give Up*.

And finally, *Hello Bastards* from Part Chimp's, *I Am Come*.'

Nye's tracks were a mixture of slipping trip hop beats with waves of ambient sound, screamed vocals over screeching metal, low rent ska, and unnervingly edgy electronica. When they finished playing, Parker congratulated Nye, 'Great choices, pal, I might have put one or two of those on myself.'

Nye said, 'They were interesting, but sadly I don't think I've found the new thing yet.'

I was on. I went down the steps to the jukebox. I stood in front of it and squeezed my eyes tight shut. I could see a few faint green blobs in the blackness. I opened my eyes but there was no green glow coming from any of the cards. I thought the green had deserted me, when the glow from the Scottish flag above the stage split into five green stars which fell onto the jukebox and gently dissolved. That was the sign. Babs had played tracks with happy titles, Rik had played the MC5, Dr Roc had gone for elite indie classics, and Nye had taken the high risk approach of playing tracks he hadn't heard before. Was any of that enough to compete with Parker's local knowledge? No, not a chance. I had to take him on at his own game, take him on on his own turf. Although I might not know much about Equally Humdrum or the other local bands, I certainly knew plenty of Scottish bands. It was perfect. The Jook was telling me to play five tracks by top Scottish indie bands. I'd have an awe-inspiring combination of local appeal and fantastic songs. I couldn't go wrong.

I pressed the buttons for my first track and the digital screen showed, 'You're listening to 38/07' which was *Blue Boy* by Orange Juice. Surely everyone in No More Heroes would know that Orange

Juice's combination of the spirit of the Velvet Underground, with Motown's rhythm, and the Byrd's jangle, was the template for indie pop. They'd know that Orange Juice were the first.

I followed *Blue Boy* with Teenage Fanclub's *Sparky's Dream*, more jangle and harmonies. It was the sound of falling in love on a spring day in a distant galaxy, like they said, 'She lived in space, man.' Next, I introduced a hint of darkness, with the Jesus and Mary Chain's *Never Understand* – pure pop glistening from waves of feedback and distortion. Unfortunately, I didn't know what kind of distortion pedal they'd used so I said, 'You know how they created this distortion – angst,' but no-one appeared particularly impressed.

For my fourth track I needed something off the wall. I took a leaf from Nye's book and took a risk. There was a compilation by Danny McGlone of Scottish rock 'n' roll band the Majestics doing cover versions, and I picked a duet of him with Clare Grogan from Altered Images singing *Love is Strange*. I didn't know that version, but I did know that *Love is Strange* is one of the most interesting tracks of all time so it couldn't fail. It was written by Bo Diddley, but he refused to be credited for it. The original was sung by a session guitarist and Sylvia Robinson, who was only about fifteen at the time of recording, and who went on to found the rap label, Sugarhill Records. It had it all, and it turned out to be a brilliant version, especially the section after the middle eight where Danny sings, 'Clare,' and she replies, 'Yes, Danny.' He asks her, 'How you call your lover boy?' and she gives a girly growl back, 'Come here, lover boy.' But if he doesn't answer, she gives him the sweetest, 'Oh, lover boy.' But if he still doesn't answer – and you'd have to say that if he hasn't answered by then, he's either crazy or dead – but if he still doesn't answer, she coos, 'I simply say, bay-bay, oh-ooh bay-bay, my sweet bay-bay, you're the one.' He's taking notice by then, no doubt about it.

Brilliant, it was a risk worth taking. I expected that to be a banker as the most unusual song, maybe even another Zeitgeist award winner for song of the night. I looked around the room but the students didn't seem to be paying too much attention. I asked Rhia what she thought of it. She said, 'I like the bit on *Dirty Dancing* where this song plays.'

I said, 'Please could you not keep referring to *Dirty Dancing* when I'm playing great tracks.' There's a time and a place. It was an inspired choice – I'd have to get hold of the Danny McGlone album, and maybe consider watching *Dirty Dancing*.

For my final selection I brought it right back home with Belle and Sebastian's *The Boy With the Arab Strap*. Belle and Sebastian and Arab Strap were both from Glasgow. They probably hung out in No More Heroes, there could even be incidents in the song that had happened in the bar. It had to strike a chord.

It was a good selection of tracks. I was satisfied. Rhia said, 'Those were great songs. I love the idea of playing all Scottish bands.'

Parker said, 'Of course you're going to be guaranteed quality music with that approach, pal, but I wonder if it was all a little bit too obvious? I hope for your sake that the crowd didn't find it a tad patronizing, but I thought you did really well. Let's see how I get on without the benefit of all the experience you've had.'

Parker stood up and waved to the crowd as Pony Boy announced him, 'We may be here in No More Heroes, but I think there's at least one hero left. Cometh the hour, cometh Parker from the Equally Humdrums, let's give him a big welcome.'

A roar came back from the crowd and a chant broke out – 'Par-ker – Par-ker – Par-ker.'

I looked at Pony Boy to see if he was going to try and calm things down. The situation could easily get out of hand if he wasn't careful, but he was actually standing at the front of the stage by the barrier, leading the chanting and whipping the crowd up even more. It was downright irresponsible.

Parker made his choices and as soon as the first track started he got another cheer. It was Arcade Fire with *Rebellion (Lies)*. Obviously he wasn't only going to play obscure tracks by local bands. He followed it up with the Pixies' *Where is My Mind*, Super Furry Animals' *Juxtaposed With U*, and Ladytron's *Seventeen*. Each of them got a cheer from the crowd, but they were songs that would be well known by any student indie audience anywhere. Where was the local knowledge coming in with those selections? I didn't recognize the final track, but the other guy from Equally Humdrum jumped onto the stage and mimed to it alongside Parker, so I assumed it was one of theirs. The track had a throbbing metronomic beat with a chorus that was something about, 'heartbeat drumbeat, the rhythm of your heart and the sound of the street.' The crowd loved it. Little Minnie was behind the bar, clapping along, and I realized that Pony Boy, Rhia and Dr Roc had started clapping. Not wanting to be a party pooper, I joined in. It was actually pretty good. The song finished. The crowd were all on their feet going wild and the outcome of JookBoxFury Round Three didn't seem to be in too much doubt. How could you compete with a local hero playing favourites from albums he put on the jukebox in the first place, and finishing up miming to his own song? Parker milked the applause then, as it faded, he sat down.

Nye leaned over to Parker and shook his hand. 'Now, that was special. I can see where you're coming from, but at the same time it's fresh, it's different. That's the thrill. What's it called?'

'*Heartbeat Drumbeat*,' Parker said.

'I've got to hear more. You do have other stuff I can hear, I assume?'

'There's the rest of the demo, and we're playing here tomorrow night if you're still around.'

Nye said, 'We're due to leave in the morning but let's talk later. Brilliant – the thrill, that's it.'

When Pony Boy announced the results, it was no big surprise that Rik came last. There was a smattering of applause. Rik gave a clenched fist salute to the crowd and shouted, 'Kick out the jams.' As he was doing that, the door to the bar opened and an enormous woman came in, probably the tallest woman I'd ever seen. Not fat, but very big-boned. She could have been made from girders. She was tanned and wearing an 'I ♥ Florida' t-shirt. As she stooped to get through the doorway, her spiky pink hair brushed the top of the frame and the Mickey Mouse ears she was wearing got knocked off and caught in a chain that went from a piercing in her cheek to her ear. Parker said, 'Shit, no-one said Big Minnie was due back.'

So that was Big Minnie. She was big. She boomed, 'What did I say to ye? I'm back, I've come back early to look fae the Guitar Man. Where is that big hunk o' love?'

168

Big Minnie looked round the room and saw Rik standing on the stage. She strode over to him saying, 'Ach, who fucken' loves Rik Peabody? You are gorgeous. I want you, lover boy.' She enveloped him in a hug so powerful you could hear his bones crack. When Big Minnie let Rik go, he flopped back into his seat like a broken doll. Big Minnie looked around and said, 'I hope you have all looked after the Guitar Man, there's going to be trouble if you havenae. It's the best thing that's ever happened in this place. I couldnae miss Rik Peabody playing the jukebox in my bar, no way. How's it going, Rik? Did ye find plenty of rockin' sounds to play?'

Rik was rubbing his arm, but he stopped and said, 'I played the MC5, there's not too much else to rock with, as far as I'm concerned.'

Big Minnie said, 'I told Little Min not to let that lazy shite Parker choose what goes on the jukebox. Is he here?'

Parker said, 'Hiya, Big Minnie, it's good to have you back.'

'It's good for me, nae so good for you, Parker Knoll.' She turned to the rest of us, 'That's what I call him, Parker Knoll – he's always around here reclining but he's nae use for anything else. Anyway, that's another story. You get on with your wee competition and I'll just settle mysel' down here, so don't mind me.'

Big Minnie crashed down onto the chair next to Rik and put her massive arm round him. Rik winced, and seemed to be struggling to hold his shoulders up under the weight.

Pony Boy said, 'Right, on with the results then. That was Rik Peabody in sixth place.'

'Not in my book,' Big Minnie said. 'There's only one place Rik Peabody should be and we're going to talk about it soon enough, aren't we, Rik?' Rik looked nervous.

Pony Boy carried on, 'In fifth, Nye Hill. In fourth, Dr Annilese Rococco. On to the top three. In third, Babs Golightly.'

How did she do it? She played happy sounding tracks without having a clue what they were and she still came third. Not that I was complaining – I'd beaten Babs at last, top two guaranteed.

'In second place, 'Sugar' Ray Mitchell.'

That was good. Second was the best I could have hoped for in the circumstances. It was a moral victory.

'And in first place, the local boy made good, it's Parker from Equally Humdrum.'

The audience started to cheer, but Big Minnie reached over and took the microphone off Pony Boy. 'Equally out on his fucken' ear,' she said, 'so you can all pipe down.' She prodded Pony Boy in the chest with a finger the size of a baby's arm and told him, 'Parker isnae allowed to take part in competitions at No More Heroes since that incident during the Christmas Quiz.'

'Parker said, 'But Tegucigalpa is the capital of Honduras…'

'Don't worry about my ass, worry about your own ass, recliner boy. Now scram.' Big Minnie put her hand over the microphone and told Pony Boy, 'He's disqualified – rule of the house.'

Big Minnie gave the microphone back to Pony Boy who announced, 'News has just come in that there is a local ruling that I wasnae – I mean, I was not – aware of, which means that our winner tonight, with his first victory in JookBoxFury, is… 'Sugar' Ray Mitchell!'

Pony Boy handed me the Jook Duke of the Juke trophy, which I received to some low level jeering, but Big Minnie glared at the crowd and it subsided fairly quickly. My first JookBoxFury victory. I should have been elated but the nature of the win left me with a nagging sense of disappointment.

Big Minnie said, 'Someone is going to have to explain to me why Rik Peabody didnae win that, but while you're thinking about it, let's have some dancing music and get this party started. You,' she said to me, 'if you're supposed to be the jukebox champion around here, you'd better chose something for us to dance to.'

I hadn't thought that being a champion would bring so much pressure so soon. You're desperate for the prize – it's what you work for, train for, dream of – but when you get it, you realize that everything's changed and life's never going to be the same again.

I said to Rhia, 'What shall I play? I don't want to get on her wrong side?'

'Don't be such a wimp, just play some good dancing music.'

'Why don't you put something on?' I said.

'I thought you'd never ask.'

Big Minnie said, 'I've waited for years hoping that one day I might get the chance to dance with Rik Peabody. Come on, Guitar Man, our dreams have come true.' She grabbed Rik and started to drag him off the stage.

Rhia turned back from the jukebox and said, 'Oh, I forgot, I need someone else to give out the Jook vouchers for a few minutes.'

Rik was trying to wriggle out of Big Minnie's grip and gasped, 'I can do that, man. Give me the fucking vouchers.'

Rhia said, 'Well, if you're sure. Most people have had them now, but if anyone asks you for a Jook all you do is give them a voucher and stamp their hand. One voucher, one stamp.'

Rik broke away from Big Minnie and grabbed the hand stamp. 'That's sweet, man. A ticket and a stamp, nice one.'

Big Minnie said, 'Aw, Guitar Man, can ye no do that later,' but a couple of girls came to the side of the stage and said, 'The barman told us we could get a free drink voucher here.'

'Too fucking right,' Rik said. 'For one night only, it's Rik 'the Voucher Man' Peabody. Tell your friends. He gave them both a drink voucher and a hand stamp.

By the time Rhia got back from picking some dancing tunes on the jukebox Rik was dealing with a small queue of Jook seekers. A few of the students had started dancing and Rhia said to me, 'Come on then, let's dance.'

I said, 'I only dance to songs I really like. I can't dance to songs I don't like – it's a kind of betrayal of the good songs.'

'Well, do you like this song? Because I think this is a brilliant song to dance to.'

I wasn't sure about it, but sometimes you've got to have a bit of flexibility in your principles. 'OK,' I said, 'I suppose we could dance to celebrate how well the Jook voucher system worked – let's hit the floor.' We danced. Rhia was really into it, she was singing the words and twirling. She was right, it was a brilliant song to dance to, and Rhia was a beautiful dancer. The songs she'd chosen kept getting better, so we danced some more, getting closer, getting in time with one another, getting slower when the track changed, getting closer. I remember every song that we danced to. I had a new top ten, and a brand new number one.

Heartbeat Drumbeat

Which came first – music or dancing? One thing's for sure, dancing without music is rubbish, so when the music in No More Heroes suddenly stopped, we stopped dancing too. I'd have liked to have carried on.

'Thanks,' I said to Rhia.

She touched my cheek with her lips quickly, but before I could work out whether it meant anything she'd walked ahead of me and sat back down at the table. After a couple of seconds, I followed her.

Big Minnie was standing by the jukebox with the plug in her hand. She shouted for Rik, 'Enough of this, what about some live music, Rik?'

Rik was in the middle of a crowd. He made himself enough space to turn round and said, 'Not now, these drink vouchers are going like fucking wildfire. I'm struggling to keep on top – and it's not often you'll hear the Guitar Man say that.'

Parker's mate eased his way out of the crowd around Rik and towards the bar. He held a wad of vouchers above his head. The back of his hand and his wrist were covered in stamp marks.

I pushed my way into the crowd. 'Rik, it was just one voucher per person. What are you doing?'

'That's not what they told me, man. That was not the instruction I received. "One voucher, one stamp," she said, and that's what I've fucking done. The Guitar Man always keeps his word, there's no-one here with more vouchers than they've got stamps, trust me.'

'You need to stop now,' I told him. 'Hopefully it's not too late.' I took the stamp and the vouchers off Rik. 'Sorry, everyone,' I said, 'the Jook's finished. No more, sorry.'

The crowd around started booing me. It was even worse than in the Queen Victoria. Gradually everyone started bouncing, like the front rows at a gig, and the booing was punctuated with shouts for Jook, which turned into a chant: 'Jook, Jook, JOOK, JOOK, JOOK. Jook, Jook, JOOK, JOOK, JOOK.'

Rik and I were stuck in the middle of the crowd and had no choice but to bounce with them. We couldn't fight the will of the people. Bottles of Jook and vouchers were held aloft all around us. The bouncing got higher and the chanting got louder, 'Jook, Jook, JOOK! JOOK! JOOK! Jook, Jook, JOOK! JOOK! JOOK!'

I looked at Rik and he was laughing and chanting too. I threw my head back and shouted, 'Jooooooooooooooooooooooookkkkkkkkk. Jook, Jook, JOOK! JOOK! JOOK! Jook, Jook, JOOK! JOOK! JOOK!'

That probably wasn't the best moment for Fran to walk into No More Heroes followed by Mike Statham, holding his reporter's notebook, and a photographer. The photographer didn't waste any time. He pulled himself up onto the side of the stage and his flash went off like a strobe, freezing moments of the Jook salutation below him. He adjusted the focus towards two girls facing him, eyes shut and mouths open as they shouted, bottles of Jook held high. Then he got one of Rik laughing insanely. The photographer turned to Fran, focused, and got a good one of her look of absolute horror. He got another as she shielded her face with her hand and turned to leave No More Heroes.

The photographer kept snapping as Rik dropped to his knees and leaned back so his shoulders almost touched the ground. He said to the girl next to him, 'Jook me, baby.' The girl straddled Rik, thrusting to the rhythm of the chant, and then held her Jook as high as she could and tipped. The green liquid sparkled as the camera flashed, and splashed onto Rik's face. He leaned back even further to catch the stream of Jook in his mouth and gulp it down. He put his index finger in his mouth and sucked. As he slowly pulled the wet finger out it glowed green. Rik reached up to the girl and touched her forehead with the finger, he drew a line and then flicked his finger round. The girl's forehead shone with a green 'J'.

The crowd were chanting louder and faster, barely even a word any more, but a primal growl, 'Ook, Ook, OOK! OOK! OOK! Ook, Ook, OOK! OOK! OOK!' I was bouncing and chanting too. I couldn't stop. I was in the tribe, I was one of the Jook people. No-one could stop. Rik was anointing everyone around him, nothing could stop the Jook, it was a primal force that couldn't be controlled…

Big Minnie roared, 'Stoppppp!' like a plane taking off. Immediately the room fell silent. The girl climbed off Rik uncertainly. I didn't know whether I really had been part of the frenzied chant.

Big Minnie shouted, 'There will be no more of this Jook nonsense in No More Heroes.'

Someone from the back of the crowd shouted, 'But what about these free drink vouchers?'

Big Minnie glared, but the voice carried on, 'The hippy said we could get as many free drinks as we wanted with these.'

Big Minnie roared again, 'I will not…' She thought for a moment. 'I will not welsh on any offer made by the greatest rocker left standing… hippy indeed.'

Rik grabbed hold of my belt and dragged himself to his feet.

Big Minnie said, 'As a tribute to the Guitar Man, you can redeem your drink vouchers for the No More Heroes speciality, the highland version of the tequila slammer, the Tartan Hammer.'

A few voices in the crowd started to chant, 'Ham-ah, Ham-ah,' but it didn't take. They stopped when Big Minnie shouted, 'Minnie!' It was like Fred Flintstone calling Wilma. 'Tartan Hammers all round, and we'll start over here with Rik and his friends.'

A few minutes later Little Minnie brought a tray of shot glasses for everyone, along with a bottle of Famous Grouse and a bright orange bottle of Irn Bru.

'There ye go,' Big Minnie said, 'the taste of Scotland. Here's highland games for ye.'

Little Minnie poured a measure of the whisky into a glass and then filled it to the brim with Irn Bru. She handed the glass to Big Minnie who put a beer mat over the top, then put her hand on that and, without any warning, slammed the whole thing down onto the table as if she was trying to break through to the other side. The glasses and bottles on the table jumped. Everyone round the table jumped. The drink fizzed furiously. Big Minnie took the beer mat off the top and handed the glass to Rik saying, 'The Tartan Hammer, down your hatch.'

It was possible that Rik didn't even remember the previous night's fizzing drink experience because, without a second thought, he threw the Tartan Hammer down. He shook his head and said, 'Phwhooo, nice one, darlin'. You don't do one with ice cream in it do you?'

Little Minnie poured, and Big Minnie slammed a drink for everyone. The Tartan Hammer hit you like a caber thrown by a big hairy man in a kilt, probably after a day up a stepladder stacking biscuits.

Everyone in the JookBoxFury team had a Tartan Hammer – everyone apart from Pony Boy, who didn't knock his back quickly enough and it fizzed out over his trousers. Big Minnie said, 'We need more music. It would be a dream come true if Rik Peabody would play a wee song for me. I hope you don't mind me asking, Rik, but it would be a girl's dream come true. Will you? Will you play *Violence is Golden*? I'd love to hear you sing. Will you play it? We all want to hear Rik play don't we?'

I wanted to hear him play. Everyone seemed fairly enthusiastic apart from Dr Roc who said, 'I suppose *Violence is Golden* is a little better than *Jook, Baby, Jook*.'

Rik wasn't enthusiastic, 'I'd like to oblige, darlin', but I'm not at my rocking best at the moment. I haven't got the guitar with me anyway, and you know the Guitar Man can't rock without his axe.'

Parker said, 'That's no problem, pal, we've got our gear down in the basement. We can set you up, no problem.'

Rik said, 'The Guitar Man has got to be in the mood, you know,' but Parker and his mate were already setting off to get their gear.

Babs encouraged him, 'Come on, Rik, don't be a spoilsport. You weren't shy about singing *Jook, Baby, Jook* this morning.'

'Well, I could give the new track a try, see if it's got the balls to work with a live audience.'

'Why not save it for another time?' Dr Roc suggested.

That was the final push Rik needed because he said, 'Where's the lad with the guitar? It's time to rock.'

Parker and his mate came back with a couple of guitar cases. Parker asked Rik, 'Acoustic or electric?'

'I'll take the acoustic for this one, man. I promise I won't smash it… not unless I have to. You can give it a bit of backing on the old Stratocaster if you fancy.'

Big Minnie said, 'I don't think that's a good idea, Rik. Parker cannae really rock if you know what I mean.'

Rik slipped the strap of the acoustic guitar over his shoulder and immediately took on a new confidence. He was like a knight taking hold of Excalibur. He said, 'He can rock if he's a sideman to the Guitar Man. This one's in G, Parkie, play it like you're jookin' with your baby. A-one, uh-two, a-you-know-what-to-do.'

Rik strummed it up, gave a Buddy Holly hiccup, and all the *Jook, Baby, Jook* that we'd heard at breakfast made sense – the line about standing by the record machine was really good. Parker started by watching Rik's fingers and stroking a few chords, but by the end of the first chorus he'd got the feel for it and was bending the chords with his tremolo arm, and the song sounded like it was one of the first rock 'n' roll records. Rik was giving it his all about his Jook obsession and cried, 'Awwww, Jook! Show me some of your good Jookin', Parkie. Take it, take it away, take it home, get a take a away, open a six pack, let's go guitar Jookin'…'

Parker took it away with a stripped down solo like lightning striking the tin roof of a Memphis juke joint. He was surprisingly good… he was good. The song finished with Rik taking it down and moaning the, '*Jook-ah, Jook-ah… Jook, Jook Jook Jook.*' It was a shame the waitress from breakfast wasn't there because she'd have seen things in a different light. Rik played a blues sequence:

A-dunga

     Dunga

          Dunga   Der

                Dunga   Duh

                   Dunga

Parker put in a few more wild notes, they looked at each other, and both leapt into the air like Pete Townshend playing with one of McFly. They windmilled a final chord and stopped it dead as they landed. It was brilliant. No More Heroes shook with applause and shouts of 'More!'

Parker said to Rik, 'Nice one, pal, what band did you say you were in?'

'The Peabodies, man.'

'Don't you know anything, Parker?' Big Minnie said. 'How can you call yoursel' a musician if you don't know about The Peabodies? You were actually quite good there, though, better than your own wishy washy noodling.'

'Do you want to do another?' Parker asked Rik.

Big Minnie said, 'You're finally starting to talk some sense, Parker. You might not be as much of a waste of space as I thought you were. Rik, please can we hear *Violence is Golden?*'

Rik started to play and Parker joined him again. A wave of joy hit me. I was with Rik Peabody, witnessing a one-off performance of *Violence is Golden.* Who knew, in years to come I might be telling my grandchildren I was in the audience when Rik Peabody from The Peabodies jammed with Parker from Equally Humdrum. I looked to my side and Rhia was loving it, too. She was captivated watching them play, but she must have realized I was looking at her because she turned to me and smiled. I blinked. I couldn't say anything. JookBoxFury was the best thing that had ever happened to me, and that included doing the Three Peaks walk with my Bam Caruso collection.

When *Violence is Golden* finished, Big Minnie jumped up and went to hug Rik. He managed to swing the guitar round his back before she got to him and turned it into firewood. When he'd broken out of Big Minnie's grasp, Rik said, 'Do you want to do one of yours, Parkie?'

Parker nodded. 'We can do *Heartbeat Drumbeat*, it's the one I put on the jukebox before. I need to get the rhythm of a heartbeat to start it off.' He leaned down to Babs and took her hand. 'Will you help me? I need your heartbeat.'

Babs put her hands to her chest like a bashful Southern belle and said, 'Oh, my, I shouldn't… but I will.' She stood up and Parker said, 'May I feel your heart?' He put his hand on her chest. His fingers were gently touching the top of her breast to one side of her cleavage, and his palm was pressed against her heaving bosom. It was an audacious move.

Babs looked about to say something, but Parker put his finger over her lips and said, 'Bom bom, bom bom, bom bom.' He looked into Babs' eyes and whispered, 'That's your heartbeat.' Then to Rik, 'Can you pick this up? Bom bom, bom bom, bom bom.' Rik started gently tapping along on the body of the guitar. Parker was still holding Babs' gaze. He lifted his hand from her chest and said, 'Thank you. Heartbeat Drumbeat.' He started to weave notes around Rik's heartbeat rhythm to create a spiralling melody, then he sang, turning the electrical version of the track we'd heard on the jukebox into a nuclear-age folk song. As the song came to an end, he put his hand back on Babs' chest, looked into her eyes, and picked up the heartbeat again. He signalled to Rik to stop, and then gradually faded his own, 'Bom bom, bom bom, bom bom,' to a whisper, and then to nothing…

No one moved.

There was no sound apart from Babs' breathing.

Nye broke the spell. 'That was fucking out – of – this – world.'

The crowd murmured and then went wild. Nye shouted to Parker over the noise, 'I've got to hear you guys play – tomorrow night, you say? Rhia, everybody, I don't want to let you down, but I think Equally Humdrum really are exactly what I've been looking for. I'm going to have to stay here tomorrow and see them. I don't want to hear about another new scene or the next big thing because I've heard it all before, but this is different, this is special. I've got to stick around and hear more of this.'

Babs was still standing next to Parker. She was almost in a trance. She gave a small sigh, 'I might stay as well.'

We stopped in No More Heroes for a few more hours, although it only felt like a few minutes. Nye was very excited about Equally Humdrum, asking Parker about their influences and whether there were any other local bands doing the same kind of thing. Parker started naming bands and styles of music that they'd taken something from. It included pretty well everyone and everything.

Nye said, 'What do you call it, though? I don't want to label what you've got because it's…' – he held his thumb and forefinger in the air and rubbed them together – '… it's indefinable, you know. It's special. But what do you call it? You've got soul, you've got the electronic heartbeat minimalism, lo-fi, hi-fi, funk, punk, folk, new wave, no wave, post-rock with a rock 'n' roll sensibility – it's everything there's ever been and it's nothing there's ever been before. Of course! It's bricolage, but it's new, like "the new bricolage".'

Parker looked bemused.

Nye said, 'I've got it, The Nouvelle Bricolage, no – the nouvelle bricolage.'

It sounded pretty much the same. Nye said, 'You're not with me yet, are you? Let me write it down.' He took out his notebook and wrote, 'nouvelle bric(01)age'. He said, 'You see, you've got the collection of everything, but there's a *je ne sais quoi* about it, and the "01", it's a new start, a new age, but it's binary – the 01 is a futuristic communication. It's a genre from the future. That's it: Equally Humdrum spearheading the nouvelle bric(01)age. I can't wait to hear you and some of the other bands in the new movement. Do you call them bands, or is it more a collective for anarchistic musical jackdaws on a journey through time? Oh, the thrill is back. Thank you the nouvelle bric(01)age.'

Nye started to make some notes. Babs, who was still hazy, asked Parker if Equally Humdrum had a video. When he told her they didn't, she said, 'I wonder if I could help you out? Maybe we could film a special performance for *Video Hits*? I could be in it if you want – I was planning to hang out around here for a few more days anyway, so we could try and sort something out, if you want to.'

Nye looked up from his notes, 'It's a new rock and pop myth. Maybe the first post-rock myth: "No More Heroes and the nouvelle bric(01)age".' He started scribbling again.

I'd been present as the first post-rock myth had happened. It was a shame no-one had been dressed as a pea, but you can't have it all. I'd won the JookBoxFury trophy, too. I picked it up off the table and tapped Parker on the shoulder. 'You should have this,' I said. 'It doesn't seem right me winning JookBoxFury because of a dispute over the capital of Honduras.'

It wasn't the kind of day when you felt like you needed a trophy.

Silver Machine

We rolled back to the hotel in the early hours, high on the best night of the JookBoxFury tour plus a carefully controlled intake of Jook and Tartan Hammers. As the night porter let us in, Rik was singing, 'Jook, Baby, Jook.' We were all singing, 'Jook, Baby, Jook.' Dr Roc even went solo on one of the verses.

Rhia tried to shush us as we tumbled into the hotel foyer. Everyone apart from Rik stopped singing when we saw Fran and Laurence in the lounge. Fran was in front of a laptop with her head in her hands. Laurence screwed up a sheet of paper and threw it onto a pile on the floor.

Pony Boy said, 'How goes it, amigos? I thought that was a rather encouraging response to the Jook back there in the Heroes bar. You must be thrilled. Just refining things for the final are we? Super duper.'

Fran coiled, prepared to strike at Pony Boy. She hissed at Rik and he stopped singing. We waited for Fran's diatribe, but she deflated. 'You must be blind,' she said, defeated. 'While I'm fighting tooth and nail to keep Jook alive, you're all treating this as a jolly. I get the impression that you aren't even on my side. I took Mike Statham back to that bar to give him another chance to report the real Jook story – people having fun sharing a Jook together. And what did he see? The place in uproar. It was awful, truly awful. I entrusted the Jook brand to each and every one of you when I made you a part of this campaign, but have you promoted Jook? No. You've done exactly the opposite, you've given that Statham man precisely the story he was looking for.

181

'James Hylton-James is taking personal control of events from here on in. Can you imagine how that feels? He's taken my campaign off me. How the mighty are fallen. After he's briefed me tomorrow I'm going to make a press announcement confirming the future of Jook – which does not look promising in the circumstances. Not that any of you seem to care enough to let that fact interrupt your enjoyment.'

I cared. 'What about JookBoxFury?' I asked her.

'What about it? If we take Jook off the market we're hardly likely to run with a promotion. The one good thing to come out of all this is that I won't have to listen to any more horrible pop songs. If we've seen the last of JookBoxFury it won't be a minute too soon. Laurence has just told me that the ridiculous jukebox game was actually your idea, Rhiannon. Now why doesn't that surprise me?'

Fran flashed Laurence a look, picked up her laptop, and walked out.

'What was all that about?' Rik said. 'I don't fucking believe it. No more Jook? That's way out of order, man. They can't put the piss out there and you get a taste for it and they just fucking take it away. That's not right, man. If anyone's been committed to Jook, it's me. What's she talking about? They're not taking my Jook away, man, no way. I'm going back to see if Big Minnie's got any left.' He lurched out into the night.

Rhia left to go to her room. I went with her to the lift.

I hadn't worked out whether the peck on the cheek Rhia had given me meant anything. As we got out of the lift to go to our rooms, she said, 'Well, I'll see you in a couple of hours.'

I said, 'Yeah, see you in a couple of hours then.' Rhia went towards her room, but I wanted to say something else. I called, 'Rhia,' and she turned round. I wasn't sure what to tell her so I said, 'You're a great dancer.' She gave a little shimmy, blew me a kiss, and went into her room.

I stood in the hall for a while, maybe five or ten minutes. I never knew what to make of those signals. I never even knew whether they were signals. Was blowing a kiss a come on, or simply a funny friendly gesture that could easily be misinterpreted and lead to an embarrassing mix-up and ultimately rejection?

The lift doors opened and a waiter stepped out with a tray of room service breakfast. When he saw me he said, 'May I be of any assistance, sir?'

He looked quite worldly, but I wasn't sure whether his remit extended to the interpretation of potentially romantic signals. I told him it was OK, and went to bed.

I couldn't sleep and then a few minutes later I couldn't wake up. I was thinking about Rhia's signals when I went to sleep, and I was thinking about Rhia dancing when I woke up.

I dragged myself down to the breakfast room to hear Nye telling Fran that, as Jook was obviously dead and buried, there was no point him travelling to London. Not when he was already at the very epicentre of the nouvelle bric(01)age.

Fran said, 'Two points for you to bear in mind, Mr Hill. One, the campaign is experiencing a serious setback, that much is true, but I will be the one who decides when Jook is dead and buried thank you very much. And two, until that point, may I remind you that you are obliged to support the Jook campaign in publicity and media relations events as per your contract.'

'Have you got a contract that I can symbolically tear up?' Nye said. 'My only obligation is a moral one. I'm morally obliged to pursue the nouvelle bric(01)age. I've got to take the new sounds to the kids, that's why I'm here.'

'Pathetic,' Fran said. 'Come on, Laurence, we need to make that flight.' She growled at Nye, 'Thanks for all your help. As for the rest of you, I'll see you all in London for the press conference and I expect your full support. As long as there is blood in my body this campaign is not over, remember, this girl is not a quitter. Pathetic,' she spat again as she dragged her suitcase into the foyer and bounced it down the steps towards a taxi.

As Fran and Laurence left, Babs, who had appeared at the breakfast room doorway, had to jump out of their way. She watched them go, then edged unsteadily into the room, wearing a hotel bathrobe and a pair of sparkly red high heels. She had her hair tied up in a scarf and could have been a weary sister of Marilyn Monroe after a couple of Tartan Hammers too many. She made her way to sit down next to Nye and said, 'Oh – my – God.' She looked at Nye's cup of coffee and croaked, 'Is that yours, can I have some?' Nye nodded and Babs took a sip of coffee, took another sip, then drained the cup.

'This might not be right,' Babs said, 'but I thought Parker was two hundred per cent pure amazing, and I'm going to stick around here for a while. I want to give him a few tips to help his career take off and maybe give him a foot up by being in his video. I know you probably think that I'm a really bad person for not coming to London with you but, you know, I always try to support new talent on *Video Hits*, and the other thing is, it's a bloody long way to London on a coach when you're feeling a bit under the weather, and if I'm honest with you, I think the whole thing's finished. Anyway, so I just… you know… ten hours on a coach… you could fly to LA in that time. I always like to help out new talent and all that, so… you don't think I'm a bad person do you? Sorry and everything but it's been good fun and, uh… I'm going back to bed.' Babs gave everyone a hug and a kiss and promised to keep in touch. She stopped in front of me as if she was going to tell me something, but then she moved on. She flicked her fingers against her palms in a little two-handed wave from the doorway, and she was gone.

Babs Golightly – I went out with her when she was Sandra Daft.

We were ready to set off for London but we couldn't find Rik. Rhia suggested that we might have to leave him behind or we'd never make it to the final, when he suddenly appeared out of nowhere, struggling to hold two packs of Jook under each arm. He said, 'I got it, but it was at a price. That was one hell of a pummelling, man.' He crawled onto the coach and crashed out, curled around his Jook.

We said, 'Bye,' to Nye. I wished him all the best with the *Nyethologies* and the nouvelle bric(01)age and told him to keep backing up his work. I got onto the coach with Rhia, Pony Boy, Dr Roc and Rik for the last leg of the journey. I'd become part of the tour, no-one even questioned me being there. Although it looked like being a futile trip, I had to see it through. I'd been with JookBoxFury from the start and there was no way I wasn't going to make it to the end – it's better to have fought and lost than not have fought at all. Even so, I was kicking myself for giving the No More Heroes trophy to Parker.

In the afternoon we stopped at a service station where the café was in a big bridge built over the motorway. We ambled up there to get some lunch. Pony Boy went to make a business call and the rest of us sat at a table overlooking the road.

'I like watching the big trucks,' Rik said.

We watched the big trucks for a while.

'Look at that one.' Rik pointed out a particularly big truck with a load of girders as it went below the café. 'A load of girders – heavy metal – now that's a fucking truck.'

A long petrol container went by. 'Hazardous fucking chemicals,' Rik said. 'Treat with caution.'

Maybe it was just that everyone was wiped out, but it wasn't the same without Babs and Nye. They'd have got into some discussion with Rik about the trucks, so I tried to compensate. 'What's your favourite truck?' I asked Rik.

'I like them all,' he said. 'It's the power, fucking driving power. They're the transportation equivalent of rock – they're silver machines, man. I don't have a favourite truck, but this is my favourite service station because you can have a nice cup of tea and watch the big trucks.'

Dr Roc had had enough. 'Oh please, trucks, service stations? Is this what we've come to?'

'Well, it is where we've come to, isn't it, darlin'?' Rik said. 'We wouldn't be here if we hadn't fucking come here, would we?'

'Oh, really,' Dr Roc said. 'I'm going to go and get the newspaper.'

After she'd gone, Rik said, 'I was only saying it was my favourite service station because of the trucks.'

Rhia said, 'My favourite service station is that one between London and Bristol. We stopped there on the way to Glastonbury once and the car park was full of people going to the festival. Instead of families going on holiday and business people and all the usual service station crowd, it had gone all alternative and was full of old VW camper vans and people in festival gear having picnics in the car park. It was really nice. In the shop everyone was buying up Rizla papers and the old lady who was serving said, "I don't understand it, we don't normally sell so many of these in a year." It was really upbeat because everyone was excited about going to Glastonbury. We stopped there again on the way back home and it had gone all quiet and miserable. Everyone was down because the festival was over and they were going back to normality. We were all covered in mud too, I still had carrier bags wrapped round my feet and sticking out of the top of my boots. Service stations are better when you're going than when you're coming back.'

Dr Roc rushed up to us with an open newspaper flapping in front of her. She said, 'Look at this, we're in the paper. She spread it out on the table and pointed to an item at the top of page three: 'Health fears over alcopop induced frenzy, by Mike Statham, Media Correspondent.' The picture beneath the headline was of Rik in No More Heroes, back on his haunches, the girl astride of him and Jook splashing into Rik's mouth. Rik was leering at the girl with a gleam in his eyes, halfway between evil and lasciviousness. The caption said, 'Rocker Peabody "Jookin' with his baby".'

Rik leered at his own picture and gave a satisfied nod. 'Fuckin' nice one. Now that is what I'm talking about. That is Jookin', man. Yeah… when did all this happen? Who's that babe? Has anyone got her number?'

'Is there anything in the tabloids?' Rhia asked Dr Roc.

'I'm afraid I only ever take the Grauniad,' Dr Roc said.

Rik said, 'Yeah, tabloids, good thinkin', man. They might have her details.'

Rhia went to buy the other papers and the rest of us crowded round Dr Roc to read the article:

Health fears over alcopop induced frenzy

By Mike Statham
Media Correspondent

Brewery chiefs are today considering the withdrawal of their new alcopop, Jook, following frenzied scenes during the drink's controversial promotional launch.

Jook is made from absinthe, greengage and a secret blend of tropical herbs and juices. The drink has a bitter, almost repulsive, taste which drinkers claim has the strange effect of making them come back from more. The aspect of Jook which has provoked the interest of the Food Standards Agency is the accusation that it can cause mild hallucination and frenzy amongst drinkers.

A spokeswoman for LNE Breweries, Fran Watson, dismissed the claims as, 'Mischief making by our competitors.' However, a clue to the real nature of the drink might be found in the name of the alcopop's launch event – JookBoxFury. While songs have been played on jukeboxes around the country in a *Juke Box Jury* style game show, fury has dogged the launch throughout its chaotic tour.

According to attendees at the JookBoxFury events, the alcopop exerts a strange power over the drinker. William Bagshaw, a morris dancer who attended the first competition said, 'They told me it was made by monks down on the south coast. Some monks. After a couple of bottles everything started to turn green. After a couple more, I found myself chanting, "Green grow the Jooksie-oh," for no reason at all. We were all chanting it.'

Mr Bagshaw says he became so worried about the drink's properties that he raised his concerns with the manufacturers the following day. 'I wasn't the only one it affected, and I wasn't the only one who rang them to complain. I told the brewery that Jook was an absolute disgrace, and they ought to send me a couple of crates as compensation. I even offered to go and pick them up myself.'

LNE Breweries say they have complied with all food standards regulations, but they refuse to supply details of tests or the full list of ingredients. Marketed as the drink 'to share together,' Jook has been at the centre of other bizarre scenes during the past week and controversial rocker Rik Peabody has never been far away. Mr Peabody, author of the Sixties classic *Violence is Golden*, is no stranger to rock's excess, but even he was seen to pass out immediately after downing a potent Jook cocktail.

Other members of the Jook launch party include pin-up girl Babs Golightly and former Radio Wonderful DJ, Simon 'Pony Boy' Rogers, along with rock obsessive (he once hauled a massive collection of obscure vinyl across the Three Peaks Walk), Raymond Mitchell. All were present in Glasgow's No More Heroes bar last night as Peabody led the audience in an almost ritualistic celebration of Jook. He then went on to sing his own paean to the drink, *Jook, Baby, Jook*, which included the words, "It's the secret of eternal youth." It seems that where the Incas used the coca leaf to attain a higher consciousness, the youth of Britain today has it's own psychedelic stimulant in the form of Jook.

Lorna Douglas, pictured with Peabody, said, 'I went along to No More Heroes with some friends who are in a band. I'd only had about three bottles of Jook when I found myself chanting along with everyone else. The next thing I knew, I had an urge to pour Jook on that hippy.'

Trading Standards officers comment, 'We are monitoring the situation closely and will make a decision within very short timescales. Anyone with particular concerns or health problems is advised to avoid this drink until we are able to give the all clear.'

James Hylton-James, Chief Executive of LNE Breweries has promised a thorough review of the Jook development and production process with the outcome to be announced later today. However, like Coca Cola's bottled tap water, tainted Perrier, and wine laced with anti-freeze, there seems to be only one possible outcome. Less than a week after its introduction, don't expect to find Jook in your local pub or club this weekend.

Rhia returned with a bundle of newspapers and asked, 'How does it look?'

'It's not good,' Dr Roc said.

'It's not so fuckin' bad,' Rik told her, 'at least I know the babe's name.'

'She's young enough to be your daughter,' Dr Roc said. 'In fact, she's probably young enough to be your granddaughter.'

'I don't measure age in years, man.'

'I'm not going to ask how you do measure it.'

'No need, darlin' – it's the heat of the meat times the angle of the dangle.'

'I might have guessed,' Dr Roc said, 'not that it has any relevance to anything. Unfortunately it seems that we have reached the end of the road for JookBoxFury. I don't foresee your employers being able to keep selling a drink that's getting this kind of publicity, Rhia.'

I said, 'Babs has gone. Nye's gone. Jook is on its way. It looks like No More Heroes was the last JookBoxFury.'

'Whoah, steady on a moment there, one and all,' Pony Boy said. 'I've never missed a show, never. Not even that time in Hunstanton when the roadshow mobile was turned over by a freak wave. We had to broadcast from the Gents by the putting green. Very difficult circumstances. My notes got washed away and I was so desperate for material that I read out a couple of nonsense limericks that were written on the wall… I ended up being taken off the air for a month.'

'What were the verses about?' Rik asked.

Pony Boy blushed slightly and said, 'I don't rightly remember.'

'Was it the usual?' Rik said. 'Shy boy with a thick nine-incher? Animals? Not that one about the mother and the son? Bloody hell. Public service broadcasting. Did you give out the phone numbers?'

Pony Boy said, 'The point I was trying to make, before I was so rudely interrupted, is that I've never missed a show. One thing's for sure, I'll be on air tonight. If I have anything to do with it we'll all be on air with the JookBoxFury final. I'll give the producer a call.'

Rik said, 'If you have anything to do with it we'll be broadcasting from a fucking toilet cubicle.'

DISC FOUR, TRACK TWO

Jump Right out of This Jukebox

Back on the bus, Dr Rococco said, 'Ray, I've got that paper I mentioned, 'mp3 and the death of pop.' I told her I'd be interested to read it, so she pulled a manuscript out of her bag and handed it to me. 'That should help pass the time, let me know what you think.'

One day Nye Hill, the next Dr Annilese Rococco – I was becoming an adviser to a different popular music commentator every day. I didn't want to risk getting into the kind of situation I'd had with Nye so I said, 'Fantastic, thanks... you have got a copy of this, haven't you?'

'I have got it backed up if that's what you mean,' she said. 'The funny thing is you'll see that I refer to Walter Benjamin's essay, *The Work of Art in the Age of Mechanical Reproduction*. Well, Benjamin wrote a letter to a colleague of his, Theodor Adorno, telling him about the essay but saying that he couldn't send it to him because he only had one copy. There's an amusing irony in that. Benjamin was writing a profoundly visionary essay on the impact of mechanical reproduction in making a multiplicity of copies, yet he only had a single copy of the essay himself. You can't imagine that happening now. As soon as you create a piece of work you can back it up, print it, photocopy it, fax it, e-mail it, you could even put it on the web and in an instant it would exist simultaneously as an infinite number of copies. But Walter Benjamin only had the one copy of *The Work of Art in the Age of Mechanical Reproduction*. Imagine if he had lost that.'

It was an irony that Nye might have appreciated. Safe in the knowledge that Dr Roc had kept a copy, even if Walter Benjamin hadn't, I settled back to read.

The Modem is the Message: mp3 and the death of pop

Dr Annilese Rococco, PhD, Professor of Popular Music Studies, The Robin Hood University of Nottinghamshire

I have recently had cause to rediscover the pleasure of playing records on a jukebox and was reminded of some words from an old Sun label recording by Onie Wheeler:

> *'Suppose that I should come to life when they play this song,*
> *I could be in a lot of places at once and see what's going on.*
> *If you believe it strong enough you'll find it will come true,*
> *And I'll jump right out of this jukebox and get a heart full*
> *of you.'*
>
> *Jump Right Out of This Jukebox*, Onie Wheeler
> Available on *The Legendary Sun Records Story*

For me, those words, in their innocence, capture the changing aura of the musical experience that resulted from the fact that popular music could, by its very nature, be in many places at the same time. From its beginning to its end, popular music – this most insidious and yet sublime, cultural form ('the soundtrack to our lives') – has been shaped by the technology that made the mass production and distribution of music possible. However, we are now in a position to say that 'popular' music, in that sense of a mass produced and commonly experienced commodity, has been replaced by something more homologous to the postmodern condition and as a result, in the parlance of the critics, pop is dead. This short paper works through an evolving formulation of this discourse.

Back to the aura. It was, of course, Walter Benjamin who considered the impact of technology on the aura possessed by a work of art. His famous essay *The Work of Art in the Age of Mechanical Reproduction* was written at a time when the media of electric communication were in the early stages of becoming mass phenomena. With the invention of Edison's phonograph, Berliner's gramophone, and the subsequent launch of the Victor Talking Machine company in 1901, the essential technology which was to shape popular music throughout the twentieth century was in place.

The act of recording and distributing music to the masses marked a fundamental shift in what it meant to experience music and it is difficult now, in the hum of the global village, to fully appreciate the implications of the change. BG (Before Gramophone – or radio), to experience music meant to be in the company of musicians and to participate directly in the musical experience; whether that was singing at a gospel meeting, playing the fiddle, hand clapping, foot stomping and dancing at the village fair, playing the harpsichord in a drawing room or listening to an orchestra in a grand theatre. Whatever the nature of the music itself, you had, as they say, to be there.

AG (After Gramophone), the presence of those making the music became unimportant; the dislocated sound and voice of the musician could be heard anywhere. For Benjamin, the consequence of this possibility was the decay of the aura, that which is the singularity, the special nature which is associated with the moment of the musical performance. Once captured on record and mass-produced, the musical performance loses its uniqueness as part of a moment. As it becomes possible to possess the object, the magical aura is no more. Ultimately, mechanical reproduction gives control of the work of art to the user, the listener, and through this liberation reactivates the work; it is the dawning of a new aura.

Now we find ourselves awakening to another new dawn as we experience a postmodern fragmentation and reassembly of styles where anything is possible. Perhaps we might witness a performance by a group of morris dancers, not on the village green on a May day morn, but in a contemporary public house, performing with reference to rock recordings for the entertainment of a hen party. Within such a context, where does the aura lie, and where is the meaning being created?

As the significance of those making the music became less a part of the musical experience, then the void was filled by those who were making the meaning. When we consider what music means, the approach of the fan community, assisted by the music press, is to determine that meaning by reference to the voice of the auteur, the romantic artist. However, the real meaning is to be found in the way listeners experience the music. The pervasiveness of popular music ensures that examples can be found in a diversity of situations: from a young woman feeling that her own chemically enhanced mood at a pop festival is reflected in the music she hears; a former radio disc jockey's reminiscences about involving the crowd at a seaside show in a 'musical performance'; or a parent experiencing a vivid memory from their past when their child sings a snatch of a popular hit.

It has become something of a cliché to say that popular music is the soundtrack to our lives, but the fact remains that for much of the twentieth century the mass of the population have lived and loved to a shared musical experience to an extent that was not possible before, and is no longer the case now. It is a trap to judge the experiences of the young through our own more world-weary eyes, just as our own parents and grandparents tutted at our youthful behaviour. So I attempt to identify difference, rather than judge the quality of experience, when I point out that the child who falls asleep to a late night episode of Hollyoaks, or events in the Big Brother house, or downloads an mp3 track for free, clearly has a different relationship to music than the teenager of the past who saved their pocket money to buy a treasured single, or fell asleep listening to songs through the static on Radio Luxembourg. We respond to the nature of the world we inhabit, but the experience is different: if it is true that popular music *was* the soundtrack to our lives, this is no longer the case today.

Music in the digital era is a simulacrum, a representation of the sound as binary code. The gramophone record's map of sound waves, made physical in the disc's grooves, has been replaced by a series of 0s and 1s in a computer file. In place of the smooth flow of the analogue record, we have an approximation of the sound as bits and bytes of data. This distance from the reality of the sound is reflected in the songs themselves, with every recording ever made providing the palette for contemporary creation: the blues singer sampled for an automobile advertisement, James Brown's *Funky Drummer* rhythm as hip hop's classic beat, the piano introduction to *Imagine* (used by Noel Gallagher in creating *Don't Look Back in Anger*), and so on and so on. Songs become less about belief and experience; they are about… other songs.

Music in the Rock era was characterized by a shared experience; listening to the radio in the car or on the beach, or even under the bedclothes, was to be part of a broader listening community. Listening to a personal selection on a Walkman or i-Pod, sheltered from the world by headphones, means quite the opposite – a retreat from the community into one's own musical solitude. Mass consumption has been replaced by micro-consumption: the smash hit replaced by the mp3 download shared by a collection of fans; the world tour replaced by the streamed basement performance on MySpace; the carnivalesque festival gathering replaced by the internet chatroom. Clearly, mass popularity can still be achieved but it is no longer the predominant feature of the current moment, which is characterized instead by fragmentation and diversity.

The 'modem is the message' is clearly a take on Marshall McLuhan's 'the medium is the message.' Through his notion of 'extensions of man', McLuhan represents all media as 'extensions of some human faculty – psychic or physical,' and it is in this sense that the medium is the message. In the global village, with i-Tunes as the jukebox in the corner, the modem, our link via the internet to every recording ever made, has introduced a greater level of accessibility to music than ever before, but at the same time we are retreating even further from the meaning and community that the music offers. Is a number one record still 'popular' if its sales figures are so low that it wouldn't even have registered in the lower reaches of the music charts in the hey day of the Radio Wonderful DJs and their hugely influential singles of the week? Is the music really 'popular' if it is experienced alone or even as part of a loose grouping of chat room participants who may never meet? What is the nature of that popularity and what kind of aura does it bestow on the experience?

We are, in McLuhan's phrase, 'moving forward through the rear view mirror', at once excited by the future and yearning for the past; like travellers in time, resting in a 1950s themed café to escape from the unpleasantness of contemporary reality into our vision of a more perfect past/future.

Whatever factors we may use to explain the development of technology, it seems that as we look back over our own lives, and into history, the changes we identify are technological. If we look at the great religions, literature or lives from the past, we see that basic human motivations remain constant, but the differences between our children's lives and our lives, and our lives and our parents' lives, are measurable by technological change. Fans and journalists have been saying that pop is long dead for as long as they have been growing up and settling down. Depending on age and inclination, they may define the time of pop's death as the year Elvis went into the army, or perhaps the date of the Rolling Stones' concert at Altamont speedway, or of course 1976 when the Sex Pistols called a temporary halt to rock's excess. Some may say the post-mortem was scheduled when Simon Cowell created his first Pop Idol as, with perfect postmodern irony, he himself became the greatest 'Pop Idol' of all.

In reality, pop didn't end with Elvis going into the army, or any other idol-led events, any more than it started with Elvis deciding to sing *That's Alright Mama* at Sun Studios, or Bill Haley releasing *Rock Around the Clock* (or even the aficionado's notion that it started with Jackie Brenston's recording of *Rocket 88*). Pop is dead because the technology that introduced the popular has been superseded by technology which has rendered the concept meaningless. Like a young man singing a new song with an old rocker, we continue to try to make sense of our world through music, but it is music that can no longer be said to be truly popular.

I finished reading and put the essay on my lap. I wasn't too happy about what I'd seen. My JookBoxFury experience was over, and now pop music was dead? Pop wasn't as good as it used to be, OK, but saying it had died was taking things too far. Dr Roc was hammering nails in pop's coffin because technology had changed. No way, surely that couldn't be right. I handed the paper back to Dr Roc and said,

'That's interesting.' I didn't know what else to say, I wasn't ready to talk. I needed some time to myself to try and come to terms with the situation.

Pony Boy bounced down the aisle, 'Great news, everybody, and I really must share this with you because I'm sure you'll be as thrilled as I am. I've just taken a call from a friend of a friend who's got a finger in a number of pies and – listen to this – he likes the idea of *Explain Your Name* very much. He's absolutely convinced that we can run with it.'

'Good for you,' Dr Roc said.

Rik grunted, 'Next time nothing happens, there's no need to wake me up to tell me about it, OK? After what I've been through, man, I need to sleep.'

'Well, don't go to sleep yet,' Pony Boy said, 'because there's more. This contact is, broadly speaking, into promotions and the like, and he thinks that we could incorporate a Bobbly Wobbler character into the *Explain Your Name* show. He was just kicking ideas around, but we might have a life-size Bobbly Wobbler bringing the guests on or maybe giving the history of the names, like a wacky Carol Vorderman type role. If that comes off, and he's quite confident that it will, then there's the very real possibility that *Don't Go Breaking My Hat* will be back on the agenda. So, as you can see, it's all rather exciting. I'm meeting the promoter later today to talk numbers.'

That was one in the eye for Dr Roc. How could she say pop was dead when *Don't Go Breaking My Hat* was back on the agenda?

As we edged our way into London, past an endless string of newsagents, greengrocers and takeaways, Rhia got a call from Fran. When the call finished Rhia said, 'Fran wanted to warn us that there's a mob outside the press conference.'

'What sort of a mob?' I asked her.

'An angry mob, apparently. It all sounds a bit tense. Fran said she expects our full support and Laurence will brief us when we arrive. I don't really know what's going on.'

DISC FOUR, TRACK THREE

Green Grow the Jooksie-oh!

We drove past the Earl's Court exhibition centre and round the corner to a fading hotel with peeling paint and a sign that said 'Duke of Ear 's Court Hotel.' Underneath the sign was a yellow vinyl banner with red lettering saying, 'Jukebox World UK with Retro South: Convention – Show – Stalls – Fun 4 All.'

It was a popular event. There was a huge crowd on the pavement who looked like they were waiting to get into the show, but as the coach pulled up someone pointed as us and shouted, 'There they are.' The line of people on the pavement surged to the side of the coach, banging on the windows and shouting. In the middle of them, was Bilbo Baggins and a couple of the other morris dancers. Some of the women looked vaguely familiar too.

'Is this a result of the press coverage?' Dr Roc said. 'A mobilization of dissatisfied consumers demanding the withdrawal of an unsafe product?'

We moved towards the front of the bus and saw a couple of policemen outside holding the crowd back. Laurence appeared in the hotel doorway. He edged halfway out and beckoned to us urgently.

'Let's go for it,' Rhia said.

As the doors opened some of the crowd started to sing, 'Green grow the Jooksie-oh!' When Rik went down the steps, Bilbo Baggins yelled, 'That's Peabody. That's Rik Peabody. Ask him.' A guy in a combat jacket stretched his arm past the policeman, grabbed Rik's shoulder and said, 'Hey, Rik, have you got any Jook, man? Where can we get some of that stuff? Don't keep it all to yourself, man.'

Rik said, 'Keep your fucking hands off, man. Jook's not a right, it's a responsibility.' He broke from the guy's grip and pushed through into the hotel, clutching a bundle wrapped in his jacket.

Laurence hurried us into the foyer. Rhia said, 'Were those people actually chanting for Jook?'

'That's right,' Laurence said. 'You can't buy publicity like this. The crowd baying for your product – this one's going straight onto my resumé. Hylton-James wants to brazen it out. He thinks we can turn this around. Fran's about to make a statement and she wants Babs alongside her – the party girl, rebellious but fun, the perfect image of Jook.'

'Babs isn't here,' Rhia said.

'Well, where the hell...? I don't need to know why right now. Uhmm? Rik – rebellious, fun – you go and sit alongside Fran in the press conference. Couple of sound bites. Job done.'

Laurence dragged Rik along a corridor to a conference room and the rest of us followed. The room was packed. Photographers at the front, men and women with pads and tape recorders at the ready behind them. Fran stood nervously in the front corner, next to a tall silver-haired man in a pin-stripe suit. Fran nodded vigorously as he spoke to her, then smoothed her hair, wiped her palms on her skirt and went to the table at the front of the room. She sat behind a microphone. Laurence dragged Rik to the front and showed him to the other chair. Fran tried to push Rik away, and shook her head at Laurence, but Rik dropped into the chair and put the bundle he'd been holding on the table. Fran sighed and poured herself a glass of water. She held out the carafe to Rik, but he shook his head and unrolled his jacket to reveal a six-pack of Jook. The room seemed to gasp, as if he'd given them a glimpse of the Holy Grail. Pens clicked and the photographers started snapping. Rik pulled a bottle out of the pack and cracked the top off on the edge of the table, splintering a chunk of wood from the side. He pulled bits of wood out of the top of the bottle, took a long drink, and looked at Fran.

In some ways the situation didn't appear too promising, but if

Fran was going to turn things around for Jook, having the drink's number one advocate alongside her might not be a bad thing. It might not be a bad thing.

Fran tapped the microphone. Rik blew into the top of the Jook bottle to make a low-pitched whistle. Fran covered the microphone with her hand and leaned over to say something to Rik who shrugged and stopped whistling.

Fran said, 'Thank you, ladies and gentlemen, for coming today. I must say that when I initiated the Jook launch I never dreamed that we would generate such a high level of interest within our first week. In response to that interest, I would like to read a short statement on behalf of LNE Breweries and then I will take questions.'

Rik leaned down to his microphone and said, 'I'll be handling any questions of a rocking nature.' The journalists laughed.

Fran coughed and started to read. 'Following the launch this week of our innovative new alocopop brand, Jook, LNE Breweries have been overwhelmed by the interest the product has generated, which has resulted in unprecedented levels of demand. We are grateful to the consumers who have supported us and who have shown their enthusiasm for this absinthe and greengage-based party drink. The support has been unlike anything we at the brewery have witnessed, either ourselves or within the beverage industry as a whole, and consequently we believe that Jook is set to become a market-leader for many years to come.'

Rik cracked another bottle open on the table and said, 'Here's a fucking toast to that, man.'

Fran didn't even look at him. 'We do, however, want to address claims made in some quarters that the drink possesses unusual side effects and we state emphatically that this is not the case.'

At that point Rik shielded his eyes and then ducked suddenly. 'Fucking close one, man.'

Fran pretended that Rik wasn't there. She ignored him, but he attracted the attention of everyone else in the room by using his jacket to swat at something invisible above his head. Then he finished his Jook and cracked open another.

Fran read, 'Following a discussion with the Food Standards

Agency, initiated by ourselves, we are voluntarily withdrawing Jook with immediate effect…'

Rik put his arms around the remaining Jook bottles and drew them to him, looking around the room suspiciously.

'… so that we can use an independent body to validate our already rigorous programme of product testing. We will relaunch Jook in a few weeks' time to our customers who can be as fully confident in this brand as we are.'

'How many weeks, man?' Rik interrupted. 'I don't know how long I can make my supply last. You'll see me right won't you? Don't make the Guitar Man go cold turkey on the Jook. I can't do it, man. Not now.'

Fran glanced at James Hylton-James, then continued to read the statement. 'No-one epitomizes the spirit of Jook more than the woman alongside me now, Babs… I mean, Rik Peabody. She is such a fun-loving…'

Someone shouted, 'Is there something you haven't told us, Rik?' The journalists started to laugh.

Fran tried to carry on. 'Rik is a fun-loving party girl… guy… who loves nothing more than a night out with the girls to share a Jook together.'

Rik said, 'Now you're talkin' darlin'.' He opened another Jook and leaned down to the microphone, 'Talking of a night out Jookin' with the girls, has anyone got the number of that babe who was in the paper with me, because..?'

Mike Statham was near the front of the audience. He stood up and asked Fran, 'Can you seriously expect people to drink this alcopop in a sensible manner after the publicity you've given it? This is a shameful experience for the drinks industry, and rather than hearing about the relaunch of Jook, shouldn't we be hearing about those responsible for this scandal being stripped of their posts?'

Fran didn't respond.

Rik opened the last bottle of Jook on the table.

Mike Statham said to Fran, 'If you really want to show confidence in your own product, Ms Watson, perhaps you would take a drink now, for the cameras.'

Fran gritted her teeth and her head started to shake.

Rik said, 'She's not having my last fucking Jook. She's the one who said we couldn't have any more.'

Fran kept shaking.

I nudged Pony Boy, 'Why don't you go up there and tell them about the other stuff. Distract them. It's not all about Jook.'

'Oh, the Bobbly Wobblers,' he said, 'good thinking.'

'No. The competition – that's the main thing.'

'You're right,' Pony Boy said, 'perfect opportunity to launch Explain Your Name.' He started towards the front of the room.

I pulled him back, 'Not Explain Your Name – JookBoxFury. Tell them the Jook campaign was a front for JookBoxFury and the final is on tonight. We've got to make sure everyone knows about the JookBoxFury final – make sure that goes ahead.'

Pony Boy went and perched on the table in front of Fran. He took the microphone from its stand and said, 'Simon "Pony Boy" Rogers here on the airwaves, if anyone out there doesn't recognize me. We've had a fabulous week on the road with Jook – just like the old Radio Wonderful days, and if you were wondering, the japes have been as good as they ever were. I think our bit of fun with Jook really got you all going for a moment there, and it's worked – here you all are. Well, you won't be disappointed. We've all had some fun with the old Jook story, but that's all been a little bit of a wind-up, because the real story is JookBoxFury. It's my new game show format and we're running the first ever final here tonight with a fantastic line-up of contestants. We've got Rik Peabody, as you can see, still crazy after all these years. Dr Roc, the rocking professor and…' He looked around. That was it. No Nye, no Babs. Pony Boy looked at me, '… and of course, our man of the people, "Sugar" Ray Mitchell… and… and, oh yes, after some impressive jukebox selections in Glasgow last night, for her first time in the competition, queen of the jukebox scene, it's Rhiannon.

'I'll tell you one more thing, you'll be thrilled to hear that the Bobbly Wobblers are back – I'm going to put them on sale here at the Retro South show. So, thanks everybody for coming along. I hope you've enjoyed the fun we've had with the Jook story, and I hope you enjoy the fun we're going to have at the JookBoxFury final here tonight.'

Rik leaned on the table and pushed himself to his feet. He held up the last bottle of Jook, knocked it back, and slammed the bottle down onto the table. 'It's about rock 'n' roll, it's always been about rocking, rocking and fury – that's why I'm here, baby.' He windmilled his guitar strumming arm, thrust his hips at the journalists and said, 'I'm burnin' with fury, baby. I'm burnin' with JookBoxFury and we're gonna rock this town tonight.'

Pony Boy said, 'Mr Rik Peabody, rocking a jukebox near you tonight. Let's hear it for Rik.' Rik windmilled his arm again and there was a gentle round of applause from the journalists. Mike Statham didn't applaud, but he put his pad and his pen away. Pony Boy left the press conference table and dragged Rik behind him.

I shook Pony Boy's hand. He was a god among DJs – he'd put me in the JookBoxFury final. I'd made it. I'd got my chance to show what great rock 'n' roll was all about.

As the journalists started to shuffle away, Fran spent a couple of moments looking at the ceiling and then went over to James Hylton-James and said, 'I'm so sorry. I am so so sorry. I don't know what all that was about. Should I call them back and make another statement?'

Hylton-James said, 'Why don't you take a few days off, Francesca, and then we'll have a chat about your future. I think Mr Rogers has bought us some time, given us a little breathing space. I think we'd be advised to keep a low profile for the time being until we see how this one's going to play out.'

Laurence approached Hylton-James. 'I think we've done what we set out to do there JHJ. We've created a brand that has got the punters talking. First thing Monday I'll get to work on concepts for the relaunch.'

Hylton-James smiled.

(What's So Funny 'Bout) Peace, Love and Understanding?

After checking into my room I went to look for Pony Boy. The least I could do after he'd put me in the final was help him set up his Bobbly Wobbler stall. There was a flip chart stand in the hotel foyer with 'Retro South' written on it in bubble writing and an arrow pointing down a hallway. I followed the arrow to the Marchioness Conference Suite and looked round the door. A guy in his sixties, wearing a bowling shirt with 'Route 66' on the pocket, was sitting at a table with a small metal cash box in front of him. I asked him if I was in the right place for Retro South.

He said, 'You most certainly are, my good sir. £2.50 entrance to you, a bargain at twice the price. Retro is the new antiques, you know. The antiques are all a bit old hat now but we've got a large range of collectables here, high quality retro merchandise, and you get all of that for the princely sum of the two pounds and the fifty pence.'

It would have been more appropriate to give him a ten bob note and a handful of threepenny bits, but instead I tried, 'I'm part of JookBoxFury, so do I get in free?'

He said, 'JookBoxFury – what's all that when it's at home? Is it one of the stalls?'

I explained about the final of the world's first JookBoxFury competition. He took a brochure from his table, put some reading specs on, and peered at a timetable. 'It's all tribute bands tonight,' he said, 'apart from Big Nev's Big Pop Quiz up in the Viscount's Cocktail Bar. That's always good for a laugh, he does it every year. He ought to be on the telly really. I can't see any of the jukebox guys doing anything this evening, though.'

'It's on at eight-thirty,' I told him. 'It's called JookBoxFury, it's going to be broadcast live on the radio.'

He had another look at the timetable. 'Ah, there it is, Juke Box Jury at eight-thirty. Well, good luck to you if you're on at the same time as Big Nev's Big Pop Quiz, everyone looks forward to that so most folks are going to be there.'

It was one thing after another. As soon as we'd got the final sorted, I found we had to go head-to-head for an audience with Big Nev's Big Pop Quiz. My disappointment must have shown because he said, 'Anyway, if you're part of the entertainment you'd better come on in.'

The Retro show was really a Fifties, Sixties and Seventies jumble sale with inflated prices. One stall had an extensive range of old Meccano and Lego sets, as well as having a bright orange 1970s black and white TV 'In good working order.' A genuine 1970s retro TV wouldn't be in good working order, it would have a picture that kept flicking round until you tweaked the vertical hold. I was drawn to a stall selling original stockings with two-way stretch tops, 'sheer, seamfree, micromesh,' but unfortunately I didn't really have any use for them – it wasn't as if I was planning a robbery. The woman on the stall saw me looking at the stockings and asked if I was interested. I said, 'No, it's changed, it's all balaclavas nowadays.'

At the next stall I bumped into Dr Rococco who was looking at a teapot with a design of alternate blocks of green and brown with wiggly black lines. 'My mother had that exact same tea service,' she said. 'Look at the price, remarkable. And that biscuit tin,' she pointed to a cream tin with a pale green lid, 'we had one of those. Isn't it strange how artefacts that were such an everyday part of our lives have become desirable again? Are we buying the articles themselves, or the memories? Either way, I'm going to get that tea service.'

Pony Boy came up to the stall, slightly out of breath. 'Ray, there you are, mate, I've been looking all over… ooh, that milk jug, we had one just like that… Anyway, Ray, look lively, the Bobbly Wobbler stall is going to be over here.'

Pony Boy had secured a stall in the corner next to the Meccano. I set out the Bobbly Wobblers on the table using the skills I'd developed earlier on the tour. Rhia wrote a sign saying, 'Spring into action – Pony Boy Rogers' Bobbly Wobblers from the golden days of Radio Wonderful – special show price…' then she asked Pony Boy how much.

He said, 'Five pounds, usual price.'

'Don't you want to give a bit of discount to try and sell a few more?'

Pony Boy wasn't happy about the idea, but in the end he agreed to four pounds each and three for a tenner. Rhia stuck the sign on the front of the table.

Pony Boy said, 'That is fabulous… Right, it looks as though you don't really need me here. I'm sorry about this, but I'm going to have to leave you two in charge for a while. I'm meeting up with the promoter I told you about before. It'll only take two ticks and I'll be back to lend a hand.' He wished us luck and off he went.

'That's a bit of a cheek,' I said to Rhia. 'He gets us to set the things up and then he clears off.'

'I don't mind, really,' Rhia said. 'It's not as if it needs three of us here, I doubt we're going to get a stampede.'

'It's not as if it needs one of us here, come to that.'

'Well, you can go and do what you want,' Rhia said. 'I'll stay here.'

'I didn't mean that. I'm quite happy here.'

'Have you seen the display of jukeboxes through in the other room?' Rhia asked me. 'Aren't they brilliant? They're going to be using some of them for the final.'

'I didn't know there was another room. I might go and have a look – just to prepare for the competition, get into the zone… if you're sure you're alright with these?'

Rhia assured me she'd be fine, so I left her with the Bobbly Wobblers and followed the muffled sound of Little Richard's *Lucille* coming from down the hall. The record was being played in an Aladdin's Cave of jukeboxes, seventy or more gleaming record machines of every shape and size. They were all round the walls, with a double row back to back down the middle of the room. Most of the jukeboxes had a card on the front showing a price ranging from hundreds to thousands of pounds. Facing me, in the middle of the room, was a Chantal Meteor 200. It stood out because none of the other jukeboxes had a Perspex dome like the Chantal's. Even so, they were all working hard to draw attention to themselves with their chrome grills, shining buttons and multi-coloured lights.

At the far end of the room, a couple of women in sticky-out satin skirts with wide elastic belts were doing a gentle jive to *Lucille*. They were old enough to have been jiving to it the first time around. A little lad was being guided round the room by his dad. The lad kept trying to reach up and press buttons on the jukeboxes. His dad was half-heartedly saying, 'Be careful now, Aaron, these aren't for playing with,' until one of the jukebox owners coldly told him, 'There is a children's play area through in the Lord and Lady Room, the little chap might be safer in there. If you hurry, you might be in time for the balloon animals.'

The other people in the room were walking slowly past the jukeboxes on display, stopping to look at each one, nodding appreciatively, and then peering inside at some detail. Occasionally they would kneel down and rub a finger across the name plate or an important part of the casing. A man said to his wife, 'I'd still go for the Rock-Ola. It plays more selections and it's easier to get parts if anything goes wrong.'

His wife said, 'But don't you think this one would go so much better with the suite in the conservatory?'

The jukeboxes were grouped together in blocks of five or six, with a table and chair next to each block. Some of the tables had a display of brochures and business cards and others were full of boxes of singles: Rock 'n' Roll, Doo Wop, Beat Groups, Soul, Ska, Two Tone, Northern. One or two of the guys selling the jukeboxes were sitting at their tables, or polishing up the chrome-work on their machines, but most of them were in twos or threes chatting about jukebox business. They were all in their late-forties or early-fifties, with shaven heads, to cover their hair loss, and wearing faded jeans and polo shirts or checked Ben Shermans.

I wandered over to the Chantal – happy memories. One of the shaven-headed guys broke off from his conversation and came over. He said, 'That's a beautiful machine, the Chantal. It's unique really, because there isn't another machine with a dome like this – it was too expensive to replace so it was impractical to keep making them. It is one of the few British designed and made boxes, of course. Highly collectable because of the rarity value, an absolute joy to play, very popular with those in the know and a sound investment. This one's a Jukebox World special, I've got it on at eight thousand, but I can do it for seven nine if you're local and you don't have too many stairs.'

'I hear they take a while to warm up,' I said.

'Who told you that? This baby won't give you any problems with warming up. I think you've been given some duff information there, mate.'

'I heard it from a guy at *Jukebox World* magazine.'

'Don't tell me – it was Warren wasn't it? Warren doesn't know bugger all about the Chantal. Just because he produces his newsletter he thinks he's a big shot expert on the jukes, but he hasn't got a bloody clue. I actually sold Warren his first machine – the Rowe R-90, not an all-time classic but a lovely starter machine – then he comes back to me saying it's not running right and he thinks the final reduction gear shaft holes are creating extra friction. Well, I tell him, "Excuse me, but I virtually rebuilt that machine from scratch, and I can tell you now that there is no problem with any gear shaft holes." I had a look at it for him – we do offer a full after-sales service – and all it needed was a tickle on the optical switch. Got it sorted in no time. Tell Warren when you see him not to go shooting his mouth off about the Chantal because he doesn't know bugger all about it.'

'I don't expect I'll be seeing him again,' I said.

'Of course you will if you're spending any time here. He's always buzzing around sticking his nose in. Anyway, were you interested in the Chantal? We can arrange finance with a reputable company?'

I said I was just browsing, then I heard a shout from further down the room, 'That is fucking beautiful, that's the exact same one, man.' Rik had fallen to his knees in front of a big old machine that had Wurlitzer highlighted on a green strip at the top, and a green glow coming from a wide grill at the front. Rik spread his arms out in front of the jukebox like someone prostrating themselves before an idol, and with the green neon glow reflecting on his face it looked like the spirit of Jook had come back to claim his soul.

I went over to Rik and asked him if he was OK.

Rik said, 'That's the same fucking one, man. When we played in Dino's, back when we started with Ricky and the Rhythm Boys, this was the jukebox they had in the café. Bloody magnificent. I must have put enough money in it to buy the fucker. Yeah… bloody magnificent. It could even be the one that was in Dino's.'

Rik stood up to look round the side of the Perspex cover. He shook his head. 'It's different. I scratched my name on the one in Dino's with my ring, just on the corner there.'

One of the jukebox owners approached Rik. 'It is stunning, isn't it? An absolute beaut. The Wurlitzer Twenty-One Four, as you probably know, undoubtedly one of the best Silver Age machines, if not the best. I've just refurbished this baby. The mech is in perfect nick. To look at it, you'd think it had come straight out of the factory. The casing is the best you're going to see. I've had all the metalwork re-chromed, just look at those trims. It's one of the best machines you'll find on offer here – it's actually been chosen for a big show that's on this evening because it's such a nice machine. I've got it on at a special price this weekend, £7,900 and that includes a three month warranty, delivery within fifty miles and a selection of records to fill it.'

'Done,' Rik said. 'I'll take it. You put a sold sign on that, man, and I'll go and get some cash. That's the exact same fucking one.'

Rik left me standing with the jukebox owner who said, 'That's the quickest sale I've ever made. Most people like to hear them play.'

'He can be quite impulsive,' I said. 'You might have heard of him, he's Rik Peabody from The Peabodies.'

'That's who he was. I knew I recognized him. I was just saying to the other guys, "I know that feller from somewhere." What a co-incidence, I used to put *Violence is Golden* on the jukebox in our local when I was a kid. Who'd have thought? I'll get a photo when he comes back. I'll have to see if Warren's about, he might want to do a bit for his newsletter… Are you in the market for a box yourself?'

'Well, I'd love to buy a jukebox, but…'

'Your first decision is CD or vinyl. Have you got much of a singles collection?'

I told him I'd got plenty of singles.

'Vinyl's probably the way to go then if you're wanting a classic machine. Cost-wise, you're looking at anything from seven or eight hundred up to ten thousand plus. Obviously the era is important, and the big thing is whether you can see the mechanism or not. People always like to see the mech so you get the full view of the record being picked up and played. On the later machines, late-Sixties, Seventies, the manufacturers hid the mech. I suppose they thought it was a bit slicker, but it's not so, not so… jukeboxy. You can pick one of those up for seven hundred if you know where to come, it's still a good machine to get you going. What sort of price range were you looking at?'

After I'd told him what my situation was he ended up selling me a solid brass record dinker. I took it back to show Rhia. 'Look what I got. It was only twelve pounds. Usually they're eighteen. It's a record dinker.'

'What's a record dinker?' Rhia asked.

'It's one of these. It cuts the middles out of singles so you can put them in your jukebox.'

'Have you got a jukebox?'

'Not yet,' I said, 'but I'm working up to it. The experts say you should get a dinker first and see if you've got an affinity for it before you take things any further. Now I've taken the first step, it's only a matter of time. Rik just bought a jukebox, the exact same type that he used to listen to in his coffee bar days. I thought about getting one too, but I decided to stick with the dinker.'

Rhia said. 'Maybe you could become a self-employed dinker operator.'

'I'm not ruling anything out at this stage.'

'What are you going to do when this has finished?' Rhia asked me.

'It's back to work, what else? I try not to think about work when I'm not there. I try not to think about it when I am there to be honest, but, you know, I keep turning up and they keep paying me. There's the pension scheme too. It might not be the most exciting job in the world, but I suppose it's some sort of security. I'd have been at work the past few days if I hadn't been off sick with facial bruising. I go to work every day and it's miserable. I come on JookBoxFury by chance, it's chaos, I get punched in the face, and it's brilliant. It's been one of the best things I've ever done. I'm even starting to look back to The Queen Victoria with some fondness. I turned up that night after hearing Pony Boy talking about JookBoxFury on the radio, and now I'm in the final. I only turned up to make sure Pony Boy didn't fix it for *Chanson d'Amour* or some rubbish like that to be voted as the greatest jukebox song of all time. Now I'm in the final. This is my chance. Playing great jukebox songs live on the radio, maybe even becoming the Jook Duke of the Juke. That's something to tell the folks back at work – except I'm supposed to have been off sick. What if Justin Quine hears it and realizes what I've been doing? Who cares? Like I said, I'm not thinking about work. The JookBoxFury final is the thing to concentrate on. If one of us wins it, that would be the perfect end.'

'Just being in the final is brilliant,' Rhia said. 'I don't really mind about winning. I'm just going to have fun because it's back to the office for me next week too, and I know what you mean about work. Being on the road this week has made me think I should pack it all in and go travelling. You don't want to spend your life being ordered around by someone like Fran.'

'Or Justin Quine. I feel like this has been the real world and all that other stuff – going to work in a dreary office and trying to please people you don't even like – that's just the world gone wrong. That's why it's been so good to be on the tour with all of you. Even though it only lasted for a week, it's always going to be a week I'll remember.'

'Which was your favourite part?'

I looked at Rhia, but I had to look away. The best part of JookBoxFury was dancing with Rhia, and when she blew me a kiss. That had to be the highlight. I said, 'The best part was when you blew me a kiss last night – that was the best part.'

Rhia picked up a Bobbly Wobbler and stroked its hair a few times. She said, 'You could have blown me a kiss back.' She gave the Bobbly Wobbler's hair another stroke.

'It seems kind of old-fashioned – blowing kisses.'

Rhia said, 'I like to think of it more as retro.'

I was about to reply when a girl of seven or eight with her hair in bunches came up to the table holding a ten pound note. She said, 'Please can I have three of your Wobbly Bobblers, please, thank you.'

I had to check. 'Three? Are you sure?'

'Three, yes please, three. One for mummy, one for Luke and one for me.'

Rhia took the ten pounds off her and said, 'You choose which colours you'd like because they've got different hair.'

The girl spent quite a while deciding, and kept changing her mind, but in the end she plumped for an orange, a green and a purple.

Rhia said, 'Tell your friends about the Bobbly Wobblers. There's nothing else like them.'

The girl said, 'I know. I'll tell Siobahn,' and left, half skipping, half running.

'They're flying off the shelves now,' I said. 'Maybe we should put some barriers up, perhaps establish a queuing system.' I wasn't speaking too soon because the girl came straight back with a friend, presumably Siobahn. Siobahn wanted three Bobbly Wobblers and got into a lengthy debate with the first girl about which one to get Luke.

'Haven't you already got one for Luke?' I asked them.

Siobahn said, 'Luke's her little brother, he's sooo cute. I am so getting him one as well.'

Rhia said, 'That's very thoughtful of you, I'm sure he'll be pleased.'

A crowd of kids burst into the room, some of them carrying balloon animals and others wearing hats made out of balloons. Luke's sister and Siobahn rushed over to them and there was lots of shrieking and squealing. The next twenty minutes were mayhem. We were rushed off our feet as all the kids came to buy Bobbly Wobblers. We'd tapped into a market of parents appeasing their children for dragging them to an event where they had to look at old stuff. For a short while, Bobbly Wobblers brought some happiness, if not a little peace, love and understanding, into the world.

Before long, we started getting mums and dads coming over to the stall and saying, 'Bobbly Wobblers – oh, do you remember those?' and, 'I got one of those from the Radio Wonderful roadshow in Clacton,' and, 'I'm going to get one of these for my sister-in-law – she was mad about Pony Boy.' At one point, the number of people round the table caused the guy with the Meccano to say, 'Can we have a bit of order there, if you don't mind? I've got some valuable construction kits in pristine condition on display here.'

Things calmed down after a while, but the Bobbly Wobblers had proven themselves to be a big hit with children of all ages. Rhia counted up how much we'd taken and said, 'You won't believe it, we've made £927.50.'

I couldn't believe it. 'How can you get an odd number when we were selling them for ten pounds and four pounds?'

Rhia said, 'I sold one for £3.50 because it had a sad expression.'

I doubted that cutting the price was going to make it feel much better, but Pony Boy made up for it by coming back with a very happy expression, which got happier still when he heard how well sales had gone. 'I knew it! I knew it!' he said. 'There were doubters, but I think we've shown them. And what is more, I've had a very fruitful discussion with my promoter friend – 't's to cross and 'i's to dot – but it is all looking rather promising. That's why I've been so long, but you don't appear to have missed me.'

Rhia said, 'You've not been gone that long.' She looked at her watch. 'You've been gone ages! It's nearly eight, we need to get ready for the show.'

I couldn't believe that. We'd been distracted from the JookBoxFury final by selling Bobbly Wobblers.

DISC FOUR, TRACK FIVE

The Hustle

We ran into the Countess Centre where the final was going to be held and were faced by an arc of five jukeboxes at the front of the room, with the last one being moved into position as we arrived. A couple of radio people were setting up microphones by the jukeboxes and running cables to a sound desk. A woman standing by the desk rushed over to us and said, 'Here you are at last. It's a good job you called, Simon. It's been a bit touch and go because of all the hoo haa about the green alcopop. I've been trying to contact Francesca Watson, but they tell me that she's on extended leave and I should talk to Rhiannon.'

She was very relieved to have found Rhia. Rhia was pleased too.

The woman said, 'I'm Carole, I'll be producing the show for London Live. We're used to doing things on the run, but I have to say I was getting a teensy bit worried that we were cutting it a little too fine.'

Pony Boy said, 'Heaven forbid, I've never missed a show. It was only this morning that I was telling my chums about one occasion in Hunstanton…'

'Good, good. Very good,' Carole said. 'As for the format tonight, obviously you know the ropes, Simon, so no concerns there. I've already run through it all with a chap called Warren who is organizing things from the jukebox side and he's…'

'It's not the Warren we know, is it?' Rhia asked.

'I don't know about that,' Carole said. 'He seems to be one of the big jukebox experts around here and he'll be introducing the

213

jukeboxes at the start of the competition. I'll get him over.' She shouted to one of the guys who had been moving the jukebox, 'Yoo-hoo, Warren, can I borrow you for a minute?' He turned round and waved.

'It is our Warren,' Rhia said. 'Well, not really "our Warren", seeing as we asked him to leave.'

Warren strutted over to us. 'So, we meet again… I must say that when the organizers spoke to me last night and invited me to do this, I was in two minds after being treated rather shabbily at your previous event. However, the powers that be were very keen for me to take part, and they made the point that I had the breadth of knowledge required to introduce the machines. Obviously being at the forefront of the jukebox media as I am, I will be very proud to do so. Is Babs here, by the way?'

'Babs had to leave to work on a video,' Rhia told him.

'Ooh, that's interesting,' Warren said.

Rhia said, 'If she was here, it might not be easy to work with you, but as she's not and it's late, we'll make the best of it. We're only interested in your opinions about jukeboxes though, nothing else.'

Warren said, 'All I've ever wanted to do is bring the joy of the jukes to as many people as possible. My suggestion to Babs was nothing more than an innocent idea to help promote the scene.'

I was going to give Warren the Chantal owner's message, but Rhia asked me if I'd go and find Rik and Dr Roc while she checked the running order with Carole and Pony Boy. As I went out of the room, I passed the guy who had been taking the entrance money at the Retro show. He said, 'Are you on in here? I'm going to give your Juke Box Jury a try. I went into Big Nev's Quiz and he's asking all the same questions again. That's the sixth year in a row that he's used those questions. How many times can you ask who played harmonica on *My Boy Lollipop*?'

'I think everyone knows that one,' I said.

'They surely do, my friend, they surely do – although you'd be surprised how many people still say it was Rod Stewart. It makes me laugh, it really does. I've decided to give your lot a try instead, so make it a good one.'

That was good news. It was a promising sign that we were winning over some of the Jukebox World UK and Retro South regulars. On the downside, it was a bit of a shocker about Rod not playing harmonica on *My Boy Lollipop*. Maybe he'd got it confused with something else. Going into the JookBoxFury final, the last thing I needed was to have my confidence shaken with a question mark hanging over a fundamental piece of pop history like that. It was all about self-belief in the latter stages of a big competition. There was still the possibility that someone listening to the broadcast would hear my selections and come in for me with a big money job offer. Carole might even want to be my producer for a cutting-edge music radio format. That was possible, and I didn't want to be distracted from stringing together some prime JookBoxFury selections by thinking, 'Well, what if Rod didn't play harmonica? What if Mike Nesmith didn't write *Different Drum*? What if Gloria Jones wasn't driving Marc Bolan's mini? What if Equally Humdrum aren't at the forefront of the nouvelle bric(01)age? What if Rhia didn't mean what she said?' I needed some foundations that I could rely on. I had to be able to trust my own knowledge and judgement.

I was surprised to find Rik and Dr Roc sharing a table in the lounge. Dr Roc was pouring tea from her new teapot and Rik was leaning down by the side of the table to take furtive sips from what looked like a bottle of Jook. I needed a Jook too – it was the spirit of Jook that guided me to the JookBoxFury final. It got me through the competition in The Blue Moon of Ken's Tuck Inn and No More Heroes… I needed one more hit to seal my destiny. One more Jook to give me the winning JookBoxFury selections.

I said, 'What have you got there, Rik?'

He said, 'It's nothing, man.'

'It's Jook, you've got more Jook.'

'It's my fucking supply, man. It's like Dave Dee, Dozy, Beaky, Mitch and Titch's roadie told me, "Get your hands on the rider and secure your own supply." I went through the fucking pain barrier to get this off Big Minnie.'

'I just want one bottle, that's all I need.'

'This is the last bottle, man. I can't share it. I need the green.'

'I only want a couple of sips. Just a couple of sips before the competition.'

'I can spare some tea,' Dr Roc offered. 'It's a big pot, and it's a lovely pourer.'

'Thanks,' I said, 'but I just wanted one last taste of Jook. Come on, Rik.'

'No can do, man,' Rik said. He put the bottle to his lips and tipped it.

I could grab it. I gritted my teeth and prepared to dive over the arm of Rik's chair. I stretched out my hand and was about to leap when Dr Roc gently pulled me back. I moved forward again but she pulled me back more firmly. I stopped. She was right. Rik licked his lips and put the empty Jook bottle on the table. It was gone. 'Sorry,' I said. 'I don't need it.'

I didn't need it. I could pick songs without Jook. I'd always been able to pick songs and if I was going to win JookBoxFury I had to do it myself. I could do it.

I led Rik and Dr Roc back to the Countess Centre. Everything was ready to go. The seats were only about a quarter full, with a collection of twenty or thirty people scattered about. I recognized a few members of the audience from the Retro Show, some had even bought Bobbly Wobblers. Mike Statham was at the back of the room chatting to a couple of photographers, but the JookBoxFury final didn't seem to be generating the same level of press interest as the psychedelic alcopop crisis. A small group of the jukebox sellers were sitting on the front row, along with Luke's sister and Siobahn who held their Bobbly Wobblers on their knees. There was no sign of Luke – obviously the responsibility of having two Bobbly Wobblers to look after was making it difficult for him to get out.

Pony Boy and Rhia were chatting to Laurence. He wished us well, told Pony Boy he'd catch up with him afterwards, and went to take a seat in the audience. Pony Boy explained how the broadcast was going to work, 'Standard format for a show like this. We'll get an announcement from the studio to hand over to us on location here. I'll pick it up, welcome the listeners and explain what it's all about, then it's over to Warren who's going to give a pen portrait of each of the jukeboxes. Then back to us and on with the final. There is a slight variation in the format this time in so far as you'll each have a different jukebox to make your selections on. So you all need to choose which one you're going to use.'

We looked at the semi-circle of jukeboxes. Rik pointed to the second one in the row. It was the Wurlitzer with the green glow. 'That one's mine, I just fucking bought that one.'

Pony Boy said, 'Shall I take it that you want to use that one then?' but Rik had already gone to bathe in the Wurlitzer's green light.

Dr Roc said, 'What's this one here, the one that looks like a piece of antique furniture?'

The first jukebox was made of polished mahogany, a cross between a radiogram and a coin-operated wardrobe, with two bands of mellow yellow light shining gently from the front. Pony Boy said, 'That's the oldest jukebox here apparently, it plays 78s and you only get twenty selections.'

Dr Roc stroked the wooden case. 'It's rather lovely. I assume that if there are only twenty discs they must all be good. It's very much mechanical reproduction as a work of art. I'd love to use this one if no-one else minds.'

I didn't mind. Twenty 78s to choose from was shooting yourself in the foot as far as I was concerned.

Pony Boy said, 'Rhia and Ray, that leaves three for you to choose from. There's the Rock-Ola, which I'm led to believe is the same model they used to have on *Juke Box Jury* on the old goggle box. The next one is a slightly more recent model, from 1977 I think it was – so you might find *Chanson d'Amour* on there if you're lucky. Then at the end of the row we have a contemporary reproduction of a Wurlitzer which plays CDs.'

I said to Rhia, 'You choose.'

Rhia said, 'It doesn't seem right to use a CD jukebox here, but I'm happy to go with either of the others. I'll flip you for it.'

Pony Boy flipped a coin, Rhia called and won. She said, 'I'll take the *Juke Box Jury* one – it looks classier.'

The jukebox was a beauty, maybe even better than Rik's. It had a large curved Perspex front, like the windscreen of a classic American car, which was wrapped around the turntable and six rows of bright blue cards. The selection buttons ran across the full width of the jukebox and below those 'R O C K – O L A' was picked out in black on yellow squares of light. On the speaker it said 'Stereo' above a jet age boomerang design.

Rhia went to check what songs she had to choose from, and after taking them in she said, 'It might be the most stylish jukebox here, but it's got a very strange combination of music on it. It looks like it's been chosen for a Nashville truck stop-cum-roller disco. Half of it is country and the other half is disco. Weird.'

I had a quick look at the list of songs and saw she was right. 'Welcome to the vagaries of JookBoxFury competition,' I said.

Even though the CD Wurlitzer had the biggest choice of music and looked like the definitive 1950s jukebox with its curved top and bubbling lights, I decided to go for the 1970s machine. Compared to the others it was plain. You couldn't see the records, and the only ornamentation were three glowing panels showing a Seventies geometric wallpaper pattern in sunset red, burnt orange and sienna. There were metal strips round the edges but the cabinet looked as if it had been covered in wood effect, sticky-backed plastic for a Blue Peter project. The selection of music was good though, 120 choices from 60 records, all from the Seventies. I glanced through the cards to see what I might play, squinting in case the green light was trying to get through to me. Nothing. I was on my own.

As I read the cards, I spotted *The Boys Are Back in Town* and thought, 'Maybe I should give that a spin.' It had been good enough to prove I was up to JookBoxFury when I'd suggested it as one of my top jukebox picks back in the Queen Victoria. Rik had said it was a rocker then, and he wasn't wrong – it was the perfect starter in my burst for glory. Then I noticed two more of the choices that had convinced the others to give me a chance: *Midnight Train to Georgia* and *Superstition*. That wasn't a huge surprise because they were pretty standard Seventies jukebox fare. Then I saw *Shine On You Crazy Diamond*. That had to be a sign. I didn't think it had even been released as a single, it was too long to be a single, but there it was, split over the A and B sides of a 45, numbers 163 and 263. The vocal part had to be the B side. It would be a gamble to play without being sure, but everything I'd suggested back in the Queen Victoria was there apart from *Seasons in the Sun*. It was a sign of what to play that was even stronger than the green spirit force had been – very superstitious. I had to follow it. Why didn't they have *Seasons in the Sun*, though? I started to look through the list again.

'It's not a bad machine, this one, for the era at least.' One of the owners had come to stand by the jukebox. He said, 'These Seventies machines are never going to command the prices of the classics, but I think they're going to become more popular with the type of people who like that kitsch thing.'

'Great music,' I said, 'just what I want to play. If it had *Seasons in the Sun* it would be perfect.'

'*Seasons in the Sun?*' he said. 'The old Terry Jacks song? Not a problem. I've got that in my record box – I can get it if you want.'

Sometimes everything falls into place. This time it wasn't about Jook, it was about me making the decisions. I was going to have the chance to prove my original list of jukebox songs in the heat of competition. The owner went off to get the single just as Carole gave us the five minute call until showtime. I tried to keep hanging about by the jukebox, but when it got to two minutes to go Carole insisted that I sat down.

There was only a minute left when the jukebox owner came back holding a single in the air. I got up and went to the jukebox, he got a key out and unlocked the top, then said, 'Shit, the single's still got the middle in. It needs the middle cutting out and I haven't got the tool with me.'

'You mean a dinker?' I said.

'Yeah, but I haven't got one with me.'

I took the record dinker out of my pocket and gave it to him. You know, sometimes…

He quickly cut the middle out of the record, pulled a disc by Bonnie Tyler out of the jukebox and replaced it with *Seasons in the Sun*. 'That's 185,' he said. He closed the lid, turned the key and went to sit down. Carole pointed at me as if to say, 'I'll see you in detention later.' She held her hands up and folded her fingers down one by one in a countdown. She got to zero, a jingle played, and we heard an announcement: 'And now, live from the Duke of Earl's Court Hotel, London, it's the very first final of the JookBoxFury competition. Here to tell you all about it, your host for the evening, Simon 'Pony Boy' Rogers.'

Pony Boy put on his radio voice, like warm condensed milk, slightly curdled. 'Good evening one and all, and have we got an absolutely fabulous trip down memory lane for each and every one of you tonight? Sitting alongside me I have a panel of some very good friends of mine who are all as mad about the crazy world of pop as I am. I've spent the past week travelling up and down the country with these girls and guys, and we've had a wild time and heard some wild wild sounds from past, present, and even future. My old pal Peelie was the one for discovering new bands, but let me be the first on air to tell you to look out for a very exciting new act called the Equally Humdrums. But that's for another time, tonight we're going down memory lane. My chums are going to play you their own selection of songs from five classic jukeboxes that we have borrowed from our good friends at the Jukebox World UK and Retro South Show. Once you've heard the songs, we want all of you out there in radio land to get involved and phone in to vote for whoever you think played the coolest, the craziest, the wildest sounds.'

I even got a decent introduction as the 'Winner of last night's JookBoxFury, so he's one to watch out for tonight.' Pony Boy said, 'Not only do we have some very special guests playing some very special music, we've also got some very special equipment to play it on. I've persuaded the world's leading jukebox expert to come along and give you the lowdown on each of the beautiful original machines that we're using. Warren, you're the Editor of *Jukebox World* magazine, so I know you will be able to give us the inside information on the jukeboxes. It's a bit like being at Blackpool Illuminations with all the multi-coloured lights on show, isn't it?'

Warren said, 'Well, Simon, one thing the jukebox manufacturers always tried to do, was to grab people's attention with their machines. They wanted to make sure the bars and diners would give them space, and the customers would notice them and put coins in the slots.'

'That's fabulous,' Pony Boy said.

It wasn't exactly fabulous, but it did sound like Warren might know what he was talking about. Pony Boy asked him, 'What's this jukebox we've got here? It seems to be made from wood, which some people might find a little surprising?'

Warren said, 'This one is from what we call the Golden Age of the jukeboxes. It's the Throne of Music, manufactured in about 1939 by the Mills Novelty Company which was actually the oldest jukebox company in the business. It plays the old 78 rpm discs but it has still got excellent mechanical reliability even now.'

Pony Boy said, 'We certainly hope it is reliable tonight because our very own professor of pop, the very reliable Dr Annilese Rococco, will be making her selections on the Throne of Music. Let's move on to the second jukebox now, which is going to be used by Rik Peabody. This one has a name that will be more familiar to the listeners, I can see that it is a Wurlitzer, and it looks like the kind of jukebox we used to see in the old films. One or two of us might even have played records on a jukebox like this ourselves.'

'That's right, this is the Wurlitzer Twenty-One Four which they manufactured in about 1957, and as you say, it's a real classic. This one is from the Silver Age of jukes. You can see there's plenty of chrome on it, so it's very silver in appearance.'

'OK,' said Pony Boy. 'The next one looks like it would be from the Silver Age as well, if I'm not very much mistaken.'

'You're absolutely right there, Simon. This is the Rock-Ola Tempo 2 from 1960, which some of the listeners will remember as the jukebox that featured on the old TV show, *Juke Box Jury*.'

'I certainly remember watching David Jacobs on *Juke Box Jury* when I was starting out,' Pony Boy said. 'David Jacobs was a big influence on me in my line of work. I've had the very good fortune to meet the Guv'nor, as I call him, on a number of occasions and he's a consummate professional and a warm and generous…'

Rik interrupted, 'It was a load of crapola on the old Rock-ola, man. *Jook Box Jury* always had some posh bird on, tapping her foot like she needed a fix, and giving it all the, "I rather like this style of record," when they played some piece of sh… some nonsense by

221

Pinky and Perky. Then they'd play a rocker and she'd say, "I'm afraid this isn't quite my cup of tea, I prefer the ballads." *Juke Box Jury* was fu… it was fundamentally flawed in my opinion.'

'That was Rik Peabody, listeners,' Pony Boy said. 'Controversial as ever, that's why we love him isn't it, folks? Talking of *Juke Box Jury*, though, I always enjoyed the way David Jacobs used the "hit" bell and the "miss" hooter, which gave everyone a laugh and was quite ground breaking for the game show format in its time. Anyway, that's enough about *Juke Box Jury*, we're playing JookBoxFury tonight so why don't you tell us about another of these hit jukeboxes, Warren?'

Warren said, 'Before I move on, can I point out another interesting fact about the Rock-Ola, because this particular machine has recently been recovered from a location in the USA. It had been left in a garage, covered in a tarpaulin, and it was untouched for years. You can see that there's a little water damage on the side, but it's a real tribute to the machine that it is still in perfect working order. It's even got the original selection of discs that were on it when it was found, so that's quite a challenge for someone.'

Pony Boy said, 'Well, that someone is going to be our very own first-time JookBoxFury contestant, Rhiannon, so good luck to her with the Rock-Ola. And what's this machine that we have prepared for last night's winner, 'Sugar' Ray?'

'This one is from the mid-Seventies and it's a very different style. It's a Rowe Ami RI-2 Canterbury, and it's the kind of machine a lot of the people at home will have seen in the pubs or clubs until the CD jukeboxes came in. You can see how things developed from the old 78 rpm machine we looked at first.'

Pony Boy said, 'We must hurry along to get the competition underway, but we've just got time for you to tell us a little about the final machine here. We won't be using it in the competition tonight, but it's an interesting one all the same.'

'That's right,' Warren said, 'this one isn't really for the purists, but it's the absolute latest in Jukebox technology. It's called the Wurlitzer One More Time, it's a replica of the original Wurlitzer Ten-Fifteen, which is probably the most recognizable of all the jukes, but it plays CDs and it also has a new feature which I must show you.' Warren pulled at a small metal rectangle on the front of the jukebox and a flat drawer slid out. 'You've got a docking station for your i-Pod there, so not only have you got a machine that looks like it was made in the latter part of the Golden Age, but it plays two and a half thousand songs on CD, or ten thousand from your digital music player.'

Pony Boy was impressed, 'That's a fabulous innovation. That really has to be the best of the bunch, I could imagine one of those chez Rogers. But the big test tonight is not how you play, but what you play. It's time for the big final – it's Jook-Box-Furyyyy!'

Pony Boy gave a quick review of how the competition worked, told the listeners about phoning in to register votes for their favourite jukebox picker and said, 'The contestants will be playing their choices in age order – oldest first. That's no offence to the very lovely Dr Rococco, it's the age of the jukeboxes I'm talking about, silly. The Mills Throne of Music is the oldest jukebox machine here so, Dr Roc, will you make your selections please? When they've finished playing, perhaps you'll tell us why you chose those particular songs. Ladies and gentlemen, Dr Annilese Rococco, in all her majesty, on the Throne of Music.'

Carole led the audience in a round of applause and Dr Roc went to make her choices – what little choice there was from twenty 78s. She was going to be playing a quarter of all the tracks available. Pony Boy watched as Dr Roc picked her first disc. He announced, 'Dr Rococco's first choice is by the lady with the big big voice, we're going to hear Bessie Smith performing *Nobody Knows You When You're Down and Out*.'

The Throne of Music became a throne of hissing and crackling as the needle started to play the 78. The music came in with a mournful horn playing a late night speakeasy intro for troubled souls. Bessie Smith sang the blues of someone who'd been hit by the depression and kept on falling: 'I done fell so low, nobody wants me round their door.' The horn solo in the middle of the song was sad, like the last night of the good times. Like JookBoxFury coming to an end.

Dr Roc's second track was the Carter Family's *The Wildwood Flower*, a simple, old timey country song from the days before country music became Country Music. The sound quality wasn't great, but hearing the old songs play through the crackles was mesmerizing, like listening to a different way of life.

Pony Boy introduced the next track, 'Quite a change of mood with this one. I'm not sure whether the younger listeners will recognize it, but listen to the words carefully because this is a very entertaining story. We're going to hear the old Stanley Holloway monologue *Albert and the Lion*.'

Dr Roc had pulled one out of left field there – if Equally Humdrum did a version of *Albert and the Lion* they'd really be onto something. Stanley Holloway started telling the tale in a thick Lancashire accent, 'At a famous seaside resort called Blackpool, that's noted for fresh air and fun…' He went on to tell how Albert, with his 'stick with the 'orses 'ead 'andle', gets swallowed by a Lion. The monologue was getting to the part where the insurance man goes to call on Albert's Ma and Pa, when Stanley stopped off in the middle of his narration and said, 'And that's not all – I'll finish story on t'other side.' A small 'Aaah' rippled round the audience as the disc crackled to an end.

You see, that's the drawback with your Throne of Music – you're not going to get that with an i-Pod docked into a Wurlitzer CD player.

Pony Boy had been caught out by the sudden ending of *Albert and the Lion* and the next record started before he could announce it. Not that there was any need for an announcement. The song kicked in with a couple of drum snaps and, 'One two three o'clock, four o'clock rock…' After hearing the earlier songs, *Rock Around the Clock* blasted out of the Throne of Music like an impatient teenager looking for a new place to go. From the late 1920s to 1954 – from the birth of popular music to the birth of rock 'n' roll, all on 78. That was about the same amount of time as there had been between the Sex Pistols in 1976 and Pop Idol in the 2000s. The twenty-two years from 1954 to 1976 had been incredible when you thought about it. Maybe Dr Roc was right, it was time to call it a day for pop music.

As the track finished, Pony Boy said, 'Of course that one didn't need any introduction. That was one of my all time favourites, but for anyone who has been sitting on a comet themselves since the 1950s, that was Bill Haley and His Comets with *Rock Around the Clock*. Let's hear Dr Rococco's final selection now, which is going to be…,' he looked at the jukebox, 'number nineteen on the selector, it's more rocking and rolling with Kay Starr's *Rock and Roll Waltz*.'

After Bill Haley's western swing rock 'n' roll, Kay Starr swapped the 'n' in rock 'n' roll to 'and' – so much nicer – to give a twinkle-toed, waltz-time treatment about, 'Mum dancing with dad to my record machine.' She sang, 'It's old but it's new,' but it sounded like a record company's last gasp attempt to cash in on the new thing without anyone getting hurt. It was a fitting finale for the Throne of Music. Times had changed.

As *Rock and Roll Waltz* ended, Pony Boy said, 'What a fantastic selection of music – it may have been old-time, but that certainly didn't stop it from being good time. Dr Roc, what made you choose those particular pieces?'

Dr Roc said, 'I wanted to capture the spirit of this lovely old machine. There are another fifteen marvellous records that I could have chosen, but I picked the ones which meant something to me. They weren't all songs of course. My father used to recite *Albert and the Lion* to us as his party piece at Christmas, so I couldn't resist hearing that one again. I also tried to give a feel for the range of music from the early days of recording, and wasn't it super to hear *Rock Around the Clock* in the way people might have heard it for the first time back in the fifties?'

'It most certainly was,' Pony Boy said. He gave out the number for listeners to ring in and vote for Dr Roc.

Rik's green Wurlitzer was the second oldest machine. His selections were all late-Fifties and early-Sixties coffee bar classics. His first choice was *Be Bop a Lula*, greasy, lock-up-your-daughters, bad boy rock 'n' roll with Gene Vincent panting lasciviously and calling, 'Let's rock,' before the stinging guitar break. He followed that with *C'Mon Everybody*, primal teen rock. Who cares? C'mon. These teenagers are out of control.

It wasn't clear whether Rik was working in a clever theme linking the songs together. He followed Gene Vincent and Eddie Cochran (in a car accident together), with three songs produced by Joe Meek, who also produced *Just Like Eddie,* which was about Eddie Cochran. It was possibly a little too contrived to win the listeners over, but the songs were brilliant. He played *Telstar*, space travel powered by early cosmic synth and a galactic coffee bar twang, accompanied by bleeps and explosions. Then The Honeycombs' Cuban-heeled stomp, *Have I the Right?* and finished with Helen Shapiro's *Walking Back to Happiness*. Girl group dream-pop done solo with a 'whup by – oh yeay-yeah.' In the same way that Dr Roc's selections were perfect for the Throne of Music, Rik's choices shone from the chrome and neon of the Wurlitzer as if they were part of the machine itself. The Wurlitzer was made to rock – and rock made it.

When the songs had finished Pony Boy said, 'I don't know about you at home, but those tracks had us bopping is the aisles here at JookBoxFury central.'

That was a lie. No-one had been bopping in the aisles at all, although there was plenty of foot-tapping and head nodding going on. Pony Boy asked Rik why he had made those selections.

Rik said, 'Those were the songs we used to listen to, man. You've heard this before, but my first band used to play the coffee bars, and the first place we played had a jukebox exactly the same as this one. So I've played the songs that took me right back to those days, you know. I've always been a rocker so I had to play Vincent and Cochran. They were like gods to me, showed me how to do it. The other three were all British groups. Hearing those the first time around made me realize that I could do it too. *Telstar*: that track is amazing, man. That was made by a guy in London and it went to number one in the States even before the Fab Four did it. Joe Meek with the Tornados was the first to take it back to the Americans. That was a breakthrough, man. It made me think about where we could go with it. *Have I the Right?* by the Honeycombs, some people might think that the Guitar Man is going soft by playing that, but you look back and they were rocking. They had a redhead playing the drums, a girl drummer. Back in the early Sixties that was stunning, man. We were on a bill with the Honeycombs a few times and when I saw them I thought, "Wow, that is far fu… far further out. And *Walking Back to Happiness*, the chicks used to play that one on the old Wurlitzer. Helen Shapiro, she was only a kid, but she sings like a woman – just hearing it again is like walking back to happiness. Those were the ones that did it for me, man.'

Pony Boy gave the phone number to vote for Rik and then called Rhia up to the *Juke Box Jury* Rock-Ola, with its weird selection of country and disco. I gave her the thumbs-up as she went by because, after what I'd seen, she didn't have much more to choose from than Dr Roc had available. A couple of tracks that stood out when I'd looked at the list were *Convoy*, the country song about being a trucker with a CB radio – 'ten four, good buddy' – and *Disco Duck*, which was about a duck that liked going to discos. There was a possible water fowl connection to be made between *Convoy*'s 'Breaker one-nine, this here's the rubber duck,' and the Disco Duck itself, but it didn't seem likely to be a vote winner, not unless London Live had a large proportion of ducks amongst their listeners. If you ever play JookBoxFury, try to make sure you're not stuck with a jukebox formerly belonging to habitués of some sort of hillbilly Studio 54 for trucking ducks.

Rhia didn't look phased by the situation. In fact, she looked surprisingly confident for a first-time JookBoxFury contender. She gave me a thumbs-up back and went to make her selections. Her first song was *Stand By Your Man*, Tammy Wynette. While it played I imagined a faded truck stop queen, perched on a bar stool in an empty roadhouse, putting *Stand By Your Man* on the jukebox. She drowns her sorrows as she listens to the message about staying true to her man, until Tammy drops the sob in her voice for a moment and gives a kick in the teeth putdown when she sings, 'After all, he's just a man.' Rhia's next track was some honky tonkin' by that man himself, Tammy's part-time husband, George Jones, singing *Swingin' Doors,* about having to leave his wife and live in a bar. While the track played, I had the sense of a big rig pulling up outside the roadhouse. The driver climbs down from his cab and ambles into the bar for a cold one while he listens to George sing, 'I've got swingin' doors, a jukebox and a barstool… I'm always here at home 'til closing time.'

Rhia's third selection was Patsy Cline's *Crazy*. Nashville smooth, but aching. The mood in the roadhouse mellows – love's crazy, life's crazy – the trucker talks to the woman, they dance. Maybe life's not so crazy after all.

After creating that mood, Rhia slammed us in to the heart of New York City. Stepping out of a yellow cab and strutting into the best disco in town, keeping time to a disco beat, to hear Melba Moore yelling an unrestrained, 'This is it! This time I know it's the real thing…' It was a feel-good record, and I felt even better when Rhia looked over at me and winked. I waved back to her.

Rhia's final track was Van McCoy's disco dance craze hit, *The Hustle*. The song's repetitive flute melody hit a groove, and when the track got to the spoken part that insists: 'DO THE HUSTLE: do the hustle… do it,' Rhia stood in front of the jukebox, gave a Travolta-esque sleeve adjustment, and hipstered into the hustle. It was basically walking backwards and forwards and sideways, but she threw in some spinning arms and some nice shoulder work. She really had got all the moves off and was getting into some prime *Saturday Night Fever* hustle action. Rhia looked good on the dance floor – she was a mover. The jukebox owners on the front row were loving it, they were possibly into it a bit too much, and I felt like going over to them and saying, 'It's not Pan's People you know, fellers.' Staying in time with the music, Rhia walked towards the audience, she got hold of Siobahn and Luke's sister's hands and said, 'Come and do this dance with me.' The girls were still holding their Bobbly Wobblers, they stood either side of Rhia in front of the jukebox and watched her feet, concentrating hard on doing the steps. They loved it, and when the song finished they jumped up and down and waved their Bobbly Wobblers in the air.

Pony Boy said, 'Well, you missed that at home, but we had a fantastic display of The Hustle here by Rhia and her two very special assistants. He knelt down to the girls and said, 'And what are your names?' They said, 'Siobahn,' and 'Lucy.' Pony Boy's memory was obviously failing him because he asked them, 'And what are these fun characters you're both holding?'

Lucy said, 'They're Wobbly Bobblers. We bought them off the lady.'

Pony Boy said, 'They're actually called Bobbly Wobblers, as I'm sure many of the listeners will recall, and I think you've been very lucky for your mummy and daddy to buy you such a special treat.'

'Luke's got one as well,' Lucy said.

'I got Luke one too,' Siobahn said.

'Lucky Luke,' Pony Boy said. 'I could spend all day talking about the good times the Bobbly Wobblers have given me, and they're not finished yet, but we must move on. Thanks, girls, for that lovely dancing. Now you two go and sit down because we're going to listen to some more music, and it's going to be played on the 1970s Rowe Ami jukebox by 'Sugar' Ray Mitchell.

Shine on You crazy Diamond

I don't know whether you can really fully prepare yourself for a moment like the JookBoxFury final. If I'd thought about it, I'd have felt like I was taking the deciding penalty in a World Cup semi-final shoot out, but I didn't think about it. I didn't think about how much I wanted to win, or how much it meant to me just being there. A calmness came over me. As I stepped up to the Rowe Ami, I knew what I had to do. Everything had fallen into place. It was serendipity. All I had to do was play the five songs that I'd suggested in The Queen Victoria. The five songs that persuaded them to give me a chance on JookBoxFury in the first place. I pressed the buttons: *The Boys are Back in Town*, *Midnight Train to Georgia*, *Superstition*, *Shine on You Crazy Diamond* and… shit – what number was *Seasons in the Sun*? What number did he say it was? There was an eight in it, eighty-something? It was a Bonnie Tyler song he'd taken out, so it had to be the same number as that. I had a quick look and found it – *Lost in France*, Bonnie Tyler. I punched in the numbers. Now we'd see. That was a jukebox selection that was my own pure inspiration. It was jukebox perfection. There was no trying to impress cowboy-booted Lonnie Donegan obsessives, hen parties, morris dancers, journalists or Equally Humdrum fans. It was time to stand up and be counted, and I was ready.

Pony Boy introduced the first track as, 'A great guitar-led rock song from the sadly departed Mr Phillip Lynott.' *The Boys are Back in Town* revved into action with the spirit of a couple of bikers pulling up outside the bar and grill on a warm summer's evening before swaggering inside – then the door of the Countess Centre opened and Babs burst in shouting a breezy, 'I'm here.' She was pulling her large pink wheely suitcase behind her and had obviously forgotten about the live radio broadcast because she said, 'Was that a bloody awful journey or was that a bloody awful journey? Don't tell me I'm late because I know, but when I got in the taxi at Stansted I heard someone on the radio talking about JookBoxFury and I thought, "I owe it to the audience to go and play some fun music instead of The Hairy Buttholes or whatever ear-aching stuff you lot are coming up with." So I got the taxi driver to come straight here.'

Pony Boy tried to cover the interruption by announcing, 'We've got an absolutely super special surprise guest for you – Babs Golightly has joined us here on JookBoxFury.'

Babs still hadn't clicked about the broadcast. 'I think they can see that I've joined you here on JookBoxFury, you fool.' She waved to the audience who applauded warmly. Warren shouted, 'Come on, Babs.'

Babs looked in Warren's direction and said, 'What's the perv doing here?'

Pony Boy was slicing his hands across each other and mouthing, 'Cut,' to Carole.

Babs kept going, 'I thought I made it quite clear when the perv gave me that thong to wear that I wasn't having anything to do with the little grease ball. Do you think I'm…?'

Pony Boy said, 'Bad news listeners, I've just spilled my coffee on one of the jukeboxes so we're going to have to take a short break while we sort that out. Let's go back to the studio for a weather update.'

Carole flicked a switch on her sound desk and gave an 'OK' sign to Pony Boy.

Babs said, 'I'll have a coffee if there's one going – my day has been an absolute nightmare.'

Pony Boy almost lost his temper. 'We're on air. That's why you heard them talking about it on the radio – this is going out live. So we don't want to hear about what sort of a day you've had.'

Babs said, 'Oh.'

'I suppose that now you've made a belated effort to get yourself here, you can play songs on the CD Wurlitzer at the end there. Make them short and we'll cut some of the wrap-up. Just remember, if you can, that we're going out live. We're back on in a few seconds, so let's not hear any more about what sort of day you've had. I'd like to see a little more professionalism from a fellow presenter if that's possible – I can tell you that David Jacobs would never have behaved like that.'

Babs said, 'I'm sorry, I didn't realize. I was just…'

'We're back on after this,' Carole said.

We heard the end of a weather bulletin about light winds coming from the North, then Pony Boy was on. 'I'm sure those winds won't be anything like the whirlwind of fun that is Babs Golightly. The great news for all the Babs fans out there is that we've welcomed that crazy lady onto the JookBoxFury panel and she'll be making the final selections of the competition. Before that, let's finish listening to 'Sugar' Ray Mitchell's selections. I'm sure you'll recognize this one, it's *Midnight Train to Georgia*.'

Gladys Knight was signing about 'Going back to find – a simpler place and time,' and *Midnight Train to Georgia* had nearly finished. For all I knew, Babs could have planned the whole thing: Parker was probably a stooge, the nouvelle bric(01)age might not even exist. It was like The Queen Victoria all over again. How can anyone seriously compete in the JookBoxFury final when someone bursts into the room complaining about their journey and then there's a weather announcement over most of your first two songs? Diabolical.

Superstition played, and the funky synthesized keyboard pumped out of the Rowe Ami's big speaker – it sounded great. Maybe the listeners had heard enough of the other songs to get a feel for them and everything wasn't lost. When *Shine on You Crazy Diamond* came on, there were some very appreciative glances from the jukebox owners in the audience and as the emotion of the song started to build I thought that maybe, just maybe, it might be possible to pull things round. Then I had a nasty thought – *Seasons in the Sun* was on next and I'd promised Babs that I wouldn't play it again. How could I have known that she was going to turn up out of the blue? When she heard *Seasons in the Sun*, all of the difficult relationship rebuilding process that had gone on over the past few days would be destroyed. I had to explain. I went to Carole and gestured for her to give me a pen and a piece of paper, then I quickly wrote a note saying, 'Sorry about playing *Seasons in the Sun*, I didn't realize you were coming back, Ray.' I folded the note in half and gave it to Babs. She read it and gave me a quizzical look. Then she folded the note back up, tore it in half, put the two pieces together, tore them in half, threw the pieces over her shoulder and mouthed, 'Loser,' at me.

I was going to write another note to give her a bit more background, but as Roger Waters pleaded for the crazy diamond to shine, the final guitar notes faded and Pony Boy said, 'That was a piece of what we used to call progressive rock from the Pink Floyd. Now we're going to hear the progressive 'Sugar' Ray Mitchell's last song, which is…' he looked at the jukebox and said, 'It's good to hear this one again, it's the Bonnie Tyler classic *Lost in France*.'

I waved my hands at Pony Boy and shook my head. I was silently shouting, '*Seasons in the Sun*,' at him, but he just held his hands out in a 'What?' gesture. The record started playing with an acoustic strum that was the same tune as the intro to *Then He Kissed Me*. I didn't remember it sounding like that. Then, instead of Terry Jacks singing, 'Good bye to you my trusted friend,' I heard, 'I was lost in France, in the fields the birds were singing…'

What? It was Bonnie Tyler's *Lost in France*. I held my hands out in a 'What?' gesture, but it didn't make any difference. *Lost in France* was playing as my last selection in the JookBoxFury final. It was like taking a penalty in a World Cup final shoot out and putting it into the top row of the stands. The shame. It was all slipping away. I had to try and do something to give myself a chance, but I'd only got a couple of minutes to turn *Lost in France* into something special. What could you do to music to make it better? It was obvious – dancing. Babs had won in The Queen Victoria when she'd got everyone dancing, things took off in No More Heroes when we started dancing, Rhia had won the audience over earlier with her Hustle. So that was the secret. I'd do something like that. The girls at the youth club used to do a thing called The Slosh – a kind of pop music line dance routine – and the lads used to join in sometimes for a laugh. I could do The Slosh.

I took to the floor in front of the jukebox. I waited for the music to get to the right place and then I started: to the left, two, three, kick; right, two, three, kick; left, two, three, kick – and then it was the tricky bit, there was a lot more to it than the Hustle – right, two, three, slap the heel of the left leg with the right hand, pivot to face sideways, slap the right knee, clap under the left leg, and off again with the left, two, three, kick. The moves came straight back, but the music wasn't fast enough – *Lost in France* just wasn't a suitable Slosh tune. The only consolation was that *Seasons in the Sun* wouldn't have been any better. It was so slow that I felt like I was dancing at a deep sea diver's ball. I looked over at the panel and Babs was slowly shaking her head, but Rik gave me a kind of, 'Good on you, man,' clenched fist salute and Rhia smiled at me. Maybe it wasn't lost. I just needed to give it a bit extra… I went to Lucy and Siobahn and said, 'Do you want to come and do some more dancing?' but they gripped their Bobbly Wobblers, pushed themselves back into their chairs and silently shook their heads. That rejection when you ask girls to dance and they say, 'No,' is hard to handle. I went back to the floor and gave The Slosh a couple more turns, but my heart wasn't in it.

Lost in France finished and Pony Boy said, 'That was the Swansea lassie herself, Bonnie Tyler there, with a former Record of the Week of mine from way way back. Excellent selection, Ray.'

That said it all. Pony Boy didn't even mention my effort on the dance floor and he actually liked *Lost in France*. It looked like it was all over and my contentious victory in No More Heroes was going to be my only JookBoxFury success. I walked back to my seat as Pony Boy announced Babs. She shook her head at me as we passed.

It was possible that Babs' journey had taken its toll on her, maybe she was jet-lagged. She had two and a half thousand selections available from the CDs on the Wurlitzer One More Time, and she chose to play Cyndi Lauper's *Girls Just Wanna Have Fun*. It worked for Lucy and Siobahn, though, because they were dancing the Bobbly Wobblers about in a routine that wasn't dissimilar to The Slosh. Hypocrites.

Babs followed *Girls Just Wanna Have Fun* with Black Box's sampled pop house smash *Ride on Time*, then played Gina G's *Ooh*

Ahh… Just a Little Bit. It was chirpily upbeat and I had a nasty feeling that she might have got the measure of the audience once again. For her next track, she bounced gently back to the Eighties with Culture Club's *Do You Really Want to Hurt Me*, and finished off with another oldie: *I'm Not in Love*. I couldn't believe it. I'd given her a note to apologize for playing *Seasons in the Sun*, and then I'd played *Lost in France* anyway, and Babs had gone and played *I'm Not in Love* for the second time in the competition without a word, not even a doodle.

I could have walked out there and then, just like I had back in the bus station, but I stayed. Things were different. For one, we were live on air, which we hadn't been at the bus station. I stayed, and had to listen to *I'm Not in Love* the whole way through. There was a section in the middle of the song that I'd never noticed before, where a woman's voice whispers, 'Be quiet, big boys don't cry, big boys don't cry…' Was Babs referring back to what she said about *Big Girls Don't Cry*?

Before I'd worked it out, Babs' selections finished playing and Pony Boy said, 'You've just heard five fabulous pop songs from the Seventies to the Noughties with the naughty lady herself – Babs Golightly.' There wasn't time for Babs to explain her choices so Pony Boy gave the numbers to call in and vote for the winner, then he told the listeners that he'd be back with the result after the news. Carole signalled that we were off air.

I turned to Rhia and said, 'Well done, you were great – I think you're going to win it.'

Rhia said, 'I think anyone could win it, everything was great, although *Lost in France* made me smile.'

'There's no need for that,' I said.

'No really, it's not the kind of song you hear very often but it reminds me of going on holiday to France with my family…'

'And you got lost?' I said.

'No, my dad made a tape for the car that had *Lost in France* on it. Still, it's probably not to everyone's taste, it's not exactly got a lot of cred so it was a fairly brave choice, but you know what you're doing.'

I was saying, 'Well, it wasn't so much a choice as a…' when the owner of my jukebox came and stood in front of me.

'That was a lot of fuss about nothing,' he said. 'Why didn't you play it?'

'I meant to play it. As far as I'm concerned, I did play it. I couldn't remember the number but I selected the Bonnie Tyler single. It was Bonnie Tyler you replaced it with, wasn't it?'

'That's right, Bonnie Tyler, 185, *It's a Heartache.*'

I said, 'Oh.'

He said, 'Ahh. You know what you've done, don't you? You know Bonnie Tyler had more than one hit?'

I nodded.

He said, 'I can't believe I changed the record for you and you didn't even play it.'

'Didn't even play what?' Rhia asked.

'*Seasons in the Sun,*' the jukebox owner said. 'I put it on the Rowe Ami specially for this guy, and then he didn't even play it.'

I took the record dinker out of my pocket and put it on the table. 'That was my lucky record dinker, but you can have it – I don't want it.'

Rhia said, 'Don't get too dramatic about it. I mean, *Seasons in the Sun*, *Lost in France*, there's not too much to choose between them, to be honest – it's not as if you meant to play a Stiff Records B side or anything like that. I like *Lost in France* because it reminds me of our holidays, but I wouldn't pretend it was an all time classic. The same goes for *Seasons in the Sun*, so I shouldn't lose any sleep over it.'

The jukebox owner said to Rhia, 'Loved your *Do the Hustle* by the way, pet. The only problem with it was giving the dancing monkey here ideas.' With that cruel jibe he went over to the Rowe Ami and started to change the records back.

Rhia said to Babs, 'It's great that you made it here for the final, Babs. What made you change your mind?'

Babs said, 'It's a long story. I'll tell you later, but Parker's a wanker. Talking of which, what were you playing at, Ray? You promise not to play *Seasons in the Sun* ever again, then you give me a note apologizing for playing it, but you don't play it anyway. What's that all about? If it was anyone else I'd say the Jook had got to you, but you've always been like that. What are you playing at?'

'It's a long story,' I said. 'I'll tell you later.'

'It better be as good as mine,' Babs said, 'and if you haven't got any Elvis impersonators in it, you're going to be struggling.'

Carole called Pony Boy over to her and seemed to be giving him some instructions.

'The results must be in,' I said to Rhia. 'I can't say I'm looking forward to this.'

'I am,' Rhia said.

Carole did her countdown again and we were on air. Pony Boy gave the listeners a warm welcome back. 'We've heard some absolutely incredible pieces from a rendition of *Albert and the Lion* to the sultry sounds of Bonnie Tyler's magnificent *Lost in France*, and I know you're all on the edge of your seats waiting to hear who the winner is. Well, we're going to keep the tension going just a little bit longer. We've taken almost five times as many calls as we expected so it's going to take a couple more minutes to tot up the final scores.'

Oh, come on, put us out of our misery.

Pony Boy said, 'While we're waiting I'm going to bring our jukebox expert back to tell us how he thought the jukeboxes themselves performed. 'Warren, any surprises from the machines this evening?'

Warren said, 'Well, Simon, they did the job they were made to do. To see the Mills Throne of Music still playing those 78s over sixty years after it was built was a real treat. I wonder if some of the mp3 players that are so popular now will still be working in sixty years' time?'

'I wouldn't want to try and put the Throne of Music in my pocket when I go out for a jog, though,' Pony Boy quipped. When he stopped laughing he said, 'So, hearing the Throne of Music was the big highlight for you, was it?'

Warren said, 'The biggest highlight for me was when Babs arrived. I felt that she really lit up the stage with her presence and I'd like to give her a small gift as a gesture of my appreciation, and as an apology for a slight misunderstanding that occurred earlier this week.'

Warren picked up a Matalan carrier bag and it looked like he was going to have another go with the lingerie. Pony Boy looked towards Babs, who was very firmly shaking her head. He said, 'Let me stop you there, Warren, because I think we might have got the results in.' Pony Boy looked towards Carole but she was shaking her head as well. The only positive vibes Pony Boy was getting were from Warren so he told him, 'Well, let's hope it's a gift that the lady is going to appreciate?'

Warren said he'd put a lot of thought into choosing it, and then pulled a frumpy grey business suit out of his carrier bag. He took it to Babs, who refused to accept the gift, so Warren laid the suit on the table in front of her. Babs looked away and said, 'That is even more insulting than the undies.'

'Carole handed a piece of paper to Pony Boy who said, 'I have just received an important update on the JookBoxFury scores and it seems that we've had a slight technical hitch. The gentleman who has been compiling the results of the telephone vote has spilled a cup of coffee on his computer keyboard and it's all gone up in smoke… So, tonight at the JookBoxFury final I am very pleased to announce that everyone is a winner. Well done to all of our fabulous contestants. Until the next JookBoxFury final, whenever that may be, it's good night from me, Pony Boy Rogers, and good night from everyone at JookBoxFury.'

Everyone was a winner? Where was the satisfaction in that?

Carole came over and said, 'Great job, Simon, and great work everybody. Thanks for that, good show. Shame about the results, but I think you got round it like the professional that you are, Simon.'

Pony Boy looked pleased with himself, but it wasn't much consolation as far as I was concerned. How could there not be a result?

I asked Pony Boy, 'Was that business about the coffee being spilled on the computer keyboard another excuse?'

'Not at all,' Pony Boy said.

'It was a latte,' Carole explained, 'so there was nothing he could do about it.'

'But it was the final. We need to be judged.'

Rhia said. 'I quite like the idea of all the listeners choosing their own winner. In a way it's true, everybody did win because somebody somewhere must have liked each of the different choices – isn't that the important thing?'

'Yeah, but… but who got the most votes? Maybe we could ask someone here to judge, just for our own satisfaction.'

Pony Boy said, 'That's not a bad idea. I'll go and ask Warren.'

Babs told him, 'I'm not having that little perv judging me. Why don't you do it, Pony Boy? You are the compère after all.'

Pony Boy said, 'And because of that I think it's important to maintain impartiality at all times. That's absolutely essential for the integrity of the host/competitor relationship. What you could do though, as it's the last event, is vote for each other.'

'Lovely idea,' Dr Roc said. 'I'll vote for Babs. Music played in the real spirit of young women having fun.'

'I'll vote for Rhia then,' I said. 'She made the best of a very poor selection of music on her jukebox.'

Rhia thanked me, and then cast her vote for Dr Rococco, 'Because she had even less to choose from, and I enjoyed hearing the old 78s.'

Rik said, 'I'm voting for myself – the only rocker on the fucking block.'

'Well, if you can vote for yourself,' Babs said, 'I'm voting for me too.'

Pony Boy raised his hands in the air as if to call a halt. 'There we have it then. Two votes for Babs, one each to Dr Roc, Rik and Rhia, and none for you I'm afraid, Ray – although if it's of any consolation, had I been voting, *Lost in France* would have swung it in your favour – so Babs is the winner.'

Babs said, 'Where's my trophy? Oh, actually, I've got a trophy here.' She reached into her bag and pulled out a JookBoxFury winner's cup. 'This is for you, Ray. Parker didn't want it… well, he didn't notice me taking it.'

I walked away from the JookBoxFury final with a trophy in my hands, a symbol of what might have been.

Are You Lonesome Tonight?

We went to watch the tribute bands in the Viscount Bar. Pony Boy said he had to catch up with Laurence but he'd see us later on. As we got near the bar, I could hear a slow and bluesy version of *Earth Mother, Moon Lover* playing. It was less crazed than the original, but it was undoubtedly *Earth Mother, Moon Lover*. The poster on the door said, 'Eddie Brutus with the Trout Replicas.'

While we watched the band, I asked Rik, 'Is it a Brutus Trout tribute?'

Rik said, 'There's no sign of Nathan Trout, and I don't know who the fuck the band are, but that's Eddie at the front alright. Where's his fucking hair gone?'

Eddie Brutus had changed completely from the way he looked in Brutus Trout. Instead of the unkempt flowing locks, his head was as smooth as a billiard ball, and the sandals, beads, scarves and kaftan had been replaced by black shoes, black trousers and a black shirt which was wet with sweat and clinging to his chest. The music was stripped down to basics, too. Eddie was still playing his trademark simultaneous rhythm and lead guitar, but he was backed only by as bassist and a drummer whose combined ages must have been less than his. Instead of the psychedelic wig out at the end of *Earth Mother, Moon Lover*, Eddie sped the song up with some chunky rhythm playing that was solid enough to build a house on. He was laying the foundations down brick by brick. Then he went into a jittery James Brown slide across the front of the stage, chopping the chords faster and faster to machine gun the audience with his guitar.

He swung the guitar behind his head and ripped out a solo, as if to prove the rumour that he'd taught Hendrix a trick or two. He swung the guitar back and counted with the neck – one, two, three, four – and the band dropped back into the slow version of the song, with Eddie playing licks that perfectly matched Rik's howling on the original. The song finished. Eddie kissed his guitar and waved to the audience as he left the stage.

'That was brilliant,' I said to Rik.

'Not bad,' Rik said. 'I liked him better when he didn't look like a fucking hard boiled egg. I don't like to see a guy suffering like that. I'm going backstage to help him out with the rider and see if they've still got the same dressing room action that they used to have.'

'I wouldn't mind meeting Eddie Brutus.'

'No can do, man. I can't risk putting you in that situation – it's not for the faint-hearted.'

Rik went looking for Eddie so I went to sit with Rhia, Babs and Dr Roc. Rhia asked Babs why she hadn't stayed in Glasgow to help Parker out with his video.

Babs said, 'Don't talk to me about Parker… What happened was, I went up to No More Heroes with Nye to meet the rest of Equally Humdrum and some of the other bands in that new brick scene that Nye was going on about. There were some friends of Parker's there who had a band called Streeteddy and they played Nye a couple of tracks and he got so excited I thought we might have to call an ambulance – or an escort service. He thought they were the best thing ever and he completely forgot about Equally Humdrum.

'I made a few suggestions to Parker about how we could do the video for *Heartbeat Drumbeat* and he said he wanted Little Minnie in it. Now, I'll be honest with you, that came as a bit of a surprise to me, because I was assuming that if I was helping him out, then I'd be in the video. Parker said it had to be Little Minnie because that's who he'd written the song for, and it only really meant anything when it was to the rhythm of her heartbeat… What a load of bollocks. I felt as though I'd been used, you know, the way he was going on when he sang it last night. So I told him he could get his own video made and I got the hotel to book me on the next flight out of Glasgow.

'I got a taxi out to the airport, but it was about fifty miles away, it wasn't even in Glasgow. When I got there I was really late for the check-in and I had to run to the departure gate. I stopped to take my shoes off so I could run better, when an Elvis impersonator came up and asked me if I'd sign a petition about changing the name of the airport to Elvis Presley International. I told him he could call it what he liked, but something Scottish might be a bit more appropriate. I said I didn't have time to discuss it though because I was running for a flight. The next thing I knew, about twenty more fat old Elvises crowded round me and they all got into that Elvis pose with their legs apart and one hand in the air. They shrugged their shoulders and they started singing *Are You Lonesome Tonight?* I said, "You'll be bloody lonesome tonight if you don't get out of my way, I've got a plane to catch." One of the Elvises said, "You seemed to change, you acted strange, and why I never knew." I said, "Don't worry, Elvis, you'll know all about it if I miss this flight," and I pulled him out of the way with his cape. A big handful of sequins and jewels came off in my hand, it was really tacky. The Elvis shouted at me, "That's the kind of lack of respect for the King that has brought so much conflict in the world today."

'I only just made the flight. They were shutting the doors as I was running up the steps. Elvis impersonators at the airport, I've never seen that before. Just look out for them, because they're probably hanging around all the airports now.'

'It must have been Prestwick Airport,' I said. 'It's the only place where Elvis ever set foot on British soil. He stopped off there when he was going back to America after being in the army. It must have been to do with that.'

Babs said, 'He probably stopped off to give a word of encouragement to all the impersonators.'

Rik came back. 'Impersonators? Fucking imposters. You don't need bloody impersonators when you've got the real deal right in front of you. You know the Guitar Man won't let you down when you want to rock. I'll tell you someone who might, though. Eddie Brutus has changed. I just saw him backstage and it was like a fucking prayer meeting back there. Eddie was doing a sudoku and

242

eating a bowl of Coco Pops. It was good to see the old bastard, but I told him he had to sort himself out, take a break from his number puzzle and get himself out here for a Tartan Hammer.'

A few minutes later a man in black wandered over and slapped Rik on the back. Eddie Brutus. Rik introduced him to all of us. Unbelieveable, I was in a conversational group with Eddie Brutus and Rik Peabody. I said to Eddie, '*Earth Mother, Moon Lover* was fantastic – it's a shame you didn't know Rik was here or you could have got him up on stage for the howling.'

Eddie said, 'Well, we've mainly cut out the howling now, man. I was in a dark place when we recorded that track and the howling was where I was at in my head, you know. Since then I've come to understand the beauty of the Earth Mother more, you know, man. It's not about howling, it's about loving. The other thing is, and not a lot of people know this, Rik never performed *Earth Mother, Moon Lover* with us live, because it isn't actually him on the record. We got him in to do the howling because of *Violence is Golden*, but when it came to his bit, he was so out of it that he could only mumble – he couldn't howl to save his life. We mic'd him up as best we could, but it just wasn't happening – the mumbling wasn't giving us the effect we wanted. We ended up getting a farm lad who was in the local male voice choir to do it. You listen, you can tell the power in his voice, that's choir training for you right there. While the boy was howling away at the microphone, there was this one chick started doing a crazy snake dance kind of thing in the studio, kind of writhing around and crawling towards him, flicking her tongue out and licking her lips…'

Rik said, 'Don't believe a word Eddie Brutus tells you. His mind's so fucking fried I'm surprised it hasn't been served up for breakfast.'

'Look who's talking,' Eddie said. 'Anyway, I can't hang around, Rik man, I've got to get off and do my thing.'

There was a lot of back slapping between the two of them, 'Great to see you, man,' 'You don't look a day over ninety,' 'You're only as old as the woman you feel.' They shook hands, hugged, said they'd have to get together in the studio some time, and Eddie went off to pack up his gear, or carry on with his sudoku.

The next band came on and it was The Beatles. It sounded like The Beatles, although there wasn't much screaming. Rik said, 'That's just four guys in Beatle jackets – that Macca isn't even a fucking lefty. I'm going to go and have a scout around backstage to see whether they've got a Cynthia with them.'

The Beatles tribute band were playing songs that The Beatles had never played live themselves. They were good, but it was difficult to get excited about them. If you closed your eyes, they did sound like The Beatles. If you squinted at them, they even looked like The Beatles, especially when 'George' did a half shuffle and almost broke into a dance like you see the real George doing on the film clips, but something was missing. Something was always going to be missing, but if pop really was dead like Dr Roc had said, then tribute bands were its future. Maybe that was the way it had always been. Mozart didn't keep playing his own stuff, did he? What was the London Philharmonic Orchestra but a tribute band? That's what it was going to be like. Pop and rock was already like classical or opera or jazz. It was fixed in its own time. All the great works had been created: *King of the Delta Blues Singers, Revolver, Highway 61 Revisited, Pet Sounds, Dark Side of the Moon, The Clash* – whatever they were. People were going to keep listening to them for ever, just like we were still listening to old 78s and folk songs and brass bands and hymns, but it was music from another time. You could bring on Equally Humdrum and as many new bands as you wanted, but it was never going to be special again. It was over. Rock 'n' roll had burned brightly, but the fire and the fury had gone out. JookBoxFury had been raking over the ashes. I loved rock 'n' roll.

Rhia asked me if I wanted to go and dance, but it was all over and I wasn't in the mood, so she went to dance to The Beatles on her own. While the Fabs were playing *Revolution*, Pony Boy came in and asked me where Rhia was because he wanted to talk to us both. I pointed Rhia out and Pony Boy took her to a table at the other side of the room and then waved me over. I went to join them and Pony Boy said, 'I wanted you two to be the first to know' – it sounded suspiciously like he was pregnant – 'because you have both been so supportive over the past few days with the Bobbly Wobbler merchandising and so on, and I think you're going to be as excited by this news as I am.'

I wasn't sure whether I could take too much more, but Pony Boy didn't seem to care. He said, 'I've been in touch with one of the big movers and shakers in the entertainment world. We've been in discussion over a possible franchise for a game show based on the Explain Your Name concept? Well, that's not going to happen. That one is on the back burner for the time being.'

That was even less exciting than I'd been expecting. I thought he was at least going to present us with a couple of Bobbly Wobblers, probably the ones with the sad expressions.

Pony Boy said, 'But something that is very much on the front burner and bubbling away fiercely, is this.' He put a legal document on the table. 'It all came together during the press conference. This is an agreement to take JookBoxFury on the road on a semi-permanent basis. I'm going to be doing pubs, clubs, student ents, business functions – you name it and I'm taking JookBoxFury there. As my promoter friend said, "JookBoxFury is the new pub quiz." There's plenty of mileage in the format yet, we've barely scratched the surface with this little tour. Don't be surprised if this time next year JookBoxFury is a prime time TV game show with a possible board game and PC version in the offing. Pony Boy's back in the big time.'

No wonder he was so excited – he was back in the big time.

Rhia said, 'That's great news, you must be very pleased.'

Pony Boy was pleased. 'It's very rewarding that all the hard work has paid off. I'm going to strike while the iron's hot because we're getting some bookings to start within the month, which is where you two come in.'

We came in? I sat up.

'I'm going to need an experienced team to back me up, and who better than people who've already got solid experience of the JookBoxFury phenomenon? Rhia, after all the good work you've done organizing the venues and taking on responsibility for coordinating the final stages of the tour, I'd like you to do the same for me. And Ray…'

This was it, it was happening. All those jukebox choices had paid off and he'd recognized them. He realized the value of having a real jukebox selection expert as a regular part of the panel, travelling from town to town, taking my jukebox magic to people everywhere. I was on my way.

'Ray,' Pony Boy said, 'the only way I can express how grateful I am for the support you've given me right from the very start, is to ask you to be in charge of merchandising – I want you to take the Bobbly Wobblers on to the next level.'

I couldn't quite take it in. He hadn't said anything about being on the JookBoxFury panel, but he seemed to want me to sell Bobbly Wobblers. How could I respond to that? I didn't know what to say.

Rhia said, 'I think Ray's a bit taken aback. I think it sounds great. I'd love to be part of JookBoxFury full time. We'll have to talk about salary and my notice from the brewery, but in theory I love it. Thanks for asking me.'

I said, 'Yeah… I need to… we need to… but… thanks.'

Pony Boy said, 'We'll have that conversation as soon as, but in the meantime, it's super to have you both on-board because we are at the start of a very exciting new phase of this adventure. Now I know I've got a quality team with me I think we can take this one all the way. I've got to go and have another chat with Laurence about ownership of the JookBoxFury concept, but we're basically there with it.' He shook both our hands and said, 'I think it's time for you two to go and celebrate.'

After Pony Boy had gone Rhia said, 'Isn't that brilliant? Organizing JookBoxFury as a job, and without having Fran to boss me about – how fantastic.'

'He wants me to sell Bobbly Wobblers,' I said. 'I can't do it.'

Anarchy in the Juke

On the Monday I went back to work. Said, 'Morning,' to the same old crowd. Showed them my black eye, told them it had actually been a lot worse when it happened, soaked up a bit of sympathy. Sat at my desk. Logged on. Started to populate a spreadsheet.

I put the JookBoxFury trophy in my desk drawer. I couldn't tell the people at work anything about Rik, or Babs, or Pony Boy, or the death of pop, or the Bobbly Wobblers. Or Rhia. I told them I'd been feeling a bit dizzy and I kept seeing stars.

JookBoxFury had become a dream. It was a dream that started when I got wound up by Pony Boy on the radio linking Bobbly Wobblers to the greatest songs of all time. Only a week before, Pony Boy had been a crap Seventies DJ, someone from the radio. He became the guy who got me into the JookBoxFury final, and then offered me a job selling Bobbly Wobblers. I couldn't accept it. Where was the security? The pension scheme? If he'd asked me to be a regular on the JookBoxFury panel, that would have been different, but being in charge of Bobbly Wobblers? I couldn't do it. I threw myself into the spreadsheet.

Halfway through the morning I got a call from Rhia. She sounded like someone from a different life. Rhia's voice was a splash of colour in the grey world, she said, 'Pony Boy's booked some time in a studio this afternoon. He's recording *Don't Go Breaking My Hat* and he wants us to go along to do handclaps.'

Handclaps or the spreadsheet? I said, 'Handclaps! Brilliant, I'm there.'

I spent the rest of the morning watching out for Justin Quine going into his office so I could get the OK to take the afternoon off. When he finally turned up I went to ask him, but he said, 'Oh, sorry, not now, Ray, I'm completely stacked up.' I had another go and he said, 'Ray mate, seriously, I've got back to back project planning huddles coming out of my ears. Must catch up though – ask Jenny to book something in next week.'

Next week? Next week was no good. I was going to be recording handclaps that afternoon.

Quine picked his briefcase up and started to leave.

I blocked him and tried again. 'It's only a very quick question. I wondered if I might be able to have the afternoon off so I can go and help some friends record a single.'

'I thought we'd agreed that wouldn't be possible. Bad luck and all that good stuff, but you know as well as I do that business requirements must come first – we wouldn't want anyone to think we weren't living the brand would we? I'm sorry, but recording a single is hardly a priority is it? Keeping this business moving forwards is more important than pop music, as I'm sure you'll appreciate.' He tried to squeeze past me but I didn't move.

The business was more important than pop music? What was he talking about? The soul-sapping pointlessness of the business, the endless meetings listening to pompous middle managers trot out the old clichés about turning the business around. The business was important for one reason only – the paycheck – and how pathetic was it that I'd got myself into a situation where my life revolved around toeing the line, doing the right thing, agreeing that we absolutely must move the business forwards, when in reality I didn't care whether the business reversed over a cliff. I was ashamed of myself for being part of it, and to suggest that all that was more important than the thrill and creativity that had come from the world of popular music was ridiculous. The business was more important than pop music? What was he talking about?

'Is the business more important than Elvis?' I asked him. 'Is the business more important than The Beatles? Is the business more important than Martha Reeves and the Vandellas? Is the business

248

more important than Bob Dylan, Bob Marley, Bobby Darin, Bobbie Gentry, The Bobettes, Bob B Soxx and the Blue Jeans, the Sex Pistols, The Clash, Little Richard, Aretha Franklin, The Stone Roses, Pulp, the Go! Team, Casper Hauser? Which bit of pop music exactly is the business more important than? Come on, which bit?'

He said, 'Look, I've got to be going, so why don't you calm down and ask Jenny to book something in for another time, hey? There's a good feller.'

I almost pushed him in the chest. 'Which bit?' I said. 'I'll give you a clue – how about Bucks Fizz? Or maybe not even a Eurovision winner, perhaps just a hopeful. How about Samantha Janus? I'd be prepared to discuss that. Is the business more important than the entire body of recorded work produced by Eurovision failure Samantha Janus? I'd be prepared to discuss that, and probably even come down on the side of the business. But is the business more important than all of pop music in its many and thrilling forms – dead or alive? No way. Not even close. If the world was about to end and I could save either the business or *Anarchy in the UK*, it wouldn't even be a contest. I'd take *Anarchy in the UK* every time. "Your future dream is a shopping scheme," that's what Johnny Rotten said. Well, that might be your future dream, Justin, but it isn't mine. You might not care about music, but to me it's everything – I've got to be in the studio this afternoon.'

'Now that's not fair,' he said. 'I like music as much as the next man. I was listening to Sting's latest disc on the way in to work this morning. I went to U2's Zooropa concert, I'll have you know. I'm a big fan of music. I can be listening to a Baroque Oboe Concerto one minute, and the next I'll be bopping away to some up to the minute stuff like Westlife, so don't come on all holier than thou about pop music. I happen to have a very good collection of pop stuff on the auto changer in the car.'

'What are you talking about?' I asked him. 'Sting? U2's Zooropa tour? Westlife? What are you telling me? You might as well walk around wearing a big hat with "Wanker" written on it. Oh, fuck it, I'm going whether you give me the time off or not. Take your job and shove it, Quine, I'm off.'

'You are off, you're fired.'

'Too late, I've already quit.'

'You can't quit, you're fired – gross misconduct.'

'Gross misconduct? I'll tell you what's gross misconduct – a grown man listening to Westlife, that's gross misconduct.'

DISC FIVE, TRACK THREE

Sweet Inspiration

I left. By the time I got to the recording studio Rik was finishing the overdubs on his guitar solo. Pony Boy said, 'Look lively, Ray, handclaps next.'

I stood by a microphone with Rhia. She winked at me. I nodded the beat back to her. We stepped up to the microphone together and put in some of the most soulful handclaps you'll ever hear on a novelty record. *Don't Go Breaking My Hat* by Simon 'Pony Boy' Rogers and the Bobbly Wobblers was destined to be a smash.

As we left the studio I told Rhia what had happened with Justin Quine. 'Being back in the office didn't feel right. I was missing JookBoxFury.'

Rhia said, 'Well, I'm sure Pony Boy's offer still stands. Don't you want to be responsible for merchandising? It won't just be the Bobbly Wobblers, there'll be the programmes and the advertising. There's all sorts you could do. You know what, if it hadn't been for you and me, I don't think JookBoxFury would have happened at all.'

'I suppose when you put it like that… we'll be on the road, part of JookBoxFury all the time, maybe even getting a chance to cover for the contestants now and then… we might even crack America… JookBoxFury has been the best… the Bobbly Wobblers aren't so bad, are they? They're quite good fun, really.'

'We'll be part of the same team,' Rhia said.

'Is that good?'

Rhia smiled. 'I think so.'

I asked her, 'What was your favourite part of JookBoxFury?'

She moved closer and kissed me on the cheek.

I kissed her back.

Later on, Rhia said, 'If you had to pick the best songs from the whole of the tour, if JookBoxFury was one big jukebox, which five songs would you choose?'

'Now we're the new JookBoxFury team we should choose them together,' I said, 'two each and one to share. You go first.'

'I'll choose *Sex and Drugs and Rock 'n' Roll* then,' Rhia said. 'Hearing a bunch of morris dancers sing that in The Queen Victoria pretty much summed up that whole experience. What's yours?'

I didn't need to think about it. 'I'd have to start with *Sweet Inspiration*. I don't even know the song, but I remember you talking about it in that exercise Laurence did, and it made me want… I wanted to hear more… And for my other choice I'll have one I played in The Blue Moon of Ken's Tuck Inn. It's got to be *Stay*, that was a turning point.'

'*Stay* was good,' Rhia said, 'but was it as good as Parker singing *Heartbeat Drumbeat* to Babs? That's my second.'

'What's the last one then? I'd suggest *The Hustle*, you were good.'

'How about *Lost in France*?' Rhia said. 'Playing *Lost in France* in the JookBoxFury final – by mistake – was pure class… unless you want to go for *Seasons in the Sun*?'

'It hasn't been a lucky number for me, so I'm going to suggest *Don't Go Breaking My Hat*.'

Rhia said, 'I won't go breaking your hat.'

Songs/tracks/albums
played, discussed or mentioned in passing
in *JookBoxFury*

Thank you for the music…

A Whiter Shade of Pale, Procol Harum
Albert and the Lion, Stanley Holloway
Anarchy in the UK, The Sex Pistols
Angel Clare, Tess and the d'Urbervilles
Angels, Robbie Williams
Are You Lonesome Tonight?, Elvis Presley
Astral Weeks, Van Morrison
At Home He's a Tourist, Gang of Four
Be-Bop-a-Lula, Gene Vincent and the Blue Caps
Bedroom Holiday, The Amphetameanies
Big Girls Don't Cry, The Four Seasons
Blue Boy, Orange Juice
Blue Lines, Massive Attack
Blue Moon of Kentucky, Bill Monroe and the Blue Grass Boys
Boring Machines Disturb Sleep, Mogwai
C'mon Everybody, Eddie Cochran
Can't Get You Out of My Head, Kylie Minogue
Candle in the Wind, Elton John
Casablanca, Kenny Ball and his Jazzmen
Chanson d'Amour, Manhattan Transfer
Chicago, John Kander, Fred Ebb, Bob Fosse
Cigarettes and Alcohol, Oasis
Come Again, Au Pairs
Common People, Pulp
Convoy, C W McCall
Crazy, Patsy Cline
Dark Side of the Moon, Pink Floyd

Diamonds on the Soles of Her Shoes, Paul Simon
Different Drum, The Stone Poneys
Dirty Water, The Standells
Disco Duck (Part One), Rick Dees and his Cast of Idiots
Disraeli Gears, Cream
Do You Believe in Magic?, The Lovin' Spoonful
Do You Really Want to Hurt Me?, Culture Club
Don't Go Breaking My Hat, Simon 'Pony Boy' Rogers and the Bobbly Wobblers
Don't Go Breaking My Heart, Elton John and Kiki Dee
Don't Look Back in Anger, Oasis
Don't Worry, Baby, The Beach Boys
Earth Mother, Moon Lover, Brutus Trout
Earth Mother, Moon Lover – for Ever, Eddie Brutus with the Trout Replicas
Earth Mutha Fucka, Wyrez XD feat Howlin' Rikky P
Ernie (the Fastest Milkman in the West), Benny Hill
Exodus, Bob Marley and the Wailers
Fun House, The Stooges
Funky Drummer, James Brown
Future Days, Can
Girl, The Beatles
Girls Just Wanna Have Fun, Cyndi Lauper
Give Him a Great Big Kiss, The Shangri Las
God Gave Rock and Roll to You, Argent
Golden Porsche, Mogwai
Greatest, Cat Power
Green Door, Wynder K Frog
Green Green Grass of Home, Tom Jones
Green Grow the Jooksie-oh!, Crowd chant from newsreel footage
Greensleeves, Henry VIII
Hairway to Steven, Butthole Surfers
Hakuna Matata, Elton John and Tim Rice
Have I the Right?, The Honeycombs
Have You Seen Your Mother, Baby, Standing in the Shadow?, The Rolling Stones
He Ain't Heavy, He's My Brother, The Hollies
Heartbeat Drumbeat (live bootleg), Equally Peabody plus Very Special Guest

Heartbeat Drumbeat, equally humdrum
Hello Bastards, Part Chimp
Hey Joe, Jimi Hendrix Experience
Hey Joe, The Leaves
Hey Joe, Patti Smith
Highway 61 Revisited, Bob Dylan
Hit Me With Your Rhythm Stick, Ian Dury and the Blockheads
Hole in the Ground, Bernard Cribbins
Halloween, Mudhoney
Hot 'n' Cold, McLuhan
I Just Don't Know What to do With Myself, Dusty Springfield
I Remember You, Frank Ifield
I Want to Hold Your Hand, The Beatles
I'm Not in Love, 10cc
Ice Cream Man, Jonathan Richman and the Modern Lovers
Imagine, John Lennon
In Love, The Raincoats
It Will Stand, The Showmen
It's a Heartache, Bonnie Tyler
It's a Sight to Behold, Devandra Banhart
It's Not Unusual, Tom Jones
Itchycoo Park, The Small Faces
Jeepster, T Rex
Jook, Baby, Jook (live bootleg), Rik and Parker
Jook, Baby, Jook, Rik Peabody with Simon 'Pony Boy' Rogers and the Jookers
Jump Right Out of this Jukebox, Onie Wheeler
Just Like Eddie, Heinz
Juxtaposed With U, Super Furry Animals
Kick Out the Jams, MC5
Killing All the Flies, Mogwai
King of the Delta Blues Singers, Robert Johnson
Liege and Lief, Fairport Convention
London Calling, The Clash
Lost in France, Bonnie Tyler
Love is Strange, Danny and Claire
Love is Strange, Mickey and Sylvia
Lucille, Little Richard
Lucy in the Sky with Diamonds, The Beatles

Mel, Casper Hauser
Message in a Bottle, The Police
Midnight Train to Georgia, Gladys Knight and the Pips
My Boy Lollipop, Millie
My La's a Sweet La, The Kirbygrips
Nairobi, Tommy Steele
Never Understand, The Jesus and Mary Chain
Nobody Knows You When You're Down and Out, Bessie Smith
Ob-La-Di, Ob-La-Da, Marmalade
Ode to Billie Joe, Bobbie Gentry
Oklahoma!, Rodgers and Hammerstein
Ooh Ahh… Just a Little Bit, Gina G
Perfect Day, Lou Reed
Pet Sounds, The Beach Boys
Peter Gunn, Duane Eddy
Pink Dust, Magoo
Pretty Vacant, The Sex Pistols
Public Image, Public Image Ltd
Purple Haze, Jimi Hendrix Experience
Ramblin' Rose, MC5
Ray of Light, Madonna
Rebellion (Lies), Arcade Fire
Revolution, The Beatles
Revolver, The Beatles
Rhiannon, Fleetwood Mac
Ride on Time, Black Box
Rock and Roll Waltz, Kay Starr
Rock Around the Clock, Bill Haley and his Comets
Rock Island Line, Leadbelly
Rock Island Line, Lonnie Donegan Skiffle Group
Rocket 88, Jackie Brenston and his Delta Cats
Rubber Bullets, 10cc
Seasons in the Sun, Terry Jacks
Seven Little Girls (Sitting in the Back Seat), Paul Evans
Seventeen, Ladytron
Sex and Drugs and Rock 'n' Roll, Ian Dury and the Blockheads
Sgt Pepper's Lonely Hearts Club Band, The Beatles
Shake, Rattle and Roll, Elvis Presley
Shakin' All Over, The Pirates

Shine on You Crazy Diamond, Pink Floyd
Silver Machine, Hawkwind
Singing the Blues, Guy Mitchell
Sister Ray, The Velvet Underground
Sisters are Doin' it for Themselves, Eurythmics and Aretha Franklin
Smoke on the Water, Deep Purple
Sorted for E's and Wizz, Pulp
Sparky's Dream, Teenage Fanclub
Stand By Your Man, Tammy Wynette
Stay, Maurice Williams and the Zodiacs
Superstition, Stevie Wonder
Suspicious Minds, Elvis Presley
Sweet Inspiration, The Sweet Inspirations
Swingin' Doors, George Jones
Teddy Bear, Elvis Presley
Telstar, Tornados
Thank You for the Music, ABBA
That's Alright Mama, Elvis Presley
The Boy With the Arab Strap, Belle and Sebastian
The Boys are Back in Town, Thin Lizzy
The Clash, The Clash
The Hustle, Van McCoy
The Jean Genie, David Bowie
The Weight, The Band
The Wildwood Flower, The Carter Family
The Wizard of Oz, Harold Arlen and E Y Harburg
Theme from Z Cars (Johnny Todd), Johnny Keating
Then He Kissed Me, Crystals
There's People Lying Dead in the Stairwell, G Plan
This Boy, The Beatles
This is It, Melba Moore
This Wheel's on Fire, Julie Driscoll and the Brian Auger Trinity
Toast, Streetband
Tom Hark, Elias and his Jive Flutes
Twist and Shout, Chaka Demus and Pliers featuring Jack Radics and Taxi Gang
Violence is Golden (But My Wounds Still Bleed), The Peabodies
Violence is Golden (live bootleg), rik peabody + equally humdrum

Virginia Plain, Roxy Music
Walk in the Black Forest, Horst Jankowski
Walk Tall, The Peabodies
Walking Back to Happiness, Helen Shapiro
Wannabe, Spice Girls
We Float, P J Harvey
We Will Become Sillhouettes, The Postal Service
What Will the Neighbours Say?, Girls Aloud
(What's So Funny 'Bout) Peace, Love and Understanding?, Elvis Costello
Where Did You Sleep Last Night?, Nirvana
Where is My Mind?, Pixies
Wherever I Lay My Hat (That's My Home), Marvin Gaye
Whisky in the Jar, Thin Lizzy
Wig-Wam Bam, The Sweet
Will You Love Me Tomorrow?, The Shirelles
Winkle Picker Shoes, Bernard Cribbins
World Cup Willie, Lonnie Donegan
You Really Got Me, The Kinks
You Send Me, Sam Cooke
You'll Lose a Good Thing, Barbara Lynne
You're the One that I Want, John Travolta and Olivia Newton-John
Your Love is King, Sade
Zooropa, U2

And all the others…

Thanks, from me to you...

Ruth
Holly and Corrina
Paul Mills
Andy Watkins
Sue Lancaster
Adrienne Gilchrist
Hugo Welsh
Tim Procter
Andrew Stafford
Ian Elliott
David McCloy
Gwen Berwick
Joe and Tom Bleazard
Philippa Major
Gavin Killip
Mike and Maria
Willie Mowatt
York Writers
John Marland
Robert Edgar-Hunt
All at York St John creative writing 2003-05
Martyn Bedford
John Murray
All at Lumb Bank, October/November 07
Lorna, Tim and Kathryn
Troubador – Terence, Amy, Julia, Jeremy
John and Elaine Stafford
Terry Jacks
Black Swan Rapper
Albion Morris
Great Western Morris
Ian at the Jukejoint, Sheffield
Sarahphotogirl
eko-create
Casper Hauser

The Jook Duke of the Juke

Your own JookBoxFury picks

LOCATION

_____

JUKEBOX (Make/Model)

_____

SELECTIONS

_____

_____

_____

_____

_____

Share them at www.JookBoxFury.co.uk